A SKY FULL OF STARS

FAY KEENAN

First published in Great Britain in 2025 by Boldwood Books Ltd.

Copyright © Fay Keenan, 2025

Cover Design by Alice Moore Design

Cover Images: Shutterstock and iStock

The moral right of Fay Keenan to be identified as the author of this work has been asserted in accordance with the Copyright, Designs and Patents Act 1988.

All rights reserved. No part of this book may be reproduced in any form or by any electronic or mechanical means, including information storage and retrieval systems, without written permission from the author, except for the use of brief quotations in a book review. This book is a work of fiction and, except in the case of historical fact, any resemblance to actual persons, living or dead, is purely coincidental.

Every effort has been made to obtain the necessary permissions with reference to copyright material, both illustrative and quoted. We apologise for any omissions in this respect and will be pleased to make the appropriate acknowledgements in any future edition.

A CIP catalogue record for this book is available from the British Library.

Paperback ISBN 978-1-83617-635-0

Large Print ISBN 978-1-83617-636-7

Hardback ISBN 978-1-83617-634-3

Ebook ISBN 978-1-83617-637-4

Kindle ISBN 978-1-83617-638-1

Audio CD ISBN 978-1-83617-629-9

MP3 CD ISBN 978-1-83617-630-5

Digital audio download ISBN 978-1-83617-632-9

This book is printed on certified sustainable paper. Boldwood Books is dedicated to putting sustainability at the heart of our business. For more information please visit https://www.boldwoodbooks.com/about-us/sustainability/

Boldwood Books Ltd, 23 Bowerdean Street, London, SW6 3TN

www.boldwoodbooks.com

To Nick, my guiding star

1

If Charlotte James believed in so-called cosmic balance (which she didn't), today would have reinforced that belief. Call it karma, equilibrium or downright law of sod, there was certainly something at play, throwing objects in her clearly defined path. Not even the sympathetic gaze of Comet, her ever-loyal cocker spaniel, was enough to raise her spirits on a dull Thursday afternoon in her minute office at the back end of the archive of the University of North West Wessex's Astronomy Department.

Comet himself was a kind of furry testament to the relative unimportance of her role in the department – things were usually so quiet in this part of the building that no one was remotely bothered that Comet accompanied Charlotte to work on the days she needed to be on site. He'd become her unofficial research associate, and the jokey picture of him next to the Morrow Telescope, the impressive device that topped the building where she worked, that she'd framed and put in pride of place on her little desk, cemented that light-hearted view. The little spaniel was sitting proudly in the picture, the white star on his chest shining in contrast with his silky black fur. So long as he kept out of the way of the equipment, and some of her rather less dog-friendly colleagues, no one seemed to concern themselves with his presence.

It was just as well, Charlotte thought, since he was pretty much her only companion either at work or away from it, apart from check-ins by her line manager, Professor Jim Edwin. Archiving could be a solitary process, and of late, for Charlotte, it had become even more so. And to add insult to injury, the first email she'd received that afternoon had been from Todd, the American senior research associate that she'd spent days, nights and most of her free time with for the past year, finally calling time on their relationship.

It wasn't as though she hadn't been expecting it: they'd made vague promises to keep things going when he'd accepted the fellowship back at his university in the United States, with even more vague promises that she'd try to find herself a post at the same institution in due course. The trouble was, jobs for historical astronomical archivists were so few and far between, especially in these straitened times for funding, that there had seemed very little prospect of that, even when she'd said it. Even though she hated to admit it, it had really only been a matter of time before he'd met someone else.

So that was one side of the cosmic balance theory, she thought wryly. Perhaps the email that had followed it was the other. Idly, since she had nothing better to do, she clicked it open again and re-read its contents:

Dear Dr James,

We would be delighted to offer you a five-week post at the Lower Brambleton Observatory, to undertake the archiving of the site's records room prior to the removal of the documentation to the School of Astrophysics at the University of North West Wessex. Your CV was exemplary, and your experience thus far is impressive. The position would be open from mid-July, subject to your department's approval, and the salary would be at the expected level...

Charlotte drew in a breath as she saw the figure that the email displayed. It was well above the rate she was on now, and for five weeks' work, over the summer, when things got quiet in the department and the undergraduate students had all gone home, she was more than happy to pack up hers and Comet's possessions and move.

When she'd applied for the post, late one night after Todd had decamped to America, she'd felt she had no hope of ever getting it. But it seemed that her pessimism had been misplaced. The organisation offering her the job, Flowerdew Homes, was not only offering to pay her a generous salary, but also to cover her accommodation costs for the time she was there. This was the opportunity she'd been waiting for and would certainly go some way to easing the sting of Todd's betrayal.

Charlotte reached down and ruffled her dog's neck. Comet, who had been lying in his basket to the right of Charlotte's chair, sniffed her hand expectantly. Smiling, Charlotte popped the lid off the cookie jar of dog treats that sat on her desk beside Comet's photograph. 'I suppose it's cause for celebration,' she added as he gently took the treat from her outstretched fingers. Then, feeling a touch peckish herself, she took a double chocolate brownie from the second jar on her desk and allowed herself to luxuriate in its taste. It was the last of a batch that she'd baked to cheer herself up, to a recipe that Todd had given her, and finishing the soft, gooey chocolate confection seemed to put a full stop to that part of her life, well and truly.

Glancing back at the email from Flowerdew Homes, she

battled with her conscience for a long moment. Much like the development companies that called in archaeologists before they could build on recently acquired sites, Flowerdew Homes had contacted her department to oversee the decommissioning of the Lower Brambleton Observatory, a building that had been standing for nearly a hundred and thirty years. Although the observatory had fallen into disuse and some disrepair over the past two decades, there had been a resurgence of interest, partly driven by nostalgia and a fair dose of nimbyism from many of the locals, in the old building and its contents. Flowerdew had borne the onslaught, though, and planning permission had been granted to develop the forty-acre site into a housing estate to enlarge the hamlet of Lower Brambleton. As with many of these developments, a new doctor's surgery and a preschool had been promised, as well as sympathetically created play areas and green spaces. The observatory's loss would be the village's gain, eventually.

Charlotte would be lying to herself if she said she was completely comfortable with the demolition of a site of such special astronomical interest, but at least, she figured, if she was in charge of the archiving she'd be able to make sure the contents of the observatory were treated with the respect they deserved. In addition, the prospect of a summer away from Bristol where the University of North West Wessex had its main buildings, in the countryside, did have an appeal, if only to get away from the painful memories of her now defunct relationship with Todd. She was due to move out of her university accommodation for the summer, anyway, as there was yet another visiting professor (this time from CERN, The European Organization for Nuclear Research, no less) who was going to be put up there for the duration of the vacation.

Charlotte was a warden in one of the newly built accommodation blocks for first and second year undergraduate students. She received a small stipend for this, on top of having accommodation in a self-contained flat on the ground floor of the building that she could live in for the duration of each academic year. The arrangement took the pressure off having to finance living in the centre of Bristol, and since there had been a drive by universities across the country to make the welfare of undergraduates, especially those in their first year of study, more of a priority, the University of North West Wessex had adopted the live-in warden scheme a few years back. It meant that students had a permanent point of contact where they lived, and Charlotte could alert the pastoral teams if any issues arose with students who might be struggling to adapt to university life. While she was sure that, eventually, being a mentor and informal 'parent' to eighteen-year-olds would lose its appeal, she enjoyed the post and she felt that it was a role that really made a difference to the lives of some of the students. Of course, there were incidents where living so close to undergraduates had been irksome – the drunken singing of a gaggle of teenagers straggling home after a student night in one of Bristol's many nightclubs had often awoken her, especially when they crossed 'Hangover Row', as the patch of green space outside her flat was known. This sometimes caused even the soundly sleeping Comet to grumble, but for the most part the students were courteous and pleased to have her on their turf. The accommodation went with the job, on the proviso that she could be 'flexible' when the university needed her to be and this flexibility meant that she often had to move out during the vacations, but this had never been a problem. She was getting a little old to return home to her parents for extended periods, but her friend, Gemma, had a spare room and never minded taking her in as a temporary lodger.

But not this summer. This summer, Charlotte was going somewhere new. It was an exciting prospect, and just the antidote she needed to the dull ache of being dumped by Todd.

'Well, Comet,' she said to the spaniel, who was looking hopefully up at her at the possibility of another treat. 'It looks like you and I are going to the country!'

2

Two weeks later, at the official end of the university's academic year, Charlotte put the final touches to her packing and prepared herself for the off. Luckily, there was plenty of storage on campus, so she was able to put most of her belongings into boxes to be returned when she moved back into her accommodation at the start of the new term in September. She was used to packing light, having spent a great deal of her time travelling the world for her postgraduate studies. But for the past couple of years she'd been relatively settled in Bristol, where she and Comet had shared the flat during term time and then decamped to Gemma's or her parents' house for the holidays. Her mother and father had started to give her *that* kind of look though: the look that, roughly translated, meant 'When are you going to get a *proper* job and buy a place of your own?' *Not just yet*. The life of a researcher and archivist suited her, and Comet was all the company she needed. Of course, for a while she'd thought that she and Todd might settle down together, but clearly *that* wasn't going happen now.

Even if she hadn't had to vacate her accommodation, a quick

look at Google Maps had confirmed to her that she'd have to find somewhere near the observatory to live for the duration of the post, anyway. She'd recently passed her driving test, on the sixth attempt, but she didn't have the spare cash to buy a car, and finance the astronomical running costs as a new driver, so she still relied on buses and her own two feet while she was living in Bristol. The city was very public transport friendly, which helped a lot. However, public transport to Somerset, especially the remote part of the county where Lower Brambleton was situated, was practically non-existent. This had worried her for a while, before she'd decided to accept the job. Lower Brambleton seemed picturesque, but it was a tiny hamlet almost equidistant, in the centre of a triangle, between the towns of Minehead, Taunton and Yeovil. Buses did run every couple of hours, but there was no direct service to Bristol, and it would take three hours to go from the university to Lower Brambleton. So, instead of having to navigate this, she'd decided to move to the countryside for the duration.

'Are you sure you've got everything?' Gemma, her best friend, and for today, moving buddy, asked as Charlotte shut the door of the flat. 'I mean, there's not a lot here...'

Charlotte smiled. 'I always travel light. It's a habit I learned when I was chasing constellations in South America. Comet's probably got more stuff than I have!'

'You're not wrong,' Gemma replied, wrinkling her nose as the pong of a well-used dog bed reached her nostrils. 'Might be time to get him a new basket.'

'He likes that one,' Charlotte grinned. 'I've tried replacing it, but he just won't take to any of the others. He's a creature of habit.'

'Like his mistress,' Gemma observed as she started the engine of her VW Touareg. 'Which makes it all the more surprising you're upping sticks for this weird job. I mean, I can understand wanting to get as far away from that tosser, Todd, as you can, but since he's already stateside, why wouldn't you just bunk with me while your flat's being occupied? I've got tons of room, and I could do with a lodger for the summer.'

Charlotte, who'd reached back to plug Comet's seatbelt lead into the socket in the back seat, gave her friend a smile. 'It's not that I don't appreciate the offer,' she said, as she turned back around, 'but, oh, I don't know, there just seemed to be *something* about the observatory project that feels right. Someone should be there to take it all apart, record the artefacts and documents for posterity; someone who actually knows what they're doing. I mean, can you imagine if they'd just gone ahead and thrown all the star charts and records into a skip?' She shuddered. 'I might not usually be on the side of a developer, but at least they seem to want to take care of the history they're getting rid of.'

'I get it,' Gemma replied as they headed south out of the city and for the open road. 'And you've always loved working on your own. I just worry that Lower Brambleton could be a bit isolated, even for you. I don't like the thought of you all alone in the countryside, licking your wounds after Todd the Twat has done the dirty, with nothing but a manky, mouldy old telescope and an archive of mildewed star charts for company.'

Charlotte saw the concern in her friend's eyes as Gemma glanced from the road to her, and then back again, and gave her a reassuring smile. 'I think the telescope's already gone,' she said. 'And besides, it's better than pining in Bristol, going back to our old haunts and wishing he hadn't hooked up with some new, better-looking model. After all, there's nothing I can do about it, is there? Might as well make good use of the summer break and supplement my meagre income as a researcher with this project.'

'I suppose.' Gemma's tone clearly illustrated that she still needed some convincing.

'Besides,' Charlotte continued, 'I've got Comet for company, and he's the only male I want in my life right now.'

'Even if he needs a bath.' Gemma's nose wrinkled delicately again. 'Promise me that's the first thing you'll do when you get there, or your new landlady'll chuck you both out on the street before you've even had the chance to get his smelly old bed in situ!'

Charlotte laughed. 'I promise. Although she did say that she was a dog lover, so hopefully she and Comet will take to one another.'

'Let's hope so,' Gemma echoed. 'Don't get me wrong, I love the old boy, but he's rather too fond of rolling in unsavoury things for my liking.'

'Yes,' Charlotte laughed. 'I'll never forget the day he barrelled in and rubbed eau de fox poo all over your living-room carpet! You're a good friend to allow us both anywhere near your home, or your car, after that!'

'Don't remind me,' Gemma groaned. 'And Copernicus will definitely be glad he doesn't have to share with Comet this summer, no matter how much I'll miss you.' Copernicus was Gemma's fat, aged ginger cat, and although he definitely had the upper paw these days, having bopped Comet more than once on the end of his sensitive nose for stealing his food, there was no love lost between cat and dog.

'So, what's the name of your landlady, again?' Gemma asked as the road began to widen, and the first of many pretty villages between Bristol and Lower Brambleton rushed by.

'Lorelai Ashcombe,' Charlotte replied. 'She sounded nice on the phone. The university put me onto her as she often has people to stay on short-term projects. She lives a stone's throw from the development, so her house seemed the best bet.'

'Strange name,' Gemma remarked. 'I wonder if she's one of those Somerset eccentrics, you know, hippies that never quite made it home from Glastonbury. I bet you'll get there, and it'll be all tie-dyed throws and incense.'

Charlotte laughed. 'She didn't sound like an ex-hippy on the phone, but I promise, if she gets too way out, I'll ring you and you can spend the next few weeks driving me from your place!'

'Just promise me you'll have a good sniff of any weird-looking tea she makes you before you drink it,' Gemma replied. 'You never know what they're likely to put in it, in the backwaters of Somerset!'

'I will.' Charlotte kept smiling. Gemma was a bit of a fusspot, but she loved her, and she was glad her friend was always in her corner. She knew that if things didn't work out, Gemma would be there to lend a friendly ear and more practical help. But as they got nearer to their destination, excitement began to mingle with trepidation in the pit of Charlotte's stomach. She couldn't help wondering if she'd made the right decision to spend her summer in such an isolated spot.

3

It wasn't much longer before the roads, wide and well maintained on the outskirts of Bristol, began to narrow, and as Gemma navigated her way towards their destination Charlotte took the opportunity to look at the landscape passing her window, which was becoming greener and more rural by the mile. She felt a little nervous: she'd lived in Bristol for ten years now, ever since she'd arrived as a wide-eyed undergraduate, and apart from the time she'd spent after her degree and before her postgraduate studies in South America, she'd barely been away from the city for any great length of time.

'Well, it's certainly going to be quiet!' Gemma broke the silence that had descended between them as she took a left turn down an even smaller lane. 'Looks like there's not a lot of phone signal out here, either. We must be in a black spot.'

Charlotte glanced up from her phone, where she was struggling to find one bar of 3G, and noticed the lane they were on was nestled at the foot of a large expanse of woodland-covered hillside. The hill loomed large above them, and again she wondered at the remoteness of Lower Brambleton. Then, she chided herself: she'd been in far more cut-off places in her career. However, she was used to being able to stream the horror films she was so fond of at the tap of a finger: she wondered if that would be out of the question, here.

'It's got to be around here somewhere,' Gemma muttered, glancing at the car's sat nav and then back at the road in front of her. 'Says we're about half a mile from Nightshade Cottage. That was the name of the place you're staying, wasn't it?'

'Yup,' Charlotte confirmed. Nightshade Cottage in deepest, darkest Somerset, where Lorelai, her exotically named landlady, lived. Where there was virtually no phone signal, and the roads were barely wide enough to get a single car down. If that wasn't the setting for a horror movie, Charlotte thought, she didn't know what was!

She had to admit though, as she wound down the window to let in a bit of fresher air (Comet really *did* need that bath), the scent of cut grass, underpinned by a muskier smell of decaying, rust-coloured bracken that thrust its fronds towards them from the high banks on either side of the road, that it was beautiful in a ragged, untamed, earthy sort of way. Pushing away the thought that sprang to mind of the movie *Jeepers Creepers*, that she'd seen, far too young, late one night on the television when her mum and dad had thought she was tucked up safely in bed, she tried not to imagine the kind of creatures that might be lurking in the trees above. *Don't be so daft*, she told herself impatiently. Her imagination really was starting to get the better of her. She had Gemma and Comet with her; no self-respecting creature of the night would dare try to attack the three of them.

'Ah, this looks like it!' Gemma's exclamation broke into Charlotte's reverie. 'I knew we'd find it eventually.'

Off to their left, there was a narrow track, and at the foot of a space that seemed barely wide enough to get Gemma's Touareg down in one piece was a beautifully written sign, black paint on a white background, announcing that Nightshade Cottage was this way. Turning onto the track, Charlotte caught Gemma's amused glance. 'And I think you can see now why there isn't a regular bus! I don't think this part of Somerset has seen any public transport since a hansom cab and two!'

Charlotte grinned at her friend. 'Well, the guy I spoke to on the phone from Flowerdew Homes warned me it was a touch, er, "rural". Seems he wasn't kidding.'

'There's rural and there's the arse end of bloody nowhere.' Gemma pressed on her brake pedal to navigate a particularly deep pothole. As she did so, her expression grew more serious. 'Charlotte, my darling, are you quite sure you want to spend the next few weeks here? I mean, you could be murdered, set in the concrete for a new patio and I'd never know...'

'Now who's letting their imagination run overtime?' Charlotte laughed. 'Just because you're a town mouse who's never lived anywhere but the city doesn't mean you can go all *Hot Fuzz* on me and start casting aspersions about murderous locals.'

'That may be so,' Gemma replied as she manoeuvred over yet another pothole, 'but I've got a feeling that things are going to change for you here, and you know what happens when I get a feeling.'

'Don't you usually just get a course of antibiotics for that?' Charlotte quipped.

'And that's another thing,' Gemma countered. 'Have you even looked into registering for the GP? For all you know, it could be all herbal remedies and hacksaws in these parts. Sprain an ankle and they'll cut your leg off, kind of thing.'

'I'd better not sprain an ankle, then!' Charlotte replied, a little shorter in tone than she'd intended. Being cautious was one thing, but she wasn't a child, and she was beginning to get irritated by Gemma's assumption that she wouldn't be able to cope out here.

The hedges on either side of the track grew thicker as Gemma drove further, and the height of them on either side of the car felt claustrophobic. It was a relief then when Charlotte spotted their destination and she breathed out. There, in front of them, was a squat thatched cottage, with a pleasingly neat lawn and waist-high wrought-iron gates attached to pillars in front of a newly tarmacked driveway. 'There.' She turned triumphantly to Gemma. 'Not a gothic turret or axe murderer in sight. I told you it was going to be all right.'

Gemma snorted. 'You're not through the door yet!'

They pulled into the drive and Gemma cut the engine. 'Now, are you sure you don't want me to come in with you? I'm quite happy to see you over the threshold.'

Charlotte grinned at her friend. 'It's fine. I'll text you when I'm tied up in the cellar!'

Rolling her eyes, Gemma pushed open her door. 'Well, at least let me help you unload your stuff.'

The two women moved to the boot of the Touareg and in very little time Charlotte's suitcase and a couple of boxes of files and assorted possessions were stacked on the driveway.

'Do you want me to wait?' Gemma said again. 'I mean, what if your new landlady's not in?'

Charlotte shook her head. 'Honestly, it's such a nice day, I can sit on the doorstep. And she gave me her mobile number to call if she wasn't in.'

'If you're sure...' Gemma clearly wasn't happy about just leaving her friend, but also knew better than to argue. 'But if you do end up shackled in the basement, try to let me know somehow!'

'I'm afraid I don't have a basement,' a dryly amused voice cut into their conversation. 'It was filled in years ago, as it played havoc with the damp course. There's a coal cellar in the back of the garden where I keep all of my victims, though, if that helps you to visualise where your friend will be!'

Charlotte jumped guiltily, and Gemma had the good grace to blush, before they both started to giggle.

'Oh, er, hi,' Charlotte said, turning in the direction of the voice. 'I'm so sorry... my friend is a little protective of me and has been teasing me all the way here about being out in the wilds of the countryside. I guess we both have pretty vivid imaginations!'

'I've heard worse, believe me. My grandson gets hives if he has to spend too much time out here. He's a proper townie, and no mistake. I'm Lorelai Ashcombe. Welcome to Nightshade Cottage.'

At the woman's thrust-out hand, Charlotte began to relax. Lorelai was a slim woman who looked to be in her late seventies. Her white hair was cut short, and she was wearing an oversized grey-green shirt and cropped trousers, and a pair of gardening shoes. Some green-stained gloves poked out of one of the pockets of her trousers, and over her other arm was a Somerset willow trug basket containing various freshly cut pastel-coloured flowers and a couple of smallish courgettes.

'Charlotte James,' Charlotte replied. 'And this is my friend Gemma Halloran.' She glanced at Gemma, whose face still showed a little colour from being caught out. 'This really is a gorgeous spot, Mrs Ashcombe.'

'Oh, call me Lorelai,' came the response. 'Everyone else does, including my grandchildren when they're cross with me.' Lorelai's eyes twinkled, but Charlotte got the distinct impression that the older woman was a force to be reckoned with. Anyone who could live out here, alone, at her age had to be pretty tenacious.

'Well, I'll be off then,' Gemma said, breaking the slight pause that had descended between the women. 'Give me a call if you've forgotten anything, and I'll bring it down.'

'Thanks, hon,' Charlotte replied. 'Let me just get Comet out and you're good to go.'

Comet, who was looking curiously and excitedly out of the left passenger window, jumped delightedly out of the car as Charlotte released him from the belt buckle lead. Wagging his tail, he started to sniff all around the driveway before lifting his leg on a vibrant clump of delphiniums. Thankfully, Lorelai laughed. 'He's obviously had a long trip.' She bent down with a slight creak and ruffled the dog's neck as he came back to where the women stood. 'Good boy. What's your name?'

As Charlotte told her, Lorelai's smile widened. 'But of course. In your job, I wouldn't have expected anything less. Now, why don't you come into the house and get settled? It's about time I had a cuppa.'

I think it's going to be all right, Charlotte thought as she waved goodbye to Gemma, who was already reversing carefully down the drive, clearly keen to get back to Bristol. Picking up the first of the boxes, she followed Lorelai through the front door of Nightshade Cottage, Comet scampering boldly in her wake.

4

Charlotte demurred on the cup of tea straight away, preferring to get her living quarters in Lorelai's cottage organised first. She was a stickler for order, which had served her well in her career, and she wanted to make sure that everything was as it should be before she relaxed. Lorelai smiled and said to give her a shout when she wanted a hot drink, and left her to it after leading her through to her room.

First impressions were definitely good. After a few minutes in Lorelai's company, Charlotte had made her way through to the spacious rooms at the rear of the cottage in a more modern extension. It ran down the side of Lorelai's gorgeously appointed back garden and was joined to the main cottage by a lockable internal door, as well as having its own exterior entrance. Charlotte realised that she'd fallen on her feet. The bedroom was light and airy, and generously proportioned, with a king-sized bed, a chest of drawers and a wardrobe all in the same aged dark wood, which had been polished to perfection. There was a desk under the window with a leather top, which would be perfect for completing any work she brought home, and, joyously, there was a good space near the desk for Comet's basket.

'There you go, boy,' Charlotte said, as she placed his shabby bed into position. A smell of dog wafted from it again, and she resolved to try to get him interested in a new one just as soon as she could.

Upon exploring, Charlotte saw a clean and surprisingly modern bathroom. There was even a small kitchenette tucked away under the staircase. The cottage, though it had looked small when she and Gemma had arrived, had depth to it, and Lorelai had made her guest quarters welcoming and private. The adjoining but lockable internal door to the space felt at once pleasingly separate but also reassuringly connected.

'You're welcome to use my kitchen whenever you like,' Lorelai had said as she'd shown her around. 'But experience has taught me that my lodgers like a few facilities of their own, so there's a hot plate, an air fryer, a kettle and a microwave that are just for you, and a fridge with an icebox, too. Just let me know if you'd like to make arrangements for dinner on a weekly basis – I'm more than happy to cook for you if you give me a little notice.'

Charlotte had smiled at that. She appreciated Lorelai's offer, but she was a largely solitary animal and guessed she'd probably end up just cooking for herself most of the time. She'd said thank you, though. This was going to be a slightly quirky living arrangement, she could see, but it was one she was more than happy with for the summer.

'And this chap will be pleased that you've got your own door to the back garden,' Lorelai had continued, giving Comet another ruffle. 'I'm delighted to have him as a guest, provided you clear up his doings from the lawn. My great-grandchildren visit a lot, and they like a game of footy on the grass from time to time.'

'Of course.' Charlotte was surprised that the spry-looking Lorelai was old enough to have great-grandchildren, but perhaps she was older than she looked. 'He – and I – are very well trained in that regard!' She always had a ready supply of poo bags with her on her belt whenever she took Comet out, and she'd brought several rolls with her for her stay in Lower Brambleton. She appreciated just how rare it was to find a landlady who would accept a dog as part of the rental, and she wanted to make sure that Comet remained as welcome as she was.

Lorelai had left her to it then, and for a little while Charlotte had just wandered about, getting to know her space, putting her things away, and trying to adjust mentally to the new place. The quiet was something that was going to take a while to get used to, after the hustle and bustle of being a house parent in the halls of residence. There was always someone around, often knocking on her door. Here, although Lorelai was just the other side of the wall, the silence was almost overwhelming.

Eventually, she'd decided to rejoin Lorelai for the promised cuppa, and now they were sitting out on the patio that ran between both sets of doors to the back garden, enjoying the late afternoon sunshine. Charlotte kept half an eye on Comet as he took his time sniffing around the secure back garden, making sure he didn't take any flying leaps into Lorelai's well-kept rose beds and herbaceous borders. The dog seemed content just to wander, though, and soon, for the first time since she'd left Bristol, Charlotte began to relax.

'It really is beautiful here,' she commented between sips of tea. 'I didn't expect it to be so remote, but it feels incredibly peaceful, too.'

'That it is,' Lorelai agreed. 'But don't be fooled, there's a decent community in Lower Brambleton, even if people are largely outnumbered by grazing sheep!' She smiled mischievously at Charlotte. 'Of course, that'll all change when the new housing estate is built. I can't tell you how many locals have been up in arms about it.'

'And what do *you* think?' Charlotte asked, figuring that she probably already knew the answer. Lorelai, after all, was a dyed-in-the-wool local. She would doubtless be opposed to anything encroaching on the sanctity of the village.

Lorelai paused, putting her mug down on the garden table before she replied. 'Well, change comes to everywhere,' she said eventually. 'And if I'm honest, it's about time something came along to wake this place up. Admittedly, a hundred houses backing up against the Area of Outstanding Natural Beauty is quite a way to do it, but I do feel, at my age, some upheaval is inevitable.'

'So you're in favour of Flowerdew Homes developing the land, then?' Charlotte was surprised.

Lorelai's expression clouded for a moment and then, like the sun breaking out again, she brightened. 'Anything that means my darling granddaughter, Thea, can finally afford to move back to the village where she grew up is all right by me. She's a school teacher, and when the houses are built she'll be able to do one of those shared-ownership things. It's her only chance of being able to return here.'

Charlotte nodded. 'I can see why you'd want that. It's difficult to get a foothold on the property ladder as it is, and I should imagine that's an unattainable dream for a lot of people around here.'

'Absolutely,' Lorelai replied. 'And what else could they do with the land? Leave it there, getting more and more overgrown, while young people are struggling to find somewhere to live?'

'But the observatory's a historic landmark,' Charlotte said. 'Isn't it worth saving?'

Lorelai scoffed at the notion. 'That place has lain unused for nearly twenty years,' she countered. 'I think it's about time it was officially mothballed and then we can all get on with our lives.'

There was something about Lorelai's tone, an undercurrent of sharpness that piqued Charlotte's interest. It was unusual to find a woman of Lorelai's years being so in favour of change, but Charlotte wondered if there was another reason she was so sanguine about the observatory being demolished.

'Well, I'm sure the university is going to be pleased with the new additions to the archive,' Charlotte said. 'I've already been doing a bit of research, and apparently there have been quite a few cosmological discoveries made in Observatory Field over the time it's been there. There was the sighting of a supernova in 1965, and it's been a hotspot for meteor shower observations for almost as long. It amazes me that after all of that history, the building hasn't been in working order for the best part of three decades.'

'Well, these things fall out of fashion.' Lorelai's tone was a little clipped, but Charlotte wondered if she was just tired. She'd obviously been out in the garden all day, and as evening started drifting softly in around the cottage, the sun's beams had also moved around the other side of the building, so it had grown a little cooler. Charlotte glanced around for Comet, who'd collapsed, panting, on the flagstones of the patio.

'I'd better get my stuff sorted out for when I start work,' Charlotte said, aware that the atmosphere between her and Lorelai had shifted somewhat. She couldn't quite put her finger on why, but then it may just have been that, as new acquaintances, they were still operating within polite boundaries.

'And I'd better get some dinner on.' Lorelai's tone sounded warmer again. 'Can I interest you in a Chicken Kiev, dear? There are two in a packet, and I so hate to open something and have to have it two nights running.'

Charlotte smiled. 'Thank you, but I tend to eat a little bit later.' It was barely six o'clock, and she was a bit of a night owl. It went with the territory, she supposed. Her academic career had entailed staying awake into the early hours, observing the patterns in the sky and making sure she noted down every change and nuance. She often joked that she was more at home in the darkness than the light.

'Well, I can keep it warm in the Aga for you if you'd like to eat it when you're peckish,' Lorelai said.

Something told Charlotte that the older woman was trying to bridge the slight distance that had sprung up between them when they'd been talking about the observatory. She smiled. 'That would be lovely. So long as you don't mind my being in the kitchen? I don't tend to eat until about nine o'clock.'

'That's fine,' Lorelai replied. 'As I said, you're free to use my kitchen when you'd like to.' She looked mildly concerned for a minute as Comet came padding towards them. 'You don't make this chap wait so long for his dinner, I hope?'

Charlotte laughed. 'No! He gets his dinner at six-thirty on the dot, and if it's not ready, he reminds me with those eyes that no one in their right mind could ever resist!' Right on cue, Comet looked up at her, and she stroked his ears affectionately. 'Half an hour longer, old chap,' she said, placing a kiss on the tip of his nose.

Charlotte rose from her chair and picked up her teacup, as

well as Lorelai's, to take through to the main kitchen. Something still niggled at her about the way Lorelai had responded to talk of the history of the observatory. *Everyone has secrets*, she thought, and she wondered exactly what Lorelai wasn't telling her.

5

The next morning, Charlotte woke feeling refreshed. The bed was extremely comfortable, and the silence around Nightshade Cottage as darkness had finally drawn in made falling asleep easy. Comet had settled well in his bed, too, and the first thing she heard as dawn broke was the rather pleasing alarm clock of wild birds outside in the trees that surrounded Lorelai's garden. Having been used to being awoken by the much less attractive sound of drunken students returning at dawn to their dorm rooms, this was a pleasant treat. She wondered how she'd feel in a week or two, though, at being up quite so early.

Comet lifted his head as Charlotte swung her feet out of bed and into her furry Ugg slippers. No matter what the time of year, she always had cold feet, and the slippers were a worthwhile luxury. Yawning and stretching, she padded over to the bedroom door, not bothering to open the curtains just yet. Comet followed her through to the kitchenette, hot on her heels.

Nightshade Cottage felt quiet. Charlotte remembered that Lorelai had said she was going out early, to babysit her granddaughter Thea's children for the morning, and so she assumed that she had already left. Charlotte flipped on the kettle to make a cup of instant coffee, then let Comet out into the back garden where he did the necessary. While the kettle boiled, Charlotte ensured she kept her word and tidied up after the dog.

'Well, old chap,' she said as she settled onto the cosy sofa that occupied the living area. 'What shall we do today? I think I'm in the mood for a bit of exploring. What do you say we take a wander and see what we can discover around here?'

Comet tipped his silky black head to one side and regarded her with his usual quizzical expression. Charlotte laughed. It never got boring, having a cocker spaniel as a companion. And she knew he'd be happy to take some exercise with her. Quickly, after grabbing a piece of toast and gulping down the rest of her coffee, she showered, dressed, and was soon locking the door to her rooms and heading out down the driveway.

It really was shaping up to be a stunning morning. The sun was already high in the sky, and the air smelt fresh, warm and inviting. Charlotte had packed a small rucksack with her phone, some water for herself and Comet and the notebook and pen she carried everywhere, and resolved to see if she could find the Lower Brambleton Observatory. Officially, she wasn't due to start for another day or so, but she wanted to get her bearings. She knew it was within walking distance of Nightshade Cottage, through the woodland incline and at the top of the hill, but it wouldn't hurt to test that distance before she actually had to be there.

As Charlotte walked along the path that seemed to double back around Nightshade Cottage, she noticed that Lorelai's home really was the only house for quite a distance. Although she'd begun following the narrow road that led to the house's driveway, she was soon directed by her phone's GPS, which, to her relief, was working, albeit intermittently, to a footpath that took her up through a copse of pine trees and up the hill. She'd expected a bit of a climb: most observatories were at a higher point than the settlements around them, but the one at Lower Brambleton was still fairly close to the village itself, perhaps because there was relatively little light pollution this deep into the countryside. All that would change with the new houses, she thought. But that wasn't really her dilemma to consider.

Making her way through the pine copse, which was heavy with the scent of warm sap and the mouldering remnants of wild garlic underfoot, Charlotte amused herself by watching Comet darting in and out of the trees, tail wagging, snout to the ground. She hoped he wouldn't find anything to roll in. No matter how fond Lorelai seemed of him, that wouldn't do him any favours with their new landlady. She loved the way he explored his surroundings, and it was wonderful to see him off-lead in a place where she didn't have to worry about meeting other people, or their dogs. In Bristol she'd had to keep a sharp eye on him, in case his questing nose got him into trouble.

Eventually, the trees began to thin, and the top of the hill levelled off to a flat plain that extended across a generous sweep of land. Charlotte spotted a red-brick building with a central tower enclosed by a high chain-link fence in the near distance, about four hundred metres from her. That had to be the observatory. From this aspect, across a field of grass that looked as though it hadn't seen a mower in months, it looked lonely and unloved. Suddenly, Charlotte felt a sense of sadness that its time would soon be over.

Not your problem, she told herself firmly. She had a job to do, and she was determined to do it. Sometimes, you just had to divorce yourself from your emotions and look at things in a scientific and factual way. Years of research had taught her that.

Making her way across the field of tall grass, wishing she'd put jeans on instead of the cut-off denim shorts she'd chosen for the walk, she drew closer to the building. First impressions were not encouraging. There was mortar missing from between the serried layers of red brick, the dome that topped the observatory and provided the opening for the telescope was green with age and, alarmingly, had what appeared to be cracks across several facets. A vibrant green ivy plant twined possessively up one side of the building, and the windows that were inset into the heavy metal door at the front of it were grimy and blackened with dust and cobwebs.

Charlotte had been warned by the contact at Flowerdew Homes that the observatory had lain abandoned for some years, and that a security company had looked after the land and the building since it had closed, but that hadn't stopped quite a few attempts by people hellbent on breaking in to try their luck on the site. As a consequence, there was a heavy chain-link fence wrapped protectively around the building, with razor wire on top, and piles and piles of junk and rubbish, obviously fly-tipped, at various points inside and outside the fence's perimeter. An old mattress, mouldy and damp, lay on its side just past the padlocked chain that marked the entry to the building. Several black bin liners, their contents spilling out like innards, obviously having been attacked by the local wildlife in need of a snack, were piled up. Charlotte wrinkled her nose at the smell of rotting refuse.

'I think I'd best put you on a lead when you come with me tomorrow,' Charlotte said, reaching down to touch Comet's soft head. It was partly for her own reassurance. She'd known the building was going to be a challenge, but the reality of it, deserted, abandoned, unloved, abused by time and indifferent locals, gave her a sense of melancholy that she was finding hard to shake. After the peace, tranquillity and wonderful atmosphere of Nightshade Cottage, it was an unpleasant contrast.

Pausing a moment longer to look at the path that led from the gated fence to the front door of the observatory, Charlotte wasn't prepared for Comet, who'd caught sight of something on the other side of the fence, to suddenly wriggle through the gap between the gate and the fence and shoot off in pursuit.

'Comet!' she shouted, heart thumping. 'Get back here, you bugger!'

Comet, however, was following his instincts. She watched as he rounded the corner of the observatory and disappeared from view.

Calling his name again, she started to panic. This place, with all of its waste hazards, would be an absolute nightmare for a naturally inquisitive dog. He could have eaten anything by the time she caught up with him, not to mention cutting his feet on discarded items. The thought of syringes, rusty tin cans and broken glass raced through her mind. She *had* to get through the gate and get him back before he seriously injured himself.

If only she'd waited until she'd arranged to meet the contact that Flowerdew Homes had appointed! He'd have all the keys, and it would have been a matter of moments to retrieve her dog. Pushing against the fence, she attempted to wriggle through the small gap that she'd managed to create. It wasn't going to be big enough, she realised. She had one arm through, but that was about it.

'Comet!' she yelled again, but frustratingly, the spaniel remained out of sight. Pushing herself harder into the gap, breathing in as far as she could and starting a rather unbecoming wriggle, Charlotte could feel the cold steel of the fence biting into her back and chest as she wedged herself between the gate and the fence. 'Just a little further...' she muttered to herself, thanking goodness she'd only had one slice of toast for breakfast. But it was no good. She'd pushed through as far as the fence was prepared to admit her in its locked state.

'Comet!' This time, there was a hitch of pain and frustration in her voice.

Then, breaking into her worry came a harsh, angry voice. 'Just what the hell do you think you're doing? Didn't you read the bloody sign? This is private property, and you're trespassing!'

6

Tristan Ashcombe wasn't having a good day. In fact, if he was being honest, the whole week hadn't been that much cop, either. Or the month. Or the year to date. And now, what was supposed to have been a brief recce of the Observatory Field site to double check a couple of details before the final planning meeting on Monday had turned into a rout of yet another trespasser. Why couldn't they just leave this bloody place alone?

'Oi!' he shouted again. 'Can't you hear me? The observatory is out of bounds.'

Striding through the long grass, his jeans-clad legs that were tucked into Wellington boots made short work of the fifty yards between himself and the interloper. In irritation, Tristan swept his curly light-chestnut hair out of his eyes, which were now fixed on the figure who was struggling, seemingly caught between the gate and the fence. As he drew closer, to his further annoyance he realised there was a small, scrappy-looking dog gambolling around the entrance to the observatory building.

'I suppose that animal belongs to you, too, does it?' he snarled as the blasted dog began to yap. 'Can't you shut it up?'

The woman, who was still struggling to free herself from the two halves of the fence, turned furious eyes to him. 'He's protective,' she snapped back. 'He doesn't like it when people shout. Especially dickheads who appear to be threatening me.'

Tristan stopped a couple of yards in front of her. 'Well, maybe you shouldn't be trespassing, then,' he retorted. It was bad enough that he'd been dragged down here on a Sunday morning, and now he had to deal with some hippy-dippy walker, who, from the look of her, probably believed she and her dog were entitled to roam anywhere they chose.

'I'm not trespassing,' the woman, whose auburn hair had caught in the links of the fence, retorted. 'I just wanted to take a look.'

'Well, you've no right to be here,' Tristan replied. He paused. 'You or your badly behaved dog. Don't you know there are hazards behind that fence where idiots have been fly tipping for years? Both of you could end up injured.'

'Don't *you* think I know that?' she replied. 'I hadn't been intending to go anywhere near the place. Comet wriggled his way through the gap in the fence, and I was trying to rescue him before he got hurt.'

Tristan's irritation subsided fractionally when he heard the concern in the woman's voice and saw the way her eyes suddenly glistened at the thought of her dog suffering a mishap. He gave a deep sigh. 'Well,' he said after a beat or two, 'it's a bloody good job I brought the keys along with me, then, isn't it?' Briskly, he unhooked the key holder from his jeans and hurried forward to unlock the padlock that kept the thick steel chain in place. As he did so, he caught the warm scent of a floral perfume emanating from the woman's body. Fumbling slightly with the padlock, he pulled it away and the chain slithered to the ground, landing coiled and snake-like in the long grass.

'There you go,' he said, pushing the gate open. 'Now you can get your dog back.'

'Thank you,' the woman replied stiffly. She looked up at him, and her clear blue eyes, the same colour as the sky above them, showed appreciation along with some residual discomfort.

'Comet!' she shouted, moving away from him. She went to go further into the compound where the observatory building was.

'Stop!' Tristan said quickly. He'd noticed, as she'd moved away from him, that she was only wearing a pair of Grecian-style flat sandals on her feet. Open toes and thin soles were no match for the potential dangers embedded in the long grass. 'Like I said, there's all kinds of stuff in there. You're not exactly dressed to get through it.' He looked down again at the woman's denim shorts and insubstantial footwear. 'You don't want to get stabbed by broken glass, barbed wire, or worse.'

'What about Comet's paws?' the woman replied. 'I can't just let him run around in there.'

Tristan sighed again. 'Give me his lead. I'll get him.'

'He won't come to you,' she said. 'He doesn't like strangers.'

'Have you got any treats?' Tristan replied. 'My gran's old Labrador would go with anyone if they offered him a gravy bone!'

'Spaniels aren't the same,' the woman replied, slightly mutinously. Nevertheless, she passed him the lead and a pouch of small, savoury scented miniature bone-shaped treats.

'Won't be a tick,' Tristan replied. For some reason, he wanted to find this dog, and it wasn't just because animal and woman were trespassers. He could see the concern in her eyes, and her very real worry for her pet. He suddenly wanted to bring the dog back to her.

'Comet, did you say his name was?' Tristan asked.

The woman nodded.

Tristan smiled for the first time since they'd encountered one another. 'Leave it to me.' He glanced down at himself. 'After all, I'm more sensibly dressed for walking through a junkyard!' He wanted to say more to reassure her, but he realised that the best thing to do would be to get her dog back.

Striding off, Tristan took a left to follow the side wall of the building and called Comet's name once, then twice. Frustratingly, there was no response, not even a whimper. At least that hopefully meant the dog hadn't fallen foul of a rusty nail or bedspring to the paw, Tristan thought. Eyes peeled for the sight of a small black dog in the shade of the building, he glanced back behind him and could just see the woman making her way gingerly, footstep by careful footstep, through the unkempt grass.

'Stay there!' he called back to her. 'Honestly, you don't want to be wandering around here if your shoes aren't armour-plated.' He was only half joking. The first time he'd visited the site after the planning decision had been made was on a grim mid-November day. He'd been wearing brogues with virtually no grip on the soles. Not only had they ended up covered in mud and rendered unwearable, but when he'd removed them that evening, he'd found a rusty section of barbed wire embedded in the heel. A tetanus jab hadn't been on his list of things to do when he took on this job, and so he'd been careful ever since to avoid wearing anything other than stout boots when he'd come to Observatory Field, whatever the weather.

'Comet!' he shouted, feeling irked now. Where was this bloody dog? From behind him, he could hear the woman shouting the dog's name, too. She clearly hadn't trained the spaniel very well: his recall was shocking. Continuing on, turning another corner so that he was at the back of the building, he suddenly caught sight of a pair of black furry haunches, wriggling frantically and whimpering in fear and frustration.

'There you are,' he murmured, picking up the pace. Raising his voice, he called back to the woman. 'It's all right. I've found him.'

Hurrying towards the dog, it didn't take Tristan long to realise that the stupid thing had got its head caught inside a cracked and mould-ridden plastic drinks bottle. Unable to see where he was going, Comet had jammed the bottle between the bricks of the foundations of an old shed and was struggling to free himself. Despite his earlier irritation, Tristan's heart sped up with a mixture of alarm and sympathy.

'It's OK, boy, I'll get you out.' Speaking softly, keeping his voice low, he approached the dog carefully. Even the most docile of canines could get aggressive and snappy if it was afraid, and Tristan didn't want a nasty bite. Stooping down, he reached out a hand, and ran it along the dog's silken black back, muttering soothing nonsense as he tried to get the dog calm enough to begin the process of removing him from the jammed bricks, and then the bottle.

'It's all right, Comet, easy now,' he said as he carefully manoeuvred the bottle out from the gap between the bricks. That was the easy bit, he thought. He didn't want to risk getting a nasty nip from the frightened animal. Smoothing down the dog's fur with one hand, he tried to remove the bottle from the dog's head, but it was jammed over his ears. If the lid had still been on it, the poor creature would have suffocated. Tristan felt a flare of anger at people's thoughtlessness and carelessness. Did those idiots who blithely dumped their rubbish here ever think about the consequences of their actions?

Mindful that Comet might bolt if he took his hands away, Tristan clipped the lead the woman had given to him to the dog's collar. Then, slipping the loop of the lead over his wrist, he reached into his pocket to retrieve the penknife he always carried with him on his visits out in the field. Flipping the blade out, he made an incision into the plastic, worryingly aware of the dog's flesh and Comet's panicky wriggling. He kept up the flow of gentle chatter as he slowly sliced through the bottle until, with relief, he'd cut it enough to pull it from the dog's head and free him. Breathing out fully, Tristan ruffled the dog's ears.

'You don't look like you're hurt,' he said, 'but I bet your mistress will be checking every inch of you over. Let's get you back to her, shall we?'

Not wanting to risk the dog's paws on the ground, Tristan scooped Comet up in his arms. The dog smelt a bit whiffy from whatever moulds and cultures had been residing in the bottle, and Tristan grimaced as Comet pushed his face upwards and gave his rescuer a stinky lick of gratitude.

'Thanks,' he said dryly, wondering how many washes it would take to get the mud and mould stains out of his green polo shirt. 'Perhaps I'll send your mistress my laundry bill!'

7

Charlotte was dying to follow this rather intimidating stranger who'd strode off to find Comet. Her heart, which had reached Usain Bolt levels of racing whilst she'd been caught in between the gate and the fence, had sped up even further when her eyes had met his across the sturdy steel padlock. It was just fear and worry about what scrapes Comet had managed to get into, she told herself firmly. After all, the dog could have stumbled upon anything if the guy who'd got her out of the fence was to be believed. Looking around her, now that she was inside the compound that made up the observatory, she realised he hadn't been exaggerating. When he'd told her to stay put, much as she was desperate to follow him and find Comet, she knew she'd be risking tetanus at the very least. Evidence of campfires, rusty tin cans, ancient rubbish sacks that overflowed with such dubious contents as dirty disposable nappies, vegetable peelings and old cans of lager and Somerset's speciality, cider, completed the grim, depressing picture. She'd been to see Banksy's art installation and parody theme park 'Dismaland' a few years back where it had been installed on the sea front of Weston-Super-Mare:

Observatory Field would have given the mysterious artist a run for his money.

Shifting impatiently on the spot, Charlotte breathed a sigh of relief when she finally saw Comet's saviour coming back with a black, wriggling bundle in his arms. She blinked rapidly as she felt tears prickling her eyes, and although she wanted to dash over the remaining ground between them, she continued to heed his advice.

'Here he is, at last,' the man said as he and Comet reached her. 'I think he's all right, but it probably wouldn't hurt to give him a bath and keep an eye on him for a day or two. Are you on holiday here? Do you have a regular vet where you live who could check him over, just in case?'

So many questions in such a short space of time made Charlotte's head spin, although that could just be the relief at getting Comet back safely. She nodded, shook her head, and then realised she must look like a total idiot.

'No, er, yes, and thank you,' she stammered as the man gently returned Comet to the ground. She noticed the streaks of mud all over the guy's dark green polo shirt. 'I'm so sorry,' she continued. 'He looks like he got into a right state.'

'He got his head trapped in a broken plastic bottle. These lowlifes who dump their rubbish here don't give animals a second thought.'

The cosy notions about the observatory that Charlotte had been harbouring in her imagination had all but gone by this point. If this was what it was like on the outside, God only knew what it was going to be like inside! She resolved to buy a pair of steel toe-capped work boots to make this trip in future. She also wondered how on earth she was going to stop Comet from hurting himself if she brought him to work with her.

'Well,' she stammered. 'Thank you for rescuing him.'

'As I said, you shouldn't be poking around in here. It's private property; parts of it are derelict and a lot of it is dangerous. The only reason it's still standing is because some boffins from the university are coming to remove anything of so-called historical significance from the records room before it gets demolished. It's certainly no place for tourists or walkers.'

Charlotte's hackles rose again at his dismissive tone. 'I'm not a tourist,' she replied shortly.

'And not a serious walker, either,' the man replied, 'if those sandals are anything to go by. Which begs the question... why are you trespassing?'

At that moment, Comet emitted a distressed whimper. Immediately, Charlotte dropped to her knees to examine him. 'What is it, boy?' she said gently. 'Did you run into something that hurt you?' Ignoring the mud and the stench from whatever it was he'd been rolling about in, she smoothed back his ears, and saw that he had a cut inside one of them. 'The plastic from the bottle must have nicked him. I'd better get him home and get the wound cleaned.'

'And the rest of him,' the guy replied. 'And I'd better lock the gate back up, or God only knows who else will come along and decide to break in.' He heaved a sigh. 'Some people never learn.'

Charlotte stood back up and made for the gate again. She dithered for a second about telling him why she'd been near the observatory, but then figured the sooner she got away and looked at Comet's ear, the better. Following him back to the gate, she stepped through and then, as he refastened the padlock, thanked him again.

'I really do appreciate you finding Comet for me,' she said. 'And next time, I'll know to be more careful.'

'Don't let there be a next time,' he said shortly. 'This is no place for a dog with zero recall and an owner with summer shoes. It's dangerous in there. You don't know what you're dealing with.'

Charlotte wanted to bite back a retort, but she decided to make a swift getaway. He had the manner of some jobsworth council worker and, grateful as she was for his rescue of her dog, she didn't want another lecture. 'Well, I'll be seeing you,' she said brightly. 'Come on, Comet, let's get you home.'

As she strode back down the field towards the woodland path that would take her back to Nightshade Cottage, Charlotte wondered why she hadn't just told him the reason she'd been there. After all, she was going to start work there tomorrow: and although she might *technically* have been trespassing since she'd been a day early, she was soon going to be spending plenty of time at Observatory Field. She supposed it had been a combination of his manner, which had been brusque and abrupt, unsurprising under the circumstances, and the fact that he really was rather attractive, with that curling chestnut hair and those long, long legs. And his eyes weren't bad, either, even if most of the time he'd been scowling at her. Gemma always said she chose the grumpy types: perhaps she was just proving true to form.

Shaking her head, dismissing any thoughts of Comet's rescuer, it wasn't until she'd got back to Lorelai's cottage that she realised she didn't even know his name.

8

It had just gone eleven o'clock when Charlotte got back to Nightshade Cottage. She hoped that Lorelai had a hosepipe somewhere that she could use to clean off her disobedient and stinky dog before he set a paw back into her accommodation. Keeping Comet close to her heels, she pushed open the gate to the back garden and was immediately greeted by two whirling balls of energy, who were racing around the immaculately mown lawn, spraying one another with pump-action Nerf water pistols. Shrieks of laughter and splashes of cold water came in quick succession, as the children, a boy and a girl, made the most of Lorelai's enormous expanse of garden.

Spotting Comet, they paused in their battle and approached.

'Ooh, what's his name? Is he friendly? Can I stroke him?' the older child, a girl of around ten, asked breathlessly, still obviously feeling the exertions of the water pistol battle.

'I wouldn't just yet,' Charlotte warned. 'He's er, he's been rolling around in some pretty stinky stuff.' She was also mindful that, while Comet loved children and was the gentlest creature in the world, a sore ear might test his patience.

'Ugh, I can smell him,' the boy, whom Charlotte judged to be around eight, observed, wrinkling his nose. 'What did he roll in?'

'I'm not quite sure,' Charlotte confessed. 'I was hoping your gran might have a hosepipe I could use to shower him off. Is there one?'

Before either of the children could respond, Lorelai came bustling out of the back door and up to them all. 'Well, he's certainly had a good morning!' she said, smiling.

'I'm so sorry,' Charlotte said. 'He raced off when I was up at Observatory Field and got himself into a spot of bother, and a lot of mess.' She thought about mentioning the man who'd rescued Comet, but didn't want to elaborate too much while the dog was still quietly reeking next to her. 'Do you have a hose I could use to wash him off? I don't want to let him anywhere near the house smelling like this!'

'I can do better than that, dear,' Lorelai replied. 'There's a low fitted Belfast sink in the utility room, just off the patio. Why don't you pop him in there and wash him down with some warmer water? Don't want to give the poor boy too much of a shock.'

'It's far more than he deserves,' Charlotte responded, giving a brief grin. 'He should learn not to roll in things he encounters.'

'Well, I had the sink put in for washing wellie boots and muddy grandchildren off when they came back from woodland walks, so he's not going to do it any harm, I promise you. What *did* he find up there?'

'I'm not really sure,' Charlotte replied, 'but the sooner I get it off him, the better.' She furrowed her brow. 'I've got some shampoo I brought with me – would you mind holding his lead while I nip in and get it?'

Grabbing the lavender-scented shampoo from her bathroom, Charlotte was soon soaping Comet down in the generously proportioned ceramic Belfast sink. She remembered her parents having one of these in their back garden as a flower trough, and it was nice to have some warm water to really scrub the lavender shampoo into Comet's shaggy fur. Making sure she got to every inch of him, she went more carefully around his injured ear, and was relieved, once she'd rinsed him off with the warm water, that the cut seemed superficial. No need to consult a vet just yet.

'I've brought you a towel.' Lorelai came back into the utility room. 'Don't worry, it's just an old one I keep for mopping up when the washing machine leaks! Should be fine for him, though.'

'Thanks again,' Charlotte replied. 'And don't worry, I promise this won't be a regular thing. I'll be keeping him on a lead when I'm working up at Observatory Field from tomorrow.'

'So, is he safe to go and frolic with Cora and Dylan?' Lorelai asked. 'They're dying to meet him properly.'

Charlotte smiled. 'I'm sure he'd love that. But tell them not to touch his ears – whatever he was doing when he was off-lead, he's managed to cut one of them.' She lifted Comet out of the sink and popped him on the tiled floor to dry him off. 'I'll come out and supervise. He's great with kids, but I wouldn't want them to get scratched or nipped if he gets too excited.'

After giving Comet a brisk rub down, so that when he shook himself there wouldn't be too much spray, Charlotte mooched out into the back garden again, Comet at her heels.

'I decided to bring the kids back here for a couple of hours,' Lorelai explained. 'Thea's current house is so small, and the garden is barely the size of a postage stamp. The children are good, but they love racing around my garden, and they don't have to worry about upsetting the neighbours with their shouting and screaming if they're here. One of Thea's neighbours isn't overly fond of children, and these two have had the rough edge of her tongue for playing a little loudly in the summer.'

'Well, they've certainly got plenty of space here,' Charlotte said appreciatively. 'They must love it, all of the lawn to run around on and the trees to climb.'

'They do,' Lorelai smiled, but there was a wistful sense to her expression once again. 'I do wish they could afford to move back to Lower Brambleton sooner, but the house prices have rocketed in recent years. Thea and her brother grew up in the village, you see, first with their parents, my son and his wife, and then, when they died, the children lived with me. Thea, especially, wishes she could come back to live somewhere in the village.'

'I'm so sorry for your loss,' Charlotte said softly. 'That must have been incredibly painful.' She looked out towards the children, who were, once again, racing around with freshly filled water pistols. Comet, keen to get in on the act, gambolled nearby until Cora leaned down and encouraged him over to her.

'Watch his ears, dear,' Lorelai interjected quickly, obviously keen to get away from the awful subject of death. 'He's cut one of them, so don't touch.'

'I won't, Granny!' Cora replied. Charlotte smiled as she heard Cora explain the warning solemnly to her younger brother, Dylan. Then, once Comet had found his paws, they continued their game.

'I've learned to make the most of these moments,' Lorelai said reflectively. 'After all, I'm not sure how many of them I'll have left.' She brushed away Charlotte's polite murmurs. 'That's why I choose to have lodgers from time to time, you see. Conversation keeps the old brain cells active, and I do so love meeting new people. Of course, now Flowerdew Homes has permission to build on the land on the other side of the wood, there'll be a lot of newcomers into the village. That'll take some getting used to.'

'And you said last night you're in favour of it?' Charlotte asked as they settled themselves in the garden chairs. 'The new development, I mean?'

Lorelai looked surprised at the question. 'Of course!' she said. 'I know that might surprise you, but as I said, Thea's got her heart set on one of the new houses, so she can move closer to me as I head towards la-la land. It'll be nice to have her nearby.' She paused. 'I suppose you thought, because I'm old and I have a nice house, that I'd automatically be against it?'

Charlotte flushed. 'Well, yes, I suppose I did.'

'Glad to see I'm still capable of surprising people,' Lorelai replied with a grin. 'Of course, it's not ideal, but Observatory Field has been a wasteland for years. Ever since the observatory itself was formally closed, it's been a magnet for the less desirable elements of the community. It'll be a good thing when it's cleared and finally put to some use.'

'But it's such a special site,' Charlotte said. 'It seems criminal just to tear it down now, no matter what state it's in.'

'Some things deserve to be torn down,' Lorelai replied, and this time there was no mistaking the dark edge to her tone, more pronounced than it had been last night when they'd first discussed the development. 'It'll be for the best when that place is gone. And then, maybe everyone can at last move on.'

Charlotte's curiosity was fully piqued now, but at that moment, Comet came trotting back to her and put two wet paws onto her knees. 'Worked up an appetite, have you, pup?' she laughed. 'Well, perhaps it's time for a treat or two.' As she felt into her pocket for the gravy bones the dog so adored, she mused on Lorelai's words. She wondered if, when she started archiving Observatory Field, she'd find some answers to the questions Lorelai's words had raised.

9

After a leisurely Sunday afternoon, Charlotte went to bed that evening in a state of excited anticipation about starting her job at Observatory Field. She was again surprised at how well she slept, and as the bird chorus woke her with the dawn, she stretched luxuriously in her bed and began running through the things she needed to remember for her first day. It was going to be a tricky job, to balance the interests of the university with those of Flowerdew Homes, and after seeing the state of the outside of the observatory yesterday, she knew she had to factor in extra care if she was going to stick to her original plan and take Comet with her. She certainly didn't want him off-lead and getting into trouble again.

'Morning, love,' Lorelai said as, a short time later, Charlotte wandered out of the exterior door that led to the back garden. Lorelai was sitting on a chair on the patio, drinking a leisurely cuppa and nibbling on a piece of toast. 'Looking forward to your first day?' she asked as they both watched Comet snuffling and sniffing around.

Charlotte nodded. 'I can't wait to get through the door and

see what's in there.' She felt a frisson of excitement every time she thought about the treasures that might be hidden in the observatory. But then her worry about Comet, who was looking expectantly at her at the prospect of another jaunt, resurfaced.

Lorelai, sharp and inquisitive, obviously noticed the way Charlotte's gaze had shifted to the dog, who, having just had his breakfast, was now champing at the bit to get going. Charlotte had told her what had happened yesterday, although she'd left out the part about the guy who'd rescued Comet. She still wasn't sure why.

'You're worried about taking this one back there, aren't you?' Lorelai said, gesturing to Comet, who was looking up at Lorelai, hoping for a bit of toast for himself. There was a slight pause.

'I'd be lying if I said I wasn't,' Charlotte admitted. 'I was hoping I could give him a bit of a free rein but the land around the observatory is in a worse state than I'd been led to believe. Until I've checked out how dog-proof and safe the actual building is, he's going to get awfully bored being kept on a lead all day.'

Lorelai glanced down at Comet, who regarded her back with bright, hopeful eyes. Charlotte suppressed a smile as an understanding seemed to pass between the old lady and the spaniel.

'Well, he's more than welcome to spend the day with me, today, if you're happy to leave him,' Lorelai said as she looked back at Charlotte. 'As you know, the garden is dog-proof and I've got no plans to go out.'

Charlotte shook her head. 'Oh, I couldn't possibly impose him on you. He can be a bit of a handful when he gets bored.'

'I'd best make sure he doesn't get bored, then!' Lorelai replied. 'I reckon a quick stroll in the woods would do us both good, anyway.' She looked fondly down at Comet. 'I used to have a chocolate Labrador who never learned to stop pulling on the lead... after that, a spaniel will be a breeze!'

'Only if you're sure,' Charlotte said, but she was already relieved at the offer. Not having to worry about Comet for her first day would be a definite plus.

'Say no more,' Lorelai replied. 'Just leave whatever he needs with me. We'll keep each other company today.'

'Thank you so much,' Charlotte replied. 'It would be a weight off my mind.' She knelt down and took Comet's head in her hands. 'And you make sure you behave yourself,' she said sternly. She grinned as Comet raised innocent eyes to his mistress. Dropping a kiss on the top of his nose, she got back to her feet.

'I'm not sure how long I'll be up there, today,' she said. 'But I'll try to get back as soon as I can.'

'Take your time,' Lorelai said breezily. 'I'm sure Comet and I will find plenty to talk about.'

After thanking Lorelai effusively once more, Charlotte shoved her lunch into her backpack and headed back out to Observatory Field. At least, she thought, having given the place a bit of a recce yesterday, she was more prepared for the hazards of the site. She'd put on a pair of sturdy walking boots and jeans and was wearing a striped T-shirt under a long-sleeved sweatshirt. It was a far cry from the sandals and shorts of yesterday.

Thoughts of the day before inevitably led back to her encounter with the brusque guy on site, and as she walked briskly uphill through the woods her mind was drawn back to what had happened. She couldn't blame him really, for being pissed off with her: she'd looked like yet another trespasser, and it had been clear from his reaction that the observatory had been plagued with them. Hopefully, that would be the last she'd see of him. She tried to put the whole unpleasant incident to the back of her mind: Comet's ear, once bathed and disinfected, seemed fine, and at least he was safely tucked away at Nightshade Cottage for the day. Charlotte was free to concentrate on the job at hand.

Picking up her pace, she was soon at the entrance to Observatory Field and covering the distance across the expanse of grass to where the building itself sat dejectedly in the centre. She could see why, in its heyday, it had been a fabulous spot to observe the stars. There would be virtually no light pollution out here, and the flat expanse made it accessible. She felt a stab of sadness that the building was going to be demolished but steeled herself to give it the respect it deserved in its final days and weeks. She cast her mind back to Lorelai's strange reaction when they'd talked about it yesterday. There was a story there. She hoped, while she was staying at Nightshade Cottage, that she might eventually be let into Lorelai's confidence. Villages like Lower Brambleton were rich with folklore and history, and while things inevitably had to change, that didn't mean the history should be forgotten.

As Charlotte drew closer to the building, she could see a figure was already at the gate. Relieved that it wasn't the same man she'd encountered yesterday, she drew in a breath and upped her pace. She'd had an email to say that someone would be meeting her at the entrance, and now her work was about to start, she felt the rising excitement. She'd do her very best for Observatory Field, and she couldn't wait to get stuck in.

10

'Hello there!' The ringing voice, with its broad, rolling Somerset 'R', was attached to a stout, grey-haired man wearing a green sweatshirt and a broad smile. 'I was wondering if you'd make it without a guide.'

Charlotte found herself smiling, but slightly overwhelmed by the expansive greeting and firm handshake of the man who quickly introduced himself as Brian O'Connor, former custodian of the observatory and current chairman of LBAS – the Lower Brambleton Astronomical Society.

'Hi,' she said as her hand was being shaken vigorously. 'It's nice to meet you.'

Brian jangled a set of keys that he'd unhooked from his belt, and as the two of them made chitchat, he unlocked the gate and then led her to the grimy-looking front door of the old observatory building.

'I'm sorry it's in such a state,' he said as he began searching for the right keys to admit them. 'It's been left to decay for a good few years now, and though LBAS still meets from time to time, none of the surviving members are as spry as we used to be, so those meetings tend to happen in the pub – especially when it's damp outside!'

Charlotte nodded. 'The observatory is rather tucked out of the way up here,' she said. 'But it still seems a shame it's going to be torn down.'

Brian gave her a tight smile. 'It is what it is,' he said. 'And to be honest, there are plenty of people around here who'll be glad to see the back of it.' He gestured around the immediate grounds. 'As you can see, it's been a bit of a draw for the parish's less, er, desirable inhabitants.'

He didn't wait for her to reply, but turned back to the door and, with a heft of his prop-forward's shoulders, he pushed it open. 'Bear with me a second while I go and switch on the fuse box,' he said as he hurried inside the building. 'I wouldn't want you to take a tumble on your first day.'

As Charlotte hovered inside the doorway, waiting for the lights to come on, a waft of damp, dust and neglect found its way to her nostrils. She hadn't been advised to wear a mask, or any protective gear, while she was archiving but she was beginning to wonder if the university really knew what she was going to be dealing with. She suspected Flowerdew Homes, despite her contract, just wanted the place emptied as quickly as possible, and they weren't too bothered about how she went about it. What she could make out from the light of the outside world, as it did its best to penetrate the gloom of the observatory, was that there was a lot of junk to contend with. But, she thought as the main area shimmered to life and the space came into view, perhaps there might be some treasure as well.

'You can come in, now,' Brian called from the back of the space. He walked briskly back to join her, a bright yellow hard hat perched atop his head, and another in his hand for her. 'Flowerdew insisted that I give you one of these for when you're working inside the building,' he said, 'and there's a hi-vis yellow vest hanging on one of the hooks on the right-hand wall. Even if you're up here alone, you should probably get used to wearing them.'

Charlotte nodded, feeling nervous all of a sudden. This was the first time she'd worked in a building in this state, and she had sudden visions of parts of the dome, which, when she glanced upwards, seemed more rust than anything else, falling down on her when she started moving things around.

'Wow,' she said, as her gaze shifted to take in the space she'd be calling her office for the next few weeks. 'It's really quite something...'

'You should have seen it thirty years ago!' Brian replied. His voice assumed a faraway timbre. 'Back in the 1990s, the observatory was one of the most important astronomical sites in Somerset, if not the whole of the south-west. Everyone thinks of the Bristol or Redland observatories when it comes to local hotspots, but here had its fair share of discoveries, too.'

Charlotte got the feeling that Brian was warming to his subject, but she was in no rush, and she was interested. 'Such as?' she asked, prompting him when he appeared lost in thought.

'Well, of course, you must know that the observatory was built in 1895 by Dr Eleanor Winslow, a pioneering astronomer of her time. She wanted a somewhere away from the city's lights to study the stars.'

'Yes,' Charlotte nodded. 'The Winslow papers form a central part of the archive for the West Country. Dr Winslow and her team made significant contributions to the study of variable stars and the mapping of the Milky Way.'

'That's correct.' Brian nodded approvingly. 'The observatory was bustling with activity until the 1960s, when, with the advent of better technology, it began to be used more recreationally than as a serious venue for research. It was kept alive by a long line of volunteers, and became the beneficiary of a number of bequests, donations, gifts, which meant that the Lower Brambleton Astronomical Society could use it as their base for the next thirty years or so.'

Charlotte could well envisage the kind of hobbyists and enthusiasts who would have kept the observatory ticking over. People who had a passion for their subject, chronicling the activities of the stars above them while they still could.

'So, what happened?' Charlotte asked as she and Brian began a slow tour of the building. 'How did it fall into such disrepair?'

Brian sighed. 'A combination of factors, really. After all, we are out in the sticks. As I'm sure you've worked out, Lower Brambleton's infrastructure isn't the best, and there's virtually no service out here for mobile phones, internet, other communications. Part of its appeal used to be that remoteness: after all, we astronomers are constantly on a quest to avoid light pollution, but what gave it its strengths back in the day eventually made it weak. Most of Lower Brambleton uses a satellite network for the world wide web, but there was no way that this place, effectively a hobby observatory, was going to have the funds to put in something like that. And so, what once gave it an advantage has become a liability.'

'I'm surprised, though,' Charlotte observed, 'that the universities passed it up. It must be a site of special scientific interest, still.'

Brian shook his head. 'Most of the Winslow papers have been removed and archived. You've probably handled a lot of them yourself in the course of your research. As for the rest...' he paused. 'Well, let's just say there are some who'd rather the more recent history of this place stayed buried. There are a few people around here who will be glad to see it torn down and built over.'

As she had when Lorelai had spoken about the subject, Charlotte felt a desire to know more. There was a story here, she was sure of it, and, fascinating as the original story of Eleanor Winslow was, it was the more contemporary history she was curious about. 'What do you mean by that, Brian?' she asked.

Brian sighed. 'Well,' he said. 'Why don't I give you the proper tour while I tell you, and then you might get to realise why getting rid of things isn't always the worst decision.'

Ears pricked, Charlotte felt a frisson of excitement.

11

Charlotte's curiosity began to rise as Brian led her carefully around the interior of the observatory. The ground floor was cracked and uneven, the tiles lifting from damp and neglect. Faded posters from the 1980s and 1990s, advertising public stargazing nights and special lectures, and photographs of celestial events and past members of the Lower Brambleton Astronomical Society lined the walls, their edges curling with age. Charlotte didn't have time to wonder why the LBAS hadn't started to clear up already: the entrance hall and ground floor felt like a time capsule. She had the feeling, though, from the conspiratorial tone of Brian's voice as he began to speak again, that she was about to find out.

'There's been a lot of legal wrangling over it,' Brian said as he led her across the floor towards the open, curved staircase that led up to the viewing gallery at the top of the dome. 'It's been locked up for the past few years and because the Winslow papers were removed in the late nineties, no one was bothered about the rest, until Flowerdew started sniffing around to develop the area. When their offer was accepted for the land, they put in high-level security, and made sure everything was safe. We at the Lower Brambleton Astronomical Society weren't allowed in to retrieve anything, either. They bought it right from under us.'

'But surely it was better for the experts to remove what's in here than just chuck it into a skip?' Charlotte asked.

Brian paused at the foot of the steps that began the ascent to the ancient, dilapidated, green-stained dome. Back in the heyday of the observatory, the dome would open like a gigantic celestial eye, to allow the telescope an uninterrupted view of the night sky. Now, since the telescope had been removed some years ago, its absence made the area seem wide, empty, devoid of purpose.

'You'd think so,' Brian replied, 'but Flowerdew weren't bothered about that. All they wanted was to get it levelled as quickly as possible. The more time it took to dismantle, the more money they were losing while the development was delayed.'

'So why did they appoint me to come here?' Charlotte asked, half to herself. But Brian, who she sensed was never one to pass up an opportunity to talk, answered it for her.

'There was an old covenant on the building,' he said. 'The owners of the land had stipulated that, should the observatory ever have to be removed, its salvageable contents should be donated to the University of North West Wessex, to sit alongside the Winslow papers for posterity. Flowerdew nearly missed it, but at the last minute the documents were found, held by some tinpot solicitor in Burnham on Sea.' He sighed. 'I'm afraid it's just another part of the very complicated history of the observatory.'

Charlotte made to ascend the staircase, but Brian reached out a hand to stop her. 'Sorry, love,' he said. 'I can't let you go up there. Since the telescope was removed, it's been condemned. Rot, rust, you name it. It's got it all. Shame, really – we had some great nights up in the dome, stargazing and chatting until dawn.' He grinned. 'But needs must, and it's far too dangerous now.'

Charlotte felt a sting of disappointment, but a broken leg, or worse, would have put an end to her work here, so she acquiesced. Turning away from the stairs, she forced a brighter smile. 'So, what else can you show me? If there's nothing left in the dome, what am I supposed to be cataloguing and archiving?'

Brian smiled back. 'Come with me,' he said.

They moved away from the staircase and deeper into the interior of the building. It felt as though they were about to enter the beating heart of the observatory, and Charlotte could see that this room, right in the centre, had been constructed to keep its contents safe and unharmed by the elements. Brian pushed open the steel door, white paint yellowed with age, and rusted from the damp. 'This is what you've really come to sort out.'

As she followed Brian into the records room of the observatory, she couldn't help a gasp of surprise. The records room was a dimly lit space filled with towering bookshelves that reached up to the ceiling. The shelves were now empty, but it was an easy leap to imagine them crammed with journals and magazines during the observatory's heyday. Dust motes danced in the light from the harsh white bulb that flashed on at the flick of a switch. A few chairs and desks were scattered about, their surfaces cluttered with stacks of books and old journals. The musty smell of old paper pervaded the room, a testament to years of neglect. There were green filing cabinets lining all four walls of the room, with handwritten labels on each drawer, which obviously formed the bulk of the paperwork and artefacts that would become Charlotte's focus for the next few weeks. Magazines from the 1980s and 1990s, such as *Sky & Telescope* and *Astronomy*, lay in piles, their covers featuring bold headlines about the latest celestial discoveries and technological advancements of the time.

To say that Charlotte was gobsmacked was an understatement.

'How on earth is this all still here?' she breathed, looking around the room in wonder. 'I mean, all of the rubbish outside... the vandalism... this part looks as though it hasn't been touched in thirty years!'

'Something like that,' Brian said, clearly enjoying her surprise. 'As I said, Flowerdew have been after the observatory for a long time. Their security was incredible, and they've had an option on it for at least a decade, even though the owners weren't prepared to sell immediately. At one point, there was a team of security guards up here twenty-four hours a day, just to keep the hordes out.' He sighed. 'That was another reason why LBAS weren't allowed in.'

'But I'm guessing this is all your stuff?' Charlotte persisted. 'Why weren't you allowed in to retrieve it?'

Brian's face suddenly looked as though it had aged twenty years. 'After everything that happened with Martin and Laura, most of us just wanted to move on. No one had the heart, or the guts, to pack it all away. Too much water under the bridge.'

'Martin and Laura?' Charlotte echoed. She was surprised by Brian's assumption that she'd know who they were, but then that tended to happen a lot in small communities, where everyone did know everyone else, or at least knew someone who did. She paused before adding, in a gentler tone. 'Who are they?'

Brian gave a sad smile. 'Sorry – since you're staying with Lorelai, I assumed you'd know.'

Charlotte drew in a deep breath, and then wished she hadn't as the taste of the dust in the air hit the back of her throat. Coughing slightly, she had time to consider her response. Eventually, she spoke again. 'Lorelai's told me a little about the developments up here,' she said, when the cough had abated. 'But I didn't like to ask too much, for fear of prying. She seemed to have some very strong feelings about it all.'

Brian paused for a long beat. 'Well,' he conceded, as if he was weighing up the wisdom of his next words. 'I suppose, since you'll be spending a lot of time at the observatory, it's only fair that you should know the whole story…'

12

A little time later, Charlotte's assumptions about the life and times of the Lower Brambleton Observatory had been blown wide apart, and then some.

'So, let me get this straight,' she said carefully, after he finally paused for breath. 'You're telling me that this place was not only the hotspot for asteroid spotting in the south-west, but also party central. A kind of nightclub for the astronomy community?' She gave a smile. 'If I didn't know better, I'd say you were having me on, Brian!'

'Where else would a bunch of astronomers come to have a good time?' Brian's eyes twinkled like the stars that, when night fell, would still gaze down at the observatory. 'I mean, your generation, with your internet and your YouTube, documenting everything at the click of a smartphone... you've no idea of the excitement of seeing something for the first time with nothing but your eyes and a telescope, and the experience of sharing those discoveries with friends of a like-minded disposition. When we knew something big was coming, it was star charts and sky maps to the ready, supplies in and nights under the stars. And if those supplies happened to comprise several bottles of good claret or a decent Scotch, then so much the better.' He paused again. 'What goes on in LBAS stays in LBAS. Until now, of course.'

Charlotte considered her own undergraduate studies, and had to concede that she, too, had experienced a few riotous nights under the stars.

'It does all sound rather idyllic,' she said.

'It was a different time,' Brian replied. 'Before we all settled down, got more stressful jobs, had families. Small children tend to put paid to pulling all-nighters in an observatory, although there were a few occasions when the children came with us as well. Of course, after Laura and Martin passed away...' He trailed off.

'What happened to them, Brian?' Charlotte asked gently.

Brian's face fell as he replied. 'They were killed in a car accident in 1995,' he said quietly. 'They'd been up here to shut the observatory down for two months, as was usually done for January and February. There's no heating up here, and we had to adhere to at least some health and safety rules, or the council would have stepped in and closed it permanently. They left their kids, twins, a boy and a girl, with Martin's mum, and were spending the evening closing things up, making sure everything was locked down tight until the weather got a bit warmer. The frost was so bad by the time they were driving back down the hill, whoever was driving lost control of the car, and they crashed into an oak tree.' Brian shuddered. 'They were killed instantly. I can't bear to think about what might have happened if the kids had been in the car with them.'

'How awful!' Charlotte murmured. 'It must have been such a shock for everyone. And those poor children.'

'It was,' Brian replied. 'After that... well, there didn't seem much point in keeping things going. None of us really wanted to, after that. We still meet, from time to time, but it was never the same. You get tainted by tragedy, you know?' Pulling himself back to the present before Charlotte could respond further, Brian shook his head. 'You'll be wanting to look around,' he said, a brisker tone in his voice. 'I'll leave you to it. I don't know what else you'll find here that the university will consider of value, but you're welcome to take what you think is worth archiving. Goodness knows, if you don't, then it'll all just go in a skip anyway.'

'I promise I'll treat whatever I find with the respect it deserves,' Charlotte said gently. 'I've been trained to look after things, and even if I don't find any more evidence for the Winslow archive, I'm sure that the more contemporary papers that have been stored here are worth saving for posterity. It's not every day somewhere with such a long history is decommissioned, and one with such amazing resources.' She still couldn't quite believe the inner sanctum of the records room had been so well preserved, given the state of the rest of the building.

She glanced around the records room again. Apart from the dust, it really was in remarkable nick for somewhere that hadn't been used in years. She wondered, again, how it had escaped the attentions of the vandals. So many buildings like this, especially those in the middle of nowhere, ended up covered in graffiti and broken beyond repair. But somehow, this part of Lower Brambleton's observatory had survived relatively unscathed. It was like a time capsule from the early 1990s.

Brian said goodbye, arranging to return and lock up in three hours' time. He'd laughed when she'd suggested that she could phone him, reminding her again about the lack of signal. She resolved not to stay for the whole day, since Lorelai had charge of Comet and she was still finding her bearings, but as Brian left her alone, she couldn't resist wandering around the room that had been the observatory's research hub. It was silent now, although she could make out the sounds of the wild birds overhead, probably nesting in the secluded nooks of the dome. She imagined what it would have been like back in its heyday, with keen astronomers congregating here to log star patterns, cosmological phenomena, and the trails and paths of comets across the sky, at all times of year. Certainly, the technology had changed, and it was easier now to document things digitally, but she felt electrified at the prospect of getting her hands on the original handwritten or typed notes that were bound to be lurking in the filing cabinets and on the shelves of the records room.

She'd have plenty of time for that. Today was about getting a feel for the observatory and its history. She'd need to develop some systems if she was to do justice to the stacks of paper and documentation that she was going to have to sift through. Pulling open the top door of an army-green steel filing cabinet, whose label, handwritten, was still attached to the front but had long since faded, she let out an involuntary gasp as she saw how crammed full of paperwork it was. Some of it was suspended in document files, hooked snugly over the rails of the drawer, while a lot more had just been shoved into cardboard document wallets of varying hues and thickness. It would take some doing to get this lot in order.

It's like Miss Havisham got a hobby and worked out how to use a telescope, she thought, giving a short laugh. The sound faded into the dim light of the records room, and, feeling oddly unsettled for the first time since Brian had left, she shivered. Maybe it was the thought of Dickens's tragic character, but the observatory suddenly felt a lot bigger, a lot bleaker, without Brian showing her around.

Best get used to it, she told herself firmly. She was a research team of one on this venture, and from the looks of it, she'd be occupied from dawn until dusk for the duration of her stay in Lower Brambleton. She realised that she was feeling more nervous now she'd seen the size of the job than she had before she'd come here. The context that Brian had given her had made her all the more aware of the imminent loss of it. She found it strange that she hadn't encountered anyone as yet who felt a sense of loss for the observatory's looming demolition.

13

After what felt like the fiftieth phone conversation of the day about the five hundred interminable details of the Observatory Field site that needed to be settled before work could finally progress, Tristan Ashcombe hung up the phone in his office and let out a long, frustrated sigh. The Observatory Field build was already a year behind schedule, and he was counting down the days until ground was actually broken and the project could begin. Then, and only then, would he be able to relax.

Tristan was, by nature, a details man. Always had been. That was what made him so good at his job. As chief project manager for Flowerdew Homes South West, he needed both the macro and micro view of a project, and while this played into his, even by his own admission, tendency to be a control freak, it also made him an excellent choice for the housebuilding company. That and his desire to constantly move forward. Tristan never looked back if he could help it. Building new homes, where people could realise their dreams for the future, was his principal driving force, and he'd been at the head of five previous developments, all of which had regenerated and revitalised their local areas, providing hundreds of people with the chance to live in the places they'd grown up.

He was, of course, well aware that this wasn't always the case with developments. They were often met with violent opposition from people who saw new houses as a threat to the status quo of their surroundings. Early in his career, he'd worked as an assistant for a number of house builders who'd ridden roughshod over the residents, and the landscape. He'd vowed that, when he eventually had the experience, he'd only work for a company that took each plot on its individual merits, not just in the interests of profit, but in the interests of the local community.

He knew that this often set him against the capital-driven goals of the businesses in question, and it had taken him a long time to find a company that aligned with his principles and personal philosophy. And up until now, he'd been extremely happy with the outcomes of the projects he'd managed. Then, Observatory Field had been earmarked as a site for regeneration, and everything Tristan believed in was now being tested to the limit.

It wasn't that Observatory Field was a bad site: far from it. The buildings on the land had lain empty for years, and the pleasing flatness of the landscape above the steeply inclining woodland lent itself well to the prospect of an estate of small, affordable, well-constructed dwellings that would enable people who were priced out of the local area to really put down some roots. The permission for the access road had been granted four years ago, and after the last deeds and covenants on the land had been recovered from the solicitor in Burnham on Sea, permission had been sought and granted for the new estate. On paper, the development was everything that Tristan strived for and would ensure that many people over the next few years would be able to settle, have families and bring new life to an area that needed an infusion of new blood to keep it alive.

There was just one problem. Observatory Field held a lot of history. Not just in the ground, but in the skies above. And when you, as project manager, were intimately connected with that history, that was when issues had the potential to arise. Despite this, he'd been cleared to project manage the development. His intimate knowledge of Observatory Field could be a benefit, and Flowerdew liked working with people who had an interest in the sites they developed.

The phone on his desk rang again, and, snatching it up in irritation, Tristan barked a terse 'Hello?' into the receiver.

'Tris? Is that you? Everything all right?'

The familiar voice of his twin sister, Thea, came down the line. Immediately, he softened his tone. 'Hi, Thea. Yes, I'm fine. What can I do for you?'

'I promised I'd pop in and see Gran tonight, but I've been called into Cora's school for a meeting. Is there any way you can swing by on the way home, check in on her?'

Tristan suppressed a sigh. He'd been hoping to stay late and iron out some of the details from the most recent land survey that had taken place on Observatory Field. There had been some question over a couple of metal compounds that had been found in the soil, and he needed to clarify a few things. If he had to call in on their grandmother, he knew he'd need to do it earlier rather than later.

'Can't you get over after the meeting?' he tried.

Thea's sigh was more audible than her brother's suppressed one. 'Not really,' she said. 'My car's in the garage, so I'm stuck until close of play tomorrow. I'm having to walk to school and back as it is.'

Realising that Thea's matter-of-fact tone was probably

hiding a multitude of woes, Tristan acquiesced. 'Fine,' he said. 'Is the car going to be all right? Do you, er, need any help?'

'Nothing I can't handle,' Thea replied. 'Just time consuming and expensive, but what isn't these days?'

'Well, let me know if there's anything I can do,' Tristan replied, knowing full well that Thea wouldn't. They were both afflicted with a stubborn, self-reliant streak, and it was the thing that drove them mad about each other. They might have been born together, but they'd strived for independence ever since.

'Just check in on Gran for me, and I'll deal with the rest,' Thea said. 'I mean, you're virtually on the doorstep these days, aren't you, for the duration of the build?'

'Not quite yet, but soon enough,' Tristan replied. Once Observatory Field was properly underway, he'd be spending a few months on site in a Portakabin office before moving on to the next project, and he was sure Thea would be calling on him a lot more regularly to check in on Lorelai. He was currently still in the office in Taunton, which was about half an hour away from Nightshade Cottage, but he couldn't say no to Thea's request. It was very rare that he denied his sister anything.

'Yup,' he agreed. 'OK, Thea, leave it with me. Hope everything goes well at school with Cora.'

'Thanks, Tris.' Thea gave a hollow laugh. 'She's been unsettled lately, and her teacher wants to talk about how that's been manifesting itself in class. It's not surprising, given what she and Dylan have been through over the past couple of years, but hopefully she'll settle down again soon.' Thea had endured a traumatic separation from the children's father, who'd shown very little interest in pursuing a relationship with them after he'd left the family home. Thea, while outwardly recovering, was finding the life of a lone parent exhausting and tricky at times.

'What's she been doing?' Tristan asked. He was ridiculously fond of his niece and nephew, and didn't like the thought of either of them being less than happy.

'She punched a boy in the face,' Thea groaned. 'Naturally, she had provocation, but I think what really took the biscuit was that she was quoting Henry V part 2 when she did it.'

'What?' Despite the seriousness of the deed, Tristan couldn't help spluttering with laughter. 'Why the heck was she doing either of those things?'

'Well, her best mate, a little boy called Harry, was getting mercilessly picked on by this kid so Cora took matters into her own hands – literally,' Thea replied. 'And as for the quote... I might have watched *The Hollow Crown* a few times lately... she obviously overheard Tom Hiddleston giving it some during the whole "God, Harry and St George" speech and decided it would be the perfect accompaniment to a smack in the mouth!'

'Well, I've got to give her points for originality!' Tristan smiled down the phone. 'Violence aside, she's got a great future ahead of her in the theatre!'

Thea laughed, but Tristan sensed the underlying worry of a mother deeply concerned for her child and upset by her actions. 'Let's hope she can channel her rage in a better direction next time,' he said.

'Thanks, Tris. You always know how to cheer me up. And thanks for popping over to see Gran. She's got a new lodger, and you know how that worries me. I don't like the thought of her having strangers in the house. The kids say there's a dog, too, so it would be great if you could just check out the latest pair of strays who've wandered into Gran's orbit.'

Tristan groaned. 'I thought she was going to stop having people staying in the annexe. It's not like she needs the money.'

'I know,' Thea agreed, 'but she says she likes the company still. You know she won't be told what to do.'

'I'll go and make sure it's not some scrounger,' Tristan replied. 'Hopefully it's just a short-term thing.'

'Hopefully,' Thea echoed. 'She's getting too old to have people she doesn't know living in the annexe. If it wasn't so small, I'd offer to move in there myself and pay her the rent!'

'You'd never survive it,' Tristan laughed. 'You'd drive each other mad in a week.'

'Yeah, you're probably right, but it doesn't stop me worrying about who she does allow to live there.'

Signing off, they both said goodbye and Tristan replaced the receiver. He reckoned he had about another hour before he'd have to head over to check in on their grandmother. He felt irritated that, despite having a talk with her some months ago, she'd decided to take on another tenant. They'd never been problem, but there was always a first time, and he didn't want to be the one who had to pick up the pieces if his grandmother had taken on more than she could handle. With a dog in the mix, too, goodness only knew what his gran had let herself in for.

Leaving his office sometime later, Tristan got behind the wheel of his Audi Q8 and drove the short distance to his grandmother's home. Soon, when he was on site at Observatory Field, it would be quicker to walk through the woods and down the hill, than to drive round to Nightshade Cottage. He resolved that he would pop in and see Lorelai more regularly when he was on the development site. For tonight, though, he still had a lot of work to do, and he'd promised to call back a casual girlfriend to firm up some plans for the following weekend – or not. He still wasn't quite sure whether or not to commit himself.

Pulling off the main road and down the track that led to the house, he eventually reached the secluded driveway. He exited the car, and just as he was about to walk through the back gate towards the door that led to his gran's kitchen, a familiar black cocker spaniel with a white star on its chest galumphed up to him, barking in a most proprietorial fashion. Before Tristan could stop it, the spaniel had placed its paws on the knees of his light-coloured trousers, covering them with mud. Tristan's irritation rose instantly. Looking towards the garden, his eyes locked with those of the dishevelled-looking woman he'd met at the gates of the observatory three days ago.

'Oh, God, Comet, not again!' the woman stammered. 'I'm so sorry. Let me get you a cloth and you can sponge off your trousers. He's been playing in the sprinkler on the lawn.'

'Don't bother,' Tristan snapped. Strolling briskly past her, he entered the door that led to Lorelai's kitchen. What the hell had his grandmother done this time? Of all the waifs and strays she'd had in the annexe, this woman and her dog were definitely the scruffiest.

14

'Well, looks like you've really done it this time!' Charlotte murmured to the not-at-all-repentant Comet as he trotted back to her, tongue lolling out in the late afternoon heat. Her heart was racing after the new confrontation with Mr Rod-Up-His-Arse, and her legs felt shaky: a combination of embarrassment and upset. She'd never been good at being told off, and this had definitely felt like a telling off. Another one. From the same guy.

All the same, she wondered what the connection was between Lorelai and the man. From the familiar way he'd come around the back of the cottage and strode past her to Lorelai's kitchen door, they must know each other. Perhaps he was the father of those adorable kids she'd met at the weekend? But would a dad of two children be quite so precious about some paw prints on his trousers?

Charlotte had returned from the observatory a little after four in the afternoon. She'd spent the time before she left unproductively opening drawers carefully and just trying to get a feel for the scale of the job ahead of her. When she'd done her postgraduate qualification in Archives and Records Management, one of her professors had warned her never to rush into an archiving project: that it was better, in the very first hours, to get an impression of a site, to tap into the intellectual lie of the land, and not to put things at risk of damage or – horrors – miscataloguing by pulling things out willy-nilly. She'd heeded that advice in every job she'd had so far, and she wasn't about to ignore it now. Besides, the collection of archive boxes and other paraphernalia wouldn't be delivered for another few days, and she wanted to make sure she had her cataloguing system up and running before she actually had to start putting things away.

As an astronomical historical archivist, her mission on a project was always complex, and had to be tailored to the specific site she was working on. Lower Brambleton's observatory had been given the once-over by the University of North West Wessex when it had initially closed a decade ago, but their renewed interest in the area, especially in the light of its proposed demolition, had meant that her job was now to catalogue, digitise and preserve any remaining artefacts of cosmological or historical importance. What if, buried deep in the reams of paper in the observatory's library and research room, there was a snippet of data, some research that had been overlooked in the first attempt to mothball the place?

She'd stopped herself just in time from gliding off on that particular flight of fancy. Chances were, she'd thought to herself firmly, that all she was going to find was a bunch of yellowing printouts from the dot-matrix printer that had been attached to one of several Commodore computers that had formed the mainframe of the observatory's internal computer network. It was highly unlikely that anything of great astronomical significance was going to be found. Whoever had archived the Winslow papers would have had ample opportunity to find things and whatever had been left would probably just end up in anonymous archive boxes or a skip.

All the same, Charlotte was excited. The novelty of working alone on this project, the first time she'd been given sole responsibility, was intoxicating, and her senses were tingling at the prospect. It wasn't just the opportunity to flex her skills as an archivist, but the chance to put her degree in astronomy into practice, too. The project was hers, all hers.

Settling back into the garden chair, where she'd been relaxing and watching Comet frolicking in the spray from the sprinkler, she picked up her phone to check her emails. She'd managed to get logged onto Lorelai's wi-fi, but it was slow. As she waited for her email to load, she couldn't help tuning in to the voices that were emanating from Lorelai's living room. Whoever the guy was, Lorelai was obviously pleased to see him, as even though Charlotte couldn't hear their conversation, Lorelai's tone sounded light. In response, he still sounded gruff and uptight.

These musings passed the moments while her emails loaded. When they appeared on her iPhone's screen, she smiled to see one from Professor Edwin, politely enquiring if she'd settled in all right, and reminding her to check in regularly with updates about anything that she might find to add to the Winslow archive. *Not as yet*, she thought.

There was also an email from Todd. He hadn't contacted her since his rather cowardly 'Dear John' before she'd come to Lower Brambleton for the summer, and she contemplated just deleting the email without bothering to read it. Her finger hovered over the screen, ready to swipe Todd's communique into oblivion, but she hesitated. What harm would it do to read it?

Just at that moment, Charlotte's attention was dragged away from her phone by the sound of the door to Lorelai's kitchen opening, and voices, still deep in conversation, coming towards her. She glanced up to see Lorelai and her visitor moving towards the gate. As they drew level with her, they paused.

'Charlotte, this is my grandson, Tristan,' Lorelai said. 'I thought it was about time you were properly introduced, although I gather you met yesterday rather less formally.'

'Hi.' Charlotte gave her best smile, despite her lingering sense of irritation. 'It's nice to meet you, Tristan.'

'Likewise,' Tristan replied shortly. Then, turning back to his grandmother, he leaned down and kissed her on the cheek. 'Think about what I said, Gran. It's important.'

Lorelai shook her head. 'And you think about what I said, Tristan, darling. I'm not ready to change my mind just yet.'

Charlotte found that she was watching the interplay between grandmother and grandson keenly as a pause descended between them, which was swiftly filled by Lorelai. 'Pop in and see me sometime next week,' she said, and from the tone of her voice, even Charlotte knew this wasn't a question, but an instruction.

'I will,' Tristan replied. He glanced at Charlotte again. 'I take it you're going to dry off that dog before it sets foot in my grandmother's annexe?'

Charlotte bridled at his tone. 'Of course,' she snapped back. 'I'm not in the habit of letting him run riot.'

The 'could have fooled me' expression on Tristan's face stayed with Charlotte long after the man himself strode out of the garden.

Sensing that Lorelai was lingering on the patio after Tristan's exit, Charlotte smiled as brightly as she could. 'He, er, seems nice,' she said, although she could hear from her own tone how insincere she sounded.

Lorelai gave a brief smile, and then sighed. 'I'm sorry that

Tristan was a little short with you,' she said. 'He's been trying to convince me to stop taking in lodgers. Says I'm getting too old. Keeps reminding me what could happen if one of my guests turned out to be a wrong 'un.' Her smile, this time, was apologetic. 'He knows I only accept people who've got good references, in your case, of course, the university gave you a glowing write-up, but he seems to think, at my age, I might be in danger of losing my marbles.'

'From what I've seen of you so far, all of your marbles are very much in the jar!' Charlotte tried to lighten the mood.

'In the jar, and packed in tight,' Lorelai agreed, and this time her smile was more convincing. 'But he worries. It's not surprising, really. He and his sister have had such a tough time of it since they lost their parents. And this Observatory Field development is taking it out of him. He has a habit, though, of, what did the therapists call it, displacing his fears. I just call it lashing out at the wrong target!'

Charlotte's mind began to whirl. Amidst all of the information that Brian O'Connor had told her since she'd begun working at the observatory, there'd been something that had nagged at her; some connection she'd been struggling to make. She drew a deep breath, wondering if what she was about to ask was going to be too intrusive. She'd only met Lorelai a couple of days ago, and she didn't want to upset her. But, she reasoned, she was going to be digging into the records of the observatory in detail soon: it would be good to know exactly what she was dealing with before she got too immersed.

'Can I ask you something, Lorelai?'

Lorelai glanced up from the roses she'd been deadheading in the flowerbed by the patio. 'Of course, love. What is it?'

'When Brian O'Connor, who let me into the observatory today, was explaining some of the history of the site, he mentioned a couple of people by name – Laura and Martin. They seemed to be pretty significant people in its timeline.' She paused, wondering whether to continue, but Lorelai nodded her head almost imperceptibly. 'Brian seemed surprised that I didn't know about them, seeing as I'm lodging here.'

Lorelai drew a deep breath. 'Martin was my son, and Laura was his wife. We lost them in a car accident thirty years ago.'

Although she already knew about the accident, Charlotte was still lost for words as Lorelai confirmed her connection with Martin and Laura. Such a tragedy, even all these years later, was shocking.

'I'm so sorry, Lorelai,' she said gently. 'I can't imagine how terrible that must have been for you. For all of you.'

Lorelai nodded sadly. 'It was. For me and their children it was the worst kind of loss imaginable. But for Brian and the rest of the Lower Brambleton Astronomical Society, it was also very painful.' She gave a brief smile of recollection. 'Martin and Laura were the heart and soul of the Lower Brambleton Astronomical Society in its heyday. They met at university, where they both studied astrophysics. Although their careers took them into industry rather than academia, they still maintained a keen interest in astronomy, and they helped put the observatory back on its feet in the late 1980s, after the first threat of demolition came onto the horizon. The observatory had been winding down in the 1970s, but there was a flurry of interest in its records when the Winslow papers were deemed to be of special interest. I'm sure you're well versed in that part of the history. That, and some minor discoveries made by astronomers in the 1960s, kept it from being torn down forty years ago.'

Charlotte nodded. 'Yes. I've studied many of the papers. For such a small site, it was a real hive of scientific activity for decades.'

Lorelai acknowledged Charlotte's statement with a brief incline of her head before she continued. 'Well, Laura, Martin and the rest of LBAS, as they became known, kept the observatory going, adding to the records with their own findings and making sure it kept its spot on the astronomical map. I'm sure Brian filled you in on a lot of the history.'

'He mentioned Laura and Martin's names, and that LBAS were known for their parties as well as their astronomy.' She smiled. 'It sounds like they were a very tight-knit group.'

'Oh, they were,' Lorelai smiled, but the smile was replaced quickly by a wistful look. 'That's why, when we lost Laura and Martin, you could say that the life went out of the observatory, and of LBAS, too. After that, things went into a decline. None of the remaining members of the society wanted to spend much time there, and it was gradually decommissioned. It couldn't be sold for a number of years, but when the right time came, its owner felt it was time to repurpose the land.' Lorelai gazed out across the garden towards the delphiniums at the bottom. Charlotte let her have a moment. She didn't want to intrude, but she was still very interested in the story.

'It all became a bit of a white elephant in the end,' Lorelai continued, finally. 'As romantic as the observatory might seem to a newcomer, it's long outlived its usefulness. It'll be good, finally, to see something new on the land.'

Charlotte was surprised by Lorelai's philosophical attitude: it seemed at odds with the huge and terrible loss she'd suffered. She would have assumed that, should something so awful happen, it would be comforting to have somewhere like the observatory as a memorial. Then she thought back to the unloved, untidy, nearly derelict site that was Observatory Field and began to see why Lorelai might think that way. What was the point in holding onto a building, when the people who brought it to life were long gone?

'I hope that having me here, doing the job I'm doing for the next few weeks won't be too painful for you and your family,' Charlotte said gently. 'Please let me know if you'd rather not talk about it. I don't want to dig up old memories.'

Lorelai leaned over and gave Charlotte's hand a squeeze. 'I appreciate that,' she said. 'It's actually therapeutic, in a strange way. I know you've not been here very long, but I already feel as though what's left of the observatory will be in safe hands. And it's about time someone who really knew what they were doing sorted through all the papers and documents. Bless Brian and his group, they did their best to preserve everything, but actually what's needed at this point is a fresh pair of eyes. I'm glad you're here.'

Feeling touched and a whole lot more at ease with the project now that she and Lorelai had spoken, Charlotte headed off to make dinner. She couldn't begin to imagine how awful the loss must have been for Lorelai, Tristan and Thea, but at least she could understand now why this development project was so important. She vowed to give it the time and respect it needed, to finally bring the strange half-life of Lower Brambleton's observatory to a close.

15

Charlotte was arranging her own hours at the observatory, and, once Brian had given her keys to the padlock on the gate and the building itself, she didn't have to stick to a strict nine-to-five schedule. For the next few days, she constructed the database that she was planning on using to catalogue the documents she found, working at the desk in her room at Nightshade Cottage. It didn't make much sense to drag all the way up the hill to Observatory Field just to stare at a computer when she could be working in the comfort and light of Nightshade Cottage's annexe. She knew she needed to be efficient, to get her systems up and running so that when she was spending time at the observatory, she was using it productively.

She'd been getting up early, before the heat of the Somerset summer sun was at full strength, to take Comet for a wander through the lower slopes of the woodland. At seven o'clock in the morning, the woods had an ethereal, unworldly air, and she was getting quite addicted to the heavenly scent of pine balsam mixed with mouldering bracken that the damp, early morning mist produced. Comet loved it too, darting in and out of the trees, snuffling and sniffing at the scents of rabbits, badgers and the roe deer that inhabited the woodlands. They were a vulnerable fringe, a buffer between the rest of Lower Brambleton and the site of the new housing estate, and Charlotte felt a sense of relief that they weren't going to be bulldozed to make way for more houses. Some things had to remain, in the midst of all of this change.

Once their early walk was complete, Charlotte began working each day. Comet, happy to stretch out in a burgeoning patch of sunlight that peered its way through the sash window in the living area-cum-study of the annexe, was usually quiet until the afternoon, when he'd request a quick pit stop in the back garden. They'd walked through the woods a couple of times in the evening, too, but Comet wasn't too fussed about a second walk. The fresh country air was exhausting him, and they were both sleeping well when they eventually turned in.

Staring at a computer screen for hours on end, though, was hardly edifying. It was the part of her job she liked the least, even though it was necessary for the successful completion of a project. Finally, after a few days of tweaking and amending, she was satisfied with the setup. By way of celebration, and because supplies in her fridge were woefully low, she decided to take Comet out for a longer stroll that Saturday morning. She knew that there was a farm shop on the furthest boundary of Lower Brambleton that was within walking distance, and so she decided it was time to check it out.

The route on foot to Saints Farm shop was meandering, and just the exercise both she and Comet needed after a few hours' work at the desk. Although she was reluctant, initially, to let the spaniel off the lead, the lane that led from Nightshade Cottage to the centre of Lower Brambleton was extremely quiet, and so, for about a quarter of a mile, she unclipped him so that he could dash up the sloping verges and have a good sniff. When she knew she was getting closer to the main road, she put his lead back on. Comet had excellent recall, despite what his early escapades at the observatory would suggest, but even the most well-behaved dog could get spooked.

The main road was quiet, too, which wasn't entirely surprising. Lower Brambleton was one of those charming little hamlets that were dotted all over Somerset: not big enough to have its own school, but to her left as she walked, Charlotte could see the austere grey tower of what looked to be a Norman church. Most likely thirteenth century, the building was still standing, but the tower was at a rather interesting angle. She wondered if services still took place there.

Charlotte had been raised in the Church of England, in so much as she'd attended a C of E primary school, and she still retained an affection for ecclesiastical buildings. Although she hadn't set foot in a church since her grandfather had died five years ago, she liked the idea that a church, and a graveyard in particular, could be grounding. She spent so much time looking at the stars, and trying to harness accumulated knowledge of the cosmos, collected by countless astronomers, that a sense of perspective about her place in the universe was comforting.

Not in any particular rush to get to the shop, she decided to take Comet for a detour. It would be lovely to get a closer look at this rather wonky church. If it was locked, she'd just amble around the grounds.

As she pushed open the wooden gate that led to the churchyard, Comet gambolled ahead, nose on alert for anything interesting, and legs running nineteen to the dozen over the grass. The graveyard looked well-tended, which suggested the church was still in use, and the close-cropped turf seemed safe enough for the dog to walk on, although Charlotte did call him back every time it looked like he might scamper too close to the gravestones. There was no one else around, but she didn't want to appear disrespectful.

Walking idly up to the heavy, curving oak door of the church, she wasn't surprised to find it locked. Most were, these days, and she suspected that even Lower Brambleton wasn't immune to the odd bit of rural criminal opportunism. She turned back down the path and decided to spend a few minutes reading the gravestones. She'd almost done a joint honours and included history in her degree, and remembered well the local history part of her A Level, where she'd spent a lot of time researching the stories behind the names on the memorial plaques inside her local church. While her mates had bunked off for a cigarette behind the enormous yew trees in the graveyard, she'd been captivated by the names of those who'd gone before, and whose families had memorialised them in stone plaques on the church walls.

Although she couldn't get inside the church today, she satisfied her curiosity by ambling down the path, reading the names and inscriptions as she went. Many of the graves nearest the entrance to the church were lost to time and the driving rain of the West Country, and were illegible, but here and there she spotted names, dates, some heartbreakingly short and some evidence of long, prosperous lives. She was particularly amused by one for an Edmund Grimes, which read:

> Here lies Edward 'Wanderlust' Grimes,
> Who roamed the world and had great times.
> He walked with adventure, and now with God,
> 'Seek and ye shall find,' says the Lord (Matthew 7:7).

Charlotte wondered if it had just been travel that had

enthralled Edmund. In his ninety-eight years on the planet, he must have seen a lot.

Moving back towards the gate, the headstones were getting newer. She was in the 1960s now, and then the seventies, until she reached the newest additions. The nineties were clearly when the churchyard had run out of accommodation, as graves she passed were dated 1995. But in truth, it wasn't the date that caught her attention on the last plot before the gate. The white-coloured marble was as clean as it must have been when it had been erected; the black engraving clear against the stark background, with no humorous verse to distract from the sadness that it signified. The names, now familiar to Charlotte from the conversations with Brian and Lorelai, were in sharp relief in the strong morning sun. They read:

> Here lie Laura and Martin Ashcombe,
> Stargazers together in life and in death.
> Taken too soon on 15 January 1995,
> Now they explore the heavens side by side.

Charlotte could feel her pulse speeding up as she read the inscription. It was pure coincidence that she'd decided to explore the churchyard, but it felt as though something had been leading her to those names again. The tragedy of their loss, and their intimate connection with the observatory would inevitably charge her research with emotion, and as she looked at the gravestone, she began to feel the weight of that responsibility. It was all too easy, when she was handling historical documents and entering them into a database, to forget that there were lives connected to the information. Living under the same roof as Lorelai, that reminder was all too clear.

16

With a thousand thoughts hurtling like shooting stars through her mind, Charlotte hurried out of the churchyard and resumed her walk to the farm shop. To get to the store, she needed to walk through the centre of the village, and it was a good opportunity to get her bearings. When Gemma had dropped her off, they'd arrived at Nightshade Cottage via a series of labyrinthine back lanes, and hadn't come through the village centre. Because she didn't have a car, she hadn't really had the chance to explore. Now, as she walked in the direction of Saints Farm, she began to notice how pretty and charming Lower Brambleton really was.

Much smaller than Roseford, its near neighbour, Lower Brambleton had a sleepy charm. The main road meandered through the village centre, and the dominant feature was a low-roofed thatched pub called the Star and Telescope. A couple of benches sat outside, and the front door was open, but it was difficult to see into the cosy darkness within. On the other side of the road was a small, independent charity shop called 'The Purrfect Paws Rescue', whose window was charmingly dressed with a selection of cat-related products and other donated items, including a particularly vibrantly patterned summer dress. Further down the road was a tea room and what looked to be a small corner shop, with a newspaper board outside bearing an eccentrically adorable headline about a rescued otter.

Lower Brambleton was small, pretty and the epitome of Somerset charm. However, there seemed to be very few people about to enjoy it, especially on a Saturday morning. She hated to admit it, but she could see why planning permission had been granted on Observatory Field. It felt as though the village needed an injection of new blood. If nothing else, a hundred houses above the woodland would achieve that.

A rumble from her stomach made Charlotte pick up her pace in the direction of the furthermost boundary of the village. It didn't take long until she spotted the rustic looking outbuilding that served as the public, commercial face of the Saints Farm enterprise, and as the road widened out towards a more major thoroughfare at the boundary of the village, Charlotte hoped she'd find some enticing things to buy. The fresh air of the countryside was making her appetite increase, and she couldn't wait to fill a basket with some locally produced, delicious food.

As she drew closer to the shop, she saw boxes and racks of fresh fruit and veg, their colours in strong relief against the pale oak of the building's construction. Crates of reddish-brown potatoes, the first of the season, grown in the dark rich Somerset soil were piled up to one side, and on the other were various succulent soft fruits, including dewy raspberries in punnets and irresistible strawberries. Lower Brambleton was only a couple of dozen miles from the village of Cheddar, the home of English strawberries, and the sign on the shelf where they lounged enticingly in their small cardboard punnets proclaimed them to be from there. Charlotte immediately picked one up, ready to put in her basket when she got through the door.

'Right, Comet,' she said firmly, looping his lead over one of the hooks on the wall to the left of the entrance. 'I won't be long. Be a good boy while I get us something to eat for later.' She noticed, with a smile, a stainless-steel bowl of water on the ground next to where the hooks had been fastened, for the shop's canine visitors. It looked fresh, too, so Comet gratefully dunked in his snout and took several large slurps.

Entering the low-roofed wooden building that, from the outside, resembled a rather upmarket barn conversion, she was immediately assailed by the sights and scents of a well-stocked farm shop. Wafts of fresh bread drifted enticingly from a rack to her right, and to her left, lining one wall, was a fridge unit full of local cured meats and cheeses. On the back wall were several thick wooden shelves full of preserves and pickles, and in the two aisles in the centre were yet more local delights, including more vegetables, fruits and several varieties of confectionery and locally produced biscuits.

What a treasure trove, Charlotte thought, and immediately regretted not having a car to ferry her purchases back to Nightshade Cottage. She'd be limited by what she could carry, today, and she'd only brought her backpack.

'Good afternoon!' A cheery voice rang out from behind the counter, which was off to the right of the door. 'How can I help you today?'

Charlotte turned from her perusal of a particularly appetising jar of pickled beetroot and saw a pretty, dark-haired woman in her mid-thirties smiling back at her. She was wearing a blue apron that had 'Saints Farm Store' embroidered in gold lettering on the front, and as Charlotte smiled back, she continued talking.

'Gorgeous dog you've got there – I'm sorry we can't let him in the shop, but after we had a Great Dane through the door who slurped up all of the samples of the local charcuterie's taster, we decided it was probably best to keep our four-footed friends outside!'

Charlotte shook her head. 'Comet's not quite tall enough to get into your cabinets, but that doesn't mean he wouldn't try!'

'I'm Annabelle Saint,' the woman went on, as she bustled about behind the counter, tidying away a few things. 'Feel free to ask if you need any help – or any recommendations.'

'Thanks, I will,' Charlotte replied, and turned her attention back to the centre aisle. She was rapidly realising there was far more here that she wanted than she could reasonably carry, and was regretting not getting a supermarket order in.

At that moment, the door that led to the back of the building opened, and a tall, striking man with beech-leaf-coloured hair and piercing blue eyes strode through the shop. He was wearing a navy-blue polo shirt with the gold embroidery, and Charlotte watched him as he progressed across the shop to the counter.

'I think that's all the deliveries done,' he called out as he reached Annabelle. 'Any more I should know about before I knock off for a coffee?'

'Let me just check the logs,' Annabelle replied, tapping swiftly on the iPad that was by the till. 'Just one for Mrs Stokes at Owl's Barn for this afternoon. She's requested a bag of those Maris Pipers and a few other bits and bobs – I'll put a box together.'

'Thanks, sis,' the guy replied. 'Coffee?'

'Yeah, that would be great,' Annabelle replied.

Charlotte, hearing their exchange, had an idea.

'Um, can I ask about your delivery service?' She approached

the counter with her potential purchases and placed them down.

'Sure,' Annabelle smiled at her. 'We charge a small fee for orders below fifty pounds, and it's free for orders over that. Usually, deliveries are for online orders only, but we do get a few customers who come in and request their shopping delivered, once they find they've bought too much to carry home!'

'That would be me, right now!' Charlotte grinned. 'I only came in for a couple of things to tide me over, but I've fallen for a whole lot more of your stock.'

Annabelle smiled back. 'It happens to the best of us.' She turned in the direction the guy had wandered off. 'Nick!' she shouted. 'Can you do another delivery this afternoon?'

Nick poked his head back through the door. 'So long as it doesn't interfere with the cricket – Roseford versus Lower Brambleton – it's a proper grudge match!'

'I'm sure you can fit it in before you have to bat,' Annabelle said dryly.

'I'll add it to the list,' Nick replied. He glanced at Charlotte. 'Where's it to?'

Charlotte smiled at the West Country turn of phrase. 'Nightshade Cottage, Buttermere Lane.'

'Oh, Lorelai's gaff? You the new lodger?' Nick inclined his head in recognition.

'Yup, just for the summer,' Charlotte replied. 'And I'd love to be able to take home more than I can carry. A delivery would be great.'

'Leave it with Annabelle – I'll drop it off on my way to Owl's Barn.'

'Thank you,' Charlotte said. 'That's great. I can really go to town now!'

Annabelle laughed. 'That's what we like to hear. We do love a happy customer.'

Charlotte, leaving her first handful of purchases by the till, set about finding more delicious things to stock her fridge and her cupboards. She had to keep reminding herself that shouldn't be too extravagant, since the prices in the farm shop were a little higher than she'd usually consider, but there were so many things she found herself itching to buy. In the end, the local lavender honey, a loaf of strong, golden-crusted sourdough and a block of butter were among the many items she added to her pile. She even picked up some freshly baked dog treats for the patiently waiting Comet to try.

'Wow, you really have gone for it!' Annabelle observed as Charlotte returned to pay. 'You're very welcome to visit us again.'

'Well, I'll be here until the start of the next academic year, give or take a week or two, so I absolutely will.'

As she tapped her debit card on the terminal, Annabelle asked her what had brought her to Lower Brambleton. Charlotte tried to give her the potted version, as she had a tendency to get too caught up with explanations and risk boring people, or so she always feared. As soon as Annabelle heard the words 'Observatory Field', though, she looked intrigued and thoughtful.

'That development's been a long time coming,' Annabelle remarked as Charlotte paused. 'There's a lot of people round here who tried to stop it from going ahead at all – said the observatory should be preserved as a site of special historical interest. Of course, most of those were well over sixty and just didn't want the village to change. We don't all think like that.'

'Speak for yourself,' a gruff voice interceded from behind Charlotte, and she glanced over her shoulder to see a tall, silver-haired man standing a little way away. He'd hefted in a wooden boxful of raspberry punnets and was clearly on his way to put them out the front of the shop. 'There's some of us who still think that.'

'Change happens, Dad,' Annabelle replied. 'And you can't stand in the way of it, especially when people need places to live.'

'People need places to live where the jobs are,' the man replied. 'What's anyone got going for them all the way out here?'

Annabelle sighed. 'You'll have to excuse my father.' She turned back to Charlotte, who was observing this exchange with interest. 'He forgets that not everyone can afford a house in town.'

'Wouldn't want to live there anyway,' the man grunted as he picked up the crate of raspberries once more. 'Let me know if anything else needs bringing up from the cold store, Annie.'

'I will.' Annabelle rolled her eyes. She met Charlotte's gaze with an apologetic smile. 'I, for one, am glad the observatory's going.' She paused and Charlotte felt that she wanted to add more. 'If you ask me, it's about time. Then maybe a few people around here can move on with their lives.'

As she paid for her shopping, and arranged with Annabelle to have what she couldn't carry delivered later that afternoon, Charlotte realised that the tragic history of the observatory really was ingrained. Annabelle wasn't old enough to have had many memories of it, but it had obviously still left its mark. She wondered how many other people would be glad to see the back of the place when it eventually came down.

17

Charlotte returned to Nightshade Cottage and put the purchases in her backpack away. She wasn't sure what time Nick Saint would be arriving with the rest, but, peckish, she made a couple of rounds of toast and a cuppa, and took them through to the garden to eat, Comet following behind her. However tired the dog was, he was always her devoted shadow, and he flopped out onto the warm flagstones of the patio while she munched on her toast and enjoyed the sunshine.

'Good walk, dear?' Lorelai asked as she emerged from her kitchen. She was wearing a battered waxed Stetson and wielding a pair of secateurs.

'Lovely, thanks,' Charlotte replied. She briefly explained where she'd been.

'Ah, yes, the Saints are one of the oldest farming families round here,' Lorelai replied. 'They used to own a lot more land, of course, but most of it got sold about fifty years back. Now it's just thirty or so acres and the farm shop, but they're doing all right out of it. Tristan and Thea were at school with Nick and

Annabelle. At one point I thought Nick and Thea might... well, things don't always turn out the way you'd expect, do they?'

'Did the Saints own Observatory Field, then?' Charlotte asked, still curious about the cryptic nature of her conversation with the family at the shop.

'Oh, no,' Lorelai replied. 'They owned all the land that surrounds it, but Observatory Field wasn't theirs.' She wrinkled her brow. 'Old Robert Saint has a right old case of sour grapes now it's being developed. His was one of the strongest voices against the whole idea. There was quite a lot of opposition to it in the early days when permission first went in, but gradually the village came around.'

'So, who did own the site, then?' Charlotte asked.

Lorelai quirked an eyebrow. 'You mean you weren't told when you took the job? I'd have thought someone would have spilled the beans by now.'

Charlotte shook her head. 'Nope. I got the brief from Flowerdew, but apart from that, I only know what you and Brian have told me about its history.'

'Well,' Lorelai said, setting her secateurs down on the patio table and sitting herself down, with a long sigh, 'perhaps you ought to know a few more details. You already know about my son and daughter-in-law and their connections to the observatory, but there is a little more to tell. Why don't you go and get another cuppa? Make it in my kitchen if you like, and while you're in there, you can grab the coconut macaroons out of the biscuit tin. You might need a sugar treat to help this rather bitter tale go down.'

Charlotte gave Lorelai a reassuring smile. 'It can't be that bad, can it?' Certainly not as awful as the parts she already knew, she thought to herself.

Lorelai shook her head. 'Bad? In parts. Sad, definitely. And now, with everything coming to an end and a new era beginning for that land, it's probably time to tell it all.'

Senses and curiosity on the alert now, Charlotte hurried to get the tea and the biscuits. When she returned, Comet had cosied up to Lorelai on the garden bench.

'Comet, get down!' Charlotte ordered the spaniel.

'Oh, he'll be all right,' Lorelai replied. 'And to be honest, I'm glad of the moral support.'

Comet stayed firmly put next to Lorelai as Charlotte sat down on the wooden chair next to the patio table. She watched for a few moments as Lorelai stroked Comet's long, silky black ears. As she did so, it was clear that Lorelai was summoning the will to begin.

Eventually, the older woman spoke. 'The Lower Brambleton Observatory has a rather tangled history. From Eleanor Winslow to the early twenty-first century is a long time for a building like that to be in operation. And as you know, it's now time to make sure that the past few decades of research are taken care of and preserved. I'm glad that Flowerdew Homes took up my stipulation that the contemporary history of the place be looked after, just as much as the more, some would say, academically worthy history of the previous century.'

'It was you who campaigned to have the rest of it archived, then?' Charlotte replied. She was somewhat surprised, given that Lorelai was so keen to see the housing development go forward.

Lorelai nodded. 'I couldn't not. I owed it to too many people, alive and dead, to ensure that the work of the past thirty or so years wasn't lost or bulldozed when the building is demolished.'

'So, I have you to thank for my job this summer,' Charlotte smiled.

'Yes, I suppose, to a point,' Lorelai agreed. 'But to be truthful, until now the development was just a pipe dream. A lot of water needed to have passed under the bridge to allow it to happen.'

'Such as?'

'Well, as you know, developers started sniffing around the site back in the late 1980s. Up until now, though, no one's been able to strike the right terms with the landowner.'

'So, what changed?' Charlotte asked, unable to resist the lure of the coconut macaroons she'd hurriedly tipped onto a serving plate and brought outside with the tea. 'How did Flowerdew finally manage to get it through?' Comet lifted a hopeful head in search of a macaroon, but Charlotte merely bopped him on the end of his shiny black nose, so he snuffled back down against Lorelai with a martyred sigh.

'One of the landowners died about two years ago,' Lorelai replied. 'Up until that point, the site was owned by a pair of siblings, a brother and his older sister, having been left it in the 1970s by their father. For years, since their inheritance, they couldn't agree about what to do with the land. The brother was a bitter old soul. He watched the observatory begin to fall into rack and ruin at the start of the 1990s, and he was fully prepared to take the deeds for the place to his grave. He had no children, and his only beneficiary was his older sister. They argued for decades. Initially she wanted to develop the site herself, to create some homes for her family, but the cost of the project was too high for an amateur to bear. It would have meant selling everything she owned, and more, and there was no guarantee that the project would be viable. The cost of clearing the land was high enough, and without the contacts, the project would have been too risky. The second route was to sell the land to a developer, and at least then, there would be money in the bank to help support them, and their family.'

'But the brother didn't go for it?' Charlotte guessed.

Lorelai nodded, her face clouding over. 'He was a mean old bugger. Always had been. He was suspicious of everyone and everything, including his sister. It didn't matter that she'd looked after him as they'd both got older, that she'd invited him to live with her as his health declined. He was ten years younger than her, but hadn't really taken care of himself over the years, so he seemed much older. He couldn't see any benefit to himself in her ideas, and in the end, as his health was failing, he accused her of nothing but cheap self-interest, of trying to fleece him out of what was rightfully his. Even when he died, he refused to acknowledge anything she'd done to make the last years of his life bearable. He went out as he lived life: alone, embittered and believing everyone was out for something.'

Charlotte was shocked at the vehemence in Lorelai's tone as she spoke. 'I'm sure he was grateful to her,' she said as there was a pause between them. 'Perhaps he just didn't know how to show it.'

Lorelai smiled briefly. 'Well, that's as may be, but in the end, it didn't matter. As the surviving sibling, and as a result of a covenant in their parents' will that stipulated, should one sibling die without issue, their share of the land would revert to the surviving sibling, the sister inherited it all. Once she had the documents in her possession, she decided, not before time, to sell it.'

'And now it's going to be developed by the professionals,' Charlotte replied, 'which, I suppose, is where I come in.'

'Exactly,' Lorelai smiled. 'It should have happened years ago. It should have happened after—' She broke off again, and Charlotte could see that she was struggling to speak.

'After what, Lorelai?' she asked gently.

'After the accident that killed Martin and Laura,' Lorelai said quietly.

Then, it all clicked into place. Charlotte nearly dropped her cup of tea. '*You're* the landowner, aren't you, Lorelai?'

Lorelai nodded. 'I think now you can see why it's taken so long to get the site redeveloped,' she said quietly.

As their conversation drew to a close, Lorelai stood up from the bench, and Comet jumped straight down, too. 'I hope this doesn't cloud your judgement about the job you have to do,' Lorelai said as she reached for their now empty mugs and put them on the tray with the biscuit plate, also now empty. 'I want you to know that you have my blessing, in the work that you're doing at the observatory. You must be free to preserve what you see as important, and unlike me, Tristan or the Lower Brambleton Astronomical Society, you don't have the emotional baggage to cloud your judgement. That's why, as part of the land sale, I stipulated that an outsider needed to come in to do the decommissioning. No one who was involved in the history would be objective enough to take those final decisions.'

'I promise I'll take good care of everything,' Charlotte said quietly. 'You can trust me, Lorelai.'

'I know I can,' Lorelai replied. 'I had a feeling about you when we first met, and I'm sure you won't disappoint me. And perhaps you can see now why Tristan can be a little abrupt at times. He's very overprotective of me, his sister, and the children. He doesn't talk about things: from the moment he found out his parents were gone, something in him just shut off. He's of a type that won't discuss his emotions, and no amount of counselling really helped. He's thrown himself into work for years and managing the building project may well be the closest he gets to an act of catharsis.'

'It must be hard for you all,' Charlotte said. 'The observatory is such a part of your family history. Won't it be awful seeing it torn down?'

'We all share one thing in common,' Lorelai replied, 'and that's the sense that moving forward is the healthiest thing we can do. We, Tristan, Thea and I, were denied that for so long. Now we can finally do it, it's an enormous relief.'

'I can see that,' Charlotte replied. She was someone who did try to cling to the past, afraid of forgetting, of letting go of things, but then, as Lorelai had correctly observed, she hadn't suffered the kind of trauma and loss that this family had. In their shoes, would she really have been any different?

18

Mind spinning from what Lorelai had revealed to her, Charlotte decided that she needed to clear her head and get some air. And possibly something stronger. She was just debating what to do with herself when there was the sound of a van pulling up in the driveway. Realising it must be Nick Saint with her delivery, she hurried out to the front of the cottage to meet him.

'Here you go,' Nick said as he unloaded the three paper bags of groceries from the back of the blue van, which had 'Saints Farm, Local Produce' emblazoned in gold on the side. 'I hope you enjoy your purchases.' He paused before adding, 'And if you want to order directly from the website, it might save you and the dog a trip next time.'

'Thanks,' Charlotte replied. 'I'll bear that in mind, although the shop's so lovely, it was great to look around.'

She declined Nick's offer to help her into the house with her bags, but as he was about to leave, he turned back to her. 'Look, er, I wanted to apologise about the way Dad was when he spoke to you about Observatory Field. He's still coming to terms with the fact that it's all going to change up there, and there are quite a few people like him, whose feelings are still running high about the whole thing. He didn't mean it personally, and I wouldn't want you to think it was an attack on what you're doing. He'll come around in time.'

'Thanks.' Charlotte, who hadn't been at all worried by the older man's abruptness, was surprised at Nick's attempt to apologise for this father. 'I didn't give it a second thought, but I appreciate the check-in. It's not surprising he feels aggrieved about it, given, er, everything that's happened up there...' She trailed off, unsure if she should allude any further to the information that Lorelai had given her. Small villages like this were notorious for folklore and gossip, and a tragedy was bound to still be very much in everyone's consciousness, even after all this time.

Nick nodded briefly, seeming to understand. 'Well, I'll be off then,' he said, then grinned. 'If I hurry, I might just catch the last few overs of the game at the cricket club. I asked them to put me in late to bat.'

'Wouldn't want you to miss your moment of glory!' An amused voice came from further down the driveway, and as Charlotte turned to see who it was, she saw the familiar faces of Lorelai's great-grandchildren, followed up by an attractive woman with brownish-blonde hair and a broad smile on her extremely pretty face.

'Thea!' Nick's grin was broad as Thea approached them both. 'Long time no see.' Charlotte watched as he gave the other woman a slightly awkward hug. Thea seemed equally pleased to see him, and Charlotte was sure she saw her blushing slightly as Nick released her.

'It's been a while,' Thea agreed. 'Time flies when you're wrangling two children.'

'Hey, guys.' Nick smiled down at Cora and Dylan. 'Nice to see you, too.'

The kids said hello and then scampered off to see their great-grandmother.

'Hi.' The woman turned and smiled at Charlotte. 'I'm Thea Ashcombe. Are you helping Nick out with his deliveries?'

Charlotte grinned. 'Nope – I'm living here. Nick's just dropped off my order.'

'Oh, right – you're the new lodger.' Charlotte felt as though she was under scrutiny as Thea glanced her up and down. 'My brother told me about you. And your dog.' Then, Thea gave a smile, which seemed to undercut the bluntness of her statement. She thrust forward a hand. 'It's nice to meet you. The kids really loved playing with your spaniel.'

Charlotte relaxed again. It was only natural for Lorelai's grandchildren to be a little cautious about anyone sharing her space, but it seemed that Comet had smoothed her path. 'Nice to meet you too. You're, er, Tristan's sister?'

'Yup, guilty as charged!' Thea laughed. 'He mentioned he'd met you.'

Charlotte wondered what exactly Tristan had told his sister about her, and wryly assumed it wasn't great. However, now Thea had met her, perhaps both siblings would be reassured.

'Well, nice as this is, I'd best be off,' Nick interjected, 'or I really will miss my chance on the wicket.' Charlotte noticed Nick looked back at Thea as he added, 'Why don't you, er, bring the kids down to the club later, Thea? There'll be a few people there if you fancy a pint and a catch-up.'

'Thanks,' Thea replied. 'I've got a few things to do this afternoon, but I'll see how it goes.' She smiled at Charlotte briefly and then headed past her around the back of the house.

'Thanks again for the last-minute delivery,' Charlotte said. She noticed that Nick was still looking towards where Thea had walked and wondered what the story was. They were obviously good friends, if the hug had been anything to go by.

'All part of the service!' Nick said, snapping his attention back to her. He said goodbye and then jumped in the van. 'See you back at the store soon.'

As Nick pulled out of the driveway, Charlotte found she was still smiling. What a contrast he was to the dour, stormy presence of Lorelai's grandson, Tristan. And he wasn't bad looking, either. She definitely wasn't in the market for anything other than some good food from the Saint family, but it was a lovely contrast to have a chat with someone who didn't spend their whole time criticising her and her dog. On cue, Comet bounded around the corner of the house and stuck his nose straight into one of the paper bags.

'Out!' Charlotte said briskly, picking the bag up. 'If you're a good boy, I'll take some of those fresh dog treats out with us on our next walk, but for now, let's get this lot safely into the kitchen.' She managed all three bags at once, and, when everything was put away, she debated where to go to stretch her legs. It was a long time until dinner, and she felt at a bit of a loose end. Working a nine to five had never been part of her career, so she wondered if she'd be better off just heading back to the observatory for a couple of hours. Given everything she'd discovered from Lorelai, she was feeling an urge to return there, to try to connect more with the ghosts of the past. She'd take Comet this time, too – he'd be all right if she kept him inside the building and on a lead inside the fence. She changed back into her walking boots, made a quick flask of coffee to take with her, as well as grabbing some snacks for herself and Comet, and set off back up the hill.

19

The path to the observatory was becoming familiar now, and as Charlotte rounded the hill, and headed up the last stretch, she felt an increased sense of belonging. It was daft, really; the observatory was going to be bulldozed out of existence soon, and she'd be back at university welcoming the next undergraduates into their halls of residence. In her more fanciful moments as an astronomical archivist, she imagined herself as some kind of great protector of the astronomical past: the one person standing between the loss and preservation of information vital to understanding the fabric of the universe. Then she'd give herself a shake and chide herself for such daft notions. Most of the time, there were no earth-shattering discoveries to be made: she was merely cataloguing things that had been seen and recorded a hundred times before, by many different people. She was a glorified house mover in her less confident moments. All the same, she liked to imagine that, sometime far in the future, some descended version of herself would find the patterns, find the links in the information she'd so carefully stored, and be thankful for the work of a scruffy researcher working in a near-derelict building in the middle of nowhere.

Charlotte gave Comet's lead a tug as she removed the padlock from the chain that bound the fence and then closed both halves carefully behind her. She didn't bother locking it again: she'd had some trouble re-attaching the padlock and didn't want to get trapped inside the compound. She was doubtful that anyone else would come here on a Saturday anyway. The developers largely did work regular hours, and LBAS were still banned from the site because of the danger, except for Brian O'Connor, of course. She'd seen Brian a couple of times since she'd started work, but he'd been keeping away, giving her space to do her job, and for that she was grateful. Archiving could be quite a solitary profession, and while it was helpful to work as part of a team when everyone was an expert, sometimes enthusiastic amateurs could be more trouble than they were worth.

'Come on then, boy, let's try to remember where we left off,' she said as she and Comet opened the large steel door. She scrabbled on the wall to the right of the door for the light switch, and after a moment's dull buzz and a flicker, the lights went on. In contrast to the bright sunlight outside, the observatory looked even more wan and unloved. The steps to the gantry that ran around the top of the dome had a fresh covering of debris, which must have drifted in on the breeze.

Hurrying through to the records room, Charlotte let Comet off the lead where she could keep an eye on him, and then placed her backpack down on the desk that she'd come to call her own while she was working. She'd finished setting up the database, but she hadn't brought her laptop with her today. This brief stop this afternoon was more of an emotional visit than a fact-finding mission.

As she wandered around the dimly lit library space, she didn't bother to switch on any more lights. When she was working up here, she had it as bright as possible, but she was content just to keep the lights low today. It felt as though the ghosts of the past were walking with her in this old, abandoned building, but she wasn't afraid. Knowing a little more about the history of the observatory's custodians felt right, and she was beginning to put faces to the names she'd seen during some of her early forays into the reams of paperwork in the filing cabinets and drawers. She'd seen the signatures – L. L. Ashcombe and M. J. Ashcombe – a few times on various star charts and logs, and the connections were starting to develop in her mind between those old documents and the humans who'd created them. She'd seen the family photos on one of Lorelai's sideboards in her living room, too – pictures of Laura and Martin's wedding, pictures of Tristan and Thea at various ages at different family functions. The links between the academic research of the observatory and the people who carried it out were getting stronger.

On her meander around the room, Charlotte was drawn to the green cabinet marked 'Q1, 1995'. It didn't take a genius to work out why. The first part of Lorelai's tragic family tale had ended on a winter's night in January. Whatever the last calculations were that Martin and Laura had made before they closed the observatory down for the rest of the winter, they'd be in that drawer somewhere.

There was probably nothing significant or terribly interesting, Charlotte thought. Lunar observations, winter star patterns, seasonal changes, all would have been noted. But she felt a need to get to know these people better, to more clearly inform her archiving. The observatory's records weren't just a stack of paper and files to her, as they might have been to an active astronomer:

the combination of disciplines she held, the research she'd done, meant that she saw things with a historian's eye, as well as having the knowledge of astrophysics that meant she could interpret the charts, calculations and data.

Charlotte carefully unlocked the cabinet using the bunch of keys that Brian had given her. The drawer, stiff from lack of use, slid with difficulty on the rails of the cabinet with a squeak that made Comet prick up his ears.

'It's all right, old chap,' Charlotte said reassuringly. 'Sorry about the awful noise.'

Comet went back to his mooch into the corners of the room, sniffing here and there and padding around. Charlotte knew he was safe in here, unlike outside: she'd checked thoroughly for any jagged edges or broken glass before she'd allowed him to come in.

She pulled the drawer out to its full extent, and then strained her eyes to see the labels on the file dividers, smiling to herself to see the neat, typewritten sections that had obviously been created even pre the acquisition of a dot matrix printer. She wondered who'd been responsible for those – Martin? Laura? Brian? Some long-suffering partner of one of the members of LBAS who could touch type? Even that little story intrigued her.

Gradually, squinting slightly, she began to search back through the tabs. They were divided chronologically with sections for each week and were clearly the forerunner for a computerised database. At the front was January, Week 1, and then right at the back, March, Week 12. Eventually, these files would all go into a box and be shut away in the university's astronomical archive room, possibly never to be seen again. She felt as though *someone* ought to spend some time looking at them before they succumbed to that fate.

Charlotte pulled out the first of the January files and brought it to the nearest desk to the filing cabinet. Carefully, she opened the cardboard divider and began to leaf through its contents. Nothing was out of the ordinary here – some printouts of logs for the first week of January, which included times, instruments used for the observation and phenomena seen. In early January, most observations centred on the planet Jupiter, and the solar storms on its surface. So far, so routine.

There were also a couple of printouts of email correspondence from various academics. Clearly the Lower Brambleton Observatory was regarded as very significant in its heyday, even if it was run and maintained by volunteers. Charlotte was surprised to see an email from the University of North West Wessex's then head of the department of astronomy proposing a data sharing exercise on the Jupiter observations. She wondered, with all of the resources at their disposal, why the university would be interested in such a collaboration. Perhaps the LBAS had more ambition and scope back in the 1990s than she had been led to believe?

A rattle at the outside door of the observatory distracted Charlotte from her musings, and she hurriedly closed the file. As she did so, a piece of plain paper, folded into quarters, fluttered to the floor. Shoving it hastily back into the folder, she put her bag over it. She wasn't quite sure why: she was allowed to be here, after all.

'Hello? Is there someone there?' A deep voice echoed through the hallway.

'It's Charlotte James,' Charlotte called back. 'I'm just, er, doing a bit of work.'

'On a Saturday?' the voice came back, lighter in tone this time. 'And I thought *I* was the only workaholic around here!'

Charlotte hurried out of the library, her ears pricking up in recognition at the voice. And there, hovering by the front door, was Tristan Ashcombe.

20

Charlotte's heart beat a little faster as she crossed the hall to the front door of the observatory, where Tristan was waiting. As she drew closer, she noticed that he was wearing tan-coloured shorts and a dark-blue Henley shirt, with a couple of the buttons undone at the neck. A glance down at his feet showed a pair of sturdy work boots, though. Clearly, even in his down time, he was taking no chances when he visited Observatory Field. A contractor had been in on Friday to begin shifting some of the rubbish but there was still a fair bit to move, so the footwear was a good idea.

'What brings you here on a Saturday?' Charlotte asked as she reached the door. 'I thought it was only me who kept irregular hours!'

Tristan smiled, and Charlotte realised, with a jolt, that it was the first time she'd seen him looking cheerful since she'd met him. She was surprised at how much more attractive it made him, as his greenish-blue eyes crinkled at the corners.

'I'm glad I caught you,' he began, and Charlotte was sure she spotted a sheepish look crossing his features. 'I, er, wanted to apologise for being so abrupt the other day. If I'd known who you were, and why you were up here, I wouldn't have reacted the way I did.'

Charlotte smiled. She wasn't one to sulk or hold grudges, and she appreciated Tristan's apology. 'That's OK. To be honest, if I'd found me stuck in the gates with a dog off the lead, I'd probably have jumped to the same conclusion.' She paused. 'Did you, er, just come back up here to apologise?'

Tristan looked surprised. 'Well, now you come to mention it, there *was* something else. I'm actually in charge of the Observatory Field development, and I remembered that you should have signed a couple of indemnity forms before you started work up here. In all of the rush of the past couple of weeks, it completely slipped my mind.' He was clutching a blue document wallet with what looked like a thick stack of paperwork inside. 'Ordinarily, I'd have emailed them to you, but the company's been having some trouble with our electronic signatory, so I thought it would be quicker just to run them over to you. I popped in to see Gran and she told me you'd come up here.'

'You're in charge?' Charlotte echoed. She thought back to the story Lorelai had told her about the ownership of the observatory, and she felt a jolt of recognition as the pieces fitted together.

'If you wouldn't mind checking and signing these, then I can tick that job off my list,' Tristan said, interrupting her thoughts.

Wrinkling her brow, Charlotte tried to think back to her first day at Observatory Field. 'I'm sure Brian O'Connor gave me a load of stuff to sign when I started here, including the indemnities. Did he not give you the copies?'

Tristan smiled again, this time showing a row of even, straight teeth as he did so. 'Brian, bless his heart, is not only forgetful but he also buggered off on holiday yesterday without handing over the forms. Flowerdew are conducting an internal audit of this site and its procedures sometime over the next few weeks, so I wanted to be sure everything was ready, should the auditors descend before we break ground. I hope you don't mind signing them again?'

'Sure,' Charlotte replied. She reached out to take the document wallet from Tristan, and as she did so, her fingertips brushed his. She felt a little flutter of something she hadn't felt since her first introduction to Todd, but tried to suppress it. She couldn't reconcile this apparent friendliness with his brusque manner when they'd encountered one another before.

Realising she was just staring at the folder, Charlotte blushed and raised her head, so that she made eye contact with Tristan again.

'I can sign these now if you want to come in and wait,' she said. 'I wouldn't want to keep you or the auditors hanging about!'

As she said this, she saw something flicker over Tristan's expression. It looked like doubt, or even apprehension.

'Er, no, I won't come in if you don't mind,' he replied after a beat. 'You can leave the folder with Gran if you like, and I can pick it up from there at some point?'

'Sure,' Charlotte replied. Given what she had discovered about the Ashcombe family's complex history with the observatory, she wasn't entirely surprised he didn't want to hang about. 'I would offer to drop them at your office, but I don't have a car, and I've discovered the public transport links in this part of the world leave a lot to be desired!'

Tristan was smiling again, the brief apprehension gone from his expression. 'You can say that again. I can't quite believe you haven't got your own transport, though, and you've come all the way out here for a job. You must feel quite isolated. Gran's house isn't exactly on the main road, and this place, well…'

'It's been a bit of a culture shock after living in central Bristol for so many years,' Charlotte agreed. 'I'm a house parent in one of the halls of residence, so I'm used to being bothered at all hours of the day and night by pissed or homesick undergrads. The quiet at Nightshade Cottage takes a bit of getting used to.'

'I keep suggesting to Gran that she sells up and gets something smaller, closer to the busier parts of the village,' Tristan replied, 'but, well, you must be getting to know Gran. She's dug her heels in and refuses to be moved from Nightshade Cottage.'

'Don't worry,' Charlotte said, 'I'll keep an eye on her while I'm her lodger. Not that she needs an eye kept on her, of course. She seems very spry.'

'Oh, she is,' Tristan said, running a hand through his hair to brush an errant lock from his eyes. 'At the moment, she's in great health, but she will insist on taking in lodgers, and while she claims they're all vetted by the accommodation company who handle the annexe, she's had a couple of close calls.'

'Oh, really?' Charlotte raised an eyebrow, then, rather to her own surprise, added, 'I'd love to hear about them, sometime. Lorelai hasn't said anything about the more, er, *eccentric* characters she's had in the annexe.'

This time, Charlotte felt a more profound flutter in her chest as Tristan laughed. 'Oh, I could tell you some stories, believe me!' He glanced at his watch. 'But they'll have to wait, I'm afraid. I've got a ton of paperwork to reconcile before the site move happens, and not a great deal of time to do it in.'

Feeling their cordial exchange was coming to a businesslike close, Charlotte nodded and tried to replicate his more formal tone. 'Well, I'll get these done and leave them at Lorelai's for you to collect at your convenience,' she said.

'Thanks.' Tristan gave her another smile. 'And I'm sorry for the hassle of having to do them again. Bless Brian, he's actually the most reliable member of the Astronomical Society these days, but even he's getting absent minded.' He paused, and glanced up towards she shabby domed roof of the building. 'It'll be a lot better for him, and for all of us, once this place has been knocked down.'

Given what she'd been discovering about Tristan's family connections to the building, Charlotte didn't feel she could disagree.

21

Later that afternoon, having signed the indemnities and put them carefully back in the folder, Charlotte decided to call it a day. She felt flummoxed by Tristan's visit to the observatory, as if its past and present had intersected like two lines on a star chart, and there had been a collision of worlds. He'd been friendlier, even if it was because he needed her to re-sign those forms, and she'd felt a definite stirring of attraction towards him. Perhaps it was the dearth of events in her love life that was making her respond that way: she'd noted to herself how attractive Nick Saint was too, or maybe it was the fresh country air, but whatever it was, she felt conflicted about leaning into it. She was fresh out of the break-up with Todd, and though Gemma would have told her that the best way to get over a man was to get under another one, she'd never reacted that way to the end of a relationship.

As she walked back down the sloping woodland to Nightshade Cottage, Charlotte reflected on how she was beginning to settle into Lower Brambleton and the observatory. She was developing a real desire to unravel its mysteries, before it was all lost to demolition, and she was looking forward to getting back up there on Monday morning, having already decided to spend Sunday putting the final touches on the computer-based filing system and organising her archive boxes, ready for transport up to the observatory. She'd asked for them all to be sent to Nightshade Cottage so that she could label them up in relative comfort, but it hadn't escaped her that she was now going to have to move them up to the observatory herself.

Letting herself and Comet through the door of the annexe, Charlotte made a cup of tea and then settled down to answer some emails. There was a check-in from Professor Jim Edwin, her head of department, to which she fired off a cheery reply, and another email from Todd, which she ignored for now. She knew he had one of those trackers that would tell him exactly when she'd opened his emails and she didn't want to give him the satisfaction of thinking she was desperately waiting to hear from him. He could definitely wait.

'Helloooo?' Lorelai's voice drifted through from the garden. 'Are you back in for the evening, dear?'

'Yup,' Charlotte replied. She was getting used to Lorelai's rather flexible notions of space and privacy, and was finding she didn't really mind the casual enquiries. 'I thought I'd treat myself to a pizza and a box-set on the laptop. There's a new series of *The Outlaws* just dropped on iPlayer and I thought I'd spend a productive evening binge-watching it.'

'Sounds good,' Lorelai replied, but Charlotte didn't miss the speculative pause. 'But if you did fancy going out, the Lower Brambleton Astronomical Society is meeting in the local pub, the Star and Telescope, from six-thirty. There aren't many members left now, but they do like to meet once a month and have a chat, especially now they're not allowed to convene at the observatory.'

A Sky Full of Stars

Charlotte thought for a moment. 'Actually,' she said, 'I've been meaning to check out the pub anyway, and it would be nice for Comet and me to have a different walk and a change of scenery.'

'If you like, I can run you down there so you only have to walk back. I don't mind dogs in the car.'

'That's a lot to ask,' Charlotte replied. Privately, she wondered just how great Lorelai's driving was at her age. She wondered if walking, even down the narrow, tree-root lined lanes of Lower Brambleton, would be safer than being a passenger in Lorelai's ancient Ford Fiesta.

'Oh, it's no trouble, dear,' Lorelai replied. 'And this little chap can still have his walk on the way home, then, can't he? Or you can just leave him with me for the evening. As I said, I'm always happy to dog sit.' She paused again. 'Or Tristan could give you a lift down – he said he might pop in later.'

Charlotte got the impression that she was being led, but she was determined not to follow. 'Oh, I'm sure Tristan's got better things to do on a Saturday evening than give some scruffy academic a lift to the local boozer!'

Lorelai raised a wry eyebrow. 'I take it he's not endeared himself much to you, then?'

Charlotte grinned. 'Well, the first time I met him, he bollocked me for trespassing, so I don't think first impressions were very good on either side.'

'He caught up with you at the observatory this afternoon, though?'

Charlotte nodded. 'Yup. And I've got his forms signed if he does drop in later.' She glanced down at Comet. 'Perhaps I'll take Comet with me to the pub. He likes a packet of cheese and onion crisps occasionally.'

'Well, the offer of a lift still stands,' Lorelai replied. 'If you fancy it.'

'We'll take our chances on the lanes,' Charlotte said. 'But thank you – it's above and beyond your duty as my landlady to offer to be my chauffeur as well.'

'Anything to get me out of the house these days is very welcome,' Lorelai replied. 'Shout if you want me to cook an extra portion of dinner for you before you head out. It's cowboy beans and sausage casserole tonight.'

'Sounds lovely, but I'll grab something when I get back,' Charlotte replied. She was grateful for Lorelai's attempts to nurture, but she felt as though she needed some space and a change of scene for a few hours.

'Come on, old chap.' She gestured to Comet. 'Let's get ourselves looking presentable and then we can go and check out the Star and Telescope, and maybe meet some more members of this soon-to-be-defunct Astronomical Society.' As she said this, a sense of wistfulness came over her. For LBAS, it really would be the end of an era once the observatory was no more.

22

'No, I'm sorry, dear, I don't know where Charlotte put the forms.' Lorelai's confusion was concerning. She was usually so whip smart and knew where everything was. Tristan tried not to feel irritated. He had to get the forms back to head office first thing on Monday morning, and his grandmother's temporary lapse of memory was most inconvenient. 'I'd offer to call her, but she's on her way to the pub, and you know how bad the reception is in the lanes.'

'It's all right, Gran, I'll pop round tomorrow morning and see her. Hopefully she'll be able to put her hands on them.' Tristan tried to push away the nagging feeling of concern that Lorelai might be losing her faculties. She'd always been so sharp up until now. He wondered if age was starting to tell on her, and yet again felt frustrated that she continued to refuse to be budged from her home.

'Well, all right then, dear.' Lorelai paused. 'Of course, if you wanted them tonight, you could always head over to the pub yourself. Charlotte doesn't strike me as the disorganised type:

she'd probably be able to tell you straight away where she's put the file.'

Tristan considered this for a moment. He really did want to get the paperwork sorted so that he could spend Sunday relaxing, maybe having lunch with Martha, whom he'd decided was probably an on-again situation, before getting to the office bright and early on Monday. If he met Charlotte tonight and she could let him know where the paperwork was, that would be one box ticked before a potential audit.

'Maybe I'll nip down to the Star and Telescope now,' Tristan said. 'I might be able to catch her before she has too much of the local scrumpy!' He leaned down and gave his grandmother a kiss on the cheek. 'I'll see you in a bit, Gran.'

'See you later,' Lorelai replied. As he left Nightshade Cottage, Tristan got the slightest sensation that he'd just been set up but, brushing aside those thoughts, he concentrated on reversing his Audi out of Lorelai's narrow front gate. He'd make this quick and hopefully he'd be back home and firming up a lunch date with Martha before the evening was out.

A little time later, Tristan had parked out the front of the pub and was heading through the red-painted wooden front door. The pub, with its name and theme of starlit skies throughout, was a rather obvious testament to how important the observatory had once been in Lower Brambleton. Successive brewery chains had managed it over the years, and poured a lot of money into its upkeep, and they had leaned into the celestial themes, including painting a rather overpowering mural on the ceiling of the night skies, circa 1895 when Eleanor Winslow had brought such recognition to the village. Brass telescopes were placed on windowsills and in alcoves, and on one wall in the restaurant there was a star chart from the 1900s. The whole effect was somewhat hokey and commercial, but even given his connections to the observatory's more recent history, Tristan couldn't help liking it. As his family had such a long association with the observatory, for better or worse, he felt at home here. It made no sense to him, but he appreciated that feeling.

'Tristan, mate! Haven't seen you in ages. How are you?'

Tristan glanced in the direction of one of the wooden tables in the bar area and smiled as he saw Annabelle and Nick Saint and Annabelle's husband, Jamie, all chatting amiably.

'I'm good, thanks,' he replied. The four of them had been at school together, and while he now lived further away, he was always pleased at the easy way they admitted him back into their circle when they saw him. Lower Brambleton was welcoming like that: links, once forged, weren't easily broken.

'Get you a drink?' Nick asked, rising from his chair.

Tristan noticed the empty glasses all round. 'I'll get them,' he said. Annabelle and Jamie raised their glasses in thanks. He'd stop for one, he thought. He wasn't a big drinker, but Carters' Cider, the biggest cider business in the south-west, had recently introduced an alcohol-free version, and he rather liked it.

Glancing around the pub, he couldn't yet see Charlotte. He was surprised he hadn't passed her on his way from Lorelai's house, but perhaps she'd taken a more off-road route to get here. There were several paths that skirted the main road and were a less hazardous route to the pub than the road he'd taken while driving. He figured he might as well sit and have a drink with his friends while he waited.

'How are you doing, mate?' Nick asked as he helped Tristan ferry three pints of scrumpy back to the table. 'Haven't seen you back in the village in ages.'

'It's been busy,' Tristan replied. 'I've been up to my eyeballs in plans and permissions for several projects, including the one in the village, and they've taken me all over the place lately.'

'Sounds like things are really taking off for you,' Annabelle interjected. 'It's about time. You've worked hard enough for it.'

The friends lapsed into a pause while they sipped their drinks. Annabelle asked about Thea, and Tristan filled her in on his sister's plans to move into the new development on Observatory Field.

'Makes sense,' Annabelle replied, although her tone sounded less certain. Tristan didn't need to ask why. Nick and Annabelle had been witnesses to his and Thea's family tragedy, and had helped pick up the pieces afterwards, and for years while they were all still at school. He knew that Thea could square living in a new home at Observatory Field more easily than he could: she had a pragmatic, practical streak that allowed her to see the advantages, despite the history. Being back in Lower Brambleton and closer to Lorelai was more important now. He still couldn't bring himself to feel the same way, but then there were some things about the tragedy he'd never reconciled himself to.

'I saw Thea this afternoon,' Nick said, after taking a sip of his pint. 'I was dropping off a delivery to your gran's house, and she rocked up with those adorable sprogs of hers. They've grown since the last time I saw her.'

'They have,' Tristan replied. 'Time flies when you're a single parent of two, or so she's always telling me!'

Nick laughed. 'She looked really well, though. I did ask her if she fancied coming over with the kids to watch the cricket, but I guess she decided against it.'

Tristan smothered a grin as Annabelle raised a speculative eyebrow in her brother's direction. 'She turned you down again, did she? Still carrying that torch from secondary school?'

'It wasn't like that!' Nick muttered, but Tristan noticed his colour rising slightly. 'I just thought it would be nice for her to have a break, that's all.'

Annabelle's *pull the other one, it's got bells on* expression wasn't lost on Tristan. 'Whatever, little brother. I'm sure she had her reasons for turning you down.' Before Nick could respond to her, she'd turned her attention back to Tristan, in a swift *volte face* that only people who've been friends forever can achieve without confusion. 'So how's it *really* all going sorting out Observatory Field, Tris?'

Tristan didn't want to get into a deeper discussion with Annabelle, who had the ability to read him better than most of his friends, over a pub table, so he was relieved when her attention was drawn to Charlotte, who'd pushed open the door of the pub. Charlotte was blinking slightly, having come in from the still bright evening sunshine. She gave a brief smile of recognition as she spotted the group of friends, and then went to the bar. His eyes followed her across the room, watching the way she walked and the way her little black and white dog trotted obediently at her heels.

'Someone caught your eye, Tris?' Annabelle teased gently.

Tristan shook his head a little too forcefully to rebut her suggestion. 'I just need a word with Gran's new lodger. She's got some paperwork I've got to take to the office on Monday.'

'Oh, the last of the great romantics.' Annabelle rolled her eyes. 'It's Saturday night and you're still thinking about work. Why don't we ask her to join us? She probably doesn't know that many people, and she might like company in this most local of local boozers.'

Tristan didn't have time to protest as Annabelle waved broadly at Charlotte, who did appear relieved to have an anchor point in an unfamiliar pub. 'Come and have a drink!' Annabelle called. 'You don't want to be sitting alone.'

Charlotte smiled, and Tristan thought what a lovely smile she had. 'Thanks,' she called back. 'I'll just grab a Coke and I'll be on over.'

Tristan sipped his cider and sat back in his chair. It didn't look like he'd be going anywhere soon, and, if he was being honest, he was quite enjoying being social on a Saturday evening. Perhaps he'd stay for another drink and see how the night panned out.

23

Charlotte's eyes took a moment to adjust to the dim light inside the pub, but when they did, she saw Tristan, Annabelle and Nick and a guy she didn't recognise sitting at one of the tables. When Annabelle called her over to join them, she hesitated for a second: would Tristan want her there given their somewhat uneven recent encounters? But, she figured, if things got awkward, she could always make her excuses and leave the friends to it.

Taking her drink, she walked over to where the four were sitting. As she did so, she noticed how much more relaxed Tristan seemed in the company of his friends, and how that smile she'd seen on the doorstep of the observatory was readier when he was with them. Perhaps she'd misjudged him after all?

'So, it didn't take you long to find the local pub, then?' Annabelle's tone was teasing, once she'd introduced Charlotte to the other guy at the table, Jamie, her husband. 'Rural life tends to be better if there's a chance of a bit of alcoholic lubrication now and then!'

The friends all laughed and Charlotte gave a grin. 'I live in university halls most of the year, so I'm well used to booze,' she replied. 'But it's nice to be out amongst actual adults and not perennially drunk undergraduates making the most of being away from home for the first time.'

'I can't think of anything worse.' Annabelle wrinkled her nose. 'How do you have the patience for all of that?'

Charlotte laughed. 'You get used to it after a while, and it's nice to know that you're helping to support the kids as they settle in. I suppose I just like university life, and I'm happy to do my bit to make sure the undergrads do, as well.'

'That all sounds very noble,' Annabelle grinned. 'Although I do hope you make the most of your freedom while you're working in Lower Brambleton, even if things are a little quieter than you're accustomed to.' She raised her glass. 'To summer adventures.'

'Summer adventures,' Charlotte echoed. As she did, she couldn't help stealing a glance at Tristan, who, to her surprise, was looking right back at her. She felt her pulse quicken, but as soon as he saw she'd seen him, he glanced back to Annabelle.

'So, Lorelai tells me that the Lower Brambleton Astronomical Society meets here on a Saturday evening,' Charlotte said, trying to move things forward, and away from the knowledge that she'd caught Tristan looking at her. 'Do you have any idea where I can find them?'

'Wrong Saturday, I'm afraid,' Nick replied. 'They have the back room of the pub for their presentations and discussions on the last Saturday of the month. Although I doubt that'll be happening for much longer now the observatory's being demolished.'

Charlotte shook her head. 'Seems a bit of a shame they can't set up somewhere else, but I suppose that's progress.'

'Certainly is.' Tristan spoke for the first time since Charlotte had joined the group. 'And speaking of which, did you manage to do those forms I gave you? I popped in to see Gran earlier, but she wasn't sure where you'd left them.'

Charlotte furrowed her brow. 'I left them for you on the table in her kitchen. I was sure I told Lorelai that's where they were.' She saw a look of concern passing over Tristan's face as she replied. 'But then again, perhaps I just forgot to mention it to her,' she added hastily. 'Sometimes I think I've done something and then it turns out I've completely forgotten.'

Tristan nodded, and then gave what she hoped was a reassured smile. 'Well, I'll pop back in before I head home and see if I can find them,' he said.

Conversation flowed easily between the group, more drinks were ordered, and before she knew it, Charlotte was giggling helplessly at yet another of Nick's stories about their escapades as kids. In spite of the tragedy that had engulfed Tristan and Thea's family, it seemed that there was still plenty of history between the Ashcombes and the Saints of an idyllic rural childhood. Lower Brambleton, with its extensive woodlands, sleepy lanes and endless fields was perfection for adventurous, growing kids.

Charlotte found herself wondering what Tristan would have been like as a child, and then a teenager, and whether or not they'd have been friends. As Nick and Annabelle assailed her with one anecdote after another, and Jamie looked indulgently on and enjoyed the stories that he'd doubtless heard a hundred times, Charlotte felt as though she was gaining admission to a rather exclusive, endearing club. She'd realised from the moment she'd sat down that Annabelle and Nick were the kind of people who extended a warm hand of welcome to all those whom they encountered, whether they were customers in the shop or friends of friends, and she was grateful for the inclusion.

'And then, if you can believe it, Tristan here had to shinny down the drainpipe and hotfoot it all the way back home before my parents found out he and Nick had drunk our dad's best, oldest bottle of whisky that he'd been keeping for his seventieth birthday. It was minus three outside, there was frost on the ground and Tristan ran all the way home in just his Ninja Turtle boxer shorts and T-shirt!' Annabelle spluttered with laughter and nearly spat the remnants of her pint on the table.

Tristan, who'd known, of course, where this story was going, turned to Charlotte with an amused glint in his eyes. 'What Annabelle isn't telling you is that I was merely a distraction tactic, because she had to make sure Jamie here escaped out of her bedroom window before her mum and dad realised he'd spent the night.'

'True, true,' Annabelle replied, 'but at least Jamie had the decency to marry me so it worked out in the end. I don't think Dad ever forgave you and Nick for drinking that bottle of whisky, though.'

'If I hadn't had it as insulation, I'd have frozen my bollocks off running all the way home,' Tristan replied. 'So, it was good for something, at least.'

Charlotte sat back in her chair and realised how relaxed she felt. She was still drinking Coke but with the addition of a shot of Jack Daniel's now, and the alcohol and the warm welcome from the friends had really put her at ease. Glancing at the clock, she realised it was getting on for 10 p.m. She wasn't bothered by the time – she was used to keeping far later hours in the course of her research, but she was aware that, if she didn't make a move soon, she'd be walking down dangerous country lanes in the pitch dark.

Comet, who'd been lying calmly under the table all night, poked up his nose when Annabelle opened a couple of packets of cheese and onion crisps and stuck them in the middle of the table for the group to share. 'Is he allowed one?' she asked as she reached down to stroke his ears.

Charlotte nodded. 'Cheese and onion is his favourite flavour, so feel free to slip him a couple if you want.' She smiled at her dog as he took the proffered crisps from Annabelle's fingers. He had a lovely, soft mouth and was the gentlest of creatures, even when food was involved.

Taking a last gulp of her drink, she shook her head when Jamie offered her another one. 'I really should get back before it gets too dark to find my way home.'

'Oh, I'm sure Tristan'll drop you off.' Annabelle's eyes twinkled mischievously and turned to Tristan. 'You said you'd got to pick up those forms, anyway, didn't you?'

'Yeah, sure.' Tristan's pause before he answered wasn't lost on Charlotte. She wondered if he was worrying about his upholstery. There weren't many cars parked outside the pub that evening, but she'd taken a fair guess that the swanky Audi Q8 4x4 was Tristan's. And she'd take another guess that he wouldn't be too keen to have a spaniel flatfooting all over his leather seats. A spaniel that now smelled of cheese and onion crisps...

'Honestly, it's fine,' Charlotte replied quickly. 'I wouldn't want to put you out.'

'It's no trouble, is it, Tristan?' Annabelle replied before the man himself could. 'I mean, two birds with one stone and all that?'

'No trouble at all,' Tristan said quickly. 'I'm, er, ready when you are, Charlotte.'

'I'll just nip to the loo,' Charlotte said, and Annabelle got up to go with her. 'Would you mind keeping an eye on Comet for me?'

'Sure,' Tristan replied, taking the dog's lead. Comet glanced at him, sighed and then put his head between his paws once more.

'It's nice to see you out and about in the village,' Annabelle said as they met at the sinks. 'A lot of incomers tend to keep themselves to themselves.'

'It's lovely to be made so welcome,' Charlotte replied. 'Makes me sad that I'm only going to be here for a few weeks.'

'Yeah.' Annabelle looked at her speculatively. 'Well, I hope you've settled in OK to Lorelai's. She's had some real waifs and strays in that annexe over the years, until Tristan and Thea put their feet down and made her go to a company and get proper references. Tris still worries about her renting the annexe out, but he seems to have taken a shine to you.'

Charlotte snorted. 'I don't think so! The first time he met me, he gave me a right bollocking.'

'He can be a bit abrupt at times, especially when he thinks something he loves is being threatened, and he absolutely adores Lorelai. She pretty much brought him and Thea up, after... well, you know.'

Charlotte noticed that, even decades on from the tragedy, the even the ebullient Annabelle didn't want to refer to it in detail. She wondered if there was still something she didn't know, but realised now wasn't the time to push for more information.

'Tristan's a good egg,' Annabelle continued. 'But he's used to his own company, and rather set in his ways. Don't take his abruptness to heart.'

'Is he, er, seeing anyone?' The Jack Daniel's had made Charlotte more relaxed, and the question was out of her mouth before she could stop it.

Annabelle raised an eyebrow. 'Well, he's got an on-off thing with a colleague of his at work, Martha, I think she's called. We met her once, but Tristan keeps his private life private. I don't think it's serious, though. I tend to know when he fancies someone, no matter how much he tries to hide it.'

'How so?' Charlotte couldn't help asking.

'Well, he hangs around in the pub and tries to hide the fact he's nervous of dogs, for a start!' Annabelle beamed mischievously. 'He got bitten on the bum by an Alsatian when he was six… he's had a bit of a phobia ever since.'

'Comet's not tall enough to bite him on the bum or anywhere else!' Charlotte grinned, although suddenly she was a little apprehensive about having left the two of them together. She also thought how well Tristan had hidden his worries when he'd rescued Comet from the horrors of the junk around the observatory.

'Anyway,' Charlotte protested, realising the full suggestion that Annabelle was making, 'he doesn't fancy me. He's been grumpy pretty much every time I've seen him, barring tonight.'

'Oh, that's just Tristan,' Annabelle replied, drying her hands. 'His sister, Thea's the only one who really *gets* him, and even she admits he can be a grouchy bastard a lot of the time. But believe me, underneath that tortured, Theo James exterior, he's got the softest heart and really just wants to be loved.'

Charlotte grinned. 'I think you've been reading too many romantic novels! I'm not in the market for a tortured soul, no matter how good looking he is.'

'Oh, so you admit he's good looking?' Annabelle teased, with the easy intimacy that a couple of drinks and an evening in the pub could create. 'I'll bear that in mind!'

Charlotte didn't reply, somehow knowing better than to protest innocence against a well-meaning friend of Tristan's.

24

As Annabelle and Charlotte approached the table once more, Tristan, Jamie and Nick all stood up. Tristan handed over Comet's lead and Charlotte smiled gratefully at him. He didn't seem nervous of her little cocker spaniel, which was something at least.

'Ready to go?' Tristan asked.

'Sure, and thanks again for offering to give me a lift,' Charlotte replied. After the conversation with Annabelle in the loos, she couldn't get the comparison with Theo James out of her head when she looked at Tristan. She'd mainlined the *Divergent* films a few years back, and adored seeing the actor in *The Gentlemen* recently, too. She told herself firmly to get a grip. It was clearly the Jack Daniel's colouring her perspective tonight.

Annabelle, Jamie and Nick all said goodbye outside the pub and headed to the battered Ford Mondeo estate that was parked a few spots away from Tristan's Audi. Chatting as they went, Jamie, who was designated driver for the evening, tooted the car's horn cheerfully as they pulled out of the car park.

Tristan unlocked the car and then opened the boot. 'Will Comet be OK in here?'

Charlotte nodded. 'Yup. He's so knackered, he'll just crash out, I would think.'

As if to contradict her, the spritely Comet jumped into the boot, looking far from tired, and Charlotte unhooked his lead. She was confident he couldn't leap over the back seat to get to her and as he settled down in the back she and Tristan rounded the car and got into the front seats.

Tristan started the engine, and for a minute or two they drove in silence. Away from the chatter and the lights of the pub, Charlotte took a moment to relax, and she leaned back on the black leather seat, taking in the dimming silhouettes of the landscape as Tristan drove back to Nightshade Cottage. She felt content, energised by the socialising, but also ready to chill by herself for the rest of the evening. She was an introvert at heart but once she felt comfortable she enjoyed the company of other people. She got the feeling, having observed Tristan tonight, that he was the same. She found her eyes drawn to Tristan's profile in the fading light. He had a prominent nose, and a generous mouth, and surprisingly long eyelashes. Realising she was staring, she turned her head back to the front before he noticed.

Very soon they'd pulled into the driveway, and Tristan briskly undid his seatbelt and opened the driver's door. By the time Charlotte had located her seatbelt clip, he'd walked around to the passenger's side and pulled open her door, too.

'Thanks,' she said in surprise. 'That's very chivalrous of you.'

Tristan raised an amused eyebrow. 'Just wanted to make sure you didn't sprain an ankle getting down. It's not a car built for, er, shorter people.'

'I'm not *that* short!' Charlotte bristled slightly, but then remembered Annabelle's words in the ladies', and decided to smile. Tristan might not have the gift of the gab, but it was still a nice gesture. She stepped down and then went to let Comet out of the boot. He jumped down and then sniffed around the front garden before lifting a leg on one of Lorelai's rose bushes.

'Thanks for the ride home,' Charlotte said. 'I wasn't really looking forward to walking back down that road in the dark.'

'It can be dangerous,' Tristan agreed. 'I tried to ban Gran from walking down it in the winter, but she ignores me and still does it sometimes.'

There was a pause and Charlotte found herself looking up into Tristan's face and wondering what to do next. Then she remembered the paperwork, which was obviously the reason he'd agreed to bring her home.

'I'll, er, see if I can find those forms, shall I?' she said, making a move for the house.

'Thanks. Gran's probably locked up her side though, so I'd better use my key.'

Lorelai was obviously still up and about as there was a warm, cosy light emanating from the small sitting room at the front of the house, and the flickering glow of the television.

'Gran's probably binge-watching *Ozark*.' Tristan glanced over his shoulder with a grin in Charlotte's direction. 'She loves a bit of drug heist drama.'

'Really?' Charlotte tried not to sound surprised. Nothing about Lorelai suggested a liking for fictional drug cartels, but the thought of it amused Charlotte.

'Oh, sure – she bookends it with episodes of *Antiques Road Trip*. Best thing I ever did, getting her a Netflix subscription.' Tristan reached Lorelai's kitchen door and fumbled to get the key in the lock. Charlotte, unsure whether or not she should follow him through to Lorelai's side of the house, hovered awkwardly on her side of the partitioned wall.

'It's all right, I'll look where you told me they were, and if I can't find them, I'll let you know.' Tristan finally unlocked the door and then paused. 'I'll give Gran a shout, too, so she knows she's not being burgled.'

'OK then. Well, thanks again for the lift, and goodnight.'

'Goodnight.' Tristan obviously had the forms on his mind because before he'd even finished speaking, he was through the door.

Charlotte got out her own keys and let herself through to her side of the house. She didn't bother switching on the main light as the moon was starting to rise and she could see well enough. She flipped the switch on the kettle, grabbed a mug from the cupboard and was just putting some fresh water down for Comet when a tap at the pane of glass in the back door made her jump out of her skin. Comet gave a protective yap and then rushed to the door, tail wagging.

'Sorry,' Tristan said, obviously having seen her jump. 'I didn't mean to give you a fright. I just wanted to let you know I found those papers, exactly where you said you'd left them.'

'Good,' Charlotte replied, once her heartbeat had slowed down. 'I wouldn't be much of an archivist if I didn't know where I'd put things.'

'It's odd,' Tristan mused. 'I mean, Gran can't have missed them – they were right there on the kitchen table.' His eyes met Charlotte's and she could see the questions in them.

'I'm sure she just didn't realise,' Charlotte replied quickly. 'Maybe she'd shoved her newspaper over them, or something.'

Tristan gave a brief smile. 'You're probably right,' he said. She got the sense he was trying to reassure himself as he said it. 'She's getting on a bit now, and sometimes people her age can be forgetful, can't they?'

'Absolutely.' Charlotte nodded and tried not to think about

other reasons Lorelai might have lapsed. Living out here in the middle of nowhere with a succession of lodgers in the annexe wasn't an ideal prospect if there was anything more seriously wrong.

'Look, I know it's a lot to ask, but would you mind keeping an eye on her while you're here?' Tristan ran a hand through his hair, looking distinctly nervous. 'I know you're just the lodger, but if you notice anything odd about her behaviour, anything at all, it would take a load off my mind if you could let me know.'

'Of course,' Charlotte replied. 'I'm sure I'll see you around the building site when you move your office up there. I'll let you know if I see anything concerning.'

'No,' Tristan said. 'I think it might be better if I gave you my number. That way, you can text me if I need to come and check on her.'

Charlotte's face flushed. She'd been hoping that Tristan might give her his phone number, but these weren't exactly the circumstances she'd been wishing for. 'That sounds like a good plan.' She whipped her phone out of her jeans pocket, and they swapped numbers. Her heart gave a little extra thudding beat as Tristan's number appeared on her phone after he called it.

'Thanks, Charlotte,' he said softly. 'I'm sure there's nothing to worry about, but it'll put my mind at rest if you could let me know if you spot anything out of the ordinary.'

'I will.' Charlotte looked up at him, and for a long moment, their eyes locked. Despite the step from the door to the patio, they were standing very close to each other, having checked the phone numbers, and now Charlotte wondered how to break the moment.

In the end, it was Comet who did it for them as he meandered past Tristan, giving him a cursory sniff on the way, as if he was saying, 'Well, are you staying or going?'

Tristan reached down and gave the dog a pat. 'I hope you both had a nice time tonight,' he said as he straightened back up. 'Annabelle, Nick and Jamie are all great company.'

'Yes, they are,' Charlotte replied. 'And it was nice to get to know you a little bit better, too.'

Tristan glanced away and Charlotte wondered if she'd made him uncomfortable.

'I enjoyed getting to know you a bit better, too,' he said softly. 'Let's do it again sometime.'

'I'd like that.' Charlotte gave a grin. 'Well, you know where to find me.'

'I do.' Tristan fumbled to put his mobile back in his pocket. 'So,' he said quietly, 'goodnight then.'

'Goodnight.' Charlotte watched as he moved away from the doorstep, rounded the corner of Nightshade Cottage and then she heard the engine start and the Audi pulling out of the drive.

For the second time that night, she jumped out of her skin as another voice floated softly across from the other side of the patio. 'Silly boy,' Lorelai said, more than a trace of humour in her voice. 'As if I'd be losing my marbles!'

Charlotte, once over the surprise, gave a short laugh. 'You hid those papers on purpose, didn't you, Lorelai?'

Lorelai, close enough for Charlotte to see the feigned look of innocence in her eyes, gave a grin in response. 'Well, what was I supposed to do to encourage the two of you to stop snapping at each other? And from what I've just seen, it worked!'

Charlotte shook her head. 'Lorelai,' she said gently, 'has anyone ever told you you're incorrigible?'

25

After a leisurely Sunday, which, for Tristan, was a rarity, he got to Flowerdew Homes' head office in Taunton early on Monday morning. He'd decided not to phone Martha that weekend: in fact, he was hoping that things might peter out between them naturally now. Martha was a lovely woman, but they'd been keeping things casual as neither wanted anything serious. She'd made no secret of the fact that she wasn't looking for anything exclusive, and so he'd give them both a bit of space.

It didn't take a genius to work out why he might be feeling that way: he'd really enjoyed Charlotte's company on Saturday night, and he'd felt that spark between them, still very faint, but it was definitely there. He wasn't going to overthink things, but the way thoughts of Charlotte kept intruding into his mind over the next twenty-four hours had to be a sign that he was ready to get to know her better, if she wanted that too.

After a morning of phone calls, paperwork and firming up the final details of his office move to Observatory Field, he was ready for a break. He checked his phone and was pleased to see that Charlotte had texted him with an update about Lorelai.

> Lorelai might have hidden those papers on purpose! She seems to think we should spend more time together.

Tristan couldn't stop the rush of relief as he read the message. Trust his gran to try to meddle in his love life. She'd been dropping hints lately that he ought to be thinking about settling down, no matter how hard he'd tried to dissuade her, and now, with Charlotte as her lodger, her imagination had obviously gone into overdrive. Lorelai clearly needed more to do with her time, he thought.

And yet he couldn't stop remembering just how easily Charlotte had slotted into his group of friends on Saturday night. She'd chatted with the four of them all evening, and it hadn't taken long before he'd forgotten how new she was to the village. The memory of their first encounter at the observatory was gradually receding in favour of the smiles and laughs they'd shared around the pub table. There was definitely a part of him that wanted to see her again.

So why didn't he text her back and suggest it? Charlotte's message certainly implied she'd be up for seeing him again, and if they didn't get on when it was just the two of them, then they didn't have to repeat it.

Grabbing his phone from where he'd put it on his desk, he drafted six possible responses before he settled on the one he finally sent:

> Glad to hear Gran's still capable of getting up to her antics. Do YOU think we should spend some more time together?

He waited for a response, trying to convince himself he

wasn't nervous. When the response came, a few minutes later, he couldn't help the grin that spread over his face.

> I'd like to see you again. Shall we say Saturday?
> Not sure I'm up for the pub though –
> Annabelle's also got her matchmaking hat on!

After replying that he and his car were all hers, and to let him know what she'd like to do, Tristan once again waited.

> How well do you know my hometown? Would you be up for a guided tour of some of Bristol's best spots?

Tristan hadn't visited Bristol in a long time, and he knew that Charlotte must know it well to make the offer. He was surprised at how keen he was to take her up on her idea, and within seconds he'd texted her back saying yes, he'd love to. They arranged to meet at Nightshade Cottage at ten o'clock on Saturday morning, but when he asked her for a few more details about what they were likely to get up to, she sent him a teasing 'wait and see'.

He was unaccustomed to handing over control of things to someone else, and for a few moments after they'd arranged things he felt uneasy. What if they didn't get on and Saturday was a completely awkward disaster? What if they had nothing in common? What if this was just a huge mistake?

Realising that he was beginning to catastrophise, he tried to shut down those thoughts. Painful past experience had taught him that going down that road wasn't good for him and he had plenty to occupy him between now and Saturday. He made a few more phone calls and arranged to pop in and see Thea on his way back home later. They hadn't seen each other for a couple of weeks, and he felt as though he needed to check in with her, especially after the debacle with Cora at the school. He knew that Thea was keen to find out about the progress on Observatory Field, and he also wanted to see his niece and nephew. As Thea texted back that she was looking forward to seeing him later, and offering to make him dinner, he looked forward to catching up with her.

26

Charlotte's week running up to her date on Saturday with Tristan had seen her making steady progress archiving the materials in the series of green metal filing cabinets. She'd managed to subdue the burgeoning curiosity she had about Martin and Laura Ashcombe's last entries in the files, and gone back to the beginning of the 1980s, when the observatory had become the responsibility of LBAS. She needed to approach the archiving with a clear head, and getting sidetracked by the tragedy of its later years would impede her understanding of the wider context of the place.

She'd been working through the cabinets and bookshelves, carefully putting things of potential historical value into the archive boxes which she'd had delivered to the observatory earlier that week. To the untrained eye, some of the objects might not seem valuable or relevant: she remembered, as an undergraduate, visiting the archives of the University of Bristol School of Drama, and being surprised to see boxes that contained such ephemera as sweet and chocolate wrappers from the 1920s, among other more obviously significant items like a handbag belonging to screen star, Vivien Leigh, complete with a cigarette burn in the lining. Every item had a story, and for the observatory it was no different.

So, it was with equal care that she catalogued the tattered poster that advertised a stargazing event dated 15 March 1983, as she did the star charts and five-and-a-quarter-inch floppy disks from that era. Sadly, the desktop computer that would have enabled Charlotte to see what was on those disks had long since been consigned to the skip, but some intrepid researcher might well be able to recover the data in future years.

Each entry into the database had a catalogue number that would tally with the main archive at North West Wessex, a brief description of the artefact and the date it was put into storage. Some items were boxed separately, and some were subdivided into sections within a single box, if they were linked. There had been some discussion in recent years about making the best use of space and reducing the carbon footprint of the archive, but for the moment she was sticking to the current way of doing things. In a few years, it might be that items would merely be stored digitally, thus doing away with the need to continually house them somewhere, but Charlotte knew the importance of being able to hold things in her hands, and she hoped that this would be a long way off.

As she reached a predetermined number of files, she was meant to contact the archivist back at the university, who would arrange for them to be collected and a new consignment of archive boxes delivered. After dragging her first set of boxes up through the wood, Charlotte had swiftly realised it would be far easier to get them sent directly to the building. Then, they'd be cross referenced against the digital records she was creating, before being carefully assigned to the archive itself, a climate-controlled space the size of a warehouse.

Progress had been a lot quicker than she'd thought it would be, initially, and she'd worked her way through the mid-eighties files quite quickly. It wouldn't take as long as she'd estimated to find herself back at the 1995 records that she'd glanced at on her first day here, but as she worked, she was beginning to piece together a more rounded picture of the life of the observatory before the tragedy. The signatures on the charts, notes and records that she kept seeing became more and more familiar, and she was building a mental image of what it would have been like to be a researcher here. The signatures of Laura and Martin Ashcombe were regularly present, and she couldn't help a little lurch of recognition when she saw one of them at the bottom of a document.

It was clear that they'd spent a lot of time here in the mid to late 1980s, but by the time 1990 rolled around, evidence of their work in the observatory was becoming less frequent. She figured that this must have been after Thea and Tristan's birth. She knew the twins had been born in April 1990, and so that made sense. Martin's signature still appeared on records for the first two quarters of 1990, and then Laura's reappeared in the final quarter of that year. It made Charlotte smile to imagine them bringing the twins up here and introducing them to their passion for the night sky.

How things might have been different if the family hadn't been hit by such tragedy. Would the observatory still be facing demolition?

By Thursday of that week, Charlotte had set to work on the filing cabinet drawer that marked the final quarter of 1994. She was getting closer to the point where Laura and Martin's names would disappear from the records forever, and she couldn't help feeling a wash of melancholy as she pulled the drawer open and carefully began to sift through its contents.

A Sky Full of Stars

The first few suspension files yielded nothing out of the routine she'd seen for the past decade of records. Star charts, photocopies of glass plates, which had long since been relocated to the North West Wessex archive and even the odd fax from other astronomers, their curling edges straightened by the years in storage, all were carefully placed in the files, as if caught in a time warp. Someone, or a long succession of someones, had been keeping things safe.

Charlotte pulled out a file marked 'November 1994, Q4, Week 1' and gently parted the cardboard covers. She'd got used to the musty aroma of documents that had been stored for a long while and ignored the scent that drifted towards her as she began to look through the file.

It was then that she saw it.

Charlotte was more than used to encountering rogue pieces of information; documents that implied one thing, but on further investigation revealed another; suggested truths that became elegantly constructed falsehoods after further investigation and research. But there was something about the document she could see, smack in the centre of the file, that stood out immediately.

'That's not possible,' she murmured as she carefully drew the paperwork out from the plastic wallet it had been shoved into. She eased the fragile, yellowed document out, pausing to carefully remove the discoloured paperclip that held the pages together. Feeling her pulse starting to race in her throat, she began to read.

> Preliminary evidence of hitherto undocumented eclipsing binary on the wingtip of Volucris. Although this may be less visible in Q1, will continue to observe over the coming

months. Will check with PP at a later date as he may be able to advise.

Charlotte knew all about eclipsing binaries – twin stars that orbit around a central mass, causing a periodic dimming of the constellation's brightness as one passes in front of the other in the earth's line of sight. The most famous eclipsing binary, Algol, often nicknamed the Demon Star, lay in the constellation of Perseus and was one of the first things she tried to look for when, as a child, she became interested in astronomy. They'd become a bit of an obsession for her over the years, and she was fairly sure that there was no documented evidence of an eclipsing binary on Volucris before the turn of the twenty-first century. The shape of the constellation, which resembled a bird in flight, wings outstretched towards the more famous constellations of Lyra and Cygnus, was documented, but no eclipsing binaries had been recorded to her knowledge.

Of course, she couldn't keep every piece of information about every discovery in her head, and the first thing she needed to do was a Google search, and then look for academic papers. It might just be that it had slipped her mind. Eclipsing binaries, while significant, were more often important because they provided data for calculations about other astronomical bodies and events. It was definitely possible that the discovery of the Volucris eclipsing binary was just a footnote in relation to another, bigger event.

Charlotte began to search carefully through the material for what was left of 1994. These included copies of the photographic plates that had been taken, printouts of calculations and, excitingly, some tentative early correspondence between Martin Ashcombe and the University of North West Wessex. An email to a Professor Jacobson at the university had been sent, but sadly, no reply to Martin's initial enquiries was in evidence from the file. Charlotte hadn't heard of Jacobson, but she made a note of his name and resolved to ask Professor Edwin, her head of department, if he had, when she got the chance.

The names aside, though, a discovery like this was so unexpected. Charlotte's job, as far as she'd been told, was merely to collate and archive the remaining materials from the observatory. How could something potentially so significant have been missed in the years since the observatory had ceased to function?

Carefully, she placed the documents down on the desk and took several photos with her phone. She needed a second opinion on what she'd found, and also a record of the information that was less delicate and damageable. After she'd stored them safely in the archive box, she entered the details into the database, but she coloured the text in red, so it would catch her eye during a search. She needed to get someone else to verify what she'd found. Briefly, she considered actually calling Professor Edwin, but she knew he was on holiday and wouldn't want to be disturbed. Then it came to her. Much as their recent history was tricky, there was no one, save Professor Edwin, who was better placed to advise. Taking a deep breath, she found a small spot where she had a little phone reception and sent a text to Todd.

27

Charlotte didn't hear back from Todd until Friday, but she had plenty to occupy her in the meantime. There were hundreds of documents in the filing cabinets, all requiring careful sifting and prioritising, and various other pieces of historical material that had escaped the prying eyes of trespassers. These had been shoved in a suspension file marked 'Miscellaneous' at the back of the current drawer she was archiving, but lots of the materials in the file were from earlier dates. They ranged from the amusing: a flyer for a 'Dancing Under the Stars' party out on the field dated 15 June 1990: a flattened paper wrapper from a tube of Polo mints that someone must have dropped by accident into the file while working on it; and, poignantly, a snapshot of the Lower Brambleton Astronomical Society standing around the telescope and raising a glass. The festive colours of the jumpers they were wearing, and the odd Santa hat, suggested a Christmas celebration, and Charlotte smiled as she remembered what Brian O'Connor had told her about the parties the group had enjoyed. She smiled more broadly when she identified a much younger Brian himself in the photo, and then caught her breath when she saw a visibly pregnant woman raising a glass of orange juice and standing next to a tall, handsome dark-haired man who had one arm protectively wrapped around her. They all had huge smiles on their faces, and with a jolt Charlotte realised that this must be one of the last photographs of the group together before Laura and Martin's twins were born. She turned over the photo and saw someone had written the date, *December 1989.*

Looking at the happy faces shining out from the photo, Charlotte saw how much Tristan resembled his mother: he had her colouring, and, having seen him looking much happier at the pub the other night, he shared her bright, all-encompassing smile. She thought about Thea, Tristan's sister, and realised that she, too, looked very like her mother. The photo would have to go in an archive box, but before she filed and catalogued it, she pulled out her phone and took the best snap of it that she could. Brian might like to see it, and she was sure Lorelai would. She paused, considering whether or not she should show it to Tristan. He hadn't really spoken much about his family to her yet, and she didn't want to presume that he'd automatically want a reminder of things from a virtual stranger. Putting the photo carefully in its own box for now, she moved onto the other contents of the current file she was working with.

A ping from her mobile some time later drew her attention away from the paperwork. She'd virtually given up expecting any kind of mobile phone service when she was inside the observatory building, but every so often a rogue data wave would meander its way from wherever the nearest phone mast was and make contact with her phone. Swiping her screen, she saw it was a message from Todd to say that he was out of the office but he'd be back in school briefly the following week. Could he give her a call then?

Rather than wait to call him, she drafted an email, attached the photos of the documents she'd found and then sent it to his work email address. He was now working at Georgia State University, which meant he'd have access to a whole lot more useful information than she did. If he could shed some light on why this potential discovery had lain unrecorded all these years, then she was prepared to swallow her pride. The shock of the discovery about Volucris could be put on hold for a few more days, until Todd had seen the papers: it had been in the filing cabinet for nearly three decades, after all.

28

Saturday dawned bright and sunny, and Charlotte woke with a combination of excitement and nerves. She and Tristan had exchanged a few texts since they'd agreed to their day out in Bristol, but she hadn't seen him since the previous Saturday evening. She wasn't surprised: the Observatory Field development was gaining momentum, and while she'd been working up at the site, she'd noticed earth movers and levellers being brought in, ready to flatten the ground, and, eventually, demolish the building. She still felt sad that by the end of the summer it would no longer exist, but at least her work was ensuring the contents of the observatory's library would be preserved for future generations.

After a quick breakfast of strawberry jam on toast, Charlotte waited for Tristan to arrive at Nightshade Cottage. Lorelai hadn't commented on their arranged date, but Charlotte had the feeling that somehow she knew about it. There was an additional warmth to the older woman's eyes when she mentioned her grandson's name in passing, and she'd offered to dog sit for Charlotte when she had said she was going out for the day.

'If you're sure that's all right?' Charlotte replied. She'd planned their day with Comet in mind and had intended taking Tristan up to Clifton Down to stretch all of their legs but leaving the dog in Lorelai's care would free them up a little more.

'It's fine, dear,' Lorelai smiled. 'He can help me do some gardening.'

Charlotte smiled back. Lorelai seemed to spend her life in the garden, when she wasn't looking after her great-grandchildren, and so she knew Comet would be fine, too. She hadn't yet had time to show Lorelai the snapshot of the photo she'd found of LBAS, but she hoped she'd get the chance over the weekend. She felt a little nervous about showing her, but she hoped Lorelai would be pleased to see it.

At that moment, they both heard the familiar sound of Tristan's car pulling onto the driveway. 'Have a lovely time.' Lorelai looked as though she was about to say something else and Charlotte paused, anticipating some hokey grandma warning about taking care of her grandson.

'Tristan's a tricky one,' Lorelai said in the end. 'I love the boy, of course, but I'd suggest you take care of your heart, should it start to flutter. He's not had the best track record with commitment, from what I gather.'

'You were the one who was encouraging us to spend some time together,' Charlotte reminded her gently. 'Are you saying you've decided it's not such a good idea, after all?'

'Oh, no,' Lorelai replied. 'But it would be remiss of me not to give you a quiet reminder that he's nothing if not complicated.'

'I'll bear that in mind.' Charlotte smiled at Lorelai, though in truth the older woman's warning had unnerved her. She was just out of a break-up… could she really cope with too much emotional baggage?

Resolving just to take today for what it was, a lovely chance to explore the city of Bristol with someone she liked, she tried to shake off those feelings. It was one date: she wasn't going to marry the guy.

Tristan came around the corner of the cottage and seemed surprised to see Charlotte and Lorelai in conversation. Charlotte didn't miss the wary look that flashed across his features as he clocked them.

'Hello, Gran,' Tristan said as he approached the two women. 'Warning Charlotte off me? Telling her what an absolute scoundrel I am?'

Lorelai gave a short laugh. 'Of course not, dear. Just wanted to wish you both a lovely day.'

Charlotte couldn't help feeling tickled by the way Tristan obviously knew his grandmother so well. 'At least,' she said, 'I suppose going out with me saves you the embarrassment of introducing someone new to your grandma! That bit's out of the way, at least.'

'Oh, Tristan very rarely introduces his girlfriends to me,' Lorelai said breezily. 'In fact, I can't remember the last time he did.' She shook her head. 'It's probably just as well. There's less for me to enquire about that way.'

'We'll see you later, Gran,' Tristan said, leaning down to kiss Lorelai's cheek. He turned to Charlotte. 'Are you ready? Any clues on our plans for the day?'

'Wait and see,' Charlotte teased. 'Just head for Bristol, and I'll guide you from there.'

'Fair enough.' Tristan's eyes softened as he looked down at her, and Charlotte felt something stirring in her abdomen that definitely wasn't her digestion. He paused just long enough for Lorelai to give a discreet cough.

'If you're not back by six-thirty, do you mind if I pop into the annexe to get the dog food?'

'That's fine,' Charlotte replied. 'And thank you for looking after him for me, Lorelai.'

'You're more than welcome,' Lorelai replied. 'Thank you for getting my grandson away from his desk!'

'It *is* Saturday, Gran,' Tristan replied, looking like the teenager he'd once been when he lived with Lorelai. 'I wasn't planning on working *all* weekend.'

'Yes, dear,' Lorelai said mildly, but she exchanged a knowing look with Charlotte. 'Have a lovely time.'

As Charlotte followed Tristan out to his car, she shook her head. Whilst the relationship between grandmother and grandson was definitely adorable, she wondered if she was ready to be a part of that dynamic.

29

'So, are you going to tell me where we're going, or shall I just drive until you scream at me to stop?' Tristan glanced at Charlotte and then pulled onto the main road to Bristol.

'Is that your usual MO?' Charlotte laughed. 'I mean, Lorelai warned me about you...'

Tristan shook his head. 'What did she say? I can never decide if she wants me to settle down or is intent on sabotaging my love life.'

'Oh, she didn't say much,' Charlotte replied. 'But she did mention you kept your cards close to your chest a lot of the time, and I think she finds that frustrating.'

'She'd love it if I confided in her about everything,' Tristan said softly. 'She can't quite get to grips with the fact that Thea and I are adults now, and we like to keep some things to ourselves.'

Charlotte wasn't sure what to say to that. Having never discussed Lorelai's place in Tristan's life, and only being on their first 'official' date with him, she wasn't sure what to reveal about what she knew about his family history. The snapshot she had on her phone would be waiting a little longer.

Thankfully, Tristan pre-empted her. 'I'm sure Gran's told you about what happened to Mum and Dad,' he said. 'I mean, I'd be surprised if she hadn't at least mentioned it, given the fact you're working at Observatory Field.'

Charlotte was taken aback by his straightforward tone. She wasn't sure what she'd been expecting, but perhaps it was worth having this conversation while he was driving: somehow it made the subject easier to broach. 'Yes, and I was so sorry to hear about it, Tristan. I can't imagine what you and your sister must have been through.'

She glanced at him as she said this, but his face seemed carefully expressionless. His hands were relaxed on the steering wheel, and he was staring ahead, focusing on their journey.

'It's all right.' He took his eyes off the road again and smiled momentarily. 'I'm not going to break down into tears, or beat my chest, or burden you with a whole pile of emotional baggage. They died. It was a long time ago. If you hadn't been lodging with Gran, I probably wouldn't even have mentioned it, at least, not on a first date, but it seemed the right thing to do to get things out there, especially since you're working at Observatory Field.'

'I appreciate you being so up front about it,' Charlotte said. 'I was worried my working at the site might be stirring up bad memories. Would you rather we didn't talk about it?'

Tristan smiled again, and Charlotte's heart did a little skipping beat that she tried to ignore. 'Since I'm going to be up there on site myself soon, it would be daft to ignore it, but, for today, it would be nice just to focus on where we're going and what you'd like us to do. How about you direct me and tell me when to stop? Do we have a deal?'

'It's a deal.' Charlotte smiled back at him, which he just saw before returning his eyes to the road ahead. She consulted Google Maps on her phone, which mercifully, had come back into range a few miles after they'd left Lower Brambleton. Perhaps she should give Tristan at least some idea as to where they were headed.

'I thought I'd take you to a few places around Bristol that I discovered when I was an undergraduate,' she said.

Tristan quirked an eyebrow. 'Missing academia already?' he teased.

'Well, the best haunts I ever found were when I was a first year in Bristol,' Charlotte grinned. 'Best pubs, best views, best nights out I could remember... or in some cases, I couldn't remember. Working for North West Wessex has its charms now I'm older and wiser, but the University of Bristol taught me how and where to have a good time!'

'I look forward to sharing a day of that with you, then,' Tristan smiled back, and this time Charlotte definitely had to tell her heart very sternly to stop messing about.

A short time later, Tristan had parked in the multi-storey car park at the top of Bristol's Park Street, which was smack in the middle of the city's university district. Known to a few million BBC viewers of the hit TV show *The Outlaws*, which was a love letter to the city, Charlotte adored this area of town for its history, heritage and the imposing edifices of the cathedral and the Wills Memorial Building, which was near to the museum. Maybe it was because when she visited these places and climbed the towers that rose like stalagmites along one side of Park Street, she felt as though she was getting closer to the skies she'd spent her academic career observing, or maybe it was just the need to get a bit of height and perspective at various points in her life.

'So, where do we start?' Tristan asked, once they were out into the sunny expanse of Clifton Triangle.

'Do you fancy working up an appetite before lunch?' Charlotte asked as they mooched towards the green space of Berkeley Square. 'How are your climbing legs?'

Tristan looked wary. 'Pretty good, so long as you're not planning on making me climb the Avon Gorge today.' He gestured to his feet. 'I don't really have the shoes on for it.'

Charlotte giggled. 'Nothing so intense in this heat. But are you all right with heights and slightly confined spaces?'

Tristan's expression changed from wary to outright suspicious. 'What have you got in mind?'

'You'll see!' Charlotte replied and Tristan shook his head.

'Just promise me that if I have a funny turn, I can hold your hand?'

Charlotte's heart sped up as, without another word, Tristan reached out and took her hand in his. Together, they crossed Park Street, the long, elegant sloping expanse that curved gently down to the harbourside, and Charlotte gestured to the imposing tower of the Wills Memorial Building.

'I was a tour guide here when I was an undergraduate,' she explained as they walked through the archway that marked the entrance to the building. 'I thought I'd give you a bit of an insight if that sounds like something up your alley.'

Tristan grinned. 'Sounds like a great way to speed up my heartbeat whilst still remaining respectable,' he quipped as he glanced at some of the facts and figures on the noticeboards in the foyer. 'Are you planning on taking me up the tower?'

'If you're up for the walk,' Charlotte replied. 'It's sixty-eight metres high, and the fifth-tallest building in Bristol.'

She noticed an expression of apprehension crossing Tristan's face before he rearranged his features more enthusiastically. 'That sounds like quite a trek.'

'Are your knees up to it?' Charlotte asked, only half-jokingly. 'We can take a break to say hello to Great George before we get to the top, if you feel the need for a breather.'

'Who's he? The tower guard?' Tristan asked.

Charlotte laughed. 'Something like that.'

Since Tristan had driven, Charlotte insisted on treating him to a ticket to the tower, and they joined a group of eight other people on the tour. As they meandered through the majestic panelled buildings of one of the best examples of neo-Gothic architecture in the UK, Charlotte slipped her hand back into Tristan's, and they found themselves moving a little closer together, not entirely due to the narrowing of the corridors. Taking in the impressive sight of the Great Hall where Charlotte had received her undergraduate degree, and several moments from famous films had been shot, the group paused before they got to the last part of the tour, ascending the tower itself.

'Now, if you're not up for climbing the whole way to the top, you can use the lift to about halfway up,' Gary, the cheery, knowledgeable tour guide, informed them with a smile. 'The first few flights of steps are fairly wide, but when you get up towards Great George, things get narrower, so don't be embarrassed about wanting to conserve your energy.'

'What do you think?' Charlotte teased. 'Fancy the stairs, or do you want to wuss out and take the lift?'

Tristan grinned at her. 'I'm game for the stairs if you are.'

'I used to do this trek three times a day when I worked here,' Charlotte replied. 'It holds no fears for me.'

'And don't worry,' Gary interrupted their banter, 'there's plenty of oxygen at the top.'

They set off on their vertical journey, and Charlotte kept up easily with Tristan's longer stride. They were passing various signs to the academic departments housed in the building, and Tristan's eye was caught by the sight of a Hogwarts-like library as they passed. Soon, however, they were heading towards the last stretch of the tour, and the building opened out as they reached the domain of Great George.

'Tristan, meet George,' Charlotte said as they walked out onto a platform that housed the tower's most illustrious resident. There, hanging in the cavity, an impressive nine and a half tonnes and cast in bronze, was Great George, whose formidable, sonorous clang rang across the city on the hour. 'He's been here since the early 1920s.'

'Almost as long as me!' Gary quipped. He turned back to address the rest of the group, asking them to spread out a little around the platform that surrounded the belfry. It was a minute to twelve o'clock, and so they waited in anticipation for the first strike.

'I forgot to ask if you were all right with loud noises,' Charlotte murmured as Gary continued to regale the group with titbits of information about Great George's creation and installation into the tower.

'I guess we'll find out in about fifteen seconds,' Tristan replied. 'Perhaps I'll keep holding your hand... it'll stop me getting nervous.'

Charlotte moved a little closer to him. 'And I'll be able to feel it if you jump, too!'

Tristan seemed about to respond to her when the creak of the bell hammer silenced him, and Great George's resounding boom rang out through the tower. Eleven more reverberating, echoing bolts of the hammer sounded until there was an equally deafening silence at the end of the chime.

'Can you still hear me?' Gary called out after the last chime had echoed away through the city air.

'Just about.' Charlotte smiled back at him, and then glanced up at Tristan, who was listening intently to Gary's facts and figures about Great George and the bell tower. Her hand still held his and she suddenly had the urge to stretch up and kiss him. Squashing the desire, she gestured to the last part of the climb up the tower as Gary paused for breath.

'That staircase is not quite a metre wide, and runs a tight vertical corkscrew to the roof – are you OK with confined spaces?'

Tristan nodded confidently. 'Seems a shame to have visited Great George and not to see the view while we're here.'

They edged around the bell cavity and headed towards the last part of the climb. Pausing to let a party of four go ahead of them, Charlotte gestured to the entrance to the spiral stone staircase and then grinned. 'Do you want to go ahead or walk behind?'

'Lead the way,' Tristan said playfully. 'I mean, I wouldn't want to get lost!'

Charlotte paused for a moment, wondering if she was ready to give Tristan such a prolonged look at her back view, before shrugging it off and putting her foot on the first step. 'I would say I'd race you to the top, but there's no room to overtake!' And with that, she began the climb.

30

Panting slightly, Charlotte emerged a few minutes later onto the flat roof of the Wills Tower and drew in a deep breath of summer air. It was cooler and breezier up here: the wind blew straight off the River Avon most of the time, but it was a pleasant remedy for the sweat they'd both worked up during the sixty-eight-metre climb to the summit.

Waiting for Tristan to emerge, she gently took his hand again when he did. 'I used to love coming up here as a tour guide,' she said as she led him to the nearest of a series of crenelations in the top of the tower. These provided those who'd climbed the tower various points at which to see the panoramic view of Bristol that the tower afforded. From their vantage point, they could see Clifton Suspension Bridge in the distance, and the many and varied rooftops of a city sprawl that spanned centuries and generations, from the Georgian edifices that lined Park Street and its environs, to the imposing neo-Gothic spire of St Mary Redcliffe and on either side the more prosaic architecture of the Bristol Royal Infirmary and the modernised façade of the Radisson Blu Hotel on the harbourside.

At this height it was easy to see how the city had developed over time, and Charlotte always felt a combination of emotions, looking down at the patchwork of rooftops, roads and rivers below, and then up at the skyline where, when night fell, she'd spent so much time staring up at the stars. She always felt that there was a symmetry between the sky and the street: patterns, equations and symbols created by men that echoed their observations of the shape of the cosmos. It was a fanciful notion, but one she often used to ground herself.

'Not a bad view,' Tristan commented as they paused in front of one of the battlement openings to look out over the west side of the tower. They lingered on the sight of the Suspension Bridge spanning the majestic Avon Gorge, and the gentle curve of Whiteladies Road as it merged into the top of Park Street. 'Almost worth the climb, I suppose.'

If Charlotte hadn't glanced at him and seen the teasing glint in his eyes, she'd have been offended by his offhand tone, but his expression suggested that he was pulling her leg.

'I'm glad it meets with your approval,' she replied. She turned towards him, away from the breathtaking vista. 'I can't believe you're a Somerset native and you've never been up here before.'

'Perhaps I just needed the right tour guide,' Tristan murmured. Charlotte could feel the warmth of his body, slightly hotter from the steep climb up the tower. His white T-shirt stretched tantalisingly over his torso, and she could smell a combination of a musky, cinnamon-infused cologne and a man whose heartbeat was elevated by exercise. The cooling breeze wafted gently around them, but Charlotte felt her own body responding to the signals she was picking up from Tristan. His eyes widened as she moved closer, and her hand moved up to his elbow. All she needed to do, in that moment, was tilt her head upwards...

'Gary would be flattered,' she murmured as their faces drew closer, all thoughts of the stunning view forgotten as their dual focus became that much more intimate.

'Then let me rephrase that,' Tristan said softly. 'Gary's been great, but *you* are also a very good tour guide.'

Charlotte smiled as she stood on tiptoe to bridge the final breath between them, and she felt a low-down fizzing tingle as their lips met in a gentle, much anticipated kiss. Tristan's mouth was warm, and she could feel his breath hitching slightly at the contact. Deepening the kiss ever so slightly, Charlotte's hand reached up to touch his cheek, feeling the warmth of his skin and the softness of the edge of his hairline under her fingertips. She was so distracted, she almost forgot to breathe, but when Tristan dipped his head so that she could step down from her tiptoes, her heels touched the ground with a bump, and she gave a gasp.

'Everything all right?' Tristan said quietly, with an evident trace of delight in his voice.

'Not a bad kiss,' Charlotte quipped to hide how jolted she was. 'Almost worth the climb.'

Tristan's eyes darted from Charlotte's to her mouth and back again. 'Would you like me to have another go?'

'I'll allow it,' Charlotte replied. 'If you make it a bit longer this time.'

'I'll do my best,' Tristan said, and before she could tease him any further, he kissed her again. She could feel the hardness of the cool stone of the tower wall at her back, in marked contrast to the warmth and vitality of the man in her arms, and she tried to brace herself against the brickwork to stop her knees from buckling at the contrasting sensations. She'd had a fair few kisses before, of course she had, but kissing someone at this elevated location seemed to enhance the sensations even more.

Gasping as they moved apart again, Charlotte realised that the rest of the group was preparing to head back down the tower, and she needed a moment to come back to earth.

'So,' she said, still rather breathlessly, 'what would you like to do next?'

Tristan was gazing down at her with a smile that broadened to a huge grin. 'Well, mouth to mouth at the top of the tower was great... but I think I might need resuscitation at the bottom of it too. After that... feel free to surprise me again.'

Charlotte noticed Gary's rather amused wink as they passed him on their way back down the narrow spiral staircase that would eventually lead them back to the ground. Once there, perhaps she should try to keep her feet on the ground, she thought. If she wasn't careful, she could see herself falling, and falling hard for Tristan, and if she felt that on the basis of just one kiss, she didn't dare imagine how she'd feel after more of the same.

31

Descending the steps of the tower was somewhat easier than the heart-attack-inducing climb to the top, and as Charlotte thanked Gary for the tour, and she and Tristan meandered out into the bright sunlight of historic Park Street, she smiled up at him. 'Fancy a coffee, or do you want to do some more exploring first?'

Tristan smiled back at her. 'Why don't we grab a takeaway and keep walking? I'm sure there's lots more you could show me.'

Charlotte didn't miss the undercurrent of suggestion in his voice, and her face felt warm as she thought back to their kiss.

'Deal,' she said. Feeling a jolt of pleasure as Tristan reached for her hand, they'd soon stopped at Brown's café and were making their way up Whiteladies Road towards Clifton Down.

Charlotte loved this part of Bristol, and she felt at home in the long, wide, sloping streets that led one way down to the city centre and the other to a haven of greenery that undulated towards the sheer, dark-brown stone drop of the Avon Gorge. Since coming back here as a house parent she'd been happier in Bristol than at any point in her life. That was why she was so keen to show Tristan some of the sights: she felt the need to share the happiness with him.

Tristan was looking with great interest at the buildings as they walked further, and again Charlotte wondered why he wasn't more familiar with Bristol as a city.

'I'd forgotten how lovely this place is,' he said as they walked towards the downs. 'I don't get into town much these days, since I'm usually based either in head office or on a site somewhere. It's nice to see buildings and not be making decisions about whether they stay or go!'

Charlotte smiled at the lightness in his tone. It was lovely to see him enjoying her tour of the city, and she was looking forward to doing more of the same.

The sun was high in the sky now and as they reached the Downs, they found themselves laughing at the antics of various dogs gambolling happily over the swathes of green space, interacting mostly amicably with other canines on their constitutionals, and sniffing around the trees and posts that marked out the space.

'Comet loves coming up here, too,' Charlotte explained. 'Although he doesn't know he's born now he's got the woodland around Lorelai's house to explore.'

'Must be good for him, being out in the countryside,' Tristan said. He paused. 'Is it good for you, too?'

They'd come to a stop by the railing that marked off the drop of the Avon Gorge, and Charlotte took a moment to gaze out, taking in the glorious view of the Clifton Suspension Bridge, and collect her thoughts.

'It's very good for me,' she murmured, 'although I'd be lying if I said I didn't miss the city. I've lived here for so long and got so used to having everything on my doorstep that it was a bit of a culture shock, moving out to the middle of nowhere!'

Tristan tried and failed to look affronted. 'If you think Lower Brambleton's remote, I'd better show you some of the places further away from the M5 – the true depths of deepest Somerset!'

He affected a long, rolling 'r' on the name of the county, and Charlotte giggled. 'Spoken like a proper native! But I'd love to see some of them.'

'Maybe that'll be our second date.' Tristan raised a hopeful eyebrow. 'If you're not completely sick of me by now.'

'I'd be prepared to give you a chance to make good on that promise to show me the more, er, rural areas of Somerset, if you'd like to,' she replied. 'So long as there's a pint of cider to refresh me at the end.'

'I'm sure that can be arranged,' Tristan said.

'So,' Charlotte said slightly nervously after a beat or two. 'Are you hungry yet? There's a café up here with great views of the gorge, or we could head back down and find something on the way.'

Before he could reply, Tristan looked embarrassed as his stomach gave a mighty rumble. 'Seems like I've worked up an appetite!' he said.

They wandered towards The Downs Café, a charming establishment where they could sit outside and still watch the world go by. As they waited for their lunch order, they chatted easily. Charlotte could sense that, at last, Tristan was starting to relax in her company, and she felt a warm rush of pleasure as he laughed more and moved closer to her as they observed the people who were out and about.

'That one's a spy... MI6 for sure,' Tristan muttered into her ear as they saw a smartly dressed woman in a lightweight grey suit striding purposefully towards one of the benches that were dotted around. 'Wearing a suit on a Saturday? Watch out if she produces a poison-tipped umbrella!'

Charlotte smirked. 'Nah,' she replied. 'She's an estate agent, if ever I saw one. Property's a cut-throat business in Bristol. Although you still might be right about the umbrella, in either case.'

Their discussions got dafter and dafter through their lunch, and by the time they were ready to walk back down the hill to the car, they were completely at ease with each other.

'This has been lovely,' Charlotte said as they meandered their way back down Whiteladies Road and onto Park Street. 'I feel as though I've been looking at Bristol with new eyes this afternoon.'

'Me too,' Tristan smiled at her. 'It's been nice.'

'Nice?' Charlotte stopped in the middle of the pavement and stared up at him. 'Is that all you've got?'

'Well, I'm never knowingly overstated,' Tristan murmured. 'I thought you might have noticed that about me by now. I am the model of restraint in all things.'

'*All* things?' Charlotte said mischievously. 'I mean, that's quite a claim...' She stood up on her tiptoes and placed a hand on Tristan's shoulder, smiling as he instinctively dipped his head towards her. 'Forgive me if I'd quite like to test out that hypothesis. I do have a background in science, after all.'

'Feel free to test it,' Tristan replied huskily. 'I promise you; the hypothesis will stand any amount of interrogation and exploration.'

'I'll definitely hold you to that,' Charlotte whispered as their lips met again.

32

The drive back to Lower Brambleton was loaded with anticipation. This was only their first real date, but it felt to Charlotte as though she was already really getting to know Tristan. Far from being the standoffish, grumpy guy she'd encountered a couple of weeks ago on her first full day in Lower Brambleton, this Tristan was funny, sexy and definitely fun to be around.

'Everything OK?' Tristan asked as they cruised along the M5. For once, the motorway was running fairly well, and as the signs for the next junction sailed past, Charlotte looked over at him.

'Everything's fine,' she said softly. 'And you?'

Tristan glanced back at her. 'Not bad at all,' he replied with a grin.

There was a pause as both seemed to be wondering how this day was going to progress. It was late afternoon and the evening stretched ahead of them, full of possibility. Charlotte was sure she didn't want their date to end just yet, but she still wasn't sure what to suggest to prolong their time together.

They were entering Lower Brambleton from the east side, which meant that they needed to wend their way to the village crossroads through a succession of smaller lanes and roads. Charlotte got the feeling that Tristan had taken a scenic route back, rather than drive straight to Nightshade Cottage, and she noticed a number of features and landmarks she hadn't spotted before on this impromptu tour. She was tickled by the vintage-looking cast-iron black and white painted signposts, which seemed like something out of *Miss Marple*. There were various pretty cottages interspersed along the lanes, and a cute wooden board with 'Purrfect Paws Feline Rescue Centre and Boarding Cattery' and an arrow pointing down another narrow driveway.

'What's that building over there?' she asked as they passed a long sweep of lawn that led to a smart Victorian manor house. She craned her neck back to read the sign by the gate, but she couldn't make out what it said.

'That's Cherry Tree Court,' Tristan replied. 'It's an exclusive venue that does mainly weddings and the odd black-tie function. Used to be owned by a branch of the Treloar family, who also owned Roseford Hall, back in the day, but they sold Cherry Tree Court in the fifties to realise some capital and it's been in the hands of a succession of people ever since.' He paused tantalisingly. 'Rumour has it that a certain Australian pop princess was considering buying it at some point in the early 2000s, but it was snapped up by a high-end boutique hotel chain and turned into a destination venue. It's even got its own helipad out the back, as the odd celeb likes to come down and use the spa facilities from time to time, or so I've heard.'

'I'll have to check it out; it sounds right up my street!' Charlotte giggled. 'I do so love an exclusive boutique venue.' She affected a posher tone, and was relieved when Tristan laughed.

'They do actually hold a winter party every year for a select guest list,' Tristan replied. 'Local business owners and the like get an invite, and those the hotel company consider to be the great and the good. Nick and Annabelle get the nod every year, along with their dad. I remember being Annabelle's date for it a few years back when Jamie was away on business, and it certainly opened my eyes.'

'You'll probably get your own invitation this year,' Charlotte remarked. 'I mean, Flowerdew Homes is a pretty big fish in this pond now that Observatory Field is underway.'

Tristan slowed down to look both ways at the crossroads that led to the village centre, and as he did so, he met Charlotte's eyes. 'If I do, you could always come with me, er, if you wanted to, that is.'

Charlotte blushed. Winter seemed an awfully long way away from this beautiful summer day, with the hedgerows in full bloom and the warmth of the season in the air, but she was flattered by the invitation. 'I'd love to,' she murmured. 'Keep me posted and I'll make sure I buy a new frock.'

Before long, having completed the impromptu tour of Lower Brambleton, Tristan was pulling up in the driveway of Nightshade Cottage.

'I had a really great time today,' he said as he cut the engine and turned towards her. 'Thank you for showing me some of the sights.'

'Any time.' Charlotte felt her pulse speeding up as there was another loaded pause between them. 'Should we, er, do it again sometime?'

Tristan smiled and she thought again how lovely and open his face was when he did. 'I'd like that a lot.' She watched as he ran a hand through his hair. 'Look, Charlotte... I'm a bit out of practice at all this. The last few relationships I've had have been pretty casual. But I've really enjoyed today.' He hesitated, and she saw him shifting nervously in his seat before he spoke again. 'Would you, er, like to come to lunch at my place tomorrow?'

'I'd like that,' Charlotte replied. 'But there's a bit of a problem with getting there. You live in Taunton, right? I'm pretty sure it's not walking distance!'

'Right,' Tristan smiled. 'I'll pick you up at twelve. And I promise I'll bring you home afterwards as well, no matter how lunch goes. If it all goes pear shaped and you decide that spending time with me was a terrible mistake, I won't make you walk back here. Scouts' honour.'

'You were a Scout?' Charlotte could well imagine Tristan as a serious little boy in the khaki colours of the organisation. She had a hard time imagining him roughing it, camping in the countryside though.

'I was, for a while,' Tristan said. 'I got caught smoking behind the Scout Hut with a mate of mine and his sister, and at that point they politely asked us all to leave!' He grimaced good-naturedly. 'Gran was livid. She'd known the Scout Leader since they were at school together.'

Charlotte laughed. 'Sounds like a good reason to get expelled, though.'

'Would have been if I'd actually liked smoking, but I was just trying to impress my mate's sister, who thought I was a dork.'

'Did it work?'

'Nope. She ended up going out with the local bike mechanic and moving to New Jersey with him, so risking ruining my lungs was a complete waste of time!'

'Well, I'd still like to come over tomorrow,' she said. 'I don't care if your Scouts' honour isn't legally binding.'

'It's a date,' Tristan grinned. Then his expression grew serious again. 'Er, could I ask you a favour?'

'Sure,' Charlotte replied. 'What is it?'

Shifting in his seat, Tristan drew a breath. 'Can you not talk about things too much with Gran? She's bound to ask you a whole load of questions when you see her, and it just feels a bit weird to know that she's going to get the low down on us.'

Charlotte smiled. 'Well, I don't know how well I'll stand up to interrogation if she gets the thumbscrews out, but I'll do my best.'

'Thanks,' Tristan replied. Then all thoughts of Lorelai were temporarily forgotten as he kissed her again.

'I'll see you tomorrow,' he murmured as they broke apart. 'Thanks again for a lovely day.'

'Thank you, too,' Charlotte replied, as, on slightly shaky legs, she got out of the car. She watched Tristan reversing out of the driveway, and then, when his car was out of sight, she reeled to the door of the annexe and let herself in.

'Good day, dear?' Lorelai, on cue, asked as not even a minute later she knocked on the internal door that separated the annexe from the rest of Nightshade Cottage.

'Lovely.' Charlotte smiled broadly, and bent down to cuddle an excited Comet, who'd dashed through to find her. 'Has this old chap been good?'

'He was impeccably behaved all day, even when he spotted a rabbit in the woods,' Lorelai replied. 'He gave chase for all of about five seconds before he came back when I called him. Such a good boy.'

'Thank you so much for looking after him,' Charlotte said. 'In the end, he'd probably have been fine mooching around Bristol, but it was good not to have to worry about him for the day.'

'Any time,' Lorelai replied, pausing before adding, 'I take it my grandson was well behaved, too?'

Charlotte grinned. 'He was.' She didn't elaborate, mindful of what Tristan had requested of her.

'And will you be seeing him again?'

'Tomorrow,' Charlotte smiled. 'Is, er, where he lives dog friendly?'

Lorelai quirked an eyebrow. 'Well, he's got a small garden, if that's what you mean.'

'That's good to know,' Charlotte replied. 'Comet can chaperone me tomorrow, then.'

Lorelai laughed. 'I don't mind keeping an eye on him again for you, if you'd rather. Anything to smooth the course of true love and all that!'

Charlotte really did laugh, then. 'It's our second date, Lorelai – hardly the stuff of romantic legend, yet!'

'Give it time,' Lorelai replied. 'Tristan's a funny one, and I say that as his grandmother, but he's a decent man, if a little, er, pedantic, sometimes.' She paused. 'But you let me know if he gives you any trouble, and I'll have a word in his ear.'

Charlotte shook her head. 'No trouble so far. He's been the perfect gentleman.'

'I'm glad to hear it,' Lorelai said. 'It's good to know he's behaving himself.'

Lorelai gave a last smile and then closed the partition door, leaving a head-shaking Charlotte in her wake. She was glad the older woman hadn't pushed her for more information – she didn't feel as though she'd given too much away. There wasn't a lot to tell, but she felt as though she wanted to hug the details to herself, to protect the little world she and Tristan had created during their time together and keep it just theirs for as long as she could.

'Well, old chap.' Charlotte looked down at Comet, who was looking expectantly up at her. 'It must be time for dinner.' She wandered through to the kitchenette and was about to get Comet's dog food out of the fridge when her phone pinged with a message. It was too soon to be a text from Tristan, who lived a good twenty minutes away, but, curious, she swiped to see who it was. She drew a breath as a familiar name appeared on her screen. Todd, at long last, was getting back in touch.

33

'Come on, little brother, spill!' Tristan's twin sister, Thea, the older of the pair by four minutes, had a teasing look in her eye as she cut him a slice of cherry and almond cake and poured him a cup of tea. 'You don't just descend on me unannounced. What do you need to talk about?'

Tristan shook his head, and, suddenly peckish, took a big bite of cake. 'I don't know what you mean, sis. Can't a guy just pop in and see his family on his way home?' He'd decided on the spur of the moment to look in on Thea, Dylan and Cora. After such a lovely day in Bristol with Charlotte he didn't just want to go home to an empty house and although he wasn't prepared to give Thea any gossip, he still wanted her company.

'Way home from where?' Thea asked. 'Don't tell me you're working weekends again? Surely that's against some kind of employment law?'

'I wasn't working,' Tristan replied. 'Although it's not unusual to have to check in at weekends once a site goes live, especially one that's got so much potential for disaster. And Observatory Field's in a tricky transitional state right now.'

'Aren't we all?' Thea replied, then sighed. 'I feel as though my life's not going to get back on track until I'm out of here and into a home the kids and I can really call our own. How long until it's going to be ready up there?'

Tristan gave her a sympathetic smile. 'As fast as I can make it happen, so you shouldn't be complaining about me working all the hours God sends on it!'

'I'd rather not be responsible for your professional burnout,' Thea countered. 'So please tell me you've been doing something fun today.'

Tristan's slight pause was all his sister needed to jump in on the attack. 'Oh, so there *is* something to tell? Come on – if I can't have my own thrills at the moment, I can live vicariously through you!'

Keeping her waiting, Tristan took a sip of his tea and then another bite of the cake. 'This is really good,' he said between swallows. 'Ever thought of becoming a professional baker?'

Thea snorted. 'That ship has definitely sailed. But thanks anyway – it's good to have an appreciative audience. Now, you were saying?'

Tristan sighed. He *had* voluntarily popped in, after all, so he should expect some questions. 'If you must know, I spent the afternoon in Bristol.'

'Oh, yes? Martha called you up for another *I won't insist on strings if you don't* date?' Thea replied archly. 'What a surprise.'

Tristan shook his head. 'Not Martha. I think we both know that was going nowhere.'

Thea raised a speculative eyebrow. 'Then who? Don't tell me you've actually met someone new?'

Tristan kept quiet. Having asked Charlotte not to spill too many beans to his grandmother, he felt like a hypocrite confiding in his sister about their first date. Over the years there had been ebbs and flows in their relationship as siblings but they'd grown closer after Thea's split from her partner, and Tristan relished that closeness. It made up for many years when he'd been unable to confide in her about anything. Especially the pain of losing their parents. Perhaps he did owe her a brief update.

'Maybe,' he said guardedly. 'But it's early days, so please don't give me the third degree.'

'Anyone we know?' Thea asked as Cora, high on the fizzy bootlaces Tristan had given both kids when he'd arrived, courtesy of a stop at the corner shop, zoomed through the living room and out of the patio doors into the small back garden.

'Charlotte, Gran's new lodger,' Tristan said quickly. 'And as I said, it's early days.'

Thea let out a whistle. 'Are you sure that's a wise move? I mean won't it get a bit awkward if it all goes south?' She shook her head, reconsidering. 'But then, to be fair, you don't often pop in on Gran these days unless I nag you to, so perhaps Gran won't notice anyway!'

'That's not fair,' Tristan protested. 'I might not be as regular a visitor as you, but I do try and see her when I can.'

'Well, at least if you're dating her lodger, you've got more of an excuse to check in on her than usual,' Thea countered. 'And even you can keep a relationship going for a few weeks, I'm sure.'

Tristan said nothing and took another bite of the cake. He'd stopped rising to Thea's comments about his love life some time ago, and he was too good a brother to carp back about the state of her own. Things weren't great between Thea and her ex, and the wounds were still raw.

'Well, little brother, I hope it all goes well for you,' Thea added. 'You deserve a bit of fun. You work far too hard, in my opinion, and if Charlotte can drag you away from your desk, then I already like her.' She sipped her tea. 'I met her the other day, and she seems nice. And, much as it squicks me out to think about it, at least one of us is getting some romantic action!'

Tristan did his best not to choke on his mouthful of tea. Some subjects were *definitely* off limits, and his sex life was one of them. 'Early days, sis,' he muttered. 'And even if it wasn't...'

'...you wouldn't be giving me details, anyway!' Thea teased. 'Believe me, Tris, I have no desire to know the, er, ins and outs, so to speak. I'm just glad you're having a good time.'

Despite his best efforts not to, Tristan couldn't help smiling. 'I am,' he said. 'And for the moment that's all you need to know.'

A little later, as he hugged Thea and his niece and nephew goodbye, Tristan reflected on how lucky he was. He hadn't always felt this way, and their family losses had taught him that he shouldn't take that feeling for granted. But, for the moment, he was happy to embrace it. And as he drove the fifteen minutes or so between Thea's house and his own, he put his mind to what to cook Charlotte for lunch the next day. He was by nature extremely cautious, but what harm would it do to be a little less so in the pursuit of pleasure and happiness? Today had been a great start, and, if he had his way, tomorrow was going to be even better.

34

Charlotte tried not to feel nervous as the hands of the clock edged towards midday. She'd attempted to walk the line between looking her best and as if she hadn't made much effort, but now she was beginning to second guess her own choices of a knee-length Jack Wills red dress and comfy but smart trainers. Was the dress too much for lunch? Did it clash with the copper tones in her hair? She wasn't *that* out of practice at dating, but she certainly felt as though she was.

Thankfully, before she could rush back to her room and change for what felt like the fiftieth time, she heard the familiar rumblings of Tristan's Audi pulling up on the driveway. She'd already popped Comet through the adjoining door to Lorelai, so, after checking her appearance in the bathroom mirror one last time, she hurried out of the back door and bumped into Tristan coming the other way.

'Sorry,' she said, face flaming as red as her dress as they collided. 'Thought I'd save you the faff of knocking on the door.'

'Or running into Gran?' Tristan gave a smile. 'Good thinking.' He glanced over her shoulder, and she thought she saw him relax a little when he realised Lorelai wasn't about to spring out on them from behind the hydrangeas. Dropping a kiss on her lips, he added appreciatively, 'Nice dress.'

'Thanks,' Charlotte replied. 'I, er, wasn't sure how smart your gaff is, so I thought I'd better make the effort!'

'Too smart for my place,' Tristan grinned, 'as you'll see when you get there, but I appreciate it.'

'You don't look bad yourself,' Charlotte replied as they walked back to the driveway. She checked out his white Henley T-shirt and dark jeans combination and smiled inwardly at his bravery for wearing white when she assumed he was going to be cooking for her.

The drive back to Tristan's flew by. Much to Charlotte's relief, conversation flowed easily, and she was pleasantly surprised when Tristan pulled into a parking bay outside a Victorian terraced house on the outskirts of Taunton's town centre. The house certainly had kerb appeal, with immaculate stonework and sparklingly clean windows, and a red-painted wooden front door.

'Home sweet home,' Tristan said as he hurried round to open the passenger door for her. 'Although sometimes parking outside can be a problem.'

'I failed three driving tests on parallel parking,' Charlotte laughed, 'so you get absolutely no judgement from me!'

Tristan led her up the small path through the front garden, which had been paved over, to the front door, and then into the relative gloom of the hallway. As Charlotte's eyes adapted to the cooler, darker interior space, she was quietly impressed when she saw the dark red wallpaper and the rich brown sloping mahogany balustrade that led to the upper floor. Underfoot were what looked to be lovingly restored original chequered tiles, and Charlotte smiled to see the mahogany hat stand and umbrella store off to one corner of the door. The rest of the hallway was pleasingly bare and swept through to a kitchen at the back of the terrace, with three doors leading off to other rooms.

'Come on through,' Tristan said as they walked down the hall. 'What would you like to drink? I've got a bottle of Chablis in the fridge if you'd like some, or something soft? I picked up some homemade lemonade from Saints' Farm when I was over there the other day, if you wanted some of that?'

'A small glass of Chablis would be great, thanks,' Charlotte replied. Now she was on Tristan's territory, she felt the need to take the edge off her nerves. It did feel strangely intense being in his space, knowing how reserved and private he was. The fact that he'd chosen to open his home to her gave her a rush of pleasure, but she also felt butterflies in her stomach at the intimacy.

'Coming right up.' They were in the kitchen, and Charlotte was surprised to see how modern it was. Housed in an extension to the original building, it had a glass roof and was a collection of glossy white units and impressive-looking chrome appliances. There was virtually nothing out on the vast expanse of counter space, except for a glass fruit bowl containing a pyramid of green apples, which looked as though they'd been put there for aesthetic effect rather than appetite.

'Have a seat,' Tristan said over his shoulder as he opened the door of the integrated American-style fridge and unscrewed the cap on the Chablis. Having poured a glass for Charlotte, he got himself a tumbler of filtered water from the fridge and then joined her at the breakfast bar.

'Thanks,' Charlotte said, and took a gulp of the wine to steady her nerves. The almost clinical look of the kitchen was a lot more what she'd been expecting to see, and it matched perfectly with Tristan's love of order and precision. She wondered what he'd make of her rather shabby kitchen in the flat at the halls of residence: whether he'd judge her for the haphazard way she lived. She tried to shrug off the feeling of inadequacy; what did it matter?

'Everything OK?' Tristan asked gently. 'This feels a bit full-on, doesn't it? Just you and me in my house, without a load of other stuff to distract us.'

Charlotte gave a nervous giggle. 'It does a bit.' She took another sip of her wine. 'I'm more used to the cluttered quarters of university academics. Your house is beautiful, but very tidy.'

Tristan gave a self-deprecating grin. 'Don't be fooled. The kitchen's a bit of a contrast to the rest of the house, but it seemed in keeping with the extension of the building to make it more modern. I promise you, the rest of the house isn't this tidy!'

'I'd love to see it,' Charlotte replied, eager to give them something other to do than sip drinks and make small talk. 'Would you mind giving me a tour?'

'Let me just put the chicken parmigiana in the oven, and then I'll show you,' Tristan said. He jumped up from the bar stool, and, clearly nervous himself, managed to knock his glass of water over, soaking the skirt of Charlotte's dress as he did so.

'I'm so sorry!' he said as he dashed to one of the kitchen drawers and pulled out a tea towel. Hurriedly, he started rubbing the towel over Charlotte's skirt, until she put a hand out to slow him down.

'It's all right,' she said, taking the towel from him and starting to pat herself dry. 'It's only water. It'll dry soon enough.'

'What a wonderful first impression,' Tristan muttered, and to Charlotte's amusement, she saw the heat rising in his cheeks. 'I'm really sorry.'

Charlotte gave one of his hands a squeeze. 'Honestly, it's fine. It's quite reassuring to see you're as nervous as I am!' She stood up from the bar stool with a bit of a squeak as her damp legs rubbed against the leather cushion. The noise made them both laugh, which seemed to break the tension. 'Why don't you show me over the house while dinner's cooking? That'll take my mind off my wet legs!'

Tristan, eventually, smiled back. 'It's a deal. But if you wanted to change, I'm sure I can find something you could put on?'

Charlotte laughed. 'Although it's nice that you try to think of everything, I'll take my chances and stick with my dress.'

Tristan paused before replying, and Charlotte wondered if he, like her, was wondering about where taking her dress off might lead. She was surprised at just how keen she was to keep imagining that scenario, as Tristan led her back out of the kitchen to show her the rest of the house.

35

'So, you renovated pretty much from scratch?' Charlotte said in appreciation as Tristan showed her the two beautifully appointed and proportioned downstairs rooms, one a cosy sitting room and the other, presumably once the dining room but now a study complete with a leather-topped mahogany desk against one wall.

'Yes, it was in a really bad state when I bought it,' Tristan replied. 'It took a while, but being in the housebuilding business, I had a fair few contacts I could call on for advice and quotes for the trickier bits.'

Charlotte was absorbed in looking at the other features of the study, which included the inevitable shelves of books and, hanging discreetly just off to one side of the bay window that looked out into the front garden, a framed picture of a smiling family. With a pang, Charlotte immediately recognised it as the same shot she'd seen on one of Lorelai's sideboards at Nightshade Cottage. Having recently found the snapshot of Laura and Martin from just before their twins were born, it was interesting to see the photo of the young family again – they looked a little older, now that they'd become parents of twins, but Laura's smile was the same as she beamed out from the photo. The twins, both with the same shade of light brown hair and the same blue-green eyes, seemed happy and relaxed too. Martin, standing alongside Laura, looked extremely proud of his wife and children.

'That's a beautiful picture,' she said softly as Tristan clocked her looking at it.

Tristan smiled. 'It was the last one taken of us all together.'

Charlotte's heart ached at the carefully neutral tone in his voice. She knew he struggled to talk about things so she replied quietly, 'I'm so sorry, Tristan.'

'I know you are.' Tristan gave her a smile. 'But I didn't invite you here to go over old ground. You're supposed to be getting away from history for a few hours, remember?' He took her hand. 'Come and have a look upstairs, and then I'd better get the rest of lunch on the go.'

They moved towards the staircase, and Charlotte noticed Tristan had put brass stair rods on a burgundy-toned Axminster carpet and painted the exposed pieces of board on each step a crisp white. She liked the nod to the heritage of the house. As they ascended the stairs, she spotted three doors leading off the landing and wondered which was Tristan's room. Her heart sped up at the thought.

'Just a quick glance,' Tristan teased. 'I wouldn't want you to think I was suggesting anything.'

Charlotte grinned. 'You don't seem the type to put a woman under pressure,' she replied. 'But I appreciate the clarification.'

Both bedrooms were neat and tidy, and the front room, obviously Tristan's, benefitted from the light and airy advantage of another bay window, through which the afternoon sun was pouring. A brass bedstead dominated the room, which was decorated in different tones of green, including an exquisite emerald flocked wallpaper. Charlotte was surprised at the opulence. She'd have had Tristan for a minimalist every day of the week.

'It's a lovely room,' she said. 'You've got a great career as an interior designer if you ever get bored of working on building sites!'

Tristan shook his head. 'Thea claims I was channelling my inner Laurence Llewelyn-Bowen in this room, but I like it.' He led her to the back of the house where there was a smaller bedroom. This one was more simply decorated and had twin beds in it. 'For when Cora and Dylan come to stay,' he said.

'Do they come round a lot?' Charlotte asked, curious to find out more about Tristan's family.

'Not so much now, but when they were younger, I used to take them off Thea's hands for a night or two. She needed the break, and I liked having them here.'

Charlotte couldn't quite imagine children in this beautifully decorated and well-kept house, but it was lovely to think of a side of Tristan who'd bond with his niece and nephew and have fun with them.

Just as she was about to ask him more, the oven timer sounded, and Tristan turned back to the stairs. 'I'll just do the last bits and bobs, and then we can eat, if you're ready?'

'Definitely,' Charlotte replied. 'I'm actually getting really hungry now.'

They headed back downstairs and in a little more time were tucking into chicken parmigiana, green beans and baby new potatoes. Charlotte had a top up of the Chablis and was definitely feeling more relaxed by the time they'd finished lunch.

'That was great,' she said, leaning back in her chair. 'Thank you for suggesting this.'

'My pleasure,' Tristan said as he whipped the plates away and put everything in the dishwasher. 'How's your dress?'

'A bit tight after all that food,' Charlotte giggled, and then blushed when she realised Tristan was asking whether or not it was still damp from the water spillage. She held out the hem of her skirt. 'And very nearly dry, too.'

'Glad to hear it.' Tristan had come back to the table and was standing in front of Charlotte, his legs almost touching hers. She looked up at him, and his expression was a mixture of anticipation and a rather adorable uncertainty. 'Do you, er, want to go into the living room and watch a film, or we could go for a walk?'

Charlotte, who knew a walk would be more sensible, but on a couple of glasses of Chablis was feeling rather too mellow to do more than mooch to the living-room sofa, smiled up at him. 'A film sounds like a great idea for a Sunday afternoon. What would you suggest?'

Tristan took hold of her hands and pulled her gently into his arms. 'Well, I'm usually a classic movies kind of guy, except when Cora and Dylan commandeer my Netflix, but I'm in your hands this afternoon. Whatever you'd like to watch, my account is all yours.'

'Now *that's* chivalry for you!' Charlotte quipped. 'How are you with horror films?'

Tristan looked sheepish. 'Not great with anything too gory,' he admitted. 'But I don't mind them when it's more cheese than torture.'

'Noted,' Charlotte replied. She wondered for a moment what might fit the bill. She felt the warmth of Tristan's hand in hers, and for a few heartbeats all she wanted to do was wrap her arms around him and bugger the film idea, but she paced herself.

She'd had some wine, and she didn't want to rush things because of it. So, settling just for one long, lingering kiss, she allowed him to lead her to the living room, and got to searching through the Netflix catalogue for something they could both enjoy.

36

A little time later, having agreed on the first of the *Insidious* films as a decent compromise for an afternoon's entertainment, they were both ensconced on Tristan's comfortable sofa, which, in keeping with other aspects of the décor, was a period piece, having reclinable arms that would turn it into a chaise lounge if the fancy arose.

'Comet would love this sofa,' she said as she tucked her feet up underneath herself and settled back into its comfy depths.

'He wouldn't be allowed on it,' Tristan replied. 'Even if he gave me that *butter wouldn't melt* look he's so good at.'

'Oh, I'm sure he'd win you around eventually,' Charlotte said. 'He has a habit of being able to get away with things.'

They watched the film in companionable silence for a while, and Charlotte found herself feeling drowsy in the comfort of a warm, cosy afternoon. Her eyelids grew heavy, and when she started to nod onto her hand, Tristan gave her a playful nudge. 'Perhaps you'd better come over here and rest your head on my shoulder,' he said. They'd been sitting a little way apart for the first part of the film – a slight awkwardness had set in, despite the kisses in the kitchen, and Charlotte was relieved when he suggested she cuddle up to him.

'What's the matter? Film too scary for you?' she teased as she snuggled up next to him. 'Need me to hold your hand?'

'Let's go with a yes for both, if it means you'll stay down this end of the sofa,' Tristan quipped. 'But I have to admit, this definitely fits the "cheesy but not gory" brief. I'm actually quite enjoying it.' Then, she felt him jump as the film took an unpredictable turn.

'You sure you're enjoying it?' Charlotte asked.

'Perhaps I'll cover my eyes during the *really* scary bits.' Tristan took one of her hands. 'Or maybe you can cover them for me?'

Charlotte gave a hoot of laughter as Tristan pulled her towards him, until they were a slightly breathless tangle of sprawling limbs as the reclinable arm of the sofa collapsed beneath Tristan and he toppled down so that he was horizontal beneath her.

'Is this one of your seduction techniques?' Charlotte asked as she found herself lying on top of him.

'I promise that's never happened before,' Tristan said, half in amusement, half in embarrassment. 'But it is an antique, so the rope ties might be a bit dodgy after all these years!'

'A likely story,' Charlotte murmured as she leaned down to kiss him. 'But I'll accept it for the moment.' Far from feeling tired, the jolt on the sofa had woken her up, and as she made a leisurely exploration of Tristan's mouth with her own, she felt him shifting beneath her, so that she was more securely on top of him. She ran a gentle hand through his hair and he reacted to her touch like a cat, pushing back against her and sliding his arms more tightly around her. Patrick Wilson's machinations against a malevolent spirit world faded into the background as they became more heated, bodies responded, and breaths shortened.

'This is rather nice,' Tristan murmured between kisses. 'I was going to get the sofa tie fixed, but perhaps I won't bother now!'

Charlotte smiled into their next kiss. 'I agree,' she said. 'You should definitely leave it broken for a little while longer.'

Their gentle banter continued along with the kisses, and only paused when they realised that the film had ended. Charlotte was lying alongside Tristan on the sofa now, and although her drowsiness had dissipated, she felt warm, safe and very, very relaxed.

'What a lovely way to spend a Sunday afternoon,' she said softly. 'Thank you for inviting me to lunch.'

'You're welcome,' Tristan replied. 'We must do it again.'

'Yes, please.' Charlotte smiled up at him. 'Perhaps at my place next time?'

Tristan raised an eyebrow. 'I'm not sure I'm up for doing this on the annexe sofa when my gran's right next door!'

Charlotte laughed. 'Fair point. Maybe I should come over here and cook for you, then?'

'I'd like that,' Tristan replied.

Charlotte watched as he stretched out on the sofa, and then caught sight of the time. 'I'd better be getting back,' she said regretfully. 'Lorelai's been dog sitting and I don't want to take advantage.'

'Gran loves dogs,' Tristan replied, leaning in to kiss her again. 'She won't mind if you're a bit later.'

'All the same,' Charlotte laughed, pushing him away playfully, 'I don't want him to outstay his welcome.'

'Fair enough.' Tristan disentangled himself from her reluctantly. 'But, for the record, I'd love you to stay longer.'

There was no mistaking the heat in his eyes when he said

that. Charlotte felt jolted by the intensity. She was beginning to realise that Tristan was an all-or-nothing kind of guy when it came to his emotions – she got the feeling that, once he fell, he fell hard.

'Let's do this again soon,' Charlotte said.

'And if it means you can spend more time here, you can bring the bloody dog,' Tristan replied. 'I'm sure he and I can tolerate each other for a few hours.'

Charlotte grinned. 'That's very magnanimous of you. He'd probably think the same!' She sat up and smoothed down her dress, watching Tristan stand up and stretch out.

'This has been wonderful,' she said. 'And I really appreciate the taxi service, too.'

'Next time, if you bring Comet with you, I might not have to drive you home?' Tristan's expression was carefully hopeful. Charlotte's pulse quickened and her expression obviously revealed her nerves, because Tristan immediately added, 'No pressure. I have a spare room, but even if you did want to stay in mine, I don't, er, *expect* anything. Just to be clear.'

Raising up onto tiptoe to kiss him, Charlotte's murmur of 'Thank you,' was soft but heartfelt. She didn't get the feeling Tristan made that offer lightly, and she was flattered that he should go to such lengths when they were just getting to know each other.

As they broke apart again, Tristan ran a hand through his hair. 'Do I need to brush it, in case Gran starts giving me the third degree?' he joked.

'Looks fine to me, considering,' Charlotte replied. 'How do I look?'

This time it was Tristan's turn to smile. 'Kind of like you've spent the afternoon snogging on my sofa.'

'Great.' Charlotte rolled her eyes. 'We'd both better tidy up a bit before we go and retrieve Comet.'

'Oh, no,' Tristan countered, 'I'm planning on chucking you out of the car and running. I'm not getting caught by Gran for interrogation.'

'Ah, so that's where the chivalry ends,' Charlotte laughed. 'I was wondering where you drew the line.'

'If you're lucky, I'll stop the car before I kick you out,' Tristan quipped. 'But if she's in the front garden, I don't plan on slowing down!'

'Good job I've perfected my duck and roll technique, then.' Charlotte was properly giggling now. 'Just say the word and I'll hurl myself out.'

It felt good to be so light-hearted. The mood lasted all the way back to Nightshade Cottage, where, thankfully, Lorelai was nowhere to be seen. As Tristan gave her a last lingering kiss in the car, Charlotte reflected that it had been the nicest afternoon she'd spent in a long time.

37

Charlotte got her head down for the next few days, mindful that time was starting to run out. She'd been diligently sifting through and archiving the records room for three weeks and she felt as though the project was beginning to head towards its final stages. She and Tristan hadn't had much of a chance to see each other because he'd been tied up with preparations for the next project after Observatory Field, but the Portakabin that was going to be his office for the duration of the build had been delivered to the site, and she knew that he was intending to move himself into it early the following week.

Friday morning dawned, and Charlotte left for the observatory early, taking Comet with her. The area between the fence and the observatory's building had been gradually cleared, although the fence had been left so that it could be locked to deter trespassers. Even at this late stage of the demolition, Flowerdew were taking no chances. Charlotte finally deemed it safe enough for Comet to roam off-lead so she started to take him with her when she worked. Lorelai seemed slightly disappointed that she wouldn't be needed to dog sit quite so much, but Charlotte was relieved. Much as Lorelai and Comet had bonded, she couldn't help feeling as though she was imposing on her landlady.

The now familiar walk through the woodland was a sure-fire way to both wake her senses and allow her a little thinking time about last Sunday's date with Tristan. Spending time with him was such a lovely experience, and a bit of a revelation. He was much more relaxed on his own turf, and although things had gradually heated up between them, he'd been the perfect gentleman. She had the feeling that they were both in sync, and she was enjoying it. In the early days of her relationship with Todd, though he'd never overtly pressured her, she'd always felt some kind of impetus to go along with what he wanted. She didn't feel that pressure with Tristan.

As she approached the observatory, her phone pinged. There were patchy spots of reception between the woodland and the observatory, and she paused to check the messages that had managed to get through. The first brought a smile to her face: it was a brief, but sweet, missive from Tristan wishing her a good day at work. She texted him back, wishing him the same.

Reception faded out again as she began to move, and as she approached the observatory, she caught sight of someone waiting outside the gate. Blinking in the sunlight that had brightened considerably upon her exit from the woodland, it took a moment for Charlotte to register who the familiar-looking figure was.

It couldn't be. Could it?

Torn between wanting to shoot back into the woods or confront the visitor, whose body language screamed nonchalance as they stood there checking their phone (good luck with that, she thought with some satisfaction), Comet took the decision out of her hands by dashing up to them, yapping in pleasure.

Comet always liked him, despite everything, Charlotte thought. Steeling herself for what seemed to be an inevitable conversation, she walked up to the gate.

'Hello, Todd,' she said, having had a few seconds to get her shock at seeing him under control. He hadn't mentioned anything in his text about being back in the country any time soon. 'What on earth are you doing here?'

'Well, if you won't call me back, what's a guy to do?' Todd gave her his best disarming smile. 'I was back in the office briefly but you haven't been in touch. So...' He trailed off teasingly.

'Really?' Charlotte raised a very sceptical eyebrow. 'You flew four thousand-odd miles just to ask me to return your call? Bit extreme, even for you.' Todd had been king of the grand gesture when they'd been together and had often surprised her 'just because'. She now suspected the 'just because' had been hiding a frequently guilty conscience.

'Well, not exactly,' Todd admitted as he leant down and gave Comet's ears a stroke. 'I was invited to give the keynote speech at Greenwich Royal Observatory last night to a group of PhD students with ambitions to work in the US and thought, since I was in the area, I'd check in, see how you were doing in the wilds of Somerset.'

'Greenwich to Lower Brambleton isn't exactly in the area,' Charlotte returned quickly. She felt off-kilter, as if two worlds had collided and she wasn't sure how to right them.

'Well, yeah, but I figured I'd take the chance. And I think you're going to want to hear what I have to say about those documents you sent me if you give me the chance to go through it in person.'

So, this was a work thing, Charlotte thought. She tried to

fight a stab of disappointment. There was a part of her that had hoped Todd had come to see her to beg for her forgiveness and ask her to take him back, irrational as that was. But she should have known better: work *always* came first with him, and it seemed now was no exception.

'You'd better come in,' she sighed, pulling the key to the padlock out of her pocket. 'Since you've come all this way, I'd value a second opinion.'

Todd smiled at her, and Charlotte willed herself not to react. She didn't need reminding how much she used to fancy him. She was surprised then how easy it was to brush past him and open up the observatory.

* * *

'So, this is what the Ashcombes might have discovered,' Charlotte began as they looked at the paperwork. 'But it's just so odd that there's no other documentation of it anywhere else. I mean, if they really were onto something, why are there no other research papers? Why is there no corroborating evidence from other labs or observatories? Their findings just seem to have disappeared into nothing.'

Todd was looking intently at the logs Charlotte had handed him, lost in the data and clearly running scenarios and calculations. A notebook to the left of him on the desk showed scribbles and sums, and a few notes that he'd made before he got here and was now amending and adding to.

'It doesn't make any sense,' he agreed. 'They obviously reached out to North West Wessex at the time of their first sighting, but no one ever got back to them. And then, back in the early 2000s, first credit for the Volucris eclipsing binary was given to Hope and Masterson in Heidelberg. Not a mention of the Ashcombes having discovered it first.' He glanced from the notes to Charlotte, and she could tell that he was as intrigued as she was. 'Why would the paper trail just stop? We're missing something, I'm sure of it.'

Charlotte had given Todd some brief background about what had happened to Laura and Martin, but they both remained baffled. The Ashcombes had died in January 1995, only two months after their initial discovery of the eclipsing binary. What had happened between those times that meant they sat on their findings? Even though evidence of their discovery was scant, it should have been reported or referenced in some journal. But there was nothing to suggest they'd ever passed on what they'd found. Instead, here Charlotte and now Todd were, thirty years on, only now putting together a puzzle that had been mouldering in an observatory that was about to be demolished.

'Unless...' Todd was thinking out loud.

'Unless what?'

'What if someone else didn't want the papers to be found? What if they *haven't* been here all this time?' Todd stood up and began to pace the records room. 'You say this place was under lock and key for most of the last decade? Who had the keys?'

'The Lower Brambleton Astronomical Society had regular access until about twenty years ago, but since then, I'm guessing just the landowners and the security company who were employed to manage it. It surprised me that the library was intact, given the potential for vandalism, but whoever my landlady, Lorelai Ashcombe, and her brother employed to look after it did a good job at keeping things secure.'

'Must have cost them an arm and a leg,' Todd observed. 'I mean, what was the point in pouring all that cash into a place that was going nowhere?'

'Family legacy,' Charlotte suggested. 'Martin and Laura Ashcombe were Lorelai's son and daughter-in-law, and they were integral to the observatory. Perhaps she couldn't bear to let anything happen to it until she was ready to let it go.'

'Even so,' Todd remarked, 'it's a hell of a long time to hold onto such a lucrative property, even for sentimental reasons. And surely, she'd want to get shot of it and move on after her family died near here?'

Charlotte stayed silent. She didn't want to divulge the intimate details of what Lorelai had told her about the fractious relationship with her brother; it wasn't her history to tell, and she wanted Todd's involvement to be purely focused on the science, not the wider family dynamics.

'Now, this is interesting,' Todd said suddenly. He was writing something in his notebook, and he reached for the initial log that Charlotte had found that documented the first potential sighting of Volucris by Martin and Laura. 'Those initials... PP... any idea who they might be?'

'No.' Charlotte shook her head. 'There's no further reference to a PP at all in any of the correspondence. The paper trail just stops after that email to Jacobson.'

'I wonder if Jacobson's still alive?' Todd was moving again. Charlotte remembered how he never could sit still when he was hashing something out. 'He might know who the mysterious PP is.'

'Maybe,' Charlotte hedged. 'I'll Google him.' She put her phone down again in frustration. 'Later.' She still couldn't get used to the lack of signal up here.

Todd replaced the documents carefully in the archive box. Charlotte busied herself with packing away the box into the larger storage container that would soon be transported to the university's archive facility.

'How about you meet me later for some dinner, and we can carry on discussing things?' Todd asked. He suppressed a yawn. 'We could Google Jacobson together. I've booked into a room above the pub, if you wanted to join me for a bite to eat when you're done here.'

Just a few months ago, Charlotte would have jumped at the chance, but things were different now. She wished she'd just bitten the bullet and contacted Professor Edwin instead. Now she had the complication of her ex-boyfriend in the village, and from the way he'd latched onto this, he wasn't going to be dissuaded easily.

'I've got a lot of work to do today,' Charlotte replied. 'And while it's great that you've taken an interest in this, it's just one small aspect of the history of the observatory, and I don't have time to get sidetracked.'

Todd said nothing for a long moment. 'It's your call,' he said eventually. 'But it would be a real shame to see this disappear into a box, never to be thought of again, don't you think? Especially when you might've really hit on something.'

'It's probably nothing,' Charlotte said. She suddenly felt keen to get rid of Todd. He was invading her space and she was finding that she didn't like it one bit. 'It was good of you to come all this way, but it might be best if you just leave me to do the job I've been paid to do.'

'You're shutting me out?' Todd's voice held a hint of petulance. He was not a man used to being thwarted, either professionally or personally, and Charlotte realised that in his total assurance of his own knowledge and expertise was an arrogance she hadn't seen before when they'd been in a romantic relationship.

'Not as such,' she said carefully. She forced a smile. 'I just think we shouldn't be jumping to conclusions. This could all be a huge pile of nothing. Surely you can see that?'

Todd fell silent again. 'If that's what you want,' he said eventually. He got up from the desk and crossed over to where she was standing. 'But call me if you have any further thoughts about it. I want to help, Charlotte.' He was turning his sincerest brown-eyed gaze on her again. 'I owe you that after everything.'

Charlotte smiled. 'You don't owe me anything,' she said. 'But I'll keep you posted if anything else comes up.'

'You do that.' He leaned forward and kissed her on the cheek. 'I'll see you around.'

As he left, Charlotte couldn't help thinking that it had been quite the gesture for him to come all this way. But then, she reasoned, he'd always been driven by a quest for knowledge: it was one of the things she'd liked about him.

38

Later that afternoon, Charlotte's phone pinged again. She was excited and pleased to find another message from Tristan, inviting her over to dinner.

> I know you said you'd cook but given the short notice, I'd love to cook for you again!

Its vaguely apologetic tone made her smile, and she texted back, accepting his invitation. Then, she packed everything up that she'd been working on, checked twice she'd secured the observatory and headed back down the hill.

Lorelai raised an eyebrow but said nothing when Charlotte mentioned she was going out to Tristan's. This time, she decided to take Comet with her. When Tristan arrived to pick her up, he gave a resigned smile when he saw Comet's eager face looking up at him.

'This fella's our chaperone for tonight, then?' His tone was amused, despite his initial expression.

'If that's all right?' Charlotte replied. 'I didn't want to impose on Lorelai for another night, and I figured he'd like a change of scene, too.'

'That's fine.' Tristan popped open the boot of his car with a smile and Comet hopped happily in as if he'd been used to travelling there all his life.

Tristan's smile turned to a grin. 'Well... shall we?'

With Comet peering curiously out of the rear window, they were soon en route to Tristan's.

When they were back in the house, Tristan hesitated after he poured Charlotte a glass of wine.

'I, er, wanted to show you something before we had dinner,' he said. 'It's a bit early to actually use it, but I thought you might find it interesting.'

Charlotte's glass paused on the way to her lips. 'I'm intrigued.'

Tristan led her out to his small, well-kept back garden. Charlotte suspected Lorelai might have had a hand in its maintenance, as there was an immaculate patch of lawn bordered by raised beds of lavender and other bee-friendly blooms. The scent, as evening drifted in softly, was divine. But it was the object in the centre of the lawn that caught Charlotte's eye.

'Oh, wow!' she breathed. 'I wasn't expecting that.'

There, on a wooden tripod, standing proudly, was a telescope. Charlotte immediately recognised it as a Unitron Refractor, popular in the 1950s and 1960s among amateur but serious astronomers. Its white casing and elegant construction were shown to great effect on a mahogany mount.

'Thought you might like to see it, and use it a bit later.' Tristan reached for her hand. 'You know that my relationship with all things astronomical is somewhat complex, but I wanted to share this with you, since you've got a real interest.'

There was that adorable understatement again. Charlotte

smiled. She ignored the 'somewhat complex' phrase and just added, 'An interest, and a career.'

Tristan grinned back. 'Well, yeah.' He shuffled on the spot. 'You know more about these things than I do, that's for sure.'

Charlotte leaned forwards and gave him a long, lingering kiss. 'I'd love to take a look a bit later,' she said. 'Thank you so much for thinking of it.' When they broke apart again, she added, 'Where did you get it from?'

'It was my great-uncle's,' Tristan said as they moved towards the tripod. 'He was a funny old fella: very private, almost reclusive. He and Gran argued a lot, especially when he came to live with her at the end of his life, but he still left everything to her. She passed this on to me some time ago, and it's been in its box on the top of the wardrobe in the spare room ever since. I didn't really know how to use it, but a couple of YouTube tutorials taught me the basics, and I thought you might like to have a go while you're here.'

'That would be great,' Charlotte breathed. The anticipation became too much, and she was impatient to take a look, even before the sky had darkened. 'May I?'

'Of course.' Tristan was obviously pleased by her excitement. 'It would be great to have an expert at the helm.'

Charlotte bent over to investigate the eyepiece of the telescope. Its lenses had been cleaned and restored and were clear and sharp. She looked into the eyepiece and made a couple of adjustments so that she had a decent view of the sky. It still wasn't dark enough to see much, but she could get a sense of the quality of the telescope and continued to tweak and amend its positioning as Tristan watched.

'That should do the trick,' she said as she stepped back again. 'Later on, we'll be able to see more. Even though it's summer, there'll be planets and some stars visible. If, er, I'm still here, when it's dark, anyway.' She couldn't help blushing as she stumblingly finished speaking – it had crossed her mind more than once that she and Tristan might be heading in a more physical direction tonight.

Tristan's expression showed that his thoughts were heading in a similar direction, as his eyes flitted between her lips and her slightly heated gaze. 'Well,' he murmured softly, 'I hope you will still be here when it's dark enough to see stars.' He reached for her hand and placed it on his chest, before drawing her closer to him for a long, sensuous kiss. Charlotte's hand, feeling the warmth of Tristan's body beneath his clothing, grew shakier as the kiss deepened. She moved even closer to Tristan, until they were pressed together, breath shortening and kisses becoming more urgent as the seconds moved languorously by.

Eventually, the oven timer pinged from the kitchen. Charlotte reluctantly broke free from Tristan's embrace and glanced up at him. 'Can dinner wait for a little while?'

Tristan nodded. 'It's nothing that won't keep. Let me go and switch off the oven.'

Charlotte stumbled slightly on wobbly legs as she followed him, watching from the doorway. She picked up her glass of white wine, which she'd left on the kitchen table, and took a big gulp, betraying her nerves. Tristan was beside her in a shot.

'It's all right.' He took the glass from her hands and put it down carefully on the kitchen table. 'If you've changed your mind, I mean.'

Charlotte shook her head. 'I haven't.' She leaned up and kissed him again. 'Now, are you going to join me and have a glass of something to give you Dutch courage?'

Tristan raised an eyebrow. 'What about driving you home? I never drink and drive.'

Charlotte wouldn't have expected anything less from this

gorgeous, serious-minded, responsible man in front of her, but his statement banished any lingering doubts. 'I don't think I'll be going home anytime soon.' *And there's always Uber*, she thought, *if things go pear shaped.*

Tristan hesitated for a long moment before moving to grab another wine glass from the cupboard. 'Well, that seems pretty conclusive.' He gave a laugh that definitely had an undercurrent of nerves. 'And a relief!'

Charlotte laughed too, but things gradually got more serious as the laughs turned to kisses, and the wine glasses were left on the kitchen table.

39

Once up the stairs in Tristan's room, things took a far more passionate turn. Their playful banter, which had banished some of the awkwardness, ceased, and their communication was softer, huskier, briefer, but even more delicious. Comet, for his part, had seemed delighted to stretch out in the last rays of sunshine that were peering in through the bay window in Tristan's living room. Charlotte had joked, when she'd seen her dog looking so cosy, that he was likely to get up onto the sofa when their backs were turned, but Tristan didn't seem to mind. Just in case, though, he threw a tartan rug over the sofa before they headed upstairs.

Charlotte was touched by the gesture and wrapped her arms around his neck and drew him in for a long, luxurious kiss, before playfully tugging his soft cotton T-shirt out of his jeans. Running her hands up his back, she felt an exquisite pleasure as he drew in a sharp breath at her touch.

'Are you sure we're not moving too fast?' Tristan murmured as they started to undress.

'I'm more than happy with the pace, if you are,' Charlotte

replied. She paused before she unzipped her dress. 'Are you OK with this?'

Tristan nodded, seemingly mesmerised at the sight of Charlotte's dress gently slipping from her shoulders. He leaned forward and kissed her neck, and she arched towards him in pleasure, luxuriating in the sensation of his lips on her skin and then his body against hers as she wrapped her arms around him.

'Shall we?' he asked, glancing at the bed a few feet behind them.

Charlotte nodded, and stepped out of her dress, which had pooled at her feet. They collapsed down onto Tristan's generous mattress, and as they did so, Charlotte felt the shift between them as their emotions stepped up a gear. She wrapped herself around him, wanting to feel every inch of him against her, and there was no doubt that he was as aroused as she was. She could feel his firm body pressing back against hers, and as her hands began to wander over his smooth, warm skin, she felt a surge of warmth and desire. This was what she'd been waiting for since they'd started to get to know each other, and although it had only been a little under three weeks since they'd met, Charlotte's body, and her heart, were telling her that this was the perfect moment to take things to the next level.

It didn't take long for both of them to lose their remaining layers of clothing, and then they began to take their time. Charlotte was glad that Comet was quiet and chilled out downstairs and completely indifferent to what was happening in the bed. She needed to fully relax and focus purely on the sensations that Tristan's hands and lips were giving her.

'That's perfect,' she breathed as his hands stroked and caressed. His fingertips were exploring her body in the gentlest way, and she felt the warmth of them as he brought her gradually closer to the summit. In return, she caressed him fully, marvelling at his heat, and thinking, in a giddy moment of heightened expectation, that she'd been right about the kind of energy he exuded.

Eventually, after a leisurely exploration, they were both ready to take that final step. Charlotte was relieved when Tristan grabbed a condom from his top drawer, and then all rational thoughts of practicality were chased away like shooting stars as he eased inside her. That intimate, immediate sensation of connection was enough to make them both draw a breath, and Charlotte matched her own on-the-edge rhythm to Tristan's. A few moments later and she'd tumbled over the precipice, and it didn't take long for Tristan to do the same.

As they lay in each other's arms afterwards, Charlotte propped herself up on one elbow and looked down at Tristan, who was sprawled, eyes half closed, totally relaxed.

'Well,' she said eventually, once he'd opened his eyes again fully. 'I'm glad we're here and not in the annexe at Nightshade Cottage. I don't think I could look Lorelai in the eye after that!'

Tristan shook his head. 'That's just what I need to be thinking about right now – my grandmother on the other side of the wall. Thanks!'

Charlotte giggled. 'Am I to assume that, should we desire a repeat performance, it'll have to be here, then?'

Raising an eyebrow, Tristan reached out and flipped Charlotte onto her back, so this time he was looking down at her. 'Absolutely,' he replied. 'And next time, I might even let you bring the damned dog again, since he's been so well behaved.'

Charlotte laughed, then looked mischievously up at Tristan. 'Well behaved, eh? Comet!' she called. 'Want a gravy bone?'

There was a patter of paws on tiles and slightly more muffled on carpet, as the cocker spaniel raced upstairs to the bed and jumped straight up to join them.

'You were saying?' Charlotte said, grinning and ruffling the dog's neck.

'Love you, love your dog?' Tristan muttered, trying to look as though he didn't really mind the dog's presence on his Egyptian cotton sheets.

'Love me, love my dog,' Charlotte echoed. 'They don't all bite, you know.'

Tristan groaned. 'I suppose you're alluding to my encounter with that German Shepherd.'

'Maybe,' Charlotte smiled into the darkening air. 'I must say, I haven't noticed that it left any scars.'

'Not physical ones,' Tristan said lightly. 'But if Comet puts his jaws anywhere near me, I'm banning him from the house.'

'He's the perfect gentleman, I promise,' Charlotte replied. As if to undercut that sentiment, Comet rolled over onto his back, legs akimbo, in a most ungentlemanly position. Charlotte couldn't help giggling. 'Well, he is most of the time, anyway!'

40

A little later on, Comet had retreated downstairs once more and Charlotte was lying in Tristan's bed in a state of post-sex bliss and contentment for the second time that evening. It had been a while since her last encounter and she had to admit, Tristan blew Todd out of the water with his passion, stamina and intensity.

'All right?' Tristan murmured, stroking her hair back from her neck in a gesture that was making her start to tingle again.

'Couldn't be better.' Charlotte propped herself up on one elbow once more and gazed down at him. His hair was tousled, his eyes were calm, relaxed and looking back up at her.

'Well, I could,' he said playfully. 'I don't know about you, but I'm bloody starving after that.'

Charlotte grinned. 'I could be persuaded into some dinner, if you're offering.'

'I kind of think we might have done things the wrong way round, tonight,' Tristan mused as he pulled on his boxer shorts and reached for his T-shirt.

'Well, I'm not complaining.' She slithered back into her own clothes and then pulled Tristan back to her for another kiss. 'I might like systems, but I'm not averse to breaking convention on occasion.'

'Just as well!' Tristan laughed. Charlotte realised that she hadn't heard him laughing very much, and she liked the sound.

They padded down the stairs to the kitchen, Comet hot on their heels.

Soon, they were tucking into Tristan's beautifully cooked beef bourguignon, mopped up with some delectable slices of sourdough bread from Saints' Farm. Comet, who'd happily lapped up his own portion of beef, lay stretched out on the cool tiled floor of the kitchen, his heart and stomach well won over by Tristan's hospitality.

Charlotte was feeling much the same, and as the wine flowed and the night drew on, she decided that she would be more than happy to do this again and again. She was so relaxed that she'd almost forgotten the mystery that she and Todd had uncovered at the observatory. She'd intended to broach the subject with Tristan but it seemed a shame to break the playful and chilled-out mood by raising the sensitive subject of the observatory. She shrugged it off – there'd be plenty of time to talk.

After they finished dinner, Tristan made some coffee and suggested they go back outside and try out the telescope. They wandered out into the garden, pleased that, as night had gently fallen, the skies had remained clear. It was a quarter to midnight, and so there were definitely things to see in the velvety summer darkness.

'Are you warm enough?' Tristan asked, as he rested his arm on her shoulder. 'I can grab you a jumper if you like.'

'I'm all right at the moment,' Charlotte replied. The wine would insulate her if it turned chilly but right now the air was still and warm. Not great for sleeping, but perfect for spending some time looking at the summer stars. She gazed up at the heavens, looking at those oh-so-familiar patterns that pinpricked the sky, adding an order to the vast, infinite reaches of space. She was frequently surprised by just how much the night sky enthralled her, even though she'd spent years studying it.

Tristan stood behind her and slid his arms around her waist, pressing up against her and warming her with his body. She leaned back into him, relishing the feeling, and, as he planted gentle kisses on the side of her neck, sighed in contentment. 'If you keep doing that, we'll never get to see anything,' she murmured. Tristan ignored her and kept kissing.

Charlotte gave a giggle. 'Come on,' she said playfully, 'you didn't go to the trouble of getting this telescope out just to get it covered in dew.' She disentangled herself from him and took the few steps over to the telescope. Comet, who had spent some time sniffing the borders of the garden and lifting a leg in a couple of quiet places, joined her at her heels.

'Now, let me just see...' She carefully adjusted the telescope again, using minute and delicate movements just to sharpen the image through its vintage lenses in the direction it was pointing. After a few moments, she secured it in place and then turned back to Tristan.

'Come and look,' she said, reaching out a hand to bring him closer.

Tristan, who had been watching her intently, seemed to shake himself out of some reverie. Giving her a shy smile, he joined her at the eyepiece.

'What am I looking at?' he asked as he leaned down to observe the skies.

'Well,' Charlotte said, 'let's start with an easy one. What

you're seeing now is the planet Jupiter, and because this telescope is really good for its age, if you look carefully you should be able to spot its four largest moons.' She reeled off the names. 'They're called Io, Ganymede, Europa and, er... Callisto.'

'You've immediately made me think of that old TV show, *Red Dwarf*!' Tristan teased. 'Didn't Dave Lister work for the Jupiter Mining Corporation?'

Charlotte couldn't help a giggle. 'I'll have to let you be the judge of that... my sci-fi knowledge isn't up to much before the David Tennant era of *Doctor Who*!'

Tristan turned away from the telescope to look at her in surprise. 'I thought being an astronomer and a science fiction fan went hand in hand?'

Charlotte shook her head. 'I've always been more interested in science fact than fantasy,' she replied. 'I was reading Carl Sagan in my teens, I'm afraid.'

'You'd have got on well with my mum,' Tristan said, a trace of wistfulness in his voice. 'Dad loved all things sci-fi, but Mum was more of a pragmatist – you're a lot like her.'

Charlotte was touched. She knew Tristan didn't like talking about the past and his parents, but she supposed in this setting comparisons and reminiscences were inevitable. Again, she thought of the photo she'd found in the observatory's files, and wondered if she should show it to Tristan tonight.

'I'd have loved to have met them.' Charlotte looked up into his eyes, and their gaze held while they both digested the weight of their words. After a short while, Charlotte turned back to the eyepiece of the telescope. 'Would you like to see a couple more things before they disappear behind the clouds?'

'Absolutely,' Tristan replied. 'And then, back in to finish our coffee?'

'Sounds good.'

Charlotte wished she could remember the position of the Volucris Binary, as she hadn't actually had the chance to observe it in the night sky since she'd discovered the notes in the observatory. Her phone was back in the house, with the photographs of the relevant documents, and she wondered if she should try to find it. Then she realised the wine must be slowing down her thinking: she wasn't likely to be able to pick it out with this telescope even if she did know where to point the lens.

As Charlotte carefully realigned the telescope to show Tristan some more celestial objects that would be easy to spot for an amateur, she was turning over his words in her mind. The more she worked at the observatory, the more attached she was becoming to its former custodians, and she wanted to make sure that she found a good time to discuss her findings in the records room with Tristan. After all, it directly concerned his family, and he had a right to know. And if he could shed any light on how the mystery of the binary stars had been buried for so long, then all the better.

41

The next morning, Charlotte woke with a slight hangover and a feeling of momentary disorientation. After their stargazing, they'd come back inside the house and finished the wine. She'd snuggled down beside Tristan and slept soundly, only waking when he left her in bed, muttering, 'I'll get some coffee on.' She'd drifted off again for half an hour, and then reawakened when he'd come back into the room.

'I *so* need this!' she exclaimed, taking a sip from the perfectly brewed flat white he handed her. 'I, er, don't usually drink so much. Must have got carried away.'

Tristan looked sheepish. 'I don't, either,' he admitted. 'Perhaps a slow breakfast is in order; to help us both recover a bit. Unless—' he trailed off before adding, 'unless you'd rather I ran you straight home?'

Charlotte shook her head, and then winced as it thudded. 'Breakfast sounds good.' She glanced down at Comet, who was waiting patiently for a walk and his own breakfast. She felt guilty that she didn't have anything for him to eat, but it would have seemed presumptuous to have packed his dog food before she knew she was definitely spending the night with Tristan. 'Sorry, old chap,' she said. 'Perhaps a couple of treats will tide you over until you get home.'

'We can do better than that,' Tristan replied. 'I nipped out to the corner shop while the coffee was brewing and got him a bag of the Royal Canin dry food – I noticed some on Gran's windowsill the other day and wondered if you'd given it to her to feed Comet when she was looking after him. I didn't want the little fella to go hungry just because he wasn't at home.'

Charlotte was touched by the thoughtful gesture. 'That's really kind.'

They drank their coffee in bed, and then Tristan gave Charlotte some privacy to have a shower. Later, they tucked into pastries and a pot of Lorelai's homemade tayberry and blackcurrant jam. 'She gives me about five pots every year and I don't have the heart to tell her I only get through one!' Tristan joked as they spread their croissants with it.

'So,' Tristan said tentatively. 'Do you have any plans for the rest of the weekend?'

Charlotte paused. She really should get back to Nightshade Cottage and do some prep work before heading to the observatory bright and early on Monday morning, but it was so tempting to hang out with Tristan a little longer. Their passion of last night had evolved into something more relaxed, and she found herself wondering what it would be like to spend every morning in his company. But, duty called, and she wanted to get some work done before the end of the weekend.

'I've got some stuff to do today,' she said, 'but tomorrow's good, if you wanted to get together again.'

'In that case,' Tristan grinned, standing up from the table

and moving so that he was in front of her, 'why don't I take you home, and we can meet at the pub tomorrow for some lunch?'

Charlotte put down her coffee cup and slid into Tristan's arms. 'That's a great idea,' she replied. She reached a hand down to ruffle the top of Comet's head. 'It'll give me time to walk this one before we have lunch, too.'

They finished breakfast and then Tristan drove Charlotte and Comet back to Nightshade Cottage. They shared another kiss before she headed back into the annexe to change.

Chatting nonsense to Comet, who was keen to get out for a walk, she threw on some shorts and a T-shirt. She and Comet headed out into the woods, and by the time they'd taken their usual route to the observatory and back, Comet was ready for a lazy afternoon in his basket, while Charlotte did her prep work. After an early night, and another walk with Comet on Sunday morning, she was looking forward to seeing Tristan again.

'I won't be long,' she said to the spaniel as she left, allowing plenty of time for the walk to the Star and Telescope. She also realised that she hadn't seen Lorelai. She wondered if she'd gone to see Thea and her grandchildren.

The walk to the pub took less time than she'd expected, and she ambled into the bar before Tristan arrived. Her eyes took a few seconds to adjust to the gloom inside, but as they did, they alighted on a figure she could definitely have done without seeing.

Todd.

'Hi,' he said, as he caught sight of her. 'Couldn't keep away, huh?'

'Don't flatter yourself,' Charlotte shot back, unnerved by the soon-to-be-juxtaposition of her past relationship and her present one. 'I thought you'd headed back to London, and your flight?'

'I decided to stick around a while,' Todd said, turning his best chocolate-brown-eyed gaze on her. 'Thought it would be worth it.'

'Not on my account, I hope!' Charlotte tried desperately to make light of this situation. 'I think I was pretty clear with you when we spoke.'

'Oh, you were.' Todd gave a brief, tight smile. 'But a guy can hope, right?' He turned away to sip his pint, and before Charlotte could conjure a suitably pithy response, he continued. 'And anyway, I couldn't stop thinking about those materials you shared with me. Something doesn't add up. With your permission, I'd like to be your research partner on this one, if you'll have me.'

Charlotte's surprise, and not a small amount of suspicion, must have registered on her face as Todd instantly raised his hands in a placatory gesture. 'Honestly, Charlotte, I'm on the level here. Ever since you sent me the photos of those documents, I've been racking my brain trying to work out why Martin and Laura Ashcombe aren't mentioned with reference to the Volucris Binary. They were in contact with Professor Jacobson at North West Wessex, for goodness' sake! Why would it just have ended there? I mean, not even a footnote in some journal somewhere? There's got to be more to it than that.'

Reluctantly, Charlotte had to concede that Todd had a point: she'd been thinking along similar lines ever since she'd found the papers. Much as she resented Todd muscling in on this, she respected his knowledge and expertise. Perhaps it wouldn't be unreasonable to make use of both if he was prepared to work with her?

'All right,' she said carefully. 'Let's research this together for a bit. It's probably going to be a dead end, and there's likely to be a rational explanation for why Volucris wasn't documented back in the mid 1990s. I suppose it wouldn't hurt to keep digging. The observatory's papers are going to be transferred to the North West Wessex archive at the end of the summer, in fact, some have gone already, so when they're in situ back at the university, I'll have more time to spend on this. For now, my job is to ensure the important documents are archived, but later on I'll have more time to look for any connections.'

'And I'll take the Jacobson angle,' Todd replied. He looked thoughtful. 'I know he worked in the US for a while before he retired a few years back. Perhaps I can track him down... jog his memory about Volucris and the Ashcombe connection.'

Charlotte raised an eyebrow. 'Wouldn't he be in his nineties by now, if he's still alive? How much is he going to remember from thirty-odd years ago? This was right at the birth of the internet, too. If the Lower Brambleton Astronomical Society hadn't kept a printout of that early email, we'd have no idea about Martin and Laura's discovery.'

'Martin and Laura?' It was Todd's turn to look sceptical. 'You sound like you knew them personally.' He gave her a faintly patronising smile. 'You get so involved when you're on a job, don't you? Almost as if you're living the lives of the people you're putting into storage.'

Charlotte realised then exactly why she and Todd would never have had a romantic future. He might be a skilled astronomer and researcher, but she couldn't put up with his 'pat on the head, what a good girl you are' routine. She knew that whatever contact she had with him now would be purely in the name of research.

'Well, I really must grab a table,' she said briskly, biting down the urge to tell Todd to sling his hook. 'I've got a lunch date, and I said I'd get us a seat if I got here first.'

'Don't let me keep you,' Todd replied. 'Who's your date? Some local you've met while you've been down here?'

'Something like that.' Charlotte beamed as she saw Tristan ducking under the low doorway of the pub. 'I'll let you know what I turn up when I've spent some more time with the papers.'

'You do that,' Todd replied. He was clearly watching the trajectory of Charlotte's gaze, and she was sure she saw a rather satisfying look of surprise and discomfort crossing his features as he laid eyes on Tristan. Todd made to move away towards the door that led to the rooms above the pub.

'See you,' Charlotte replied. Not wanting to face the awkwardness of her past and present romantic lives colliding, she hurried over to meet Tristan halfway across the bar.

'Hey,' she said quickly, raising her face to his for a kiss of welcome. 'I think I spotted a table out the back by the window if you fancy it.'

'Great,' Tristan replied. He appeared not to have clocked the interaction between Charlotte and Todd as he'd arrived. 'I hope you're hungry,' he said as they made a beeline for the table, away from the main bar. 'The Star and Telescope does a mean Sunday roast.'

'Sounds perfect,' Charlotte replied. She was glad when they'd rounded the corner and taken their seats, out of Todd's line of sight. She'd fill Tristan in this afternoon about everything, she thought. After all, this concerned his family; he had a right to know. All the same, she felt a nagging sense of worry about raising what she thought she'd found before she was truly certain. What if she told him about his parents' link to Volucris and it turned out to be a trail that led to nothing? As a scientist, she was trained to test hypotheses and create theories based on hard evidence. Was she really at the stage where she actually had anything she could even call evidence yet? And what if Todd was right and there was more to it than they'd hitherto discovered? Resolving to enjoy lunch and then think about how she might raise the subject with Tristan, she settled down to make the far easier choice about which type of roast to go for.

42

'You weren't joking,' Charlotte said as she put her knife and fork together on an empty plate, 'that really was the best roast I've had in ages!' Living alone, she never cooked the full Sunday lunch with all the trimmings, but when she felt the need for a bit of good old English tradition, she'd slink down to one of the university's canteens and avail herself of theirs. The Star and Telescope's incarnation of the meal, however, knocked spots off any university's attempt. Succulent, locally reared roast pork, complete with crackling and homemade apple sauce, was the centrepiece of a plate that brimmed to overflowing with root vegetables, stuffing and even, to a non-purist's delight, a gigantic, feather-light Yorkshire pudding. She'd devoured it all, and now was feeling replete.

As a result of last night's wine, neither she nor Tristan had fancied alcohol, so they were both drinking elderflower cordial and feeling a whole lot better for it. Leaning back in her chair, Charlotte waved away the dessert menu. 'Honestly, I couldn't, but go ahead if you can.'

Tristan grinned. 'How about a slab of apple pie and custard and two spoons?'

Charlotte tried to demur, but in the end, she had a good few mouthfuls of the most delectable shortcrust pastry that encased more locally grown Bramley apples, and a gloriously silky homemade custard.

'I will *never* eat again!' she proclaimed a few minutes later as she pushed her spoon away from her.

Tristan shook his head. 'I'm so glad you're someone who likes to eat well.' He paused, obviously debating whether to continue. 'My, er, my previous girlfriend was always on some diet or other. I could never work out what to cook her, and although she grinned and bore it a lot of the time when I got things wrong, I never felt as though I got it right. But that was her decision, of course – each to their own.'

'Were you together long?' Charlotte asked. She was curious about who had held a place in Tristan's life and his heart before her, and hoped that an insight might give her more of a handle on this rather complicated man.

Tristan shook his head. 'It was a casual thing.' He looked a little rueful. 'I've, er, I've never been particularly good at commitment.' He rushed to clarify. 'Don't get me wrong. I don't screw around, and I've never cheated when I've been involved with someone.' His face coloured slightly as he continued. 'It might sound like a bit of a cliché, but I've never really met anyone I've felt able to see myself being with in the long term.'

'It's not a cliché,' Charlotte said softly. 'Sometimes, people come into our lives for different reasons, and at different times, and then they go again. Not every relationship has to start with the vision of a lifetime commitment.'

Tristan leaned back in his chair as if he was trying to lessen the sudden intensity of the conversation. 'I suppose you're right,' he said. 'My, er, my parents had that once-in-a-lifetime thing: they met at university, when they were both studying something they loved, and for them, the stars just seemed to align.' He gave a laugh. 'Sorry, I'm back to speaking in clichés again!'

'With that kind of an example, it's easy to assume that all relationships work that way,' Charlotte replied. 'I've never been able to imagine my parents at that passionate, carefree stage. I know they love each other, but it's a quieter form of love: they're best friends more than husband and wife, I suppose. I've never heard them argue, in front of me, not once.'

'You've had a lifetime of watching that relationship, though,' Tristan observed. Then, obviously realising how wistful he sounded about his own situation, he cracked a mischievous grin. 'Perhaps, back in the day, they were the plate-throwing, devil-may-care, wildly passionate types!'

Charlotte laughed. 'I can't see it somehow! If you ever meet them, you'll know exactly what I mean!'

Tristan moved forward again and reached for one of Charlotte's hands. 'I'd like to, one day, if you want to introduce me to them.'

There was no mistaking the emotion in his eyes and Charlotte wondered whether there was a more permanent place for Tristan in her life. With Todd she'd never really felt as though their future was assured, but sitting here with Tristan, seeing the look on his face, and spending time with him felt different, felt right. Chiding herself inwardly for taking too many steps down that path, she gave his hand a squeeze. 'Maybe I will, one day.'

Charlotte paused, considering what else she should say. Perhaps, since Tristan had so casually referred to his former girlfriend, now was the time to bring up the fact that her ex was actually in Lower Brambleton at this moment. 'My, er, my ex-boyfriend grew up in Georgia, in the USA,' she began tentatively.

'He was someone who really loved to eat. I don't think he ever quite got over the culture shock of coming to the UK and seeing the size of our dinner plates in comparison!'

'Were you together long?' Tristan asked.

'A year or so,' Charlotte replied. 'He accepted a post back home and left a couple of months ago. We said we'd try to keep things going but it didn't work out.'

Tristan nodded. 'I can understand that. Must have been hard when he left, though.'

'It was, at the time.' Charlotte took a deep breath and prepared to drop the minor bombshell that she'd been keeping to herself about Todd's actual whereabouts right now. It seemed silly to keep hedging around it, since they'd broached the topic in conversation.

'The thing is...' she began.

'I'm so sorry to interrupt, Charlotte, but may I speak with you?'

Todd's voice, with its distinct transatlantic intonation, cut through their conversation like a tail of a comet bisecting the night sky and Charlotte felt a sharp prickle of irritation.

43

Perfect timing, as ever, Charlotte thought crossly as Todd appeared by the table. Couldn't the guy take a hint? Research buddy or not, now was not the time to gatecrash. She'd been on the verge of telling Tristan that Todd was in Lower Brambleton and the possible discovery she'd made about the eclipsing binary, and now Todd had obviously taken it upon himself to intervene.

'Forgive me,' Todd said, giving them both his best apologetic smile. 'I don't mean to interrupt, but I just wanted to let you know, Charlotte, that I'll be heading out on the next flight from Heathrow. If you wanted to talk anything through in person before I leave, we could meet at the observatory this evening?'

Charlotte glanced from Todd to Tristan and back again. The intimacy of the last few minutes had vanished if Tristan's expression was anything to go by. He was looking at her expectantly, clearly waiting to be introduced.

'Tristan, this is Todd,' Charlotte said quickly. 'He, er, he's been assisting me with some of the archive work up at the observatory.'

'I thought you were working alone?' Tristan's brow wrinkled.

Charlotte's face began to flame. She didn't like the intersection of her private and professional lives one bit.

'Todd's been looking into a few anomalies for me. I was going to fill you in when I was sure about what we might have found.' God, this was awkward. She didn't want to reveal Tristan's family links with the observatory to Todd, who had no idea that Tristan was Martin and Laura's son. And she certainly didn't want to divulge the specifics of the binary star discovery to Tristan like this.

'Yeah.' Todd continued to smile, although Charlotte could tell he was somewhat surprised by his introduction as 'research buddy'. 'Charlotte contacted me to come on board with the archive project in an advisory capacity. We just need to tie up a few loose ends before I head home.'

'And where's home?' Tristan asked. Charlotte didn't miss the tighter quality of his voice. She sensed that Tristan might be putting two and two together.

'Atlanta,' Todd replied. 'I'm currently working for Georgia State University.'

Tristan's quirked eyebrow in Charlotte's direction told her it had all clicked. 'Fascinating work,' he said. 'Funny... we were just talking about you.'

'All good, I hope!' Todd's smile became more fixed.

Tristan didn't grace him with a reply. He glanced at his watch. 'I'd better be off,' he said. 'I, er, promised I'd look in on Thea and the kids this afternoon.' He made to stand but Charlotte tried desperately to delay him.

'What about the bill? We should split it.'

'No need.' Tristan gave her a brief, guarded smile. 'I'll take care of it. I'll, er, leave you two to discuss your research. No time like the present.'

'Hang on.' Charlotte rose to follow him. 'Let me walk you out.'

Todd stepped back from the table, and Charlotte was sure she spotted a flicker of triumph in his eyes. Tristan reached out a hand to shake Todd's briefly. 'It was good to meet you,' he said.

'You too,' Todd replied.

Then, in a formal gesture that spoke volumes, Tristan leaned forward and kissed Charlotte's cheek. 'Lunch was great,' he said. 'Text me when you've finished discussing your research.'

Charlotte felt a pinprick of frustration at the back of her neck. Why was Tristan the one to walk away? The last thing she wanted was for him to leave, and to be stuck with Todd until he buggered off to get his flight. Taking a deep breath, she turned back to Todd. 'I'm sure whatever you've found out can wait,' she said. 'Or even better, be put in an email. I'm busy right now, as you can see, and I was enjoying a pleasant lunch. Why don't you contact me when you're back in Georgia and we can discuss things further. You did say you needed to check a couple of things?'

Todd was the one looking surprised, now. A man unused to being given the brush-off, his face assumed an irritated expression. 'If that's what you want,' he said, after a beat.

'It is,' Charlotte replied. Nothing Todd could have discovered was worth leaving Tristan with an incorrect impression about her and her relationship with her ex. She kicked herself for not being up front with Tristan at the start of lunch and making it clear that, although Todd might be in Lower Brambleton, it wasn't because she'd invited him. She'd have to make sure that he knew that now. Without pausing to say anything else to Todd, she hurried out to the bar area, where Tristan had finished paying the bill and was heading for the door.

'Tristan!' she called as she crossed to follow him.

Tristan stopped, but Charlotte could tell he was reluctant. His posture was stiff, mannered, as if he was trying to act as though he hadn't been bothered by meeting Todd, but he couldn't quite pull it off.

'It's OK, I got the bill,' he said, going to walk out of the door.

'That's not why I stopped you, and you know it,' Charlotte replied hurriedly. 'Look, I know you said you've got to get to Thea's, but can we talk?'

Tristan's eyes flickered past Charlotte, clearly to see if Todd was still lurking. 'Yes, all right. Why don't we leave the car here and walk off some of that apple pie?'

Charlotte felt the first stirrings of relief at his response. She smiled. 'That sounds good.'

There was a public footpath across the road from the pub that many Sunday dog walkers used to burn off the excesses of their lunch so without further ado they headed out towards the path.

'Look,' Charlotte said when they'd crossed the road and were out of potential earshot of any other walkers. 'I'm sorry about what just happened. I should have levelled with you from the start that Todd had decided to make an unannounced detour from Greenwich to come and see the Lower Brambleton Observatory.'

'And you, presumably?' Tristan added.

Charlotte glanced up at him, but his face gave nothing away. She felt another pinprick of frustration that he'd put what she was beginning to realise was his 'game face' back on. She'd thought they were past that. They had been until this lunchtime. Taking a deep breath, she realised that she had to be honest.

'I emailed Todd recently,' she said. 'I wanted a second opinion about something I'd found in the observatory's records. My boss at North West Wessex, Professor Edwin, was my first choice, but he's on annual leave and I didn't want to bother him. Since time is of the essence, I decided to swallow my hurt feelings and contact Todd. Despite the way things ended between us, I still respect his scientific opinion. I sent him some anomalous data that I'd uncovered, and the next thing I knew, he'd rocked up here.'

'Convenient that he was in Greenwich at the time you emailed him,' Tristan observed.

Charlotte didn't like the implication. 'He wasn't until a couple of days ago. And I didn't know he was there, just to be clear.' She stepped around a fallen branch on the footpath. 'As far as I was aware, he was still in Atlanta. I thought it would just be a quick email exchange: I'd send him the information; he'd give me his opinion and that would be it. I was shocked when he turned up at the observatory on Friday.'

Tristan's head shook slightly, and if Charlotte had been looking ahead of her, she'd have missed it. 'It's true, Tristan, I promise you.' She didn't like having to repeatedly justify herself and was growing frustrated by his apparent scepticism.

'So, you knew he was here. Did you know he was staying at the Star and Telescope?'

Charlotte drew in a quick breath. 'I did. But I thought he'd checked out on Saturday. I saw him in the bar just before you arrived, and I should have mentioned it to you straight away that he was here, but I just didn't think it was worth it. He's going back to Heathrow later, and he'll be back in Atlanta by the end of tomorrow. Apart from communicating about our research, I don't anticipate seeing him again.'

'So, what are these findings?' Tristan asked, clearly keen to get off the touchy subject of having an ex-boyfriend sprung on him.

Charlotte took a moment to consider her next words carefully. She still didn't really know how aware Tristan was of the relative historical importance of the Lower Brambleton Observatory. It would be a fair bet, given how young he and Thea were when their parents were killed, that unless he'd made the effort, his parents' astronomical work would have remained a fairly abstract, distant concept for him. Lorelai might have enlightened them both over the years, but she was no expert, and given the somewhat parlous relationship between Lorelai and the only other member of the family, her brother Philip, who had also been an astronomer, she wondered how much Tristan would really understand. All the same, she knew she had to try to explain things to him: she would need to explain to all the surviving family members eventually, if what she suspected did indeed turn out to be true.

Charlotte waited until a young family, complete with chocolate-brown Labrador, had passed, before she turned back to Tristan.

'While I was sorting through the observatory's records for the last quarter of 1994 I came across something that surprised me.' She proceeded to explain, in as clear a way as possible, the observations made by Tristan's parents about the eclipsing binary and the fact that there had been no reference to its discovery before or in 1995.

Tristan looked deep in thought as she recounted the story, and as she paused, he took a seat on a nearby tree stump.

'So, what you're telling me is that my parents should have been credited with the discovery, but due to the rather inconvenient event of their sudden deaths, that didn't happen?'

Charlotte's heart gave a lurch at the strange tone of Tristan's voice: a tone she couldn't interpret and was struggling to understand. 'Well,' she ventured, 'I wouldn't quite put it like that.'

'Then how *would* you put it?' Tristan sprang up again from the tree stump. 'You're the expert. Do tell me.'

'I'm *trying* to tell you.' Charlotte tried to keep her voice as calm as she could, but she suddenly felt as though Tristan was telling her off again, like the first time they'd met. 'I don't know why this wouldn't have been documented at the time.' She reached out a hand and tried to touch Tristan's arm, but he stepped away from her, out of reach. 'There should be at least a footnote in a journal, a reference to your mum and dad in relation to the discovery, but there's nothing. The professor who was at North West Wessex at that time, Professor Jacobson, should know more. Your dad emailed him back in the day, to ask for his assistance in corroborating the potential discovery, but then the trail ends there. It doesn't make any sense. Todd's going to try to track him down as he moved to an American university and had tenure until he retired a couple of years ago. He wants to work out why the paper trail went cold after that email from your dad.'

Tristan stood stock still, his expression unreadable as he took in what Charlotte was saying. Eventually, he broke the rather uncomfortable silence that had descended between them.

'I appreciate that this is important to you,' he said. 'And perhaps, if I'd spent the past few weeks immersed in the project as you have, I'd be champing at the bit to find the answer to what's clearly a bit of a puzzle.'

'It's more than that!' Charlotte couldn't disguise her irritation at Tristan's understatement. 'It's a significant discovery that potentially should have been attributed to your parents. Aren't you even a little bit excited or energised by that?'

'Do you want the truth?' Tristan asked, and Charlotte immediately noticed a different, more brittle tone in his voice.

'Of course I do,' she said, trying to keep her own tone calmer than she felt. 'Tell me, Tristan, please.'

Tristan's eyes met hers for a long moment before he averted his gaze to look down the long, straight track of the next stage of the woodland path. There wasn't anyone on the horizon, and for a moment, it felt to Charlotte that if there had been, Tristan might not have been so honest.

'I've spent my life trying to move on from what happened to my parents,' he began quietly. 'I wanted to manage the Observatory Field project because, to my mind, razing it to the ground was the best way to get away from the stranglehold it has on my family. And now, when we're literally days away from the final phase in that process, you're telling me that the book might not be closed, after all?'

Charlotte's shock at his words must have registered on her face, because before she could respond, Tristan continued. 'Thea, my grandmother, and I have all rebuilt our lives after what happened to my parents. The last thing any of us needs right now is for an over-enthusiastic archivist to go digging about in the past, raking up memories that we've all tried to move on from. When Mum and Dad died, we all needed to put some distance between ourselves and the observatory. Even though the bloody place stayed in the family so long, what was left of the family needed the space. Gran's brother didn't make that process easy; he blocked every attempt she made to sell the land and I never really knew why. When he finally died and left his share to Gran, we discussed what should happen next. Painful as it was on some levels, it was agreed that the best thing to do was to sell it. Everyone made peace with it, and although Gran was determined to ensure its contents were preserved for future academics to study, none of us had any intention of becoming immersed again in a past that was so painful for us.'

This time, when Charlotte put out a hand to touch Tristan, he let her. 'I understand what you're saying,' she said gently. 'And I can't even imagine how difficult and traumatic this final stage of the observatory's history has been for you. For all of you.' She paused, considering her next words carefully. 'But wouldn't you rather know that your parents got the credit for the discovery that they deserve? If it does emerge that they found the binary first, their names should go alongside it.'

Tristan shook his head. 'Can't you see, Charlotte? It doesn't matter. So what if they found this eclipsing binary thing first? It doesn't bring them back. Even if they do get credit for it, it'll be just another footnote in a scientific journal that no one will bother to read. It means nothing.'

'Are you telling me to just forget about it, then?' Charlotte retorted. 'Because at the end of the day I'm an astronomical historical archivist, and spotting things like this is part of why I do what I do.'

'I can't tell you to do that.' Tristan's tone was gentler now, and his eyes were locked on Charlotte's, pleading with her to understand. 'But please... tread carefully. The last thing my family needs is to be dragged back into the past. We've tried to escape it for so long. If you can't leave it where you found it, then at least grant us the courtesy of not involving us.'

Charlotte nodded. 'I can try not to.' She gave a brief smile, trying to reassure Tristan. 'Besides, all of this was before the internet became commonplace... there might not be anything more to tell.'

'Does it sound awful that I hope there isn't?' Tristan asked. He suddenly looked incredibly tired and vulnerable, and Charlotte thought she saw a trace of the small boy who'd lost his parents all those years ago. 'I've spent the best part of thirty years trying to get away from the horror of what happened that night. I'm not sure I'm ready to revisit it.' He stepped forward and Charlotte was enveloped in a warm embrace. She rested in his arms, a combination of relief and frustration battling within her. Her heart told her to respect Tristan's strong wish for her potential discovery to be abandoned, but her head and all of her academic training were screaming at her to keep following the trail. Tristan's feelings were one thing, but sometimes emotions had to take second place to science. She still didn't know which territory this particular conundrum could claim to be in.

44

Monday morning arrived with mixed emotions for Tristan. It was his first day in the Portakabin office on the Observatory Field site, and he'd spent most of it getting his papers into the right places, setting up the wi-fi router, which, irritatingly, wouldn't be connected until the following week, and making sure everything was in order for the commencement of the build. Charlotte wasn't on site today, having chosen to work from Lorelai's, but he felt relieved. It would have been difficult enough to concentrate as it was, knowing she was at the other end of the site, after yesterday.

He believed Charlotte when she'd told him that it was all over between her and Todd. Why wouldn't he? She'd stated in no uncertain terms that there was nothing between them, and he had no reason to doubt her. That she'd neglected to mention Todd making a flying visit to Lower Brambleton nagged at him, but he trusted Charlotte and he knew he could take her at her word when she explained why she hadn't said anything. They were still in the early days of their relationship, after all: she didn't owe him an explanation about everything she did, and everyone she chose to see.

On the other hand, he'd seen that acquisitive look in someone's eyes before, and he didn't like what he saw in Todd's gaze when he'd been wrapping up his conversation with Charlotte. She'd tried to reassure him that there was nothing to worry about, but his insecurities ran deep. He'd felt as though he might finally be allowing himself to take risks with his emotions, and it was a cruel twist of fate that the day after he'd come to this realisation, Charlotte's ex had shown up. He might trust Charlotte, but he definitely didn't like Todd one little bit. Something about his perma-smile and the confident way he'd approached them at their table rankled.

And then there was the information Charlotte had dropped about the potential binary star discovery made by his parents. While this wouldn't be an earth-shattering discovery in the grand scheme of things, and the canon of astronomical revelations, it had been enough to set his world even more off-kilter. Tristan liked order, and his mantra was always to move forward. He didn't want to be dragged back into a past he'd spent so much of his life trying to get away from.

So now here he was, about to sign off on the demolition of the observatory building and consign whatever it was his parents had discovered to the dusty annals of history. But what did it matter? He'd lived with the tragedy of their death for decades; why should he now start caring about the place that had, indirectly, been the cause of it? He remembered, as a young child, being almost jealous of the hold the observatory had over both of his parents: how he'd got bored just hanging around up there while they spent what felt like hours aligning instruments, making calculations and discussing their observations with each other and the rest of the Astronomical Society. With the imminent demolition of the observatory, he could finally lay all that to rest.

It was ironic, then, that out of the greatest tragedy of his life the greatest potential for happiness had sprung. He wasn't enough of a romantic to think that he was head over heels in love with Charlotte yet, but she was clever, funny and seriously attractive. He wanted to spend more time with her, to get to know her. He was astute enough to realise that the potential was there for him to fall deeply in love, if the daft smile that he could feel creeping over his face whenever he thought back to this weekend with Charlotte was anything to go by. He'd even grown to like her dog.

The paperwork he had onscreen was enough to banish all further thoughts of romance from his mind and concentrate it on the future of the observatory site. A DocuSign copy of the agreement for the demolition of the building was staring him right in the face, confirming the date that had been set, which was a fortnight from today. After he'd signed off on this, the observatory would be closed to everyone and no one would be allowed on site until the demolition was complete.

He looked at the screen for a long, long time before he signed it. As the document updated, he felt a visceral sense of loss, of letting go of things, of ideas and thoughts that would now, truly be consigned to history. But it was for the best. This was going to be the start of a new phase for Lower Brambleton, and also for him and his family. He knew it would be a great start for Thea and her children, and many others who'd benefit from the new development.

As if she'd been aware he'd been thinking about her, Thea's name flashed up on his phone. Swiping, he spoke.

'Hi, Thea? Yeah, I'm fine. What's up?'

'Can you come over later? I need to talk to you.'

Tristan wrinkled his brow. He had hoped he'd be able to see Charlotte tonight, if she wanted to see him. He felt uneasy about the way they'd left things after their walk, but not wanting to appear needy, he'd given her some space and not pestered her with texts or calls. She'd told him how busy she was going to be in the run-up to the demolition, and he didn't want to be the cause of any distractions. He had, however, hoped that she might be free for a drink later.

'All right,' he said, when he realised that Thea was still waiting for an answer. 'What do you need to talk to me about?'

'I don't really want to discuss it over the phone. Can you just come over? Please?'

It was rare for his sister to be so cagey, and Tristan's alarm bells started to ring. He knew he didn't really have any other choice but to agree.

'Of course,' he said gently. 'I'll be over as soon as I've finished up here. Do you want me to bring anything?'

Thea gave a short laugh. 'No. Just yourself. And don't worry about dinner – I'll sort you something out.'

They said goodbye and ended the call. Tristan's attention shifted back to the paperwork on his desk, and the inevitable arrival of new emails. After ten minutes, though, he found he was just staring at things, and not really taking anything in. His mind felt as though it was being unravelled in at least three different directions, and he couldn't concentrate. Sighing, he shut down his computer and shoved the papers on his desk into the top drawer. There was no point trying to do anything else today. Locking the door behind him, he headed off to see Thea.

45

It took fifteen minutes to drive from the observatory site to Thea's house, and Tristan spent most of it trying to calm his racing thoughts. He was someone who needed to focus on one thing at a time: he'd always found multi-tasking overwhelming, and his laser focus on individual projects was what made him so good at his job. The problem was, when things came at him simultaneously, it took him a while to be able to separate out the strands. In an attempt to calm himself, he ran through what the planned layout of the Observatory Field site was going to be once the demolition started. The land around the building had already been flattened, and was a wide, long, smooth stretch of compacted rust-orange Somerset earth, ready for the heavy loaders and JCBs to come in. Off to the far side, where the access road had already been laid to hardcore, was his Portakabin.

His thoughts progressed to his own professional path for the next couple of months. He would be on site, and then back in head office, checking in remotely and in person from time to time. His involvement with the site would gradually taper off as it began being populated with houses, and the sales team, already selling off plan even before a brick was laid, took on the bulk of the management. Then, it would be pastures and projects new. That strange state of limbo between the breaking of the first earth and the day the first owners and tenants moved in always felt surreal: as though he couldn't fully move on until the places came back to life with their new occupants, having been razed to the ground and rebuilt. The rise from the ashes, and the sense that he was helping to create something new was what drove him and gave him passion for the job.

Once he was outside Thea's house, he parked up behind her car on the driveway. He didn't have to knock as Thea was at the door before he'd even locked the car.

'Thanks for coming over, Tris,' she said, giving him a nervous smile. 'I'm sorry about sounding so dramatic on the phone.'

'What's up?' Tristan asked as he followed Thea back through the small hallway and into the kitchen, where she'd put the kettle on to boil. 'You did sound a bit cloak and dagger. Is there a problem with one of the kids?' He listened for the familiar sound of footsteps on the stairs, but the house was surprisingly quiet. 'Where are they both, anyway?'

Thea, despite her serious demeanour, relaxed a little. 'I've had a bit of a parenting result tonight,' she replied. 'They're both at sleepovers so I don't have to go and get them until tomorrow morning.'

'So, were you planning a wild night on the town, then?' Tristan teased. 'Don't let me stop you if you've got a hot date!'

'The only hot date I've got is with another cup of tea and the last series of *Cobra Kai*!' Thea smiled. 'I've always had a thing for brooding blond types, as you know.'

'TMI, sis.' Tristan's expression grew serious again just as hers did. 'So, what is it you need to talk to me about? Is Cora having trouble at school again?'

Thea shook her head. 'No, it's nothing like that.' She poured hot water into two mugs and left the teabags to infuse. Leaning against the kitchen worktop, Tristan waited for Thea to enlighten him.

'I'm worried about Gran,' she said. 'I popped in to see her earlier, and she seemed a bit, oh, I don't know... discombobulated, I suppose. She had a whole load of paperwork out on her kitchen table, but it was old stuff, not current. She kept looking through it while I was there, but when I asked her what it was, she wouldn't tell me. She just said that she thought she had some stuff that Charlotte might find useful for the observatory's archive, and then changed the subject.'

Tristan felt the encroachment of unease, just as he had a couple of weeks back when he'd asked Charlotte to keep an eye on Lorelai. At the time, Lorelai had brushed off their concern, but that, added to Thea's description now, suggested that they might have cause to worry about their grandmother. 'Could you get a look at the paperwork in more detail while you were there?' he asked, accepting his cuppa and a chocolate bar from Thea's novelty dog biscuit barrel. It had been a long time since lunch.

'Nope,' Thea replied. 'It all looked old, though – handwritten letters, and the kind of stuff that was churned out of one of those dot-matrix printers in the eighties and nineties. Had the punched edges around the borders and everything. Before I could ask her about it, she'd shoved it back in an old blue document wallet and into her bureau. But whatever it was, it seemed to be unsettling her.' Thea sipped her tea. 'I might be over-reacting, but this can be the way dementia starts, can't it? Odd, repetitive behaviour? Fixations with things that seem irrelevant? What if Gran's getting Alzheimer's or something similar?' She paused, as if saying it out loud was akin to swearing in church.

Tristan knew he needed to reassure his sister, and fast. She had a lot on at the moment, with Cora's behaviour, and the stresses and strains of buying a new house that hadn't even been built yet. He didn't want Thea to worry about their grandmother until they both knew there was a real reason to.

'I'll check in on her more often from now on,' Tristan replied. 'I've moved to the site now so for the next few months it'll be easy to pop down after work, or even walk down at lunchtime and see how she is. If she is starting to go downhill, it'll be easy to spot.'

'But perhaps not so easy to get her to acknowledge it.' Thea picked at a flake of glaze on the side of her mug. 'They say that people in the early stages of dementia can be very reticent about admitting it and seeking help. And we both know how stubborn Gran is, even without taking that into account.' She shook her head. 'I just don't know how we should proceed.'

'For the moment, I think we just need to keep an eye on her,' Tristan said as calmly as he could. 'It might just be that she was frustrated because she couldn't find what she was looking for. She's always joking about how we're going to have our work cut out for us, clearing her house, when she's gone. Maybe that's not so far from the truth. Now that Observatory Field is well and truly out of the family, too, perhaps she just wanted to go through the paperwork and start getting rid of it. It could be as simple as that.'

'I hope you're right,' Thea replied. 'Gran's always been so strong, so together. I can't imagine what it's going to be like if she really is beginning to decline.'

'Let's cross that bridge when – and if – we come to it.' Tristan sipped his tea. 'We'll both be a lot more hands-on over the next few months, and as soon as your house is ready, you'll literally be across the woods from her. If there is something to worry about, we'll see it, and we can deal with it. Together.'

'Thanks, Tris.' Thea gave him a shaky smile. 'You can always talk me down off the ceiling. I suppose, if I'm being honest, Gran might not be the only one getting the collywobbles about the observatory. I know it sounds mad, given what we've all lived with for the past few decades, but now it's really, truly, all going to change, I wish I felt more excited. Instead, I just feel... numb. I mean, Observatory Field has loomed over us all for our entire lives, like a mausoleum. It's been a constant reminder of what happened to Mum and Dad, and in the next few weeks it's going to be gone. I just don't know how I'm supposed to feel. Does that make any sense?'

Tristan nodded, but only because he wanted to reassure his sister. She was always so much better at putting things into words than he was. In truth, he still couldn't articulate his emotions in a way that made a tenth as much sense. All he really knew was that it felt as though there was something unfinished inside him, something that would, he hoped, wrap itself into a neat little parcel and disappear to the back of his mind once he witnessed the observatory being demolished.

'Not knowing how to feel seems perfectly reasonable right now,' he said eventually. 'I think we all just have to take things one day at a time, just like we did when Mum and Dad died. But I'm here for you, Thea, and we'll both be there for Gran, whatever happens.'

'Thanks, Tris.' Thea blinked a couple of times before she grabbed their now empty mugs of tea. 'Do you want to stay for dinner?'

'Thanks, but I'm hoping I'll have plans.' Tristan couldn't suppress a quick smile at the thought that he might see Charlotte later.

Happy to move onto a cheerier subject, Thea grinned at him. 'Oh, yes? Things going well with Charlotte, then?'

'Yes. So far, so good... mostly.' He didn't want to go into the conversation he'd had with Charlotte yesterday. That was another one to be filed away for when he was ready to deal with it.

Thea, with that sixth sense she always seemed to have for when to push Tristan and when to leave well alone, didn't choose to comment on the 'mostly'. 'Will wonders never cease?' she teased. 'Do keep me posted, brother dear, or I'll be forced to interrogate Gran for the details.'

'Don't you dare!' Tristan grinned back at her. 'The last thing I need is the third degree from Gran about my love life.'

'Well, enjoy it while it's good,' Thea replied. She gave a melodramatic sigh. 'I remember those early days of hormones, hearts and flowers. How quickly they give way to dirty socks, farts and arguments over which brand of beans to buy!'

'Maybe if you'd agreed on the beans, things would have been different,' Tristan teased, and earned himself a swat with the tea towel Thea was using to dry off the mugs she'd rinsed. Tristan remembered to double check that she'd included a dishwasher on her list of appliances for her new house.

'Certainly would have helped with the farting!' she giggled. 'I wonder if I could have cited that as grounds for divorce, if Carl and I had ever bothered to tie the knot?'

'And on that cheerful, optimistic note, I'll leave you to it.' Tristan found himself still smiling as he walked to his car. Spending time with his sister never failed to cheer him up, and even though what she'd said about Lorelai was nagging at him, it had been nice to speak to her. He resolved, as he always did, to make this a more regular occurrence.

46

All the way home, Tristan pondered what Thea had said about Lorelai's strange behaviour. He couldn't just shrug it off. Perhaps it was the recent talk with Charlotte about unearthing information from historic sources that was unsettling him, but he kept turning things over in his head. Sighing, halfway back to his house, he pulled into a side road, turned the car around and headed back to Lower Brambleton. He knew he'd spend the evening worrying if he didn't swing by Nightshade Cottage, and if, as he hoped, Lorelai was fine, it would also be a good excuse to see if Charlotte was about. He wanted, he needed, to see her again. There was no point trying to dismiss what he was starting to feel for her. If anything, the discussions they'd had yesterday after that weird encounter with her ex had clarified his feelings for her. He wouldn't have been half so bothered by Todd if he hadn't been starting to fall for Charlotte. He'd loved spending time with her over the past few weeks, and he wanted to continue seeing her, even when she moved back to Bristol. He really hoped she was feeling the same way.

Pulling into the driveway, he noticed the light on in the

annexe, and his heart sped up. He'd definitely knock on the door later. He headed around the back of the house, trying to rehearse how to broach the subject with Lorelai. She could be the most easy-going person in the world, but when the mood took her, she could also be the most stubborn. She wouldn't take kindly to the suggestion that something was wrong with her memory, and he knew he'd have to handle things carefully.

Reaching the back door that led into the utility room, he paused and peered in. He wasn't sure what he was expecting to see. Lorelai was more likely to be settling down in her living room at this time of the evening. He'd intended to give a brisk knock of the door and then go in for a chat. What he saw, however, made him freeze in the act of knocking.

It was as if what Thea had told him was being rewound and replayed, right in front of his eyes. Lorelai was sitting at the kitchen table, with a huge, disorganised pile of paperwork in front of her, frantically rifling through it, and clearly looking for something. She looked agitated, and more stressed than he'd ever seen her. Observing her for a few seconds longer, Tristan's heart sank. Maybe Thea was right: it looked as though they did have cause for concern.

Gently, not wanting to startle her, he tapped on the window-pane. Lorelai glanced up, and as if a switch had been flipped, her expression changed when she saw him. He pushed open the utility room door and moved quickly into the room, before she could struggle out of the wooden kitchen chair.

'Hi, Gran,' he said gently. 'Don't get up.' He pulled out the chair next to her and sat down. 'What are you looking for?'

Lorelai gestured vaguely to the papers that were strewn over the table. 'Oh, nothing,' she said. 'I was just, er, just hoping to...' She trailed off in apparent confusion. 'It can wait. What can I do for you, my darling?' And there, behind the befuddlement, was his grandmother. Tristan fought an inexplicable urge to burst into tears. He had no idea how long she'd been sitting there, but there was no evidence of her having cooked dinner for herself, or any other signs that she'd been away from the kitchen table.

'I was just passing,' he said softly, 'and I thought I'd see how you were.'

Lorelai smiled knowingly. 'Making a duty visit to your grandmother before you pop next door to see her tenant?'

Tristan smiled back, feeling more reassured by Lorelai's tone. 'Perhaps.'

'Well, I'm sure Charlotte will be as pleased to see you as I am.' She reached forward to try to bundle up the papers, but as she did so, several of them fell onto the floor between herself and Tristan. 'Bugger,' she muttered, leaning down to retrieve them.

Tristan was swifter. He picked up the fallen documents and couldn't help but notice some very familiar handwriting on the one nearest to him; handwriting he hadn't seen for a long time.

'What is this, Gran?' he asked carefully. His eyes were drawn to the page he was holding, not just because it was so recognisable, but because the penmanship became sloppier the further down the page it went, as if the writer was in an increasing state of frustration. It was a section of a handwritten letter, but not the beginning of it, and Tristan's brow furrowed in confusion as he began to read.

'Just give it back to me, darling,' Lorelai said quietly, but there was an undercurrent of tension in her voice. 'It's something I should have binned years ago. That's all I was doing now when you came in. It's nothing important.'

Eyes glued to the page, Tristan ignored his grandmother. In mounting confusion, as the words he was reading began to sink in, he found he couldn't tear his eyes away. Eventually, he reached the bottom of the page and looked up.

'This is from Great-Uncle Philip,' he said softly. 'I recognise the handwriting. Who's it written to?'

Lorelai's silence extended between them. Impatiently, Tristan looked at her, willing her to answer.

'It's nothing,' Lorelai eventually insisted. 'Just an old love letter to a girlfriend, that's all. Give it back to me, there's a love.'

'I never knew Uncle Phil had a girlfriend. He kept that close to his chest.' Tristan gave a brief grin, which faded from his face when he saw the expression of unease on Lorelai's face. 'Gran... what aren't you telling me?' He glanced down at the rest of the papers he'd retrieved from the floor and saw the first page of the letter. Before his grandmother could snatch it back, he began to read. As he did so, the amusement that his uncle might have had a secret girlfriend morphed into something entirely different.

'Tristan...' Lorelai said again. 'Just give them back to me. They don't concern you.'

Impatiently, Tristan shook his head and continued reading. As he did so, his hands started to shake so badly, he nearly dropped the letter again.

'Darling,' Lorelai murmured. 'Let me try to explain...'

It was as if Lorelai's voice was light years away. Tristan's world had shrunk to the words on the page he was holding. The writing began to blur before his eyes as he read further, trying to stem the rush of emotions that threatened to overwhelm him.

'He was in love with Mum...' Tristan heard his own voice as if it was outside his own body. 'All those years, he was in love with her.' From the corner of his eye, he could see Lorelai nodding.

'Yes,' she said simply. 'Your mother was the only woman Philip ever loved.'

A terrible thought occurred to Tristan as the possible repercussions of what he was holding sunk in. 'Did she... did she ever feel the same way?' With a struggle, he raised his gaze to look Lorelai straight in the eye. He had to know she was being truthful.

Lorelai didn't hesitate when she shook her head. 'No. She never felt for him as he felt for her.' Lorelai tried to reach for the pages in his hand. 'Let me have those. It's all ancient history. An old man's desire for someone he knew he could never have.'

'Why didn't you tell us, Gran?' Tristan said. He could feel a pain in his throat that refused to go away, no matter how hard he swallowed. 'All those years that Uncle Philip kept his distance from us... and we couldn't work out why. Was it because of this?'

Lorelai nodded. 'Your mother was Uncle Philip's best and brightest student when she was at university. She was all set for a career in academia, under his tutelage, when she finished her postgraduate degree. Philip adored her, thought they'd make a wonderful research team. He'd never been in love before: he was forty years old when she came to work with him, and he fell for her, hook, line and sinker. Your mother was twenty-five.' She paused. 'Somehow, though, she always seemed to be the one who was wiser about the world. He'd spent his whole career in labs, in libraries, pursuing the abstract and chasing the unknown. He had very little idea about life outside his subject.'

Tristan nodded. The perception he'd had of his great-uncle tallied very much with Lorelai's account of him. The man had been so bound up with his research, with his books, that Tristan and Thea had always been slightly intimidated by him. When he'd come to live with Lorelai at the end of his life, he'd been a remote figure, and had shunned any attempts by the twins to get to know him better. 'So, what happened?'

'They'd secured some funding from the European Union to

extend the research she'd carried out for her doctorate. It wasn't quite enough, but Philip convinced Laura to stay on for the two years of the project – he assured her he'd find funding from other sources to make it work. Really, he just wanted to be with her, and the prospect of another two years' study with her was a great reason for him to keep pushing for the money. She even moved into his spare room – he was living in Redland in Bristol at the time – and they spent day and night together.' She paused, searching Tristan's face for a reaction before continuing. 'I suppose he thought that, eventually, with them both in such close quarters, she'd fall in love with him, too.'

'But that didn't happen.'

'No.' Lorelai sighed. 'You could say that it was written in the stars. Your father, who was a couple of years older than your mother, as you know, had graduated before she'd come to work in Philip's department. He'd been working at Greenwich Observatory since he'd graduated, but he wanted to get back into the research side of things. Being far more commercially minded than Uncle Philip, though, it was a means to an end – his goal was to go out into industry, eventually, and he saw a short-term placement at North Wessex as a good string to his bow to achieve that aim. He and Uncle Philip could never see eye to eye about that: Philip was an academic through and through: he lived for the intellectual challenge of discovery and research. Your father saw research as a means to an end, and his goal was to work for a corporation, at the cutting edge of commercial research, if he could. They often argued about the merits of their own paths. It was never an easy relationship.'

'So Dad came to work in Uncle Philip's lab?' Tristan let out a breath, feeling as though he was bracing himself for what he knew was inevitably coming.

'Yes. He was everything that Philip wasn't... charismatic,

confident, charming... your mother, of course, was smitten. Uncle Philip watched it all happen; observed the woman he adored falling in love with his own nephew, and he couldn't do anything to stop it.' Lorelai brushed at her eyes impatiently. 'When your parents decided to get married, it was the final straw for him. He cut off contact with them both, and with me, for a long time. By the time you and Thea were born, he'd retreated so far into his work that he was a virtual stranger to us all. As far as I know, he never told your mother how he felt but when he died, I was sorting through some of his old paperwork. That's when I found the letter. He obviously never sent it to her, but it was all there.'

'So Mum never knew?' Tristan asked. He was trying to keep a foot on the bottom of the pool, but the abrupt intersection of the past and present was sending him off balance. He'd spent most of his life trying to get away from the traumatic undercurrents of the past, and now it felt as though the waves were once again rising around him.

Lorelai smiled sadly. 'I have no idea. Your Uncle Philip was intensely private: rather like you, in fact. Played his cards very close to his chest for his whole life, never letting anyone in.'

Tristan winced at the comparison: his memories of his uncle were of a person who seemed embittered by experience, and reluctant to let anyone close to him. Was he, himself, really like that?

'The accident destroyed your uncle almost as much as it did the three of us,' Lorelai continued. 'But he could never talk about it. The maudlin side of me wonders if it was a broken heart that killed him, in the end. After your mother died, he just seemed to give up. By the time he came to live with me, he was damaged beyond repair.' Lorelai looked as though she was about to add more, but at the last moment she stopped herself.

This did not go unnoticed by Tristan. 'What aren't you telling me, Gran?'

'Nothing, darling,' Lorelai replied, a little too quickly. 'Heavens!' she then exclaimed, rising from the chair with a creak. 'I had no idea it was that far past dinner time. I'd better get something together. Did you want to stay for a bite?'

'Gran, please.' Tristan reached out a hand and covered one of Lorelai's, hoping to stay her progress before she started buzzing around the kitchen. 'I know when you're not being truthful with me. There's something else, isn't there?'

'Don't be daft!' Lorelai's smile looked forced, and Tristan became worryingly aware that he didn't know the whole story.

'Gran,' Tristan said, keeping his tone as gentle as he could. 'Whatever else you need to tell me, I'll understand. I promise you.' Mindful of his earlier conversation with Thea, and wanting as much clarity as he could get now, for fear of what might happen in the future if Lorelai really was in danger of losing her memory, he pushed again. 'You've always been there for me, and I want to be there for you now. You shouldn't have to keep things to yourself any longer.'

Drawing a deep breath, Lorelai's expression was bleaker than he'd ever seen it. He knew she was steeling herself to give him the final part of the puzzle. As she faced Tristan, and looked him straight in the eye, he felt the warning creak of Pandora's Box being fully opened, and for a moment, he wanted to slam the lid shut again.

'Tristan, my darling, darling boy,' she began. Tristan felt the warmth of her hand as it closed over one of his, and he braced himself for another revelation.

47

The rapping on the door that led out to the back garden made Charlotte start awake in shock. She'd been in a heavy doze on her sofa, having dropped off after she'd finished working for the evening in front of some unmemorable drama on Netflix. Heart racing, she struggled off the sofa. With a pang of concern, she wondered if Lorelai had locked herself out of her side of the house. As she moved, still half asleep, to the back door, she was doubly shocked to see not Lorelai, but Thea Ashcombe, an expression of worry etched on her face, getting rapidly soaked in the heavy downpour that had obviously started while she was asleep.

'Charlotte, I'm sorry to pop round so late,' Thea said. 'Can I come in for a sec?'

It was coming up to eleven o'clock, and the greyish-blue colours of the cloudy, rainy night sky were beginning to give way to a velvety blackness as the stars emerged. Orion, who always led Charlotte home, sparkled cold and brightly through a shawl of cloud like a signpost directly above Lorelai's garden, and the rising moon caught the blondish-brown hue of Thea's hair.

'Sure,' Charlotte replied, admitting Thea into the annexe. 'Is everything all right?'

Thea shook her head. 'Not really, no.' She began to fidget with a bracelet on her wrist, as if she was weighing up whether or not to tell Charlotte something.

'What's happened?' Charlotte asked. 'Is it Lorelai? Tristan?'

Thea took a deep breath, and Charlotte got the distinct impression she was trying not to cry. 'Gran called me about an hour ago, in a hell of a state.' She blinked rapidly. 'She and Tristan had a really difficult conversation earlier, about some family stuff. Tristan, well, Tristan doesn't handle things to do with the family very well and he was incredibly upset when he left her. I was hoping he might have come straight around to you...' She trailed off, hope flaring in her eyes. 'Is he here?'

Charlotte shook her head. 'No. I haven't seen him. I didn't even hear his car earlier, but then I was wearing noise-cancelling earbuds while I was working, so I may have missed him.'

Thea looked downcast. 'I've got that Life 360 app, and so has Tris. He likes to keep track of me and the kids, and he even persuaded Gran to get it on her phone, although that's no help when she forgets to take it out with her. He definitely tracked here about four hours ago, but then he went off grid. It can drop in and out round here because the signal's so crap, but something feels off. I've been trying to call him but his phone's just going to voicemail. I'm starting to get really worried, Charlotte. Gran told me what she'd told Tristan, and from the way he reacted, he's in no state to be on his own.'

Charlotte's heart began to beat a little faster. She desperately wanted to know what the revelation was that might have set Tristan off, but she didn't want to pry.

'Look,' Thea continued, 'I know it's a lot to ask, but if he gets in touch, please can you call me? I just want to check in and make sure he's OK.'

'Why wouldn't he be?' Charlotte asked.

'He can be very, very good at falling down mental rabbit holes, and I just want to make sure he's not tripped into one after talking to Gran.'

'Why would he have done that?' Charlotte asked. 'Thea... you can tell me to bugger off if you want, but it might be useful if you told me what it was that you think might have upset him.'

Thea paused for a long few beats before she answered. 'Tris told me that you've been chasing down some information about Mum and Dad, haven't you? To do with their time at the observatory?'

'That's right,' Charlotte said. She hesitated before adding, 'That's kind of what Tristan and I were talking about yesterday. He wasn't completely at ease with me trying to gather the facts about a discovery they may have made.'

'When I popped in to see Gran earlier, she was looking through some paperwork of her own. Personal stuff that belonged to Great-Uncle Philip – Philip Porter, Gran's younger brother. He was a professor of astronomy back in the day, and he and Gran owned the observatory site after they inherited it from their father.'

A faint spark of recognition flared in Charlotte's mind when she heard the name. Could Philip Porter have been the 'PP' in the notes from the first recording of Volucris by the Ashcombes in 1994? 'Lorelai told me she was the one who sold the site to the developer after her brother died. Tristan mentioned that your great-uncle was an astronomer, but he gave me the impression it was more of a hobby for him than a profession. I had no idea he was an academic.'

'Yeah,' Thea replied. 'He never really spoke much about it

after he retired.' She gave a nervous laugh. 'He didn't speak to us much, in fact. He wasn't interested in the family, and even after Mum and Dad died, he didn't offer Gran any help when we were growing up.'

Charlotte felt a pang of sympathy for the woman in front of her. The support and love of a family was what both Tristan and Thea had so desperately needed after the death of their parents, and she couldn't imagine what it would have been like to know that another member of that family was so uninterested in them.

'I'm so sorry, Thea,' Charlotte said gently.

'I know,' Thea said sadly. 'But what's worrying me now is where Tristan's gone. Gran, er, Gran tried to stop him from leaving but he bolted out of the door, and he was in no state to be driving. I have to find him, Charlotte. If you have any idea where he might be, please tell me.'

'I don't mean to pry, Thea, but if you are able to tell me what Lorelai said before he left, it might help us to find him.'

Thea's eyes glistened with tears, and she blinked them furiously away. 'Gran was getting rid of some papers, as I said. One of them was a letter from Great-Uncle Philip. Tristan read it before Gran could stop him. It was a love letter. To our mother.'

'Oh, God,' Charlotte breathed. 'Did they? I mean, were they...?'

Thea shook her head. 'No. It was unrequited. But it explains a hell of a lot about why Uncle Philip kept his distance from us. He worked with Mum for years, they were close, and then Dad came to work at the same lab. The rest is history.'

'And you never knew?'

'No. Gran kept it a secret. I suppose she didn't see the point in giving us any more emotional baggage.' She gave a short, nervous laugh. 'I mean, it's not like we didn't have enough already.'

'She seems like the kind of person who'd want to protect you as much as she could,' Charlotte said gently. 'She obviously loves you both very much.'

Thea looked thoughtful. 'She says that even she didn't know until she was going through Uncle Philip's papers after his death.' Thea bit her lip: the conversation with Lorelai had been distressing. 'She's really upset, but I've told her to go to bed. She'll probably ignore me. Thankfully, the kids are both at sleepovers tonight so I can get out there and see if I can find Tris.'

'Is that wise?' Charlotte asked. 'It's bucketing down out there, and these roads are dangerous enough in the dark. I'm sure he's fine and his phone'll just blip back on when he hits a decent spot.' Even as she said it, she knew Tristan's sister wasn't going to listen to her. She, herself, wouldn't have.

'I'll be all right. To be honest, I'm not worried about driving in the rain. But I *am* worried about Tristan, and what finding all of this out might have done to him.' Her eyes glistened, and Charlotte could see that she needed a few seconds before she spoke again. 'After Mum and Dad died, I talked to everyone and anyone the bereavement charity who supported us could give me. I wasn't going to let this awful thing dominate my life. And although it still hurts like nothing else I've ever experienced, I've learned to walk alongside that pain: to live my life in a way that allows me to think about them, and how much they'd have loved to have seen me grow up, to meet my own children. It's never easy, but I think it's been healthy, for the most part.' She paused.

'Go on,' Charlotte replied. She got the feeling that Thea felt as though she was breaking a confidence by talking about Tristan to someone who was only in the early days of a relationship with him, but circumstances seemed to make it necessary.

'Tristan wasn't the same,' Thea said flatly. 'He refused to talk to anyone, no matter how hard Gran or I tried to persuade him. He sat in the room with the counsellors, but he wouldn't say a word. He talked to me, of course, but we had both experienced the same thing: we became our own echo chamber. What he needed, more than anything, was an outside perspective. But he ploughed himself into his studies, into his social life, into everything he could to try to blot out the pain of our loss. And to a point it worked. What he's achieved has been extraordinary. He's the youngest project manager in his field. But it came at an emotional cost. He repressed everything to do with our parents' death. He never looks back, and he never lets anyone get close to him.' Thea leaned against the wall. 'Gran and I have always worried that one day he'd crack, and when he told us he was going to manage Observatory Field, we were even more concerned. He's the perfect person to do it, because he knows how to create beautiful, sustainable places, but he's also the worst because of how bound up in its history he is. He jumped through the hoops, satisfied everyone he could do it without any kind of conflict of interest, and now everything's signed and sealed, it looks as though he's almost made it.'

'Almost?' Charlotte queried.

Thea took out her phone again. 'I wasn't being completely honest with you when I said I hadn't heard from him.' She fiddled around with her phone until she found her voicemail. The reception was terrible, and the caller had obviously been driving when the call was made as the engine sounded loud and familiar. But overlaid against the engine noise and the sound of the rain hitting the windscreen and the car roof was another unmistakeable sound: the heartbreaking sound of someone sobbing.

'Oh my God,' Charlotte breathed. 'He sounds absolutely broken.'

Thea nodded, and this time she couldn't stop the tears falling, even as she wiped them away. 'I'm sorry,' she said quietly. 'It's so awful, hearing him like this.'

Charlotte put an arm around Thea, but as she did, Thea spoke again. 'Gran didn't just show Tristan Uncle Philip's letter,' she said. 'She also told him that...'

'That what?'

'That the night our parents had the car crash, Uncle Philip was up at the observatory with Mum and Dad.'

Charlotte's stomach turned over. 'Was he in the car with them?'

Thea shook her head. 'No. He'd walked up through the woods to the observatory. Gran remembers him turning up here late, drunk, and passing out in her spare room, in no state to drive back to his house in Bristol. The morning after, when he found out what had happened to Mum and Dad, he left here and she didn't see him again for months.' She gave a sniff. 'He didn't even come to the funeral.'

'Why did he go up there?'

'No one knows. Perhaps he finally snapped and had to tell Mum how he felt about her, although by that point I've no idea why he thought it would change anything. Maybe it was something else. Who knows?' Thea glanced at Charlotte. 'Maybe there's something in the observatory archives that could shed some light on it all.'

Charlotte's mind began to tick, and even though her immediate worry was Tristan and his whereabouts, there was a thought tapping in her brain that wouldn't go away. 'Thea,' she said tentatively, 'your great-uncle's initials were next to the notes your mum and dad made about a discovery they were documenting a couple of months before they died.'

'So?'

'You said that Lorelai mentioned your great-uncle was up at the observatory the night your parents had their accident. Could it be that he was trying to help them with their discovery?'

'Possibly,' Thea shrugged. 'But relations were so bad by then between him and Mum and Dad, I don't see why he'd put himself out to help them.' She shook her head in frustration. 'To be honest, I couldn't care less about that right now. I just want to find Tristan.'

Charlotte nodded. 'You're right. I'm sorry. It'll keep.' Now wasn't the time to be thinking about the whys and wherefores of a past tragedy: the focus was to try to avert another one. 'When I get back to the university archive, I can take a look,' she said. 'But right now I think our main priority has to be finding Tristan.'

48

Charlotte shook her head in frustration. Why hadn't she saved up and tried to buy a car? She felt hopeless, useless. 'Tell me what I can do.'

'I'll drive from here towards Tristan's house,' Thea said. 'His Audi's pretty distinctive, and if he's had a shunt on the way home, I'm sure I'll spot it. If the signal comes back on his phone, it should be easy to track him via the app, as well.' Thea looked intently at Charlotte, and Charlotte could see how much Thea was hoping for a positive outcome. 'I've never heard him sound like that,' she said quietly. 'He's bottled everything up, for our whole lives. If the dam's broken now...'

Charlotte reached out and put a hand on Thea's forearm. 'We'll find him,' she said. 'You know him better than anyone. Where could he be?'

Thea sighed and regarded Charlotte with a gaze that suggested she was weighing up whether or not to tell her something. Eventually, she spoke. 'When Tristan was a teenager, he disappeared for three days. It was shortly after Gran had had yet another blazing row with Great-Uncle Phil over the future of the observatory. He overheard them arguing about what should happen to it late one night, and when I'd gone to bed, he walked out of the house and vanished.'

'Oh my God,' Charlotte breathed. 'Where did he go?'

'He never told us. Honestly, I don't think he had much memory of it. We searched high and low, and there was no sign of him. Then, three days later he walked back into the kitchen, kissed Gran on the cheek and went to bed for twenty-four hours. He never told me or Gran where he'd been or what he'd done in that time. But something must have triggered in his brain to make him leave that night.' Thea ran a slightly shaky hand over her face. 'When someone you love does something like that, it doesn't matter how many years later it is, you are always on your guard that the same thing might happen again.'

'He was in his car, this time, though,' Charlotte said. 'And we know he wasn't in a good state. He could have gone a lot further. What if he's in a trauma loop and doesn't know what he's doing?'

Thea's face paled as she digested that possibility. So much so that Charlotte had to reassure her. 'But even with that voicemail, it doesn't mean that's the case.'

'I hope you're right,' Thea replied. She shook her head. 'I'm going to go up to the observatory as well and check it out. It's dark, but I might be able to spot his car.'

'Hold on,' Charlotte said as Thea made to open the door and leave. 'I know the observatory better than most. I've been working up there for weeks, after all.'

'Are you sure?' Thea asked. 'It's a lot to ask of you, and the site's dangerous in the dark.'

'I'm not going to get any sleep tonight, anyway,' Charlotte replied. 'And I'm used to working at night.' She glanced out of the window. 'Looks as though the rain's not going to stop any time soon. I'd better grab a coat.'

The two of them, with Comet in tow, headed out to Thea's car. As they drove quickly through the lanes to Observatory Field, neither said much. They didn't want to voice their hopes or fears about what they might find. Thea sped as fast as the old car could take them on the hardcore access road to the site, but Charlotte knew she was as disappointed as she was to see no sign of Tristan's Audi parked anywhere.

'Looks like I was wrong,' Thea said, her voice shaking. 'God, Charlotte. What if he *has* had an accident somewhere?' She brushed away sudden tears, and Charlotte's heart ached for her.

'I'm sure he's fine,' Charlotte replied. She turned to Thea. 'Look, it's almost longer for you to drive back to Lorelai's than it is for me to walk. Let me out here. I'll have a quick scout around and I'll let you know if I find anything.'

'Are you sure?' Thea asked. 'The weather's still bloody awful.'

'I've never minded the rain,' Charlotte replied. 'And Comet loves splashing about in puddles. Honestly, we'll be fine.'

'All right, but keep me posted,' Thea said as Charlotte went to open the passenger door. 'If you spot anything that might help locate Tris, though, let me know. I don't care how late it is. I'll drive back in the direction of Tristan's house, and I'll call you if I find him.'

'OK,' Charlotte said. They swapped phone numbers and then Charlotte gave Thea a quick hug. 'One of us is bound to find him.' Hurrying out of the car, she opened the boot of Thea's ancient Volvo estate and let Comet out. 'Come on, old chap,' she said. 'We're going to form a search party.'

49

The warm, swiftly soaking summer rain began to fall harder as Charlotte and Comet strode across the flattened earth that formed the Observatory Field development site. Her work was done, and in a few days the building that housed over a hundred years of astronomical observations would be wiped out of existence. Charlotte had only been here a few weeks and the sense of history in the place, enwrapped by the decay of years of neglect, had permeated her thoughts and emotions. She couldn't even imagine what might be happening inside Tristan's head.

The rain was getting heavier. That, combined with the now-fallen darkness, was making it even harder to see. Struggling to get her phone out of her pocket, Charlotte pressed the torch icon and pointed it a few yards in front of her. She approached the Portakabin but a quick rattle of the handle demonstrated that it was still locked. Undeterred, she peered in through the window of the temporary structure, but all looked neat, tidy and undisturbed. There was no sign that Tristan had returned here. It hit her, as hard as the rain was pounding the hood of her jacket, just how heavy the weight he'd been carrying with him his whole life was. Their paths had intersected at a crucial time for him, and now she was being pulled into his traumatic orbit, and that of his family's history. She had the feeling that tonight he'd reached a tipping point.

'Tristan!' Charlotte's voice was lost to the driving rain as she dashed from the Portakabin across the scarred and flattened width of the levelled land in a desperate, soaking wet search.

Not a sound came back to her.

The rain lashed down on her back as she stomped across the ground which was starting to run with mud and rivulets of water in the ferocity of the summer storm. Comet bounded ahead, sniffing, zigzagging in the rain and then coming back to her to check in. His fur was soaked, but he didn't seem to mind too much. The air was still warm, and as a threatening rumble of thunder rolled overhead, Charlotte's heart sped up. She'd heard too many stories about people being struck by lightning at the top of hills to feel anything other than panic at being out here in the middle of a storm.

Shouting Tristan's name again, Charlotte shook her head, feeling her sodden hair thrashing her face in rats' tails as she did. She *had* to find him. She didn't know why, but she had a gut feeling he was here. She was making progress towards the observatory building now. Luckily, she still had the keys to the padlock, so she dug in her coat pocket to find them. As she did, her phone began to ring. Whipping it out of her other pocket, she saw Thea's name flashing up onscreen.

'Thea? What is it? Has he been in touch with you?'

It was a minute before she could make out what Thea was saying. The wind and the rain were deafening, the reception was intermittent and Thea's voice was breaking up.

'Charlotte? C-can you hear me? I've just found Tristan's car...'

Oh, shit. Charlotte's knees went so weak she nearly fell onto the muddy earth. 'Wh-what?' she stammered. 'Where is it? Is he OK? Are *you* OK?'

Thea clearly wasn't. She was struggling to speak, choking on the words. 'It's slipped off the side of the road. He must have misjudged a corner. The car's at an angle in the rhyne.' Thea's voice broke up on the other end of the line, but Charlotte could just about catch what she was saying.

'Is he still in the car, Thea? Can you see him?'

An agonising moment passed as Thea's signal dropped out again. Charlotte cursed out loud, but her voice was whipped away by the rising wind. It was still horribly humid, despite the rain, but the atmosphere was crackling with pent-up energy, and as a second rumble of thunder rolled over her head, she knew she was standing in the path of the mother of all Somerset summer storms. Charlotte punched out Thea's number, willing her phone to reconnect, but it cut straight to voicemail.

Then she noticed Comet had scampered off. Damned dog! That was the last thing she needed. His recall had been much better since they'd been living in the countryside, but he'd picked the worst possible moment to go AWOL. The rain was growing heavier, and there was a nasty mist drifting in from the hillside that Charlotte didn't like the look of, either. The second Comet came back to her, he was bloody well going on his lead.

'Comet!' she yelled across the wide expanse of the building site. Where had he got to? She shone her phone's torch in a wide arc around herself, trying to make out the dark shape of a mostly black spaniel against the midnight-black sky and land. 'Comet! Come here, boy!'

Nothing. And she still couldn't get hold of Thea. If Tristan was in the car, then she'd turn tail and get back down the hill.

She prayed he wasn't hurt. Should she call an ambulance? *How?* she reminded herself. *I've got no bloody signal!*

She walked as briskly as she could towards the observatory building. Comet had to be around here somewhere. The rest of the area was flat and provided little cover for an inquisitive dog. He had to have headed towards the building he knew so well. 'Comet!' she yelled again.

As she approached the observatory, she could see that the chain that housed the padlock was on the muddy ground, and the gate was skewed open. Someone had been up here tonight. Perhaps was still here. Pushing through the gate, she shouted again and was rewarded with a distant bark.

'Comet! Come here!' she shouted, not in the mood for games.

The bark came again, but it was clear, this time, that he wasn't sniffing around outside. Flashing her phone torch at the door of the observatory, she saw it had been left ajar. Vowing to keep trying Thea's number the second she had Comet back on the lead, she pushed open the door and called out again.

The electricity had finally been disconnected earlier in the week, and the only source of light Charlotte had was her rapidly diminishing phone torch. Glancing at it, she realised that the battery wasn't going to last very long. Without the stark glare of the strip lights overhead that she'd taken for granted while she was working there, the observatory felt haunted by the ghosts of all of the people who'd passed through. Charlotte shivered, despite the humidity. She'd never minded being alone up here when she was working, but now it seemed to reek of something maudlin. It felt like being in a tomb.

'Comet!' she called again and was unsurprised to hear the tremor in her voice. The creaks and rattles of a building destined for demolition seemed to creep into her mind, making her pulse race and her palms sweat with every passing second. She needed to get out of here, before she started catastrophising about the injuries she could do herself on an uneven floor in the pitch black in a condemned building in the middle of a thunderstorm.

Finally, an answering bark made her jump out of her skin. Pointing her phone in the direction of the bark, she raised it slightly to follow the direction of the stairs that led to the platform that had once housed the observatory's prized telescope. Brian O'Connor had warned her, back on her first day at work, not to go up those stairs, and she'd heeded that warning rigidly all the time she'd been working here.

But now, as Charlotte tracked her torch upwards, she knew that this time she'd be ignoring Brian's advice to avoid the gantry. The metal gate that had been put in place to stop anyone going up was at a strange angle on the staircase, as if something or someone had pushed their way through. The thunder, right overhead now, growled menacingly, and a brilliant flash of lightning infiltrated the cracks in the observatory's dome, poking long fingers of light through the building, as if it was reaching out to claim her. Panning her torch light around the area at the top of the stairs, between the viewing platform and the dome, she called Comet's name again.

It was no good: she'd have to get up there. The dog had clearly got spooked and scuttled to the top level of the building. That was definitely where the barking was coming from, and as she strained her eyes in the diminishing light of her phone's torch, she thought she caught sight of a soggy black tail wagging in the darkness. It was enough to harden her resolve. She began to ascend the steps, testing the weight of each one gingerly before she put a foot fully down. She huffed out a breath as she painstakingly made progress towards the platform. With one hand gripping the handrail, and the other clutching her phone, she moved further upwards, praying the structure wouldn't give way beneath her.

'When I get you home, I'm going to give you such a talking to!' she muttered, feeling the adrenaline prickling over her skin as, with the next step, the staircase gave an alarming creak. What the hell was she doing?

Just as she was about to give up and head back down, what was left of her bravery having been virtually shredded by the careful ascent up to the viewing platform, she caught a more definite glimpse of a dark, wriggling mass of sodden fur at the far side of the structure. There, about thirty feet away on the curve, was Comet. And the little spaniel with the white star on his chest wasn't alone. Huddled against a recess in the wall, knees drawn up to his chest, was Tristan.

50

'Oh, thank God!' Charlotte breathed, trying to stop her hands from shaking. Her nerves were already shot to pieces, but the sight of Comet and Tristan sent her senses into overdrive. How had he ended up here, when his Audi was in a rhyne a mile away? And why the hell did it have to be in the most dangerous part of the site that she, or rather Comet, had found him?

'Tristan?' she said softly. 'Tristan? Can you hear me?'

The figure thirty feet away on the gantry that was curving away from her in the gentle swirl of the circular dome didn't respond, although, she reasoned, he must have heard her shouting for Comet, who was now nosing Tristan's huddled form in concern and mild annoyance that he couldn't raise even a pat from him.

Charlotte's heart sank. She knew she was going to have to make her way over to Tristan, and try to rouse him, try to get him off this blasted platform. The floor underfoot was spongy and damp, neither great signifiers of the safety of the wooden boards. The handrail that ran around the platform was in varying stages of rust, the white paint having flaked off almost entirely and, as Charlotte put out a hand to grip it, terrifyingly unstable. She rapidly withdrew her hand again. The rail up the stairs had felt more secure, but it would be safer not to trust it now she was at the top.

'Come on,' she said to herself. She had no idea if the platform would take the combined weight of two people, but what choice did she have? Thea was unreachable at the moment, and in the absence of Tristan's sister she might be the only person who could talk Tristan down off the ledge.

Step by step, testing the rotten floor before she put her full weight on it, she carefully began to close the gap between herself and Tristan. Her legs were trembling from the adrenaline that was coursing through her body, and she found herself counting each breath as she inhaled and exhaled. She'd been terrified when she'd done a high ropes challenge on a friend's hen weekend at Longleat: this felt infinitely scarier, thirty feet in the air without the aid of a safety harness and a hard hat. Trying to push those thoughts away, she continued moving, hoping with each step that Tristan would raise his head and acknowledge her presence. With every passing second, she grew more and more concerned for him.

'Tristan,' she said softly. 'Tristan, can you hear me?'

Still nothing. Charlotte moved a couple more steps forward. She was now only about twelve feet away from the huddled figure in the alcove. Another clap of thunder warned her the storm wasn't abating any time soon. As the lightning swiftly followed, she took a few deep breaths to stop herself from hyperventilating. Having a panic attack right now would be the icing on the proverbial cake.

'I'm coming towards you,' she said gently, hoping that the sound of her voice might elicit some kind of response from Tristan, whose head was still buried in his knees. 'If you can hear me, try to let me know.'

No response. She was about eight feet from him now. Edging closer, she jumped as her phone rang. Scrabbling to answer it, seeing it was Thea, she prayed the reception, and her battery, would hold out so she could tell Tristan's sister that she'd found him.

'I'm with him,' she said as Thea began to speak. 'We're at the observatory. Yes, please, as soon as you can.' She glanced at Tristan, who still showed no signs of having heard her. 'He's, er, he doesn't seem to be in a good way. No, not hurt, but we're inside the observatory on the viewing platform.'

Charlotte ended the call, hoping Thea had picked up enough of what she'd said to make her way back to Observatory Field. She was so busy trying to put her torch back on that she didn't notice the appallingly rotten board she'd stepped on. As her foot went through with a sloppy, crashing groan of aged timber, she screamed. Her phone dropped out of her hand, bounced and tumbled to the ground floor of the observatory, its light extinguishing as it smashed apart on the concrete floor thirty feet beneath.

Comet gave a surprised and concerned bark, and Charlotte called out in fear. Her heart was hammering in her chest as she found herself with one foot dangling beneath the platform, the other knee forced into a bend only inches from the rest of the rotten board. Tears of pure terror streamed down her cheeks as she tried to pull herself back up, but she was too afraid to put too much weight on the boards around her, which had been weakened by the collapse of the one she'd stepped on.

'Tristan!' she yelled again. 'For Christ's sake, help me!'

For a long, agonising moment that to Charlotte felt like years, he remained still and uncommunicative. This is it, she thought. I'm going to break my neck falling from this bloody gantry, and my name will be added to the tragedy of the observatory, just in time for it all to be knocked down. Why the fuck hadn't she just stayed put at Nightshade Cottage? Why had she come out here on some godforsaken heroic journey just to find a man who could do what he wanted? This was not how she wanted it to end. If Tristan needed to be here, that was his business, not hers. Why hadn't she just waited for him to come back to her in his own time? This had been a fool's errand, and one that now seemed to be the stupidest, most dangerous errand of her life.

And then, as Tristan finally raised his head from his knees and, as the lightning flared once more, her eyes, in that split second of illumination, locked with his and she knew exactly why she'd done it. It had been stealing up on her, like the quiet emergence of Arcturus in the velvet darkness of the summer night sky, and, like Orion, the brighter companion, it had come to guide her home. 'I love you!' she yelled across the eight-foot gap between them. 'I bloody love you, Tristan Ashcombe, and if you don't come and get me out of this hole, I'm never going to be able to tell you that again!'

51

Tristan didn't know how long he'd been sitting at the top of the viewing platform. He didn't even know how he'd got there. The last thing he could remember was climbing through the woods to the observatory, having abandoned his car after it had slipped off the road in the rainstorm.

Lorelai had tried to stop him from leaving Nightshade Cottage, but he'd had to get out of there, put as much distance between himself and the memories that had suddenly confronted him after they'd spoken. 'Tristan, we need to talk about this,' she'd said to him, but he couldn't. They'd never really discussed what had happened the night his parents were killed on the road by the observatory, and that, combined with the knowledge that Great-Uncle Philip might have been the trigger for the tragedy, was enough of a push for him to have to get away. Why had his uncle been at the observatory on a freezing cold January night, and what had been said between Philip and his parents? He could go around in circles forever trying to work it all out, but, in truth, he'd never know. Had Philip finally told Tristan's mother how he felt about her? Or was it something to do with the discovery his parents had made, that binary star? It felt impossible to escape what was in his own head. 'No,' he'd kept muttering. 'No, it's not like that. It can't be like that...'

All he knew now was that, through the fog of his own thoughts, through the barriers he'd erected to keep the outside world at bay, something had slowly, painfully brought him back to the present. It took a few moments for him to re-associate with the moment, to get out of the maelstrom of his own thoughts and emotions, but as the fog began to clear, he became aware of Charlotte's terrified voice. His eyes met hers across the short distance between them, and then the darkness fell again, as the lightning disappeared with the flip of an atmospheric switch. It was enough, though. Charlotte was in terrible danger, and he knew he had to do something to try to help.

'For fuck's sake!' she was screaming at him. 'Did you not hear what I just said? Tristan, help me, please!'

It was the uncharacteristic swearing as much as the declaration of love that brought him back. The storm was right over their heads, and another sheet of lightning lit up her pale face, and showed her caught in the rotten wood of the platform, likely to fall through at any moment.

'What are you doing here?' he shouted, raising himself from the sitting position he'd been stuck in for God knew how long. His knees told him it had been a while.

'What do you bloody think?' Charlotte was almost snarling with fear now, and Tristan knew he had to make his next moves extremely carefully indeed, or he was at risk of both of them hurtling to the ground, and Comet, too. The little dog was looking frantically from him to Charlotte, clearly unsure which way to run.

'I'm coming over,' he said as calmly as he could. 'Try not to move.'

'I don't plan to,' Charlotte hissed. Her gaze shifted from Tristan to Comet. 'Stay, boy,' she commanded.

Tristan gave a smile. 'I said I was coming over.'

'Not funny!'

The only light he had was the flashes from the storm, but it would have to be enough. Carefully, he edged towards Charlotte. There was one way off the platform, and it was the way they'd both climbed up. If the floor gave way... he tried not to think about it.

'Charlotte? Tristan? Are you there?' Tristan froze as Thea's voice echoed up from the ground floor.

'We're up here,' Tristan called back. 'Have you got a torch?'

'I brought the one from my emergency kit in the car,' Thea replied.

A sickening creak from the board underneath Charlotte's knee made her cry out. It was a sound that was beyond even fear, and Tristan knew there wasn't a lot of time.

'Thea, can you call Comet down to you?'

'I can try,' Thea replied, and then she called the dog's name. For a few seconds, Comet looked in bemusement from Tristan to Charlotte and then back again.

'Go on, boy,' Charlotte said. 'Go and find Thea.'

Giving them both a last glance, and clearly finding the atmosphere as scary and unnerving as they did, Comet scuttled past Tristan, somehow dodged his way to one side of Charlotte and scampered down the rickety staircase.

'He's with me,' Thea called.

Tristan's shoulders relaxed a fraction. 'Keep hold of him,' he said. 'And point that torch up here. Charlotte's gone through the floor.'

'Shit!' Thea aimed a shaky torch beam at the gantry and, in her haste, dazzled Tristan with the LED bulb.

'Not in my eyes,' snapped Tristan.

'Sorry,' Thea replied. Tristan looked at the rotting wood of the platform as Thea adjusted where she was pointing.

'I'm going to come to you,' Tristan said gently to Charlotte. 'I'm going to move very slowly. Try not to make any sudden movements yourself. We're going to get down those steps together.'

After hours of swirling numbness in his mind, he now felt complete clarity. There was one thing he needed to do, and that was get Charlotte back on the ground. Step by slow step, foot by foot, he moved carefully back towards her. At four feet away, the wood splintered and squelched beneath his left boot. He drew in a sharp breath and tried to stop the trembling that was making his whole body shake.

'All right?' Charlotte called out to him. She hadn't taken her eyes off him since he'd stood up.

'Yeah,' he murmured. 'Just got to be careful.'

'You're telling me!' Charlotte gave a nervous and slightly hysterical laugh.

Thea was tracking the torchlight along the floor of the gantry, lighting up a path to lead Tristan to safety. His gaze flickered between Charlotte and the path, and he suddenly felt an incredible gratitude for these two women in his life, who'd found him and brought him back from the brink of something terrible. But there would be plenty of time later to think about that. Focusing back on the immediate task at hand, he moved forward again.

Three feet. Charlotte was almost within touching distance.

'Nearly there,' he said, trying to project a calm he didn't feel.

He had no idea if the area she was stuck in would bear his weight as well as hers. 'Keep still. I'm coming.'

Two feet, and another crack of thunder made them both jump. The lightning flared, and he was progressing forward again.

'When I get to you, I'm going to move around and behind you,' he said. 'Don't try to grab hold of me until I'm on the other side. I think that's the best chance I've got of pulling you out without the floor disintegrating under both of us.'

'All right,' Charlotte said. Her face was so pale it looked almost green in the stark light of Thea's torch, and Tristan desperately wanted to rush to her, and hold her in his arms. But he couldn't risk it. He had to stick to his plan. 'But hurry... please.'

Tristan nodded. 'It'll be all over soon, I promise.'

He was a foot away, and he called down to Thea again. 'Shine the light on Charlotte, but keep it low. I need to see how stable the boards are around her.'

'Got that,' Thea confirmed, and then did as Tristan asked. 'OK?'

'Perfect.' Gingerly, Tristan edged around the gap that held Charlotte captive. He reached out to the handrail, but it gave an alarming wobble, so he let go again. He moved slowly, inch by inch, trying not to dislodge any more of the wood.

'Nearly there,' he murmured. He looked down to see the top of Charlotte's head, her hair plastered to her scalp, and the back of her neck looking pale and vulnerable in the torchlight. He took another step, until he was round Charlotte and nearly onto the more stable area of the platform.

A warning creak from the aged wood made them both gasp.

'Why the fuck didn't they take this down years ago?' Tristan muttered, standing stock still, trying to work out which step to take next.

'Bit late to be asking that now,' Charlotte said, but there was no hiding her terror.

'OK,' Tristan said, committing himself to one of two last steps that would enable him to get a more secure foothold and hopefully pull Charlotte to safety. 'I'm going to turn around now, and then I'll—'

A loud, sickening crack cut him off mid-sentence, and as Thea's torchlight wobbled erratically around them, another part of the gantry gave way. There was a scream, a crash and a frantic-sounding bark, and then everything was silent.

52

'It's all right. It's all right, I'm here. We're safe...'

Charlotte could hear the words, but she couldn't respond to them. She couldn't do anything except cling to Tristan, as adrenaline flooded her body and she trembled in his arms. She felt Tristan shaking as uncontrollably as she was: the past few minutes had been terrifying for them both.

The gantry where Charlotte had been caught had fallen away just seconds after Tristan had pulled her to safety. It had been one of those moments that had simultaneously slowed down and sped up, until Charlotte couldn't be sure what it was that she'd experienced. As Tristan had stepped around her, there had been a warning groan, and in the moments before the walkway fell thirty feet to the ground floor, Tristan had reached out and pulled Charlotte out of the broken floor with such force, her release had sent them both hurtling backwards. Fortunately, the top of the staircase, sheltered somewhat by the lip of the dome, was less rotten than the rest of the viewing platform, and as they'd hit the deck, Charlotte knocking the wind out of Tristan on impact, they'd instinctively clung together.

Now, they sat at the top of the stairs, waiting for the trembling to subside enough to find their way back down.

'Tristan! Charlotte!' Thea's frantic voice echoed through the air, making them both jump again. 'Are you all right? Can you hear me? Are you hurt?'

Tristan cleared his throat, and Charlotte could tell he didn't want to betray how scared he was to his very worried sister. 'We're good,' he managed. 'We're coming down.' He glanced down at Charlotte, who was still clinging to him, unwilling to let go. 'Are you all right to move?'

Charlotte nodded. She didn't want to speak. She was afraid if she opened her mouth too soon, she'd begin to scream. She couldn't process what had just happened, and now she was the one who felt detached from reality.

'Charlotte?' Tristan was saying her name softly, gently, and as if there was no one else in the world to hear him. 'Please. Say something. I'm not going to let us move from here until you do.'

Charlotte looked up at him again, and as her eyes met his, she felt the adrenaline starting to subside. His blue-green eyes were so full of love, so open that for a few seconds she forgot all about the seemingly disassociated state she'd found him in at the top of the gantry.

'Are you all right?' she said eventually. 'When you were up there, with Comet, it was like I couldn't reach you. You didn't seem to be there.'

Tristan's expression clouded briefly. 'It's not something I've ever really discussed,' he said. He wrapped his arms more tightly around her. 'But if you want to, we can talk about it when we get off this bloody staircase!'

Charlotte felt the nervous rumble of laughter in Tristan's chest. She nodded. 'I think that would be a great idea. Two great ideas, talking and getting down from here.'

Carefully, they stood up, which was tricky since neither was prepared to let go of the other. But they made it to a standing position, and then began the nerve-racking descent down the rickety wooden staircase.

'Sis?' Tristan called before they put the first foot forward. 'Can you shine the light on the stairs?'

'Absolutely!' Thea replied, and her guiding light moved just ahead of them. Slowly but surely, step by step, somehow keeping hold of each other in the process, they arrived on the ground again.

'Thank God you're OK!' Thea exclaimed, putting the torch down carefully on the concrete floor before engulfing first Tristan, and then Charlotte, in a hug. 'I thought I'd lost you both when the platform gave way.'

'No such luck.' Tristan's voice was muffled in another hug. 'Takes a lot more than that to get rid of me.'

Charlotte, who still had an arm around Tristan, watched as a hundred different emotions passed over Thea's face.

'You stupid wanker!' Thea's voice, raised in fear and frustration, betrayed how terrified she'd been. 'Why the fuck did you go up there? Do you have any idea how worried we've been about you?' Thea's voice broke, and tears started coursing down her face. 'I thought I'd lost you, Tris. I was so scared…'

Charlotte moved carefully away from the twins as Tristan gently disentangled himself from her and took Thea in his arms. Pulling her close, he wrapped his arms around her, stroking her hair and speaking gently, trying to calm her down. It was painfully clear that Thea had been worried sick, terrified that she was going to lose her brother as well as her parents, and the dam she'd been holding together for the sake of Lorelai and her own children had broken at that thought.

'It's all right. I'd never leave you, Gran and the kids.' Charlotte could hear Tristan's low reassurances as she knelt down and gave Comet a huge hug. The little dog looked both delighted to see her and completely bewildered by the situation as she picked him up and drew strength from his wriggling, still-damp little body. Her own emotions were perilously close to overspill, and all she wanted to do now was get the hell out of the observatory and sink into a warm bed. Whatever residual affection she'd had for the place had all but vanished after this horrifying experience.

When Thea had calmed down a little, Tristan moved away from her. Charlotte could tell that the siblings had a lot to talk about, and suddenly felt like the outsider she was in this complicated family. Tristan crossed the small space between them and reached out a hand to cup her face. 'We need to talk,' he said, his voice rough with the emotions of the recent minutes. 'But let's just get out of here and get back to Gran's. I don't want to spend another minute in this place.'

'Me neither,' Thea replied. She picked up the torch, and the three of them, as well as Comet, made their way back to Thea's car.

Charlotte said nothing. She could already feel the wheels starting to turn, time moving on from the horrendous experience of being trapped, suspended on a rotten platform above a concrete floor, and she had no idea how to make sense of any of it.

The short journey back to Nightshade Cottage wasn't an entirely comfortable one. Charlotte knew the discussion she needed to have with Tristan would come later; it was only right that the Ashcombes spent time putting the pieces of this evening together just as a family, but they had enough to work through without having to explain things to her, as well. She resolved, as soon as she got back, to give them the space they needed, however long that took. In the meantime, she'd work on the information from the archive and Volucris.

53

Charlotte woke the next morning to the merry sound of the dawn chorus in full tweet. The cheer outside her window did little to raise her own spirits, though. The sound felt like the dying days of the season, and the golden light that was spilling across her bedroom floor, just warming her bare feet where she was lying on top of the bedclothes, reminded her that summer, and her time in Lower Brambleton, was coming to an end.

She, Tristan and Thea had got back to Nightshade Cottage last night and spent some time with Lorelai, who was still up and already boiling the kettle. After a rather uncomfortable cup of tea, Charlotte had made her excuses and gone to the annexe. It had been clear that the family needed to be alone. None of them had said as much, but she knew she had to give them some space. She wanted space, too. The events of the past few hours kept cycling through her mind, and she wanted to be alone to get a handle on all that had happened.

Leaving the Ashcombes on one side of the house, she'd given Comet's coat a brush to get rid of the worst of the rats' tails from the torrential rain, brushed her teeth and then crashed out.

She'd fallen asleep in minutes and was unsure whether Tristan had returned to see her before he'd left Nightshade Cottage. She wondered if he'd spent the night, with his Audi still in a ditch at the side of the road, but didn't rush to find out. This situation was so bizarre, and the evening had been so traumatic, that she needed the headspace herself.

In truth, she wasn't sure what she was going to say to Tristan when he did make contact. Last night had been terrifying almost beyond her limits, and it was only now, in the admittedly warm light of day, that she could begin to process what had happened. If Tristan hadn't yanked her to safety in time, she'd have been waking up in a hospital bed... or worse, not waking up at all. And if it hadn't been for him, she'd never have ended up in that situation in the first place. These thoughts warred in her head: she'd only known Tristan a few weeks; did she really want to immerse herself into his now very obviously active trauma? There was a huge part of her that just wanted to call Gemma, pack up her stuff and get the hell out of Lower Brambleton and back to her regular life. Technically, she still had a week to go of the placement, but the observatory was empty, ready for demolition, and she'd be better off back at the North West Wessex archive, overseeing the permanent storage of the artefacts she'd spent the past four weeks collating. Her scientific efficiency and her ability as an archivist had served her a little too well, but there was still work to do. Just not on site.

Despite her gloom, she couldn't hide a smile when Comet came ambling over from his still very whiffy bed and nosed her hand, eagerly requesting his breakfast. At least he wasn't showing any ill effects from the previous evening. Swinging her feet over the side of the bed, she meandered through to the kitchenette to make a cup of coffee. She'd collected the pieces of her phone from the floor of the observatory, and it lay on the table by the window. That would be another thing to sort out today. Flipping up the lid of her laptop, she clocked a series of notifications that had come through as it fired up.

Todd, back in the US and finally seeming to be in work mode, had emailed her with some information about the departed Professor Jacobson, who'd worked at Georgia Tech as a tenured professor until he'd retired and who he'd finally managed to track down. Todd had contacted him and had attached an audio file he'd made of the conversation between Jacobson and himself. As she listened to it, Charlotte forgot all about her coffee.

Professor Jacobson's accent, light Somerset with a smattering of transatlantic vowels, filled the annexe as he recounted a story of academic rivalry, professional jealousy and finally intellectual dishonesty in relation to the Volucris Binary.

'Philip Porter was a senior professor at what later became the University of North West Wessex. He'd once been a rising star in the field of astronomical research, having several projects to his name, but none that really broke any new ground. By the time I met him, his star was on the wane. Funding was more and more difficult to come by, and he seemed to lack his earlier ambition. I also felt he wasn't to be trusted. He'd claimed lead author status on several papers that should have been attributed to others, including Laura Myers, his extremely bright and able research partner.'

Charlotte shook her head. Credit on academic papers could be a murky business, and she'd heard too many stories of senior professors snatching the limelight from their hard-working research assistants. She wondered if Philip's claims of lead author status had coincided with Laura falling in love with Martin. Given what Lorelai had told her about Philip's bitterness towards the young astronomers, she would have taken a punt on it.

Jacobson's voice continued to fill the air. 'When the tables were turned and Philip's nephew, Martin, and Martin's wife, Laura, made the initial discovery of an eclipsing binary, he was consumed with jealousy. It really seemed to push him over the edge. This was a discovery Porter would have given his whole career to have made. And now, here it was, documented by his – and I quote – "young upstart of a nephew" in Somerset. Porter couldn't abide it. He asked me to destroy the paper trail, until such time as we could claim it as our own. It was quite easy to delete the electronic records of our communication – back in the 1990s email was in its infancy and servers were regularly scrubbed at the end of each academic year. What you didn't save on a hard drive was lost. What neither of us counted on, however, was that Martin Ashcombe would have kept hard copies of our initial communication. He clearly knew his uncle's tendencies and wasn't taking any chances.'

Charlotte paused the recording and poured hot water into the cafetiere. Her heart was racing. The only tangible proof that could be attributed to Martin and Laura Ashcombe about the Volucris Binary was a yellowing email and their early observations. The rest, it seemed, had been deliberately obscured by none other than Martin's uncle, Lorelai's brother. Now that she knew some of the tortured emotional history between Philip, Laura and Martin, Philip's anger and jealousy about the discovery made a whole lot more sense.

'Of course, after Martin and Laura's terrible accident, everything was put on hold. Philip persuaded me that it was ridiculous to retrospectively attribute the discovery to Martin and Laura. I, to my shame, let it go.'

Todd's voice interjected on the recording. 'What accident?'

Jacobson's sigh was long, drawn out and spoke volumes in itself. 'Martin and Laura Ashcombe died on a January night on the road that led to the Lower Brambleton Observatory where they'd made the discovery. Philip Porter had pursued them there in a rage, driving down from his home in Bristol to confront them about their discovery, which I'd emailed him about that evening. Later on he told me, off the record, that they'd argued, and Martin had been so adamant that he and Laura were going to claim Volucris as their own that Philip had lost the plot, and driven off to the pub, where he'd proceeded to get thoroughly drunk. Leaving his car at the pub, he'd staggered back to his sister's house and passed out, only to be woken hours later by the news of Laura and Martin's death. He was racked with guilt about the part he might have played in the accident, whether the row he'd had with his nephew had contributed in some way to their dreadful end, but, in the cold light of day, his ambition took over again. Once he'd calmed down, he decided to bury Volucris, and told me to forget of its existence. I only had a speculative email from Martin and I was preoccupied with other research, so I agreed. Porter was my senior. What choice did I have?'

Charlotte shook her head in frustration. She'd never know for sure, but Philip's actions smacked of a man who'd lost everything: the woman he loved had fallen for his nephew, and that same nephew had discovered something that Philip had spent his whole career aiming to find. Perhaps the jealousy and bitterness became too much for him? A stronger man might have risen above his emotions and given credit to Martin and Laura as a kind of memorial, but Philip Porter wasn't that man.

'So, what happened next?' Todd's voice, gentle, probing, got Jacobson back on track. Charlotte poured a little double cream into her coffee.

There was a very audible sigh on the recording. 'What do you think happened, my boy? A year after the death of the Ashcombes, Philip Porter and I were about to go public with the discovery. He'd done his own calculations and was ready to present it. I'd kept the original paper copy of the email from Martin, of course. It was my insurance that Porter would include me in the paper as co-lead researcher. If he didn't, then I was going to reveal the information that it was his nephew and his wife who should take credit for the initial discovery. Porter had fleshed out the initial data and was preparing to publish in one of the most prestigious astronomical journals in the world.'

'And?' There was no mistaking the excitement in Todd's voice as he asked. Charlotte, too, was frozen in place, her coffee cup halfway to her lips.

Jacobson gave a laugh that had an edge as bitter as the Columbian blend Charlotte favoured in her cafetiere. 'Would you believe it? The bloody Germans got there first! Made the calculations, named the two stars in the binary the Geflügeltes Wesen! All the funding went to Heidelberg, and we were left with nothing.'

Charlotte shook her head. It felt like poetic justice, of a kind. Philip Porter was denied his last act of satisfaction, and had been left festering with that knowledge until the day he died. Even as she thought this, she was already a step ahead of herself, though. There had to be some way to reclaim Volucris in the name of the Lower Brambleton Observatory. Despite the traumas of the previous night, she was already thinking about how she could do it.

There was still a little left of the audio recording, and after a moment Charlotte realised Todd had spliced on a message of his own.

'I hope that's enough evidence for you, Charlotte. I have to admit, it's been kinda fun pulling the threads on this one. It's certainly kept me outta trouble before the new year starts. Call me if you wanna talk about any of this. Or don't. But take care of yourself. And don't let that English wanker – as you might say – yank your chain too hard. See you soon.'

Charlotte smiled. It was easy to forget what a smooth bastard Todd was when she listened to that Atlantan drawl. But she was grateful for his help. He'd given her some more pieces of the puzzle, and, hopefully, a potential solution. If Jacobson didn't mind going public, perhaps between them they could get Martin and Laura the recognition they deserved.

She was just wondering whether she should nip around to Lorelai's, both to check in on her and to see if Tristan had indeed spent the night, when there was a knock on the pane of the annexe door, and there stood Tristan, an expression of deathly seriousness on his face.

54

'Can I come in?' Tristan asked as Charlotte opened the door.

'Sure,' Charlotte replied. 'Er... why didn't you just knock on the adjoining interior door? Would have saved you getting your shoes on!'

Tristan gave a brief smile. 'I didn't want to presume.' He crossed the threshold and shook his head when Charlotte offered him a coffee. 'I've had a couple at Gran's, and I've got to talk sense to the AA when they come and pull my car out of the ditch later on.'

'I never got the chance to ask,' Charlotte replied, sipping her mug of coffee, 'how did it end up there in the first place?'

Tristan gave an embarrassed smile. 'I, er, lost focus on the road during the rainstorm and forgot about the rhyne. Thankfully, there's been no rain for weeks so it had virtually dried up, but the deluge last night meant I couldn't get the car back out again once I'd skidded off the tarmac. If it'd been full and running, it could have been a hell of a lot worse.' He dropped his gaze from hers. 'I shouldn't have rushed off from Gran's last night. In hindsight, I was in no condition to drive.' He paused, obviously choosing his next words with care. 'Thea, er, told me about the voicemail she found on her phone. I should never have got behind the wheel, the state I was in.'

'You sounded really upset,' Charlotte replied. 'You had us worried sick.'

'I know,' Tristan replied. 'You might say I deserved to skid off the road.'

'I wouldn't say that,' Charlotte chided. 'I'm glad you weren't hurt.' The events that happened after Tristan's car accident were replaying through her mind vividly again, and, as Tristan glanced back up at her, she could see he was thinking about the same things.

A long pause elapsed between them. Charlotte had never been good at filling silences, so she kept quiet. She was waiting for Tristan to make the first move, to acknowledge the true extent of what had happened last night. Eventually, he spoke.

'Look, Charlotte,' he began, his voice sounding more nervous than she'd heard him in the short time they'd known each other. 'I don't know where to begin with what happened on the gantry. You could have been killed if that platform had given way.' He blinked furiously, and Charlotte heard an undeniable tremor in his voice. 'Thea and Gran spent a long time with me last night, trying to get everything into a kind of shape, but if I'm being honest, I know that what they did is barely the beginning. There's so much to process and I've got a lot to work through about Mum, Dad and the rest of the family, too. All this stuff with Great-Uncle Philip has pulled me right back into a place I'm not sure how to navigate.'

'I'd be lying if I said last night wasn't terrifying.' Charlotte ached to reach out a hand and touch Tristan's hand, but she held back. The events of the previous evening seemed to be acting as a barrier between them, and she wasn't sure how, or if, they'd be able to break it down.

'You risked your life to try to get me down from there,' Tristan continued. 'I should never have put you in that position. I'd completely understand if you decided you never wanted to see me again because of it.' He gave a shaky laugh. 'I feel lucky that we're both here, having this conversation. If things had gone differently up there...'

That was when Charlotte knew she had to take the lead. The air between them felt suffocating, and she'd barely clawed herself back to a sort of calm before Tristan had knocked on the door. She knew she just wasn't ready to relive what had happened between them.

'Tristan...' she began gently.

The flare of love in his eyes was almost enough to make her change her mind. But she had to stay resolute. 'Last night was the scariest thing I've ever experienced. The thought that you, or I, or both of us, might not be sitting here having this conversation keeps running through my mind.' She drew a deep breath, and then she did reach out to hold his hand. 'If I'm being honest, I need to process everything. And if you're being honest, I think you do, too.' She squeezed his hand and felt the warmth of Tristan's other palm closing over hers.

'So, what are you saying?' Tristan asked softly.

Charlotte took a deep breath. 'I'm saying that...' She swallowed. 'I'm going back to Bristol tomorrow. And I think some space might be what's best for us right now. You need to spend some time with Lorelai and Thea, and, as you said, work through the family stuff, perhaps with the help of someone who's qualified to help you. I have to get my head around what happened last night, and I've got to finish the observatory archiving project and start a new term. I think we've both got plenty to think about.'

Tristan's look of shock turned into one of resignation as he took in Charlotte's words. 'I understand,' he said, and gently disentangled his hands from hers. 'And for what it's worth, I'm so sorry for putting you through all of this.' He stood up from the table. Charlotte rose too, and for a second there was an awkward silence as they both felt their boundaries readjusting.

'Can I text you?' Tristan said softly.

Charlotte's throat ached as she looked at him, and she heard a little voice of doubt whispering inside her mind. Was she doing the right thing, calling a pause on their relationship? She thought back to her screamed admission of love for him on the splintering viewing platform and was surprised he hadn't brought it up. But then, he'd been so far inside his own head when she'd shouted at him, perhaps only the noise, and not her words, had registered? Her face began to burn as she realised that he might just be ignoring it, waiting for her to make the first move and tell him now their feet were on the ground again. But much as her heart was screaming at her to do it, her head was very firmly reminding her that she just didn't have the emotional bandwidth to cope with it all.

'I'd like that,' she said quietly. 'Tristan... I...'

It was the hope in his eyes that nearly broke her. 'Yes?'

'Never mind.' She couldn't find the words. Instead, she stepped forward and wrapped her arms around him in a hug that she hoped communicated more than she could verbally. His arms around her in reciprocation felt warm, right, and achingly familiar, and her sense of conflict grew about leaving things on hiatus between them. But it had all been too much: this whirlwind of a summer romance had swept her up and taken all of her control, and the drama of the past hours had thrown her back to earth with a bump. She needed time, space, and her normal, familiar world around her. She needed North West Wessex university, the archive and the counsel of her best friend, Gemma. She needed to go home.

They broke apart and Charlotte steeled herself not to kiss him. If their lips met, she knew she'd change her mind.

'See you soon,' she said sadly.

Tristan nodded, and then, before either of them could say any more, he'd opened the door and walked through. Charlotte sagged back against the tabletop, feeling it solid against the back of her legs. She knew she'd done the right thing, so why was her heart aching so much?

55

'Right, hon, well, if you're sure that's what you want?' Gemma's voice was laced with concern, and Charlotte felt her throat constricting again as she tried to reply.

'It is,' she managed. Gemma had collected Charlotte and Comet from Nightshade Cottage the following morning, and they were now on their way back up to Bristol. Charlotte had said a fond goodbye to Lorelai, after filling her in on the information that Todd had recovered from Professor Jacobson's interview. Lorelai had been devastated at the part her brother had played in the death of her son and his wife, albeit indirectly, but now Philip's withdrawal from the family made a lot more sense. She'd promised to send Lorelai a copy of the audio file, and in return, Lorelai had given her the documentation that her brother had withheld from the observatory's records room, that she'd been sifting through when Thea and Tristan had called in. It contained, to Charlotte's trained eye, valuable information about the first discovery of Volucris by Martin and Laura and gave a very good case for getting them recognised as its locators. Charlotte promised it would take its rightful place among the papers in the North West Wessex archives, and was looking forward to finishing the story. Charlotte had also sent Lorelai the photograph of LBAS she'd found – she hoped it would be of some comfort to all the family.

As she sat in Gemma's car, watching the miles mount up between her and Lower Brambleton, she couldn't help ruminating on the twists and turns that had brought her to this point. At the start of the summer, she had had no idea of the secrets she was going to be uncovering in Lower Brambleton Observatory's past, and how they were so heavily intertwined with the family of the man she'd fallen in love with. Those two facts felt now like the eclipsing binary itself: she'd uncovered the truth about a major discovery, but in the process the truth had triggered a response in Tristan that showed just how far he needed to travel along his own path of healing before he was ready to love and trust again. The two realities were in orbit together, one affecting the other as they took turns at taking precedence in her life and in her mind. She'd called a pause in their relationship, but she'd had enormous provocation to do so, having faced the very real prospect of her own death in a condemned building.

'You know you and Comet can bunk with me anytime, though, right?' Gemma said, breaking into Charlotte's gloomy thoughts. 'You don't really want to be all alone in the halls until the students descend, do you?'

'I could do with the solitude,' Charlotte replied. 'It's always chaos when the students arrive. It'll be nice to have some peace before then.'

'I get that,' Gemma said, putting her foot down to overtake a tractor and trailer laden with a crop of cider apples that was meandering up the A38 at a snail's pace. 'But after everything you've been through... are you sure being alone is what you really need?'

Charlotte forced a smile. 'You know me,' she said, reaching back to ruffle Comet's head. He was stretched out on the back seat of the Touareg as though he owned it. 'I'm never alone with this fella. And I've got enough to organise, overseeing the observatory papers into the archive, anyway. Not to mention the last-minute additions. There's a transcript of Professor Jacobson's interview to sort out, and I need to talk to Professor Edwin when he's back about getting some posthumous recognition for the Ashcombes... I'll have a lot to do.'

'Well, if you change your mind, you know where I am,' Gemma said. 'And at least come round for dinner tomorrow night. We'll have a proper postmortem of what happened between you and Tristan over a bottle of wine. You can bring the mutt, too.'

'Thanks.' Charlotte smiled at her friend. 'That I *will* take you up on.'

Gemma helped her take her boxes and cases to her flat on the ground floor of the student accommodation building, and then hugged her goodbye. 'I hate leaving you here when it's so empty,' she grumbled. 'It's like a bloody ghost town.'

'Rather these ghosts than the ones in Lower Brambleton,' Charlotte said ruefully. She felt relief at being back on familiar territory, but that relief was tinged with sadness. Her time in Somerset hadn't all been awful: she'd made friends in Nick and Annabelle Saint and grown fond of Lorelai. Thea was on the way to being a friend, and Tristan... well. That was a thought for another time. For the moment, she needed to get herself set back up in the flat.

'Come on, old chap,' she said to Comet, who was already sniffing hopefully at the back door of her flat. Being on the ground floor, she had two entry points to her accommodation, one which led directly out to the communal green space known as 'Hangover Row' where first year undergraduates could be seen trying to mooch off their nausea after a heavy night in Bristol's hotspots. It was also a good space to give Comet his morning and evening constitutionals, and while it lacked the scope and beauty of the woodland behind Nightshade Cottage, it was expansive enough for Comet.

Comet bounded around, sniffing and rediscovering all his familiar spots, while Charlotte tried to readjust to the sights and sounds of the city. The traffic felt too loud, and the frequent roaring of the planes overhead, coming in to land at Bristol Airport, intruded on her thoughts. She hadn't realised how accustomed she'd got to the quiet until she was back in the noise of the city.

At least the sun was still out, she thought. She sat down on the bench that was placed alongside the path that ran from the green space to the entrance to the halls. Comet, after checking in with her, scampered away again, but remained within sight. Charlotte sighed. She thought being back here was what she needed, but now she wasn't so sure. The thought of the new term, which was just around the corner and usually filled her with such hope and optimism, now just seemed to fill her with dread.

'No,' she said firmly. 'This isn't going to be how you deal with things.' She stood back up from the bench and pulled her phone out from her back pocket when she felt it buzz.

Todd had written:

> Jacobson's willing to go on the record. Looks like Martin and Laura Ashcombe will get their footnote for Volucris after all.

Charlotte's eyes blurred with tears. If nothing else, she thought, that was a result. She instinctively began to text Tristan with the news, but then paused. After everything that had happened between them, she wasn't sure whether telling him by text was the best option. But now she was back in Bristol she couldn't exactly pop down and break the news to him in person, either. Putting her phone away, she called Comet and wandered back into the flat. She needed to think, and she always did her best thinking in one place: the archive.

'Come on, old chap,' she said, grabbing her backpack and filling up her water bottle. 'Let's get back to work.'

And work she did, for the next four weeks. The archive boxes had been periodically arriving all through the summer, and she now had to make sure they were filed appropriately in the North West Wessex Astronomical Archive. Having sifted through everything on site, this should have been a fairly straightforward process, but Charlotte kept lingering on things as she double checked them before putting them away in the slots that had been allocated for the archive boxes. She felt as though she wanted to keep the memories of the summer alive. It might have ended traumatically, but Lower Brambleton Observatory had been a turning point in her life: it was her first solo project; she'd unearthed some findings that had hitherto been forgotten; and she'd fallen in love into the bargain.

'Everything all right?' Professor Jim Edwin, her boss, poked his head around the door.

'Yup.' Charlotte forced a smile. 'I think I've just about finished here.'

Professor Edwin nodded. 'You did a great job. Shame there weren't any nuggets to add to the Winslow papers, but chasing the thread of Volucris was inspired.'

Charlotte felt her face burning at the praise. 'Thank you,' she replied. 'I didn't expect to be coming back here with a discovery, but it's exciting to have played a part in righting a historical wrong, or an oversight, at least.'

Professor Edwin went to leave her office, but just before he did, he added, 'Oh, I almost forgot – there's a parcel down in reception for you. Courier dropped it off an hour ago. I'd have brought it up, but I had my hands full with a month's worth of post.'

Rather mystified, Charlotte wondered what might be waiting for her. She sometimes had the odd Amazon order delivered to work, since she'd had parcels go astray when they were delivered to the halls of residence, but she couldn't recall ordering anything recently.

'Thanks, Prof,' she said. 'I'll pop down and see what it is.' Closing the door on Comet, who was snoozing peacefully in his basket, she ambled down the stairs to reception. There, waiting by the staff pigeonholes, was a large brown box, securely wrapped with thick parcel tape, with a handwritten label. The address read:

Dr Charlotte James, Department of Astronomy, University of North West Wessex

From the date mark on the stamp, which she could just about make out, it had been around the houses before arriving here.

Curiously, she took hold of the box, feeling its substantial weight and wondering what she'd been sent. There was no return address, and the post mark had been smudged where the location would have been. Hurrying back up the stairs to her office, she placed the parcel down and hunted for a pair of scissors to cut the tape. Carefully, in case whatever was inside could be caught by the scissors, she sliced the tape on the box flaps and opened it up. It was full of polystyrene packing chips, and, smiling at the memory of Comet crashing through a box of them when he was a pup, she plunged her hands in, trying not to spill any on the floor.

The first thing she felt was an envelope, which had her name on it. The small, slightly spidery handwriting wasn't familiar, but at least she knew whatever had been sent to her definitely wasn't from Todd. She'd seen his signature many times over the course of their relationship and his flamboyant scrawl was easily recognisable. Thumbing open the seal, she drew out a letter on the same high-quality cream paper as the envelope. There was only one page, but as her eyes scanned what was written, her hands began to tremble.

Dear Charlotte,

I hope you're well and enjoying the new academic year. I've been meaning to send this on to you, as, in light of everything you discovered over the summer about my parents and their connection to Volucris, I thought it was only fitting that you became its custodian. To be frank, I don't really know how to use it anyway, as you saw that starry night at my house over the summer. I don't know whether it's better in the archive or in your care – it's up to you whether you want to see it as a gift or as another artefact for the Observatory Field collection, but in view of the part Great-Uncle Philip played in Mum and Dad's lives, I no longer feel as though it belongs with me. It's a beautiful instrument, and I wanted someone to have it who would be able to make the best use of it. If you want to keep it, then I'm happy for you to do so, but if you'd rather put it in the archive, then that's fine by me, too.

I also wanted you to know that I've been seeing someone.

That sentence, right at the bottom of the page, made her stop in her tracks. Charlotte's heart did a little painful thump as the words registered with her entire body. She and Tristan had called a pause, that was true, but she hadn't imagined he'd move on so quickly. Maybe he wanted to just forget it had all happened? The way things had been left between them had been traumatic, but she still faintly hoped that they'd see each other again eventually.

Realising she was just staring at the letter, she gave herself a mental shake and turned over the sheet of paper.

Thea and Gran were haranguing me about talking through some of the things that might have led to that awful night at the observatory, so I've decided to see a therapist (God, I HATE that word!), to help me to come to terms with the stuff I've been running away from for all these years. It's early days, but one of my therapist's first suggestions was that I try to find ways to process the little things, find the wins, as a way to tackle the larger things, and so I thought that sending this to you was a good way to start. This isn't to put pressure on you, though. I know that you've also got a lot to work through, and our broken pieces won't automatically fit back together.

Charlotte felt the relief washing over her, both that her first assumption was wrong, and also that Tristan was obviously trying to work on the issues that had dogged him for so long. That could only be a good thing.

I do miss you. I'd love to see you again, if you'd like to see me. If you'd rather not, though, please just accept the enclosed as a gift. I think it will have a better home with you than if it stays with me.

Yours,
Tristan

Putting the letter down on her desk, Charlotte delved back into the parcel and drew out a wooden case. In a flash, she knew what the box contained. Carefully, she put the case down on her desk next to the letter, flipped the brass catches and lifted the lid. And there, nestled in its protective black velvet lining, was the Unitron Refractor telescope.

Charlotte knew better than to try to lift it out of the case. One of the first things she'd learned when she did her qualifications as an archivist was never to just delve in and grab any artefact, to make sure your hands were clean, and you were as calm as you could be. Her hands were trembling too much to risk it now. So instead, she just gazed at the beautiful instrument as the tears started to fall.

56

'So, what do you reckon I should do?' Charlotte was sitting on Gemma's extremely comfortable sofa, nursing a glass of wine and brooding quietly. She'd left the telescope at work for the time being, still undecided as to whether to donate it to the archive or keep it herself. There was no conflict of interest – Professor Edwin had read Tristan's letter and confirmed that, since Tristan was giving her the choice, she was indeed free to decide where the telescope ended up. The question was, did she want to possess an artefact that was so intimately connected to Tristan and his family? On the one hand, if they decided not to continue their relationship it would be a reminder of what had happened between them; on the other, if they did meet up again and decide to pick up where they'd left off, Tristan might not want the continual reminder of the role his uncle had had in his parents' personal and professional lives. The gift, though thoughtful, was now causing her head to ache. Perhaps the best thing to do would be to just put it in the archive and forget about it.

But Charlotte couldn't forget about that wonderful night they'd spent stargazing in Tristan's garden. She didn't want to forget. Her heart was telling her one thing, and her head, as usual, was telling her another.

'Well, you'd better at least text Tristan to thank him,' Gemma replied. 'If nothing else, he'll want to know that the parcel got to you all right, and in one piece.'

'I've been drafting and redrafting a text since I opened the bloody thing!' Charlotte said, taking another sip of her wine. 'I just can't seem to get the tone right.'

'Perhaps that's because you're not as decided now as you were when you left?' Gemma observed. 'I mean, let's face it, you're back doing your house parent thing and when you're not looking after pissed undergrads you're in the archive sorting out the Observatory Field papers. Now, Tristan's sent you this gift and it's put your mental planets out of orbit again, after just managing to get back on an even keel.'

Charlotte winced at the mixed metaphor, but she knew what Gemma meant. 'I guess so,' she conceded. 'But it's difficult to reply with anything other than a "thank you, it got here safely" when I still haven't decided what to do with it.'

'Then just do that,' Gemma reasoned. 'You can always follow it up with something more detailed when you're ready.' She topped up both of their glasses. 'Now,' she continued. 'How did the first time out in the new car go?'

Charlotte grimaced. 'About as well as you'd expect.' She'd decided to brave the world of motoring again since returning to Bristol. Being out in Lower Brambleton for the summer had reminded her just how useful it would be to be more mobile, especially when she couldn't rely on public transport or Gemma to get her places. Her parents had gifted her some money as an early Christmas present which, combined with her pay for the Observatory Field job, allowed her to buy a second-hand car and insure it. After much stalling and crunching of gears, she'd gradually stopped shaking and taken a first proper drive around the city.

A little voice in her head had reminded her that, should she have her own car, it would be easier to travel to see Tristan, too, but she'd hushed it firmly. This wasn't about Tristan. All the same, she hoped that if she gained some confidence in her driving she might be able to take a trip under her own steam to Lower Brambleton again. She quite fancied visiting and staying connected with the new friends she'd made. And if she was ready to see Tristan, so much the better.

'I'm happy to sit in your passenger seat, too,' Gemma said. 'Although I'm not sure how good a support I'll be!'

'Thanks.' Charlotte smiled at her friend. 'I'll bear that in mind.' She took her phone out again and was looking at the text in her drafts folder. Would 'thank you, the telescope arrived safely' really be enough to send to Tristan after such a heartfelt letter? She sighed and put her phone down again.

'Stop overthinking it!' Gemma said firmly. 'And either send it to him now or put your phone out of reach. One more glass of wine and you'll be drunk-texting something you'll regret.'

'All right,' Charlotte grumbled. She put her phone back into her backpack. 'I just wish I knew what to do.'

Gemma tilted her head to one side, and Charlotte realised she was under scrutiny. 'Well,' her friend said eventually, 'this sounds like a cliché, but what is your heart telling you to do? Forget *knowing*, and try *feeling* for a bit. Maybe you'll find the answer.'

Charlotte shook her head. If only it were that easy. Taking another sip of her wine, she settled back against the sofa and tried to focus on the television, where Gemma had selected another episode of their guilty pleasure viewing, *Outlander*. Watching Sam Heughan wooing Catriona Balfe across the wilds of time, Charlotte, feeling drowsy, began to wonder if the situation with Tristan really was as complicated as she was trying to make it. Perhaps it was simply a case of trusting the stars.

57

A week and a half after Charlotte had taken delivery of the telescope, Tristan still hadn't quite got used to getting decent reception in his Portakabin office, and actually getting messages and WhatsApps through on the site's newly established wi-fi was almost intrusive. For the first couple of weeks on site the inconvenience of a patchy connection had been counterbalanced by the fact that he could only really be reached when he got out of Lower Brambleton's black spot, and it was almost liberating. Now everything had gone live, and he was reachable wherever he was, he felt a little cornered. It hadn't helped that he'd left his phone in the office on Saturday afternoon when he'd popped in to check a couple of last-minute details on the heavy plant machinery that was arriving on Monday. Now, on Sunday morning, he should have just picked up his phone and left again – he had a lunch date with Lorelai and Thea and the kids, but he found himself compelled to check a few more details for Monday, while he was here.

Grabbing his phone where it was face down on his desk, his heart raced when he saw it was a message from Charlotte. She hadn't been in contact since she'd gone back to Bristol, and so it was with some trepidation he'd sent her the Ultron Refractor telescope and his letter. What had happened between them had felt unfinished, and he wanted to offer her his perspective on things, just as a way of providing his own full stop. Whether she chose to respond was up to her. For days after he'd sent the package he'd been on tenterhooks, but now, at last, that waiting seemed to have come to an end.

> Hi Tristan,
>
> Thank you so much for the telescope – it was a very thoughtful gift. I still haven't quite decided whether I should keep it or give it to the archive, but I promise it's in safe hands either way. I hope you are well.
>
> Best wishes
>
> Charlotte

Tristan was perturbed by the perfunctory nature of Charlotte's response. Perhaps she hadn't wanted to mention any more details of the letter he'd sent with the telescope over text, but it still seemed a little lacking. They hadn't spoken in the weeks that Charlotte had been in Bristol, and he was disappointed and a bit hurt that she hadn't referenced anything he'd actually written in the letter. Then he shook his head. They had agreed to put a pause on things: perhaps this was just Charlotte's way of reminding him of that. Before he could continue second guessing, he decided to send her a reply.

> I'm glad it got to you OK. I hope you find the answer you're looking for!

He pressed 'Send' before he could add any more. There was

so much he wanted to say but it didn't seem right to reiterate what he'd already written in the letter. Then, grabbing his phone and locking the office, he headed off to lunch with his family.

Later that afternoon, replete with roast beef and Lorelai's famed sticky toffee pudding, he slumped on the sofa in Lorelai's living room, idly watching Cora and Dylan arguing over who got to go next on the old Nintendo DS that he'd dug out of his attic for them. Cora, who had control of the stylus, was threatening to poke her younger brother in the eye with it when he felt he should intervene.

'Why don't you two go and count how many conkers have fallen off Gran's tree and bring some back in? We could make something out of them.'

Cora rolled her eyes, but a warning look from Thea compelled her to give a conciliatory smile to her uncle. 'All right, Uncle Tristan. Come on, Dylan, let's get a bag out of Gran's cupboard and we'll go and collect some.'

'Thanks... I think!' Thea grinned at her brother. 'So long as you take what they find home with you. I've still got a bag of last year's going mouldy in the shed!'

'It's a deal,' Tristan replied. He'd enjoyed spending time with them all. Since he'd started seeing the therapist, he'd gradually felt able to be more present in the moments with his family, and although it was early days, it definitely seemed to be helping.

'That text you got from Charlotte seemed a little cold,' Thea said, once the two of them were alone. Lorelai was in the kitchen, putting the pots and pans away, having waved off her grandchildren's offers to clear up, and with the children down the bottom of the garden, Thea obviously wanted to discuss it. Tristan, unusually for him, had shown his sister the message before lunch, and she'd expressed surprise, but then hadn't said anything else.

'It was a bit,' Tristan admitted. 'But I suppose I shouldn't really expect anything else, after everything that happened.'

'Hmm...' Thea looked sceptical. 'I don't think she's being entirely fair. I know you called a pause, but you didn't call it off between you altogether, did you? She owes you a little more than that response, I think.'

'She doesn't owe me anything,' Tristan protested. 'If it wasn't for me, she'd never have ended up on the gantry that night.'

'Yeah, that's true, but you had a good thing going before then – I mean, you'd actually spoken to me about her, and that *never* happens!' She grinned.

Tristan sighed. 'I know you mean well, sis, but I think Charlotte just needs some space. I don't want to push her.'

'Like sending her Great-Uncle Phil's telescope wasn't a push?' Thea countered. 'I mean, don't tell me you weren't hoping she'd come back with something other than "Thanks a lot, I haven't decided what to do with that incredibly thoughtful gift you sent me"!'

Tristan hadn't told Thea about the letter he'd written to go with the telescope. He got the feeling, if he had, that she'd be even more on his case than she was now. Besides, he was conflicted enough about the whole thing, now he'd had a couple of weeks to think about it. Perhaps it had been a daft idea, and he'd put her under too much pressure.

'I don't want to force her into something she's only doing because she feels guilty,' Tristan countered. 'The telescope felt like the right thing to do, but now... I kind of wish I hadn't sent it.'

'You can't keep second guessing yourself,' Thea said. 'The ball's in her court.' A funny expression passed over her face as she spoke, which Tristan didn't miss. Before he could ask her what had occurred to her, though, Thea continued.

'That night on the gantry, you were in a hell of a state. At least you're doing something about that now. Didn't the therapist suggest some coping strategies to help you next time you feel as though there's been a trigger?'

Tristan nodded. 'Yeah, but sometimes it all seems so ridiculous. I mean, I should just be able to cope, shouldn't I?'

Thea sat back up again and put a hand on her brother's arm. 'Tris, we've both been through so much. There's no harm in taking some time to get to grips with it all. You've waited long enough to be able to do that. Don't rush things.'

Tristan gave a slight laugh. 'You sound like my therapist!'

'I was, for years, but I clearly wasn't a very good one!' Thea's eyes shone momentarily before she added, 'It's a good job you've got a professional to turn to, now.'

'You did the best you could,' Tristan said softly. 'It's not your fault I'm a stubborn bastard who doesn't know what's good for him.'

'Yeah.' Thea looked shifty, and this time the expression remained. 'About that...'

Tristan was suddenly on the alert. He and Thea had always been finely tuned to each other's changes of emotion, and now he definitely knew something was up.

'Sis?' he said quickly. 'What have you been up to?'

Thea sighed, but then tried to hide a smile. 'I, er, might have taken things into my own hands a bit...'

Tristan's pulse started to race. 'What have you done, Thea?'

At that moment, Lorelai's doorbell rang.

Tristan turned to Thea, who seemed to be preoccupied by something on her phone. 'Do you want to get that?' she asked.

'Nah,' he responded. 'Probably just someone selling something. I mean, who calls round on a Sunday afternoon?'

Thea raised an eyebrow. 'Are you sure you won't just go and answer it?' The doorbell rang again. 'Could be important...'

'Oh, for fuck's sake!' Tristan muttered, then glanced around guiltily in case his niece and nephew had come back into earshot. 'I'll send whoever it is away with a bloody flea in their ear at this rate.' He pushed himself off the sofa and meandered reluctantly towards Lorelai's front door, silently cursing his sister under his breath as he went. If it was a cold caller, he'd make sure they knew they shouldn't be inconveniencing his grandmother, especially on a Sunday afternoon.

Unlocking the door, he took a deep breath before he pulled it open, but the words died on his lips when he saw who was standing on the doorstep, looking almost as nervous as she had the first time he'd seen her.

'Charlotte?' he said, his heart suddenly in his mouth. 'What on earth are you doing here?'

58

This was a terrible idea. The look of shock on Tristan's face when he opened the door to Nightshade Cottage was enough to make Charlotte want to jump back into her second-hand Volkswagen Polo and scuttle back to Bristol. Comet, though, had no such reservations and was scrabbling frantically at the back window of the car, eager to escape and greet his old friend, Tristan.

'Er, hi,' Charlotte said, twisting the ring on the middle finger of her left hand, just for something to do. 'I came as soon as I could. Thea sounded pretty stressed on the phone when she called me earlier. How can I help?'

Tristan's blank look of incomprehension made Charlotte twist the ring on her finger even more tightly. He looked as though he didn't have the faintest clue what she was talking about.

'You've spoken to Thea today?' Tristan eventually replied. 'What about?'

Charlotte's heart sped up. 'Er, about the papers Lorelai found in the attic? The ones that she needed some help to decipher? She asked if I could pop down and spend a couple of hours looking through them, since there were too many to post. I said I'd see if there's anything I could do to help.'

Tristan wrinkled his brow. 'First I've heard of it.'

'And me.' Lorelai's slightly amused voice emanated from the kitchen, where she was helping Cora and Dylan to separate their newly collected conkers into two carrier bags. 'Come in, dear. Tristan, it's rude to keep a guest on the doorstep.'

Charlotte began to realise what had happened, a split second earlier than Tristan did. Her face burned with embarrassment and not a little awkwardness. 'Look,' she said, 'there's obviously been some sort of misunderstanding – I'll get going...'

'Don't be daft!' Thea emerged from the living room. 'Tristan's getting sleepy and lazy on the sofa this afternoon, and he could do with a walk. Why don't you take Comet over the woods? Don't you think it's about time you talked?'

Charlotte shook her head. 'When you called me this morning, you said you needed my help. You lied to me to get me here. I'm up to my eyeballs in work, Thea, and I haven't done much driving since I bought my car! I dropped everything, scared the bejesus out of myself on the A38, not to mention the horrible lanes around here, and now you're pushing me to talk to Tristan when you know damned well we called a pause? What the hell were you thinking?'

Thea, clearly shocked by Charlotte's outburst, dropped her gaze first. 'You're right,' she said quietly. 'I'm sorry. I shouldn't have interfered. But when I saw that text of yours, something inside me just snapped. Can't you see what everyone else does? You two need to talk things through. I've never seen Tristan so happy as he has been this summer, and I'm willing to bet, despite how things ended, that you were happy too. I don't know much about romance, but I do know a good couple when I see one, and I know my twin brother. I'm sorry I lied to you, but now you're here, don't you think it's worth at least having a chat?'

It was rare that Charlotte couldn't think of a logical answer for something, but standing on the doorstep of Nightshade Cottage, a place where she'd spent so much time over the summer, in front of a man she knew she was really falling in love with, despite everything, all she could do was concede that his meddlesome twin sister might just have a point.

'All right,' she muttered. 'But I can't stay long. I've never driven in the dark.'

Tristan, who'd clearly been as taken aback as Thea had been by Charlotte's outburst, finally spoke. 'Do I get a say in it, or am I just expected to go along with this scenario?' He turned to look at Thea. 'Charlotte's right – you shouldn't have interfered.' He shook his head. 'You were literally just talking to me about triggers, and you spring this on us? After all the hassle that the last lot of paperwork Gran found caused?'

Thea's face fell, and Charlotte could see that Tristan's words had really hit home. Reluctant to interrupt, but unwilling to see them descend into an argument, she put a hand on Tristan's arm. 'Look,' she said gently. 'Thea might not have been right to get me here like this, but since I am... how about we go for that walk? What harm could it do? To be honest, I need to relax a bit after that drive, and Comet's great company but I could do with some conversation too. What do you think?'

Tristan turned back to face her, and Charlotte felt her mouth going dry, and her palms starting to sweat. She'd forgotten just how much of an effect he had on her when they were close, and she knew she had to get moving before the adrenaline really did kick in and scupper her resolve. 'Come on,' she said gently, 'let's get Comet out and have a wander in the woods, shall we?'

'OK,' Tristan said after a beat. He glanced over his shoulder.

'Don't go anywhere until we get back, sis. You and I will be having a word later.'

Charlotte suppressed a smile. She might not have known Tristan that long, but she detected a distinct note of levity in his voice, now he'd decided, like her, to make the best of an unexpected situation. She popped open the boot of the Polo and clipped Comet's lead to the dog's collar before he could escape into the familiar territory of Lorelai's back garden. Something told her, by the end of this walk, she and Tristan would both have to decide where they stood.

59

'So...'

Charlotte's heart, already slightly elevated from the incline through the woods, sped up as Tristan broke the not-entirely-comfortable silence between them.

'So?' Charlotte echoed. She glanced ahead of them, to ensure that Comet wasn't likely to go dashing off in pursuit of any local wildlife, or to greet other walkers in his usual enthusiastic way, before pausing to catch her breath and meet Tristan's gaze.

'I'm sorry about Thea,' Tristan said. 'You were absolutely on the nail when you said she had no right to interfere. Sometimes, though, she just can't help herself.'

Charlotte shook her head. 'To be fair to Thea, she was right to get irritated by that text. It was a little, er, *to the point*, and was less than you deserved for sending me the Ultron.'

'It was up to you to choose how you responded to it, not my bloody sister,' Tristan muttered. 'She can't help sticking her oar in, sometimes, and I'm just sorry you were on the end of it.'

'That's as may be, but I should have replied a little more

sensitively.' Charlotte paused by the stump of a newly felled pine tree. Its sweet balsam scent seemed to calm her thoughts. She needed to keep her feet on the ground for the next few minutes, at least. 'That letter you sent, with the telescope... it meant a lot to me that you could be so honest about yourself and your feelings. The reason I didn't mention it in that text was because I didn't want to just write off everything you'd said. It felt wrong just to shoot back a WhatsApp, when there was so much else I wanted to tell you.' She rummaged in the back pocket of her jeans. 'So much so that, after I got Thea's call, I finished off a reply of my own that I'd been drafting to you.' Pulling out an envelope, slightly crumpled from where she'd been sitting on it while she was driving, she handed it to Tristan. 'You don't have to read it now,' she said. 'Just stick it in your pocket and read it when you're ready.'

Tristan's mouth gave a little upward twitch when he saw how crumpled the letter was. Charlotte immediately knew he was thinking back to their first meeting and how scruffy she'd looked. 'I'd like to read it now if you don't mind.'

'Sure.'

Tristan perched on the tree stump. Feeling incredibly awkward, Charlotte searched the immediate vicinity with her eyes for Comet and noticed he was disappearing in the direction of the building site. Determined to give Tristan a couple of minutes' space to read her letter, she took her time meandering over to Comet.

When she'd located him, she turned back to see Tristan was still sitting on the tree stump, but he'd shifted his gaze from the letter in his hands to where she was. The look on his face, from this distance, was difficult to make out. Drawing closer, she could see that his eyes were fixed on her, and much to her relief, he was smiling.

'Do you mean it?' he said gently, as he stood and closed the remaining distance between them.

'I do.' Charlotte's knees, only just recovering from coming face to face on the doorstep with Tristan that afternoon, began to shake again. And when Tristan dipped his head, and she felt his lips, tentatively at first and then with increasing assurance, meeting hers, her knees very nearly gave way altogether. It was just as well he'd slid his arms around her, to give them both some stability on the uneven forest floor, as by the time they broke apart again it was difficult to tell who was trembling more.

'I've missed you,' Tristan murmured. 'You've no idea how much.'

'I've some idea.' Charlotte smiled into another kiss. 'And I think it's time to press play again on things, don't you?'

'Definitely.' The kisses could have gone on all afternoon, with the odd gently falling copper-burnished leaf fluttering from the beech trees that interspersed the pines in the wood, had Comet not returned with a large stick, and butted Charlotte on the back of her legs with it.

'Timing, dog,' Charlotte muttered as she was pushed even closer to Tristan.

'I don't know.' Tristan's eyes sparkled with amusement and love, never breaking her gaze as he stooped slightly to give the errant Comet a pat. 'His timing seems pretty perfect to me.'

EPILOGUE
A YEAR LATER

At number sixteen Orion Close, a small, three-bedroomed house tucked into the corner of the Observatory Field development, and a stone's throw from the woodland that the new owner had explored as a child, the champagne cork popped and fell a long way short of the back fence. Cheering followed, almost as swiftly as the small black and white cocker spaniel, Comet, did after the cork.

'Congratulations, Thea.' Lorelai raised her glass, which was the first to have been filled, in her granddaughter's direction. 'This has been a long time coming, but I wish you every success in your new home.'

'Thanks, Gran.' Thea passed a glass to Charlotte, who was standing off to one side of the patio table with Tristan, and then filled her own. 'I can't believe we're finally here!'

Thea had been one of the first owners to move into her new home on Observatory Field. The house, big enough for herself and the two children as they grew into teenagers, was part of a tasteful development that her brother had overseen from start to finish. The garden, while not enormous, was substantially bigger than the small courtyard plot she'd had in her rented property, and ensured that Dylan could practise his penalty kicks for the Lower Brambleton Under-9s without fear of losing his ball to the road or the house behind. Cora, who'd loved the woodland since she was old enough to walk, now spent a great deal of her time exploring the surrounding countryside, and had a chart on her new bedroom wall which detailed the different kinds of British wildlife she might expect to find. She'd ticked off many of these already. The estate, still in the process of being built, was welcoming new residents regularly, and a community was beginning to form. In a few years' time, it would ensure the survival of this charming little Somerset hamlet.

Charlotte looked over at Tristan, who was sipping his champagne and gazing out over the garden, seemingly lost in thought.

'You OK?' she murmured, slipping closer to him.

'Absolutely,' he replied. 'You know, it's nice to think about the changes that have happened here and just be happy.' He shook his head. 'I don't know what that says about me, that I had to watch a building being razed to the ground to feel that, but that's how it happened.'

Charlotte smiled up at him. She knew what a concession that was for him to admit out loud, even though they'd had a lot of discussions about it over the past year. Losing the observatory but gaining a sense of peace about the past had been a worthy exchange, not just for Tristan but for his whole family. A family that now included Charlotte, unofficially at least.

Charlotte herself had seen out the academic year in her flat in the halls of residence, but had been pootling up and down the A roads between Bristol and Lower Brambleton on a regular basis to visit Tristan, and almost as regularly, Lorelai. Still not quite ready to take the plunge and move in together, Charlotte had commandeered a space in Tristan's study for some of the

A Sky Full of Stars

days during the university vacations when the students had gone home and she couldn't be bothered to drive back to her flat, and they'd been moving their relationship along slowly, giving each other the time and space they needed to progress at a pace that suited them both. Things had been getting more serious lately, though, with more of Charlotte's possessions finding their way into Tristan's house, and Tristan quietly rearranging them whenever she went back to Bristol. Despite Thea's none-too-subtle hints that Cora was desperate to be a bridesmaid, Charlotte and Tristan were content with their own timeline, for now.

While Tristan had now moved on to mastermind the next Flowerdew Homes development, Charlotte still worked in the North West Wessex archives, where she was putting together a research paper proposing that the Volucris Binary's German name be given an additional identifier called the 'Ashcombe Formation'. From across the Atlantic, Todd had been her research partner and was even now using the vast resources of his university's astrophysics department to provide up-to-date calculations of the pair of eclipsing stars, to ensure that, unlike thirty years ago, Martin and Laura's discovery would not be forgotten. Even if the identifier never took, their names would be recorded as the first astronomers to have observed and noted the discovery.

The small housewarming gathering at Thea's had been the perfect excuse to get friends and family together, and along with Lorelai, Thea and the kids, and Charlotte and Tristan, Thea had invited Annabelle and her husband and Nick Saint, too, who, having just split with his girlfriend, was pleased to get out for a chat and a drink. Nick spent most of the afternoon saving Dylan's goal kicks, and Annabelle was heard to remark to her husband that it was good to see him smiling again.

After a little while, Tristan stood from the patio chair he'd been sitting in to drink his champagne. 'I could do with stretching my legs,' he said. Charlotte saw him glancing at her. 'Do you fancy a quick walk?'

'Sure,' Charlotte replied. She went to put down her glass, but Tristan had refilled it.

'Bring it with you,' he said. 'I'm sure no one's going to grumble about street drinking if we're subtle.'

Charlotte shook her head. 'Who are you, and what have you done with Tristan?'

Both clutching their glasses, they headed out of the garden gate and walked along the newly tarmacked footpath that snaked its way through the development, past saplings that had been planted on sympathetically designed patches of green space, and towards the centre of the site, where the Lower Brambleton Observatory had once stood.

'That's better,' Tristan said as they walked. 'Don't get me wrong, I love them all, but if I sat around any longer, Dylan would have been subbing me for Nick and I'd have been saving penalties all afternoon.'

'What, you're not up to throwing yourself around in a goal?' Charlotte teased. 'You must be getting old.'

Tristan grinned down at her. 'I'll remind you of that when it's your turn to take a shift!'

They'd reached the centre now, and they paused. One of the things that made Observatory Field unique was the fact that Flowerdew were very aware of the site's history and heritage. Some of the touches felt a little arbitrary: there were road names that seemed to come out of the *Junior Encyclopaedia of Space*, of which Orion Close was definitely the least cringe-inducing, but something Tristan had been clear had to be included, reinforced by Lorelai's wishes, was a subtle memorial to what had hitherto stood on the site. In the end, a well-known design company had created a plaque, inset into the ground where the centre of the observatory had been. Its simple yet poignant inscription read:

> This plaque is dedicated to the tireless efforts and passion for discovery of the members of the Lower Brambleton Astronomical Society.
>
> In 1994, Laura and Martin Ashcombe, esteemed members of LBAS, made the remarkable discovery of an eclipsing binary star, expanding our understanding of the cosmos. Their dedication and contribution to the field of astronomy continue to inspire future generations of stargazers and scholars.
>
> 'Per Aspera ad Astra'
> Through hardships to the stars

'It's good to know there'll always be a part of them that's remembered here,' Tristan said quietly. He'd seen the plaque at all stages of its design, and he and Thea had stood together with Lorelai when it had been installed. It had been a deeply emotional moment for all three of them, but it truly felt as though it was the perfect footnote to round off the history of the place.

'I think they'd have been really happy to see how pleased Thea is with her new home,' Tristan said as they sipped their champagne.

'It's the perfect memorial,' Charlotte replied. 'And I think you're right.'

'So, now I've brought you out here, there's something I wanted to ask you,' Tristan continued. 'I, er, wanted to do it somewhere that I know became as special to you as it did to my parents.'

Charlotte's heart began to race as Tristan knelt down and placed his still half-full glass of champagne down next to the plaque. When he didn't immediately get back up, her heart raced even faster.

'I never thought I'd be asking this of anyone,' Tristan began as he reached into his pocket and pulled out a ring, 'but then I never thought I'd fall in love with someone as special as you. Charlotte James, will you at least think about being married to me?'

Charlotte looked down at Tristan, and at the exquisitely cut pair of diamonds in the slim white gold band, and, silently thanking the stars that had brought her to Lower Brambleton, she responded with a very enthusiastic, 'Yes!'

And somewhere far above them, at least one set of binary stars moved in perfect harmony.

* * *

MORE FROM FAY KEENAN

The latest book in another feel-good, romantic series from Fay Keenan, *Coming Home to Roseford Villas*, is available to order now here:

www.mybook.to/CHRosefordVillasBackAd

ACKNOWLEDGEMENTS

Starting a new series of novels is always a daunting prospect, but I felt hugely reassured by the amount of support and encouragement from so many people during the process. New places, new characters and new complications in a story take a lot of thinking about, and a lot of discussion, and there are lots of people to thank for helping me to get this book out there.

Firstly, a huge thank you to all at Boldwood Books, who put their trust in me time after time to deliver a manuscript that's worth sharing. To my wonderful editor, Sarah Ritherdon, for encouraging, pushing and supporting me through what is now our twelfth novel together – you are the best and I'm so grateful. The whole Boldwood team make this process so much easier, and I feel so valued as an author for your time and patience. My thanks, also, to the brilliant Cecily Blench, copy editor extraordinaire, who has such a light touch and an eagle eye for the details. The same goes for Rose Fox – I really appreciate your hard work and keen ability to spot things I've missed!

When I conceived this novel, I knew I wanted to take myself out of my comfort zone, and as an English Literature specialist, there were fewer places further away than Astronomy and Astrophysics! I've asked the advice and indulgence of quite a few experts while I've been writing, and I can't thank you enough. Erin Hollington, I am so grateful for your patience, insight and expertise, and your explanations about binary stars and telescopes, as well as a number of other astronomical phenomena, which has been invaluable and so interesting. My thanks, also, to the science department at Backwell School, headed up by the knowledgeable and approachable Michael Lake, for the conversations about exoplanets and other astronomical things. I feel so lucky to have specialists on my doorstep to call upon. Also, thanks to Rob and Carly Kilby for the stash of astronomy books, which were so useful for checking out even more details about space and the universe. All scientific errors and inconsistences, and any incidences in this book where I've bent time and space to suit the plot are entirely my own!

I also owe many thanks to Chris and Pamela Peters, who are not only avid readers of my novels, but also have the pleasure of owning the gorgeous Levi, who provided the inspiration for Comet the spaniel in this novel. I'm so grateful to you both for reading, and for giving me free range to pet and cuddle your wonderful dog!

Thanks, also, to the University of Bristol Teachers as Writers group, headed by the fabulous Lorna Smith, who provide endless support and inspiration. The group's recent excursion to the top of the Wills Memorial Building tower provided a fabulously romantic location for Tristan and Charlotte's first kiss! I must also thank Wills Memorial tower guide Gary Nott for his brilliantly informative and entertaining tour – I highly recommend a visit, if you happen to be in Bristol.

To the friends and family who have been with me on this journey, thank you, once again, for your patience and indulgence while I've been in the Lower Brambleton headspace. Nick, Flora and Roseanna, you are very patient with me! And finally, to you, the readers and listeners, who walk alongside me as I tell you the stories – I am so grateful to you all. I aim to invite you in and make you feel welcome, and it's a privilege to have you with me. Thank you.

ABOUT THE AUTHOR

Fay Keenan is the author of the bestselling Little Somerby and Willowbury series of novels. She has led writing workshops with Bristol University and has been a visiting speaker in schools. She is a full-time teacher and lives in Somerset.

Sign up to Fay Keenan's mailing list for news, competitions and updates on future books.

Visit Fay's website: https://faykeenan.com/

Follow Fay on social media here:

- facebook.com/faykeenanauthor
- x.com/faykeenan
- instagram.com/faykeenanauthor
- bookbub.com/authors/fay-keenan

ALSO BY FAY KEENAN

Willowbury Series

A Place to Call Home

Snowflakes Over Bay Tree Terrace

Just for the Summer

Roseford Series

New Beginnings at Roseford Hall

Winter Kisses at Roseford Café

Finding Love at Roseford Blooms

Winter Wishes at Roseford Reloved

Coming Home to Roseford Villas

Brambleton Series

A Sky Full of Stars

BECOME A MEMBER OF

THE SHELF CARE CLUB

The home of Boldwood's book club reads.

Find uplifting reads, sunny escapes, cosy romances, family dramas and more!

Sign up to the newsletter
https://bit.ly/theshelfcareclub

Boldwood

Boldwood Books is an award-winning fiction publishing company seeking out the best stories from around the world.

Find out more at www.boldwoodbooks.com

Join our reader community for brilliant books, competitions and offers!

Follow us

@BoldwoodBooks

@TheBoldBookClub

Sign up to our weekly deals newsletter

https://bit.ly/BoldwoodBNewsletter

Printed in Great Britain
by Amazon